DARK MATTER PRESENTS

HUMAN MONSTERS

A HORROR ANTHOLOGY

First Dark Matter INK paperback edition October 2022.

Copy Edited by Rob Carroll, Marissa van Uden
Book Design and Layout by Rob Carroll
Cover Art by Olly Jeavons
Cover Design by Rob Carroll

ISBN 978-1-958598-00-9 (paperback)
ISBN 978-1-958598-10-8 (eBook)

darkmatter-ink.com

DARK MATTER PRESENTS

HUMAN MONSTERS

A HORROR ANTHOLOGY

EDITED BY
SADIE HARTMANN & ASHLEY SAYWERS

To Rick & Jack,
Love you, guys. Best family ever.

—Ashley

Dedicated to my Stackhouse and Hartmann families.
We've made homes full of love; our safe places.

—Sadie

Contents

Content Warning

This anthology contains content that may be unsuitable for certain audiences. Stories include foul language, disturbing imagery, and graphic depictions of sex and violence. Reader discretion is advised.

Introduction

By Christopher Golden

I'll tell you a little secret. I almost never write stories about human monsters because they disturb me deeply. I've edited a lot of anthologies, but never one like this, for that very reason. I know horror is supposed to get under my skin, to dig deep into my softest, most comfortable places and tear them to shreds, but I prefer monsters of the inhuman kind. I like metaphor and questioning the nature of belief and the fabric of imagination. When it comes to reading these stories, or watching movies in the same vein, I've got to be in the mood.

TL;DR...this shit freaks me out.

But when it's done well, it's always worth it.

When I heard about this volume, I was instantly intrigued. Sadie Hartmann and Ashley Saywers have made their mark in the horror community by being passionate about the genre, but even more so because of their comprehensive knowledge and impeccable taste where horror fiction is concerned. These days we use the term "influencers," but once upon a time the word of choice would have been "tastemakers," and I like that one so much better. I have such admiration for the positions they have staked out for themselves in the genre, and confidence that this is only the beginning of a much larger impact to come in the future. So, when Sadie asked me if I'd be interested in writing the introduction to *Human Monsters*, I immediately said yes... even though I knew these stories would freak me out.

And they certainly did.

There are too many stories in here to run through them one by one, and I always feel it's sort of unfair to pick favorites while writing an intro to an anthology. For a single-author collection, it's fair game, but in an anthology, it's bad form to name-drop half of the authors and not mention the other half. That's okay in a review, but not here.

Even so…just to illustrate my reaction to this book, I'm going to mention one story. "Prototype" by Leah Ning is the kind of human monster story I most adore. When you read it, you'll see what I mean. Nasty, yes, but also just fucking weird. But the best thing about the story, for me, is that I had never heard her name, much less read her work, before reading *Human Monsters*, and now I'm *paying attention*. Not only to Leah, but to so many of these writers.

That's the real value of an anthology like this, and the work that Sadie and Ashley are doing and have done here. Of the authors in this book, there were twenty-two I had literally never heard of before. There were eight others whose names and reputations were familiar to me, but whose work I had not yet gotten around to reading. That leaves only five writers I had already read. That is the gift that Sadie and Ashley give us here—a broad cross-section of contemporary horror authors from superstars to rising stars to the very first sparks of hoped-for careers. There are so many small presses out there, and every year there are loads of horror anthologies of varying quality, which is the kindest way I can say that the bar is sometimes set quite low for inclusion. This is not that. Sadie and Ashley have higher goals, and as a fan, I'm grateful to them for that…and to all of the writers who contributed these deeply unsettling stories.

I hope they freak you out as much as they did me.

Terror loves company.

Christopher Golden
Bradford, Massachusetts
July 14, 2022

Kill Me With Lipstick

By Cynthia Pelayo

Blood on a wall, but not that sort of blood. Written in wasted perceptions, spiral bound.

What was the year? Punctuated by a massacre of newspaper clippings.

And what were their names? Women who were murdered again in ink.

In June 1945, let's recall spin back into that past, our parallel.

Josephine. Stabbed. Head-wrapped round. Choked with her own pretty dress.

Months later, Frances found. Knife protruding from her throat. A bullet in her head.

Our memory is a tangled video tape. No, a newsreel. Remember them.

Remember when in that red, not that red, of panic-stricken killer's call.

No dial tone, so sing us the high-pitched news jingle, or a symphony of worry.

Nothing is taken. Promises of sad notes displayed. They were his cutting board.

"For heavens Sake catch me Before I Kill more I cannot control myself"

And so, his infamous scrawl, a coward's plea imprinted, the Lipstick Killer.

In 1946 Suzanne was just six when a troll crawled into her tower, leaving behind

a cold ladder leaning against a bedroom window, arrows flashing the red flag of menace.

"Get $20,000 ready & wait for my word. Do not notify the FBI or police. Bills are in 5's & 10's. Burn this for her safety"

Nothing was burned, except for her. Newspapers later wrote in white, black and red of

Suzanne's head in a sewer. Her little pink and blue leg in catch basin. Other parts in a drain.

A broken doll scattered across a great city, a child as scavenger hunt, a killer's breadcrumbs.

Suspects followed witnesses morphing into empty ransom calls.

A 17-year-old burglar interrogated and drugged.

Our monster in headline:

HEIRENS CONFESSES TO THREE MURDERS

Confessions cycle on and off, cries of guilt and pleas of innocence, blinking in and out.

Results deemed inconclusive, or conclusive? Sixty-six years later and death slips into his cell.

Those buildings still stand, but what do we really know? There's crumpled, yellowed, faded newspaper in archives. Perhaps evidence in moldy boxes as morbid curiosities.

A cast of character witnesses all dead with time. Was Heirens innocent? Or Guilty? Do you remember Josephine, Frances and Suzanne? Do we really remember anyone anymore?

7 P.M. Awards Ceremony, Followed by Girl Scout Auction at 8

By Sam Rebelein

At six o'clock, the moms start putting shit on tables. They spread Solo plates and plastic cups and thin paper napkins from the dollar store. Everything is gold and green, the official color scheme of the Annual Awards. Crepe streamers, balloons, the banner over the stage: "129th Annual Awards," all of it in leafy green and champagne-foil gleam. Even the M&Ms are color themed. Mrs. Dabrovitz, the Scout Troop Leader, got monogrammed ones that say "CONGRATS" on one side.

The entire event hall of the American Legion in Wallow Valley, Ohio, is bedecked. The moms have stripped Party Central of all its greens and golds. But that's okay—Party Central buys it all in bulk a month before, to prepare.

They take the Awards very serious, here in Wallow Valley.

The dads stay home while the moms set up. They'd only get in the way. They'd fold the napkins all wrong. But dads *do* have the very important job of holding down the forts at home while the kids get ready and hang out in their rooms until it's time to go. All across town, dads sit downstairs in their wood-paneled living rooms, watching the game, drinking cans of Lenny's Lager from a brewery in Kentucky, which is the only beer they can get from outside Wallow Valley, but there are rumors that Sam Adams might start importing, too. Wallow Valley gets liquor, of course, but most of the moms'll smell whiskey on your breath if you drink and drive like that. Or the kids'll smell it, and they'll blab. Beer's a safer buzz, and besides, cocktails are gay

("I mean, cock's right there in the *name*"). If one of the dads brought White Claw to an event, the rest'd fuckin' laugh in his face. "What, your balls fall off?" But White Claw doesn't sell in Wallow Valley anyway, so it's a moot point.

At about six-thirty, the dads should start getting ready to head to the American Legion. The moms start getting nervous about everyone being late, so they text all the dads that it's time to go. The dads, per tradition, ignore the first text. It's like hitting snooze. But when they get the *second* text, they better get off their ass. They grumble as they turn off the game, dump their empties in the recycling. They don't text the moms back as they shove into their shoes, and so the moms call, which of course only delays the dads even more. The moms say *way* too nonchalantly, "I think we're all set up here, so please lemme know when you're on your way. And oh. My. God. Remind me I have to tell you. Ronnie is getting under my fuckin' skin. She is *so* anal."

The dads manage to herd the kids into the car, and almost all of the kids have a last-minute emergency, like, "Dad, I can't get my tie right!" Because all the kids have to wear ties to the Awards. Dads don't, but it's *highly* encouraged, according to the moms. Highly. Or, "Dad, I spilled ice cream on my shoes!" Kids gotta wear shined shoes, too (with buckles, is the tradition). Or, "Dad, I can't find my shears!" Because, of course, all the kids bring their shears.

It's a pain in the ass, but the dads finally hustle the kids into the cars. This is an important bonding moment, the getting ready, because the dads get to spit on your stained shoe, rub it clean, or fix your tie knot, find your shears, and they wink at ya, say, "Good as new," and for a second, you're like, *Dad's actually pretty cool.* It's easy to think that because you're ten, your first time being a double-digit (and no turning back now). Most of the things your parents do still seem like magic. And as you drive to the Wallow Valley American Legion, staring out the window while Dad listens to the country station on the radio, you wonder when these adult-superpowers and their odd side effects will transfer to you. *When will I be able to magically locate random items in drawers, but constantly misplace my phone, like Mom? When will I be able to tie my own tie, but also get really hairy, like Dad?* As you ponder these mysteries, you hug your shears to your chest and wonder what the future will be like.

Let me tell you: things will be smaller than you imagine them. You'll return to your third-grade classroom five years from now and believe that someone has shrunk the chairs to squirrel size. You'll visit your old favorite playground (where you got that infamous splinter) and it'll be, like, knee high. It used to be as tall as trees. What happened? Or, better yet, you'll look back at life itself and think, *How did it get so small?*

The dads feel a jerk of anxiety as they turn into the American Legion parking lot. This arrival in the lot is the first very social thing they'll have to do over the course of a very social evening. Smile and small talk. Horrible. But invariably they'll see, pulling up at the same moment as them, Henry or Jeremy or Putts ("Still *mini* golfing, Putts, or didja piss your pants again? Oh, come on, don't be sensitive, it's just a joke," but it's the same joke they've been telling since middle school). They'll feel relieved, because even though they have to be very social now, at least it's with guys they know. As long as they can avoid getting sucked into some weird-ass conversation with Ronnie (who *is* extremely anal), it'll be a fine evening. Free food. Havin' beers with Henry and Jeremy and the gang. Maybe their kid will even win an award.

While the dads shake each other's hands, the kids greet each other tentatively in the parking lot. They admire each other's suits and dresses and shears. Most of the shears still have blood on them.

"Think you'll win anything tonight?" one eight-year-old boy asks.

"Nah." His friend shakes her head. "I only got *one* sinner this year."

Inside the event hall, the moms are all aflutter. They descend on the kids as they enter, and the kids stand Medusa-ed for a moment while the moms floof dresses and adjust hair and ties and tucked-in shirts, and then line them all up so they can take pictures under the balloon arch, posing with their shears. The green and gold balloons shine in the reflections of a hundred camera snaps. Lightning rips through the hall as picture after picture after picture flashes. But the kids don't mind the fuss. It's a chance for everybody to see everybody else dressed up. Some of the boys eye the girls, and the girls eye the boys. A couple of the girls eye the other girls, and some of the guys catch each other eyeing them, but that kind of thing isn't allowed in Wallow Valley. Ain't natural.

Everyone finds their tables (Anal Ronnie has given everyone specific places, which some of the boys flat-out ignore). Everyone carries their paper plates to the troughs along the back wall by the kitchen, where they scoop up pulled pork, lasagna, and Mrs. Dabrovitz's mac and cheese in big steaming dung heaps. Everybody eats, and by the time the youngest kids (the younger siblings) are running around blowing off calories, the cake has magically appeared. This is the magic of the moms: to make food magically appear.

While everyone is eating their cake, Ronnie goes up to the podium by the stage. She adjusts the mic and gives everyone a plastic smile. She says "Good evening" in that way that just *tells* you this is gonna be boring. But you have to hand it to her, she also *knows* how to say, in a way that gets you pumped every time, "Welcome. To the One Hundred and Twenty-Ninth Annual Awards."

Applause. The dads pretend to be chewing still, so they can look disinterested in the applause. A little girl has fallen and skinned her knee on the hardwood floor. She cries over Ronnie's voice. "Every year, every child aged seven through twelve in our great town of Wallow Valley is nominated for five awards." She goes on, but she doesn't say that they also *all* get an award now, which the dads call the Gimme Ribbon. "When I was your age, you weren't rewarded for just participating. That's counter-fuckin'-intuitive." The dads think it's some real liberal pussy bullshit, these Participation Ribbons, but the moms don't care. "Everyone deserves an award."

Gimme a break.

As Ronnie explains, the five major awards are given in order of social clout, like the Oscars. First, though, Anal Ronnie gives the whole spiel about the reason *behind* the Awards. It's stuff you can mostly tune out, you know, like you're eating your cake with the TV on in the background. Really, it's for *her* benefit she gets to say all of this. She doesn't have kids of her own.

She goes on to recite the part about how, every year, Wallow Valley's youth are sent out into the world on an excursion, to seek and cleanse, blah blah blah. They're given seven days, armed with a pair of shears, yadda yadda. When the week is up, the children return to Wallow Valley using only their wits and an allowance of seven dollars (one dollar for each point of the Wallow Valley Star). Then, of course, she explains everything about the Star's history. How She fell that night in September, 1885, and took the form of "a woman made of light, striding down from the hills." And this Star-woman? She "made demands" of the farmers and tanners and cidermen of Wallow Valley. "Build a fence," She said. "Block the roads into the Valley," She said. "Shun the never-blessed." Blah blah, yeah yeah.

I mean, we all *know* the story.

Henry looks up from his pulled pork, chewing. He catches Jeremy's eye, cocks an eyebrow. Jeremy rolls his eyes. Henry laughs silently, takes another shovelful of pork. The children sit around, eager to hear who won. They grip their shears tightly. One of the girls reaches over to her friend's shears and scratches at a clump of hair stuck there.

"Cool," she says.

The friend grins, proud. "You shoulda heard him scream."

At the podium, Ronnie gives the crowd another plastic smile. "And now," she concludes (she was *born* to say, "And now," into microphones), "it's time to announce this year's winner of Best Light."

Scattered applause. Best Light is an honorable award to get. You don't have to try very hard for it, but hey, it's nice to be acknowledged. You just have to blatantly draw attention to yourself, then slip away, make it back over the fence and into the Valley before you're caught. Don't worry, the police never go past the fence. Not after What Happened Back in '83. A night so awe-inspiring, it's always referred to in hushed tones and capital letters: What Happened Back in '83...

So Sarah McGinnis wins Best Light, which is fair. She's short and slick. She can maneuver fast across the soccer field. She's proud to win this award. She holds her shears up for everyone to see. It's an impressive display. These shears have been in her family for a long time, almost since She first came into the valley. They're rusted and the handles wobble, and years upon years of caked sinner blood are spattered 'cross their surface.

Sarah McGinnis takes her small golden trophy and returns to her table, where her dad squeezes her bare shoulder.

Best Clip goes to Benton Carr, a beefy kid who smiles without showing any teeth. He has a doughy face and the dads don't trust him. The moms love him, but the dads can't shake the feeling that he's...up to something. It's that weird, close-lipped smile. No wonder he got Best Clip. "Anyone with that kind of face," Henry texts Jeremy under the table, "knows how to hack off limbs easily." He almost wants to ask Benton what happened out there, but he knows that's against the rules. Nobody knows what happens on the excursions except the kids and the Awards Committee. You only go on the excursions five years running, from seven to twelve years old, and some dads miss the rush of it. Some moms, too, but they won't admit it. Henry wants to ask Benton so bad, "Was it a finger, a toe, a whole arm? I clipped a whole arm once when I was your age. Walked right up to the bus stop and just *shick*. Clipped off some guy's arm and his tweed sinner sleeve. Star as my witness." Henry likes to think of that time as his glory days, which is sad because, you know, he was nine.

Best Mimic goes to the kid who can blend in the best. Over the years, the police in the towns surrounding Wallow Valley have wised to the annual dispersal of dirty children from that fenced-in town. They set up roadblocks and post warnings. "For the first week of September, stay in your homes with the doors locked as much as possible. Beware of alleys, as they may contain what appear to be homeless individuals but are actually WV children." Local celebrities even film commercials warning everyone in the local towns to stay indoors. There are hashtags: #WallowValley. #StopWallowValley. Some of the Valley children are even "rescued" during their excursions and foisted on foster families on the outside, "safe from that abominable cult." This is a fate worse than death, according to Wallow Valley, and the families of these children are shunned.

Simply put, the outside-people know Wallow Valley is a problem. "We shouldna even let it get this far." But that fence? The electrified eight-footer with guard towers that Wallow Valley erected many years ago "to keep the sinners out?" The police will *not* go over that fence. Not after What Happened Back in '83. The way the stars moved that night—it drove men mad.

In the wake of all this outside interference during the excursions, Best Mimic is the kid who does the best job of slipping unnoticed into nearby towns. They're the one who manages to pass as a local and sneak into a school or a Walgreens or a Burger King. They're the one who slips right up behind you as you're pushing your cart down the Wal-Mart aisle, slides those shears from their shirt, slips them round your ankle, and *shick*. Drains the sin from your leg. Or *shick*, snaps an arm in half, drains the sin in great red gouts from the stump of your elbow. And then scampers away before you even know what hit you.

Throughout Ohio, there are many campfire stories about Wallow Valley kids. Even adults in the nearby towns won't sleep with their hands drooping over the side of the bed. Anything could be waiting under there, shears at the ready. Some people say you can tell sometimes, a second before it happens, but by then it's too late. Because right before they cut you, the children whisper, "Star be my witness." And then you'll feel that metal *slice*…

So Danielle Talbot gets Best Mimic. She got, like, four people in a single evening by pretending to be part of the Cincinnati Children's Choir. She even brought the fingers home to show. Her dad taught her how to dry them and hang them on her wall for good luck. She wanted to wear them tonight, but her mom said they didn't go with her dress.

Best Remainder goes to that girl with the clump of scalp stuck to her shears. She deserved it, really. It's a gnarly leftover, that clump. She holds the shears high so everyone can see the long dark hairs, the shred of skin.

Applause.

"And now," says Anal Ronnie, "the moment we've all been waiting for." A dramatic pause. Everyone's done eating now. Ronnie smiles. "Best Live Capture."

She slides a long finger into the green envelope, neatly pops the gold wax seal. She reads the name, "Tucker Graham."

Everyone applauds again. Tucker tromps onstage. He's a tall blond smirk. Very handsome. He bows several times, knowing how handsome he is.

Henry's daughter huffs, crossing her arms. "I woulda won that one if she'd stopped *squirming*."

"Well, you know the saying," says Henry. "Only sinners squirm."

The previous four winners from tonight join Tucker onstage. They all beam and bow. Then they head backstage to retrieve the catch. Brian Graham, Tucker's dad, has parked his truck out behind the American Legion so they can haul the catch right from his truck bed to the stage door. It's a large burlap sack, five ropes stretching out of it. The ropes, of course, are painted green and gold. The five children each take a rope in hand and pull. The sack thumps off the truck onto the ground. They drag it across the floor, onto the stage. With a flourish, Tucker removes the burlap, and the catch lies there, hogtied, blinking against the lights and the *flash* as all the moms snap pictures with their phones.

Now the five winners lift their shears up high. They beam out at all the parents, siblings, grandparents, aunts and uncles, and Mrs. Dabrovitz. The moms begin to film as Tucker leads them in the prayer: "This we offer, in all our grace. We hope this off'ring's to your taste. Star be our witness, feel our light. Drain the sin from this man tonight. We are blessed, he is not. Help us cleanse him, of his rot."

And they begin to hack. To *slice*. The catch screams. He screams for a long time, longer than anybody would expect. Blood is already cascading off the stage, and still he's screaming.

"Yes," yells Henry, cheering them on. "Yes!"

When it's done, the stage is covered in steaming ribbons. Ronnie leads everyone in another round of applause. The blood-soaked winners get to join their parents again, who hug them and peel the guts off their hair to stick on their lapels. Henry gets a piece of skull, tucks it in his breast pocket like a handkerchief. The parents say what a good job everyone's done. There are more pictures. It all goes on Facebook, and it's all evidence, of course. The police could arrest everyone on sight. But what can you do? *Nobody* is willing to cross that fence. Not since What Happened Back in '83. The way the gate in that long solid chain-link motherfucker slid open *slow*, and the things that came through…

Mrs. Dabrovitz and a handful of other moms mop up the stage and the floor. The rest of the moms take a breather and slip out of their heels. They're drinking white wine straight from the bottle now. "Well, we did it. We pulled off another Awards." It's done now. Good job everyone. "I never want to see green and gold *again*."

Ronnie turns down the lights and steps outside the hall to the parking lot. She smokes a Camel in the twilight. It's the only brand that'll send its trucks through the gate in that fence. Sometimes it's hard to get good products, down here in Wallow Valley.

Some of the families break off and head home to shower, enjoy their own private celebrations (i.e., more cake). About half the crowd remains. The dads get another drink from the bar, and the kids all run around playing with chunks of the catch.

The Girl Scouts wash up in the bathroom. The bathroom only has one flickering light, and it makes them nervous. "Star protect me," they murmur. "Lend me your light." But if ever there's a time and place when they feel She can't hear them, it's in this bathroom, on this night.

When they're all sparkly in their Girl Scout uniforms, they line up on the shiny wood stage. They beam. It's dim now in the hall, half-empty and eerie. All the fathers stand in shadows in the back, by the bar, holding drinks, whispering lewd compliments to each other. "Your little Casey really filled out this year, Putts." The moms at the tables all clasp their hands together proudly and grin, lobotomized and unvaccinated. They were Scouts once, too. It's a rite of passage.

Lined up on the stage, the Girl Scouts smile. They flick their eyes nervous but steady over the crowd. Perky in their little sashes, skirts, and knee socks.

It's Mrs. Dabrovitz's turn to speak now. She goes to the microphone, adjusts it with her red nails, and says, "Welcome, everyone, to our annual Scout Auction. This year, we have some exciting items lined up for you. The first item…is Casey Ciotta. Casey likes watching reruns of *The Bachelor* and horseback riding. Casey Ciotta, everyone. We'll start the bidding at five hundred."

One of the dads lifts a paddle. Dabrovitz inclines her head. "I see one thousand. Do I hear two thousand."

Another dad puts up his paddle. Casey's smile falters for a second, but she holds it. If you were up close, you'd see her lips quivering.

By eight-thirty, every item at the Scout auction has been sold. Dabrovitz flicks off the rest of the lights, and everyone puts on their masks for the next event at nine. Dabrovitz goes outside to bum a cigarette off Anal Ronnie. They never participate in the nine o'clock event. "It's too silly for me," claims Dabrovitz. "Not enough action," claims Ronnie.

Which is a shame, because this is always a fun one, I think. Except they're tuning it down this year. Did you hear that? I know, I know, they've been tuning it down *every* year. It's the moms' fault. They're getting sucked into more and more of that liberal pussy bullshit. Those fuckin' participation ribbons were just the beginning of the end.

Get this: This year, when the clock strikes nine, only *four* people get knives, and only *three* of the Scouts are gagged.

Can you believe that?

I know. You ask me, Star as my witness, Wallow Valley's goin' downhill fast.

The Heartbreak Boys

By Andrew Cull

If you're really gonna murder someone, there comes a time, a moment, a millisecond, when all the talking, all the planning, the nightmares, when all of that is done, and there's nothing but the cold weight of the hammer in your hands and that look in their eyes. They know.

That moment, it'll test the depth of your hate. The depth of your anger, your greed, whatever it is that drove you to think murder would be the answer. I was twelve years old, standing in the corn field behind the Randall place, sun so bright I could barely see, sweat streaming into my eyes, holding a hammer so large it took me both hands to raise it over my head. In that moment, you better hope your hate runs deep. That it runs to the bone. Because if it doesn't, everything after that is hell, broken loose and hungry.

I held the hammer above my head, my arms shaking. I could have just as easily dropped it on my own head, it weighed that much. Greg Hayward knew it was coming.

"Fucking do it already!" spat Zeke.

We'd talked about it. Planned it. Planned all the details. We'd sat in that same cornfield, talked it through every evening for two weeks. The four of us. Four boys. Three ten-year-olds and me, the older one, the ringleader, I guess.

We'd acted it out. Taken turns to be Hayward. Worked out who'd be best to play each part. Lucas was fast. He'd be the bait. He'd flag down Hayward's truck. Tell him that Zeke had had a fall, a bad one, and that he needed help.

Zeke was stocky, muscular. He'd be waiting, a way into the field, hiding between the corn rows. He'd have a shovel. When Hayward was far enough in, Zeke would rush him from behind. Hit him across the back of the head, or the legs, just take him down. Hard.

Once he was in the dirt, Lucas, Zeke, and Ethan would hold him down. I'd deliver the final blow. That was my right.

When it was done, we'd empty his pockets. We knew he'd be carrying plenty of cash on him. Takings from the scout stall at the county fair the day before. We'd take that and split it up. Then I'd drive his truck to Three-Mile Creek and roll it off the edge, sink it. No one would ever believe it was us. That four kids, from four of the most respected families in Carver, would team together to murder their Scout Leader.

I'd never been a scout. Never saw much point in learning to tie knots or navigate by the stars. Most times any knot will do, and you can keep your stars, I'll take a map with me. I didn't see any point in it, but Jesse did.

Jesse learned every damn knot, and insisted on following me around the house, showing me how every damn knot got, well, knotted. Jesse was about as much a pain in the ass as any younger brother could be. He followed me everywhere. Sometimes I'd open my bedroom door in the morning, and he'd just be standing there. Some toy, or comic book, or that damn rope in his hands, waiting for me to wake up so he could show me.

It was Jesse who told me about Hayward's trip with the county fair money. That was a month ahead of that day in the cornfield. Hayward had told Jesse about the money run because, at that time, he'd planned to take Jesse with him.

It's called a spike maul. Big like a sledgehammer, only the head's thinner, I guess closer to a pickaxe. They use them to hammer the spikes in along the train track. I'd found mine left in the dirt while I was walking the tracks. I was listening to Jesse's tape of *Born to Run*. Dad would've killed me if he ever found out I'd bought it for him. It felt right that I found the hammer there. Like it'd been left for me. Like I'd know what to do with it.

Each day for a week, I bought a watermelon from Gerry Gatlin at the general store. Each evening, I took that watermelon out to the cornfield, lay it on the ground, swung the hammer, and drove the steel head of the spike maul through it.

A watermelon's bigger than most people's heads. I took to carving a face into them, to give me a better idea of what I was aiming for. It took practice. I couldn't hold the hammer in the air for long, almost drove it through my foot more than once. On the fourth day, I hit the watermelon first time. Hit it on target and it'd crack right open, red flesh bursting out the sides, the face caved in by the impact. I wondered if the first blow would kill Hayward outright. Truth was, most times I could raise that hammer in a row was three. If I missed twice, we didn't have a back-up plan.

Jesse could talk. Oh yeah, he could talk! He could and would talk about anything and everything. He talked about those damn knots, about how to build a campfire, about how Batman was better than Superman, about music, about the weather. If the sun was up, it was likely he was gassing. He was the worst possible person to tell a secret to. There was no malice in it, mind. He just couldn't keep it to himself. I knew what I was getting for my birthday, for Christmas, long ahead of those days coming round. In the end, Mum and Dad stopped telling Jesse what I'd be getting so he couldn't spoil the surprise.

It was more fun when Jesse knew.

The fact that Hayward told Jesse about the money run shows how fucking little he actually knew him.

• • •

Saturday, July 13, 1985. That was the day Jesse stopped talking.

There was nothing strange about Jesse getting back late from his Saturday morning Cub Scouts meeting. He'd often hang out with his friends after they left the den, bike up the creek, or just sit out in the sun. Zeke's dad coached the football team, and Zeke had gotten hold of an old stopwatch of his. They'd gather round, see who could tie and untie their knots the quickest. That game could go on for hours.

But that Saturday, he knew we'd been invited to lunch at Pastor Callahan's house. So, when Jesse still wasn't home by the time we had to leave, and Dad slammed the car door so hard it made Mum cry out, I knew that no excuse, short of divine intervention, was going to save Jesse from the belt when Dad got hands on him.

For three courses, Dad stewed on it. When we'd finally waved our goodbyes and pulled out of the pastor's drive, the smile dropped from Dad's face as quick as if someone had flicked a switch. He gripped the wheel with white knuckles the whole way home.

Jesse was waiting at the end of the porch. He looked so small. Dad had his belt off before he'd even made it to the house. He dragged Jesse off the porch and out to the garage.

Now, I'd heard Dad angry. I'd been in that garage and taken a beating more than once myself. But I'd never heard him scream the way he did at Jesse that afternoon. I couldn't make out everything he said. I was so terrified, I spent most of Jesse's beating in my room with my hands clamped tight over my ears. But I did make out one word. One word screamed again and again: *liar*.

When it was over, I heard tires squeal and Dad's car tear out of the driveway. It took me fifteen minutes more before I could get the nerve up to go check on Jesse. I found him curled into a corner of the garage. Dad had beaten him so bad he could barely walk. I gently picked him up and carried him back into the house.

I was sobbing as I carried him up to his room. I was scared, I was angry, but most of all, I was sorry. I was so sorry I hadn't done something to stop Dad. I remember Jesse wiping the tears from my face. He was trying to comfort me, after everything he'd just been through. I laid him down on his bed. In a quiet voice, he asked me to leave him alone.

That was the last thing he ever said to me.

Saturday stretched into Sunday, and I didn't sleep at all. I heard the car return around ten. I heard Mum and Dad head to bed, but I didn't hear a sound from Jesse's room. No crying, no getting up to pee, nothing.

At 6 a.m., I got out of bed, left my room, and went to stand outside Jesse's bedroom door, the way he'd done to me so many times before. I wanted to be waiting for him when he woke up.

I was still waiting there when Mum and Dad came down the stairs from their room an hour later. I hated them that morning. I hated him for hurting Jesse. I hated her for letting it happen. I hated myself for the same reason. After they'd gone, I knocked quietly on Jesse's door. When he didn't answer, I knocked again, louder. Come on, Jesse! I didn't try a third time. I grabbed the handle and flung his door open.

He was gone.

We still went to church. Dad was convinced Jesse would be back. Said kids ran away all the time. That he was probably out in the corn fields, sulking. I prayed that he was okay.

Jesse didn't come back. At 2:37 that afternoon, my baby brother walked in front of the express train to Edison.

Mum and Dad made excuses. Said Jesse had been listening to his Walkman and hadn't heard the train. Said they'd told him about walking on the rails. Said maybe he'd slipped and fallen. I knew different. I knew, because while we were at church, Jesse had gone back to the house. He'd written me a letter and left it on my bed. *If we'd stayed at home, I might have been able to stop him!*

I knew what he'd told Dad in the garage the day before.

Jesse had stuffed a pair of his underwear down the side of his bed. He'd done that because they were covered in blood. I burned them so no one would ever know what had happened to him.

On the morning of Jesse's funeral, I stood inside my bedroom, looking at my bedroom door. I couldn't open it. I couldn't stand to open it and face that he wouldn't be waiting in the hallway for me. No more knots, no more arguments about comic books, no more stories, no more laughter, no more spoiling my birthday. No more of the things that had filled my days and my heart. I ground my teeth, trying to fight back the angry sobbing that made my whole body shake.

I climbed out my bedroom window, onto the porch roof, hung off the guttering, and dropped onto the driveway below. I left my bedroom door closed.

A couple of days after the funeral, I waited for Zeke outside Gerry Gatlin's store. I knew he'd stop in on his way home from school. I shoved him down the alley beside the store. I just wanted to ask him if he'd known anything about what happened that Saturday. Did he know Hayward had kept Jesse back at the den after their meeting? Did he think it was strange? Why hadn't he told anyone? Jesse was his friend, wasn't he? Why hadn't he done something? Why did he leave Jesse there on his own? I had so many questions, but I couldn't get one of them out for crying.

Then I hit him.

I hit again and again. I beat him till he wailed for me to stop. Till he told me everything.

Jesse hadn't been the first. Zeke, Lucas, Ethan. They'd all reached their tenth birthday before Jesse. That was when Hayward took them into his office at the back of the den. He told them that at ten, they had responsibilities. That at ten, they were now men. That men did things that boys didn't.

Of course, part of being a man was being able to keep a secret. Men had secrets.

Jesse never could keep a secret.

I held Zeke as he cried. I told him it would be okay. I told him it was over.

I told him we were gonna kill Hayward for what he'd done.

There are a lot of reasons in the world to murder someone. It might have looked like money, but mine was a broken heart.

The first day in the cornfield, it was just me and Zeke. He talked, and I listened.

The second day, Zeke brought Lucas with him. The next, Ethan joined us.

In a small, religious town like Carver, no one was gonna take the word of a ten-year-old boy over a respected member of the community. Hayward knew that. In my heart, I wanted to believe that my father had believed Jesse, that he just couldn't stand what he was hearing, that his rage was somehow driven by sheer horror. Every single day, as we met in the cornfield, I waited for my father to act. I waited to hear he'd spoken to Sheriff Owens. I waited to hear he'd been to the scout den. I waited. And the weeks passed. Then Zeke, Ethan, and me were standing in that field, Lucas out on the road, waiting for Hayward's truck to materialize out of the heat haze that snaked across the distant highway.

The high sun made my head pound. I wiped the sweat from my eyes. My fingers were wet, slippery on the hammer's handle.

"I can see him!" Lucas yelled.

I Did a Thing

By Caroline Kepnes

She's crazy to let them in, but it's fun, you know? There's that hour before they arrive. They could be anyone. A psychopath. A rapist. They know where she lives, and they know she's expecting them, and who does this? Who opens their house to strangers? She prepares. She stashes a kitchen knife under a white towel on the table in front of the chair. She keeps a straight razor in her back pocket, and she pictures the stranger in her house, in her chair. The stranger pulls a gun, but she pulls her razor. Blood everywhere, like *Sweeney Todd*, her favorite thing in high school, the image she holds onto for no reason. The story that made her know who she was. What she wanted. To lay a tarp on a person, to slice a throat. No interest in what comes next, the hole in the floor, the partner baking human pies. Just the blade and the blood, and why? Why ask why? It's baby's first sugar. Baby smiles because sugar is good. The *why* is irrelevant, made of science and molecules. But the fixation. The comfort in wanting one thing and one thing only. She did it, you know? She's a stylist, and it's her job to set a white tarp on the future corpse. The trusting client, and the demon "barber." Something sticks with everyone—her cousin Abigail loves dolphins—and *Sweeney* is *why* she went to beauty school, each day flush with the possibility of a single efficient blade, blood squirting and sputtering, opera minus orchestra, no English teacher framing the depravity, squashing it in historical context and moving on to lesser stories, no peers laughing, unaltered, closing their books. Imagine not feeling that play in your bones. She can't.

She's not a sicko. She's never has done it. Thirty-six years on this planet, fourteen of those years, with countless daily opportunities to do it, and look at her cousin. Abigail wanted to swim with dolphins, and she did it. Abigail sent everyone photos—*I did a thing*—and how horrible that part of the desire was rooted in other people knowing. Abigail didn't just want to swim with a dolphin who has no use for her, a dolphin trapped and trained to put up with her. She also wanted people to know what she did. All of it is anathema to the stylist. Visual proof that you did it, like a photo of a haircut. She shudders at those reductive sad dolphin photos in circulation. *I did a thing.* What the hell is wrong with people? What the hell is right with people?

Soon, a client is coming, and this could be it, the day *she* swims with the dolphins. Abigail really did it, and she can too. She learned from her cousin. You can't just jump into the Atlantic and tread water and hope the dolphins come your way. You do your research, hatch your plans, find out where the dolphins are trained, warm, and waiting. The stylist is doing all that. She quit the salon four months ago, started working from home. Easier to kill someone if you're home than if you're in a crowded room, around all those distracting people. Because again, that is *not* what she wants: to be caught, to be seen.

People would get it wrong. They'd say she "snapped"—the spontaneous combustion of a private tradeswoman. But no. This is not a snap. It's a long-fostered dream. A curiosity. It's for her and her alone, and that's what's right with her. She turns on some music, soft and subduing. Won't be long now until her first client of the day rolls up, and will this be it? Going solo was the right move. Salons haven't been good to her. Always some owner, some older broad with a chip on her shoulder, telling her what to do, what not to do. Better to work at home, on her terms, on her schedule. She has a solid clientele. Loyal, giggling women and a few lonely men who are happy to follow her wherever she goes, even to this new little house, if you can call it that. More like a shack really. Wrong side of a nice road. All the good houses on the water, all of the smaller bad houses on the other side of the street, pushed into the woods, as if someone didn't want them to see the water. Smell it, yes. See it, no.

This could be it. First client is due at eleven. A new woman. She doesn't want to "kill" a longstanding client. I mean, she would, if it came to that, but it's preferable to do it to a *stranger*. She has no agenda, no vendetta against any one person. She didn't ask for this. No dolphins are born *wanting* to swim with lousy humans. The same for her future corpse. Sometimes, you get picked for no reason.

But who is she to think today's the day? No day has ever been the day, and her will is a receding hairline. She'll never do it. All people picture things. Things they wouldn't tell you about. Right? Maybe. Hopefully. Nothing in her background points to her urges. Remember her dog Alfie? Trusting Alfie, sweet boy. All the things she could have done to him, all the things she never did to him, never wanted to do to him. Alfie died by the vet's needle, not by her hand, and it's funny how the social contract chooses *this* moment to rear its ugly head. 10:46. The client will be here any minute, and she's wimping out already, striving for normalcy, the commonplace comfort of checking boxes at the doctor's office—no, you don't have this; no, you don't have that—an average patient handing over a clipboard packed with proof that she's no big deal.

Who is she kidding? She'll never do it.

10:49 and here we go. The slow creep of a sedan, wheels crushing the broken shells on the driveway. Hesitant. A woman this time. She probably told her friends she was nervous about today, trusting a stranger, going to someone's *house*. They all like to start out by telling her that someone knows where they are, and this woman is no surprise, emerging from the sedan, waving. Not a serial killer or a rapist. Slightly crooked nose. Careful not to step on the flowers. Humble. Hesitant.

The stylist calls out—*Door's open, come on in!*—and the client does as told, and it's the hellos and how-are-yous, and the autopilot small talk and the reliable irritation, another reminder of what all people do: render themselves unkillable without even meaning to do it.

11:03 a.m. The client wants what most of them want. *Cut a little, but not too much, no big changes, just a trim.* She goes to work, first washing the hair, and there's always the possibility that the client is sicker than her, that it's all an act. The client closes her eyes, nervous and laughing, *I've never had a haircut anywhere except a salon.* The stylist says the right things—*I'm harmless, I promise*—and the client believes her. The closed eyes, the exposed flesh of the neck, and does she do it? Does she slash her skin? Nope!

And then it's off to the other chair. The client is confident now. Quick to relax, to assume the stylist is a fellow normal. They talk about movies, about all the bad drivers, and all the while the razor is in her back pocket, just in case they turn on her, but there is no case. Ever. And remember...That's not what she wants, how she wants it. She doesn't want a *fight.* She wants the blood, not the war. She doesn't want it to be an act of self-defense, so why should she be mad when they don't give her a "reason" to act?

All done cutting, and she sets her scissors on the counter and picks up the blow-dryer. Loud white noise. Painstaking. Monotony. The plastic, decapitated, neckless heads at beauty school coming back to her. Separate the hair into chunks. Pull. Blow. Repeat infinity.

And then the client rejoices. *I love it here. What a great spot! See you in six weeks, or maybe a year. Ha!*

Always the same dumb jokes, no idea how close they came to death, but the stylist doesn't mean to be cruel. She doesn't look down on these people, not really. It's human nature, the way she saddens when they leave, alive and restored. It's no fun being left, ever. The sedan that held so much promise now backing out, leaving the same way it came in, proving that it was all transactional, that the client got what she paid for but, once again, the stylist did not.

Twenty-four minutes until the next client, and weeks of this now, six women a day sometimes, four men a week, spread out, and something has to change. There are things she can do. Be like the English teacher and frame things differently. The universe is a psychopath, watching and aware. As long as she is prepared, the chance will never come. The will is destined to recede. She deserves to be punished. So, she does it. She stashes her razor and her knife in her safe. And now even if someone does attack her, she'll die, likely. Weeks of this nonsense. Defenseless with regulars and strangers. Every day devoid of possibility. People going on about their brother's wedding, a parking ticket. No one attacks her, and she attacks no one.

And then a new message on the online marketplace. A man. No photo.

Do you have time Saturday?

I have a family event Saturday. (It's a funeral, but he's a stranger, and you don't do that to a potential client; you don't tell them you have to go to a *funeral.*) *But I could do Sunday, 10 a.m. does that work?*

Yes, it does! See you then. I'm Mark, by the way.

I'll text you to confirm day before. See you then, Mark.

Mark. A literal mark. *Sunday Bloody Sunday!* An offering from the universe! No woman in her right mind gives faceless *Mark* her home address. But she does it. The night before *Mark,* she texts him again to confirm. No response. Nothing. Phone is dead. Chills. Joy. *Mark.*

Sunday morning. Happy. Alert. Up early, searching for anything about Mark and his life online. Nothing. The phone must have been a burner. He is on his way, expecting her to be alone—she is online, knowable, and she has no one, no partner, no kids—and she almost feels bad for Mark, so trusting, possibly innocent, undeserving. But then, she is righteous. Maybe he really *is* a baddie. And let's face it. Life is always going to let you down, force you to compromise. Young Abigail wanted to *be* a dolphin, but older Abigail wanted to swim with them.

Time passing faster now. What will he look like? Will their eyes lock in the mirror right before she does it? Will he see her for who she is, will he know what she is capable of, or will he mistake her for a normal and close his eyes, lean back, thinking he has all the time in the world to kill her? Hard to picture without knowing what he looks like but that's part of the fun.

Wheels on shells. He's fifteen minutes early. He steps out of the car—a coupe—and waves. A letdown. Unsuspecting sandy hair. Soft shoulders. Slow, unsure steps, fussing with his keys. He's not the violent type. He didn't come here to kill her. He's just going to sit in her chair and talk about his breakup. This is a sad man, and he sits, he talks. She was right. The ex-girlfriend cheated on him, betrayed him, but there's more. She is stalking him, calling him at all hours, so he deleted all his social media and got a burner phone. Saying too much. Swallowing. Adam's apple swollen, daring. Would her razor cut through it? Eyes closed when he gets to the punchline. *My life is a mess, but a haircut's one way to fix it!*

Painful, the way he cracks a joke to lighten the mood. They all do that, and they're all the same. You want to smack them, not slaughter them. And then it's over. Mark is a new man, likes what he sees in the mirror. The stylist is *amazing*, and she takes the compliment, the tip. He looks around her house. She can feel him liking her, and why can't he feel her wanting to be Sweeney Todd? Here it comes. Predictable. He asks if she ever worries about letting strangers know where she lives.

She laughs. Polite. Warm. Open to a nice guy. "I have good instincts about people, so I don't worry that much."

The way he believes her. Clueless. Scarlet cheeks. Adam's apple bobbing beneath his skin. And then, the words. "Maybe you'd like to get a coffee sometime."

She doesn't want to get a coffee. She wants to take her switchblade to someone's throat. No music soaring. Demon barber. Mark has bad instincts about people. No idea who she is, what she is capable of, if only she could do it. He's so nice. It was too hard for him to ask her out, and he deserves a yes. Good guy. She smiles. "That would be great."

And then the goodbye. He's going to get a new phone and he'll text her later. Poor guy. Devoid of all demons except the one he fails to recognize. Terrible taste in women. But then is she any better? Capable but inert. Always waiting. Backing away. That's what he's doing in her driveway, backing out, no idea of how close he came to his end. She waves goodbye. Like a normal, like a woman who met a man.

A quick sad standing lunch in the kitchen. Ritz crackers and cheese. Not together. Separate.

And now another car in the driveway. New girl. Twenty something. Long greasy hair. A furrowed brow. Beeline for the house. The stylist wants a story. She wants this to be Mark's ex. She was following him, she's onto them. She came here to tell the stylist to stay the hell away from her man. At some point, the darkness has to knock on her door, barge in, howling.

No such luck. The woman isn't Mark's ex. She's just *going through it, you know?* Trouble at work, her stylist moved away, worst possible timing. Drama queen. Unkillable because enough with the *drama*. The woman would be in heaven screaming. *Of course I was murdered by a random psycho for no reason! Story of my life!* The stylist can't do it. This woman is too fragile. Talks too much. Frenetic apologies. *I'm so embarrassed. I should have washed my hair. You must think I'm gross. It's so greasy. But of course they shut off the water in my building.* The stylist understands. Comforts this woman, this teacup on a card table in an earthquake. She assures her that most people ruin their hair by washing it *too much*, no shame in a little grease. The words help. The water runs. The eyes close. The neck is right there, and maybe she was wrong. Maybe she could do it. Imagine Mark if she did it. Pulled the razor. "Snapped."

I met this woman, she cut my hair in her house, and she seemed great and an hour after I leave...She murders a perfect stranger. And I had no idea! I was right there, and I had no clue!

Can't do it. Can't bear the idea of Mark with a "story." And no trap door. Car in the driveway. Why didn't she rent a house with a garage? Why no trap door in the floor?

Combing the hair now. The client has an idea. She wants bangs. *Is that crazy?* The stylist says what you have to say when people want bangs. *Yes, it is crazy.* The client laughs. It's the *good* kind of crazy. *Let's do it.* Oblige. Pull the hair forward. The client is blinded by her own mane. Neck covered but easily manipulated. Grab the head by the face, yank, pull the razor, that's it. Could be it.

Nope. She cuts the hair. Miles of it on the floor. A mountain. The shock of the bangs. Too short. Irreversible. The client hates it, but she knows it was her choice, and she needed something new to hate. *Do you know what I mean?*

The stylist smiles. *They'll grow out. And they look better than you think. It's always a shock.*

A mountain of lies, and the client stares at herself in the mirror. As if the stylist isn't here. The bangs were a mistake. The client wants to keep going. The bangs are too short, and now the hair is too long. *Can we take off a few more inches?*

It's like she *wants* to stay, to die. This could be it. Do this, and the client doesn't have to deal with her bangs. Do this and Mark wakes up. But then what? Police. Tedium. Handcuffs. A trial. Cutting hair in a prison, eventually, way down the road. Actually, no. Scratch that. No warden is going to give her a pair of scissors.

Walls closing in. Failure. How did Mark get in her head? She drops the scissors. She bends. She stays like that. Head down. All the blood rushing. The trap of the world.

"Are you okay?"

The client's voice. An intrusion. She gets back on her feet. Too fast. Dizzy. The client bites her lip. The client knows she isn't safe. Something is off. Bangs, but something darker. The client pulls the white sheet off her body, her living body. Scrambling for her phone. No eye contact. *I forgot I'm supposed to pick up my friend now. Can I Venmo you later?*

Venmo is okay, and the client is out the door, almost jogging, like she's on the run from a psychopath. No proof, just a feeling. A gut instinct. She's going to tell people about the weird feeling she had in the chair. The bad bangs. Shorter than she wanted. Her friends aren't going to come here. They'll stick to the salon, where they feel safe. *Even with a woman, you just never know.*

Barren hours. Turn off the radio. Silent house. Nothing new from Mark, not yet. The afternoon will be another bust. A loyal client due at 3:00, not the kind of person she wants to kill. Midday blues. Low blood sugar. She can't slash the throat of an acquaintance, and she can't do it to anyone she *doesn't* know.

Yesterday, her cousin's funeral. Cousin Abigail. *I did a thing.* Abigail was like that. She did things. She went down to Florida and swam with dolphins, and then she came home and died of a heart attack two weeks later. They weren't close. Eleven years apart. But the stylist went to the funeral. A two-hour drive, and the whole way there, *why, why, why* was she going? If she died, she wouldn't have expected Abigail to show up. And then she was there. Too many people—Abigail was married, kids, *I did a thing*—and then after, in the meeting room, all the sad whispers: *why, why, why*? Abigail was young! Healthy! No family history! The stylist nibbled on a Danish and watched the door. A mass of any kind is a neck below two closed eyes in a home salon, an over the shoulder wink to a shooter, a dare.

What a waste. No one stormed the gates with guns blazing. Why did her mind do this? Pressing a blade into the flesh of a human, oh God yes, yes please. But arbitrarily blowing away mourners? Oh God no, never. And *why, why, why* with Sweeney thoughts here, now? Alone in a sea of pastries and strangers and not one of them afraid of her. Stupid people. Blind. All the loud performative *whys.*

On the way home, it was simple. I'll tell you *why.* Abigail was dead because dreams are tricky no matter their size, their substance. A razor in your pocket, the idea of bangs, a dolphin in the water. Go after them, and you wind up in a casket of bobby pins. Give in to a dream, and you might go to *prison.* Better to leave dreams alone, like bangs that grow out as you grow into them, as you outgrow the need for them. Maybe one day, for no reason—*why, why why*—maybe she won't want that razor in her pocket. Dreams are dolphins are bangs are fixations. They don't last forever. If she watched *Sweeney Todd* right now, would she even like it?

Shake it off. 2:46. A familiar client due at 3:00 and Mark already texted—he really didn't sense anything off in her—and the client with the bangs is the same. *Sorry I snapped. You were great, and I'm actually loving my bangs!* Nothing to say to either of them, no time to say it. Pavlov's dog barking in the yard, tires rolling over cracked seashells. The slam of a car door, footsteps.

Happier now. The sweet spot of life, when the dolphins are trained and ready, when the next client is knocking on the door. *Come on in!* She could do it. The client is at ease, already sitting in the chair by the sink. Again, this is not what the stylist wants, not exactly, but now she sees it, the trick to getting through life. She's not *exactly* what Mark wants, and nobody "loves" their new horrible hair. But you deal with it. Abigail on the boat. The wind had teeth, and the dolphins didn't glisten and smile the way they did in pictures. Maybe she bought time. Chalked it up to nerves while she waited for the flicker of darkness to pass. And then she did it. She chased her dream into the sea and smiled that unbearable showcase of a smile.

The woman in the chair is an Abigail type of woman. Married, kids, *I did a thing.* At her funeral people will be aghast. *Why, why, why?* The sweet spot is souring, and the stylist pulls the razor. This is it. She could do it. Never been this close. Too close. The stylist wants to slash a throat, yes, but she also wants to talk to someone *after* she kills them, to *why, why, why*? Impossible as wanting to be a dolphin. Horrible to realize what she wants, for the person she kills to tell her why she killed them.

The client opens her eyes. She laughs. Howling, fearless. "You crack me up, Holly."

This is what she is, a joke. "Oh?"

The pre-corpse closes her eyes, as in *get back to work.* "Your razor," she says. "I know that's a thing now, slice and dice the hair to thin it out, but I'm not up for anything new today. Not in the mood for any big risks. Maybe next time?"

Holly slides the razor into her pocket. "Definitely."

Different now. Everything. She runs a comb through the hair on the head, still attached to the neck. Sticky and clean. A final feeling. Happy and triumphant, like un-cutting bangs. No desire to *why, why, why* with this client, not anymore. And okay, she didn't do *the* thing—it's not baby's first sugar—but she did *some* things. She killed the insecure human part of the dream, and she trained the dolphin, and she bought time to figure out what to do with the body, with the car. If things go well with Mark, who knows? Maybe she'll invite him to the funeral.

The Bystander

By LP Hernandez

My mother said I came out incomplete, that the best parts of me dribbled down her leg when my father was finished. This was meant to hurt me, I think. I'm not skilled at understanding interactions like that. I nodded, waited for her to say more, but instead, she took a long drink from the bottle of gin she'd been nursing for a few hours. I think that was supposed to hurt me as well.

I understand physical pain just fine. I've been brought to my knees from a stubbed toe more than once. It's that other interpretation of pain, the one you can't see, that never really resonated.

"Don't you love me?" Mom asked.

I peeked around my hand, held in front of my face so I wouldn't see her breasts floating on top of the pink water. She smiled, eyes swinging lazily between me and her arm as if wanting me to notice it. The blood wasn't flowing as quickly now. I almost told her she didn't cut deep enough, but it felt like one of those things she would get mad at me for.

"Yes, Mom."

I did. That wasn't a lie. I loved my mom.

She smiled.

The tendons in my shoulder felt like warm string cheese, so I dropped my hand. I blurred my vision, so Mom's breasts were out of focus, but even fuzzy and glimpsed peripherally, warmth pooled below my belly button.

"Then why don't you stop me?" she asked, gesturing at the razor blade on the porcelain next to her ear.

I swallowed. I usually messed these moments up, said the wrong thing. Mom wanted to kill herself. She said so more times than I could count. Other than telling me my father was only good for his money, that was probably the most common phrase uttered in our house. I understood she wanted to die. I understood when she did die, there would be no more Mom. I would have to live with Uncle Dale because Dad said I wasn't allowed around his real family.

"Mom?"

She sat up in the tub a bit, breasts creeping back into view.

"Yes?"

"Will I have to change schools?"

She frowned, hope draining from her eyes, "What?"

"I really like the lunches at my school, and I don't know if I would like them as much at another school if you kill yourself and I have to move in with Uncle Dale."

"Lunches?"

I nodded, "The tater tots are the best."

She sank into the water until it touched the bottom of her chin.

"Do…do you *want* me to die?"

"No."

"But you won't stop me?"

"No."

She took a deep breath.

"Can you leave, please?"

I stood, took a step toward the door, but hesitated there. "Mom?"

"Yes?"

"Do you know if the new school will have tater tots?"

Gary 2 is almost ready. He's asleep at the moment, the cat he named Mr. Gray, like fresh-from-the-dryer laundry, between his legs. It's kind of funny he named the cat Mr. Gray when his name is Gary 2. They're almost the same. Maybe he hasn't made the connection.

I named him Gary 2 because when I made it back to the Gs, I couldn't think of another name that started with G. (Later I thought of George, but he didn't look like a George) It's like how they used to name hurricanes, I think. That's probably where I got the idea. I'll admit, I skipped over the X. All X names are really Z names anyway.

I've learned so much from Gary 2. We've been through a lot together. Gary 2 doesn't know he is almost ready, probably thinks this is just what his life is now. Considering what he endured in the past year or so, the prospect might be comforting.

He was scarecrow-thin the day I picked him up. A junkie, obviously, which is not my first choice among subjects, but they're easy pickings.

My dad came around more after his wife divorced him. Uncle Dale spilled the beans about Dad's other family after Mom died. I think Dad was okay with it, as he was ready for something new.

It was through my dad I learned if you present a certain image to the world, you can get away with pretty much anything. It isn't *wealthy*, either. Many people make that mistake. Do you think an addict or runaway pregnant teenager would get into a Porsche? No. I would have my hackles raised as well. Surprisingly, I've had the most success with my pickup truck. It's modern but not new, comfortable but not top-of-the-line. Maybe it reminds people of their own fathers or grandpas.

There was nothing special about Gary 2 when I found him off Grand Street, other than he was alone. He wore more layers than the weather required and rubbed his hands together either to keep them busy or warm. I told him I would get him some clean needles and food, said he could use my shower. Though I didn't have any drugs for him, I would drop him off on Grand Street with money to carry him through the weekend. That was enough, the hope of another fix, more than the prospect of a meal or shower.

There he is now, sleeping with Mr. Gray, the cat flipping his tail in the midst of a dream. I am anxious to push Gary 2 across the finish line, but not so anxious I need to wake him unnecessarily. I want the realization to be organic. I want him to put the puzzle pieces together, with no outside influence. It's what he's here for, after all.

While I wait for him to wake, I access the Gary 2 file with all my favorite moments. It's a big file. He's been here longer than any subject, by a margin of six months. Junkies present a specific challenge in that it is difficult to predict what combination of drugs, and in what amount, will incapacitate them without killing them. Most of the downtown junkies are on heroin, and I have a pretty reliable cocktail for them, but I've been wrong before.

On the day I found him, Gary 2 was obviously on heroin, and the cocktail left him draped over the kitchen island before it was half consumed.

There are four cameras in Gary 2's room. The ceiling-mounted camera offers an overall view but is blurry in the corners. Another behind Gary 2's bed is trained on the door I use to enter and exit. A third covers the bathroom area. Gary 2 woke an hour-and-a-half after his cocktail. I guess he needed the sleep. In the recording, he starts pawing at the collar around his neck. The fourth camera is zoomed on Gary 2's face, though it is actually programmed to follow the sensor in his collar. This is my favorite view. He hasn't blinked for over a minute. What's going on in that mushy brain of yours, Gary 2?

He jolts as I enter the room, eyebrows dancing between fear and hope. Here he is, collared, a chain fastened to the hasp on the back of the collar, which vanishes into the floor, and he still smiles when he recognizes me. He thinks I am here to save him. Must be the plaid shirt, maybe the slight paunch of my belly. I don't look like someone who would do this. That's fair. He doesn't look like someone who would survive as long as he has.

"Your name is Gary 2," I tell him.

"What? My n-name is—"

"Your name is Gary 2."

He slips a finger inside the collar and tugs. I pluck the remote from my pocket and show it to him. I flip the switch and the chain retracts, plastering Gary 2 to the bed, cutting off his air as the gears begin to squeak at the resistance. He yelps, and I flip the switch to reverse the chain, giving him a little slack. Each time I demonstrate the remote for a subject, I am reminded of Oprah.

Now, you're going to conjure a mental image of Oprah, and I would advise you to examine your prejudices. When I got to the Os, it was the first name I thought of. I made the mistake of leaving the remote in my front pocket as I went about my day, and I guess the switch flipped inadvertently. I hadn't even checked the monitor when I entered the room with lunch (turkey sandwiches), so it was quite a surprise. Her roommate was just as surprised. He cried while cleaning Oprah's hair and blood out of the gears of the contraption, which was very peculiar; as to my knowledge, he didn't even know her.

But he did get an extra turkey sandwich for lunch, so that's something.

"Wh-what is this? Why am I here?" Gary 2 asks.

He doesn't perceive me as a threat yet.

"Whatever happens, just behave as you normally would. You don't need to perform," I say, indicating the cameras in the room. "It won't change anything."

"I don't understand."

"That's fine," I say, turning to leave.

"Wait!"

I stop, hand on the doorknob.

"What about my fix?"

For all the problems they present, junkies are endlessly fascinating. Their thoughts always travel in the same direction, even when they're cleaning Oprah's flesh and gray matter from the teeth of a gear the size of an eighteen-wheeler's hubcap.

I check the live feed. Gary 2 stretches his twig arms over his head. He calls for Mr. Gray, watches the doggie door I added to the main door, but the cat is no longer in the room. Mr. Gray's food and water dishes are in the kitchen. I do not interact with the cat beyond filling its dishes. It is not my cat, after all.

Gary 2 inspects the floor. He swallows, Adam's Apple like a baby's fist trapped in his throat. He looks at the camera, expression blank but his eyes are screaming. Gary 2 has not eaten in three days. His belief this is an oversight is buckling. We have a history with food, and as Gary 2 considers the emptiness of his belly, I open another file.

It was Gary 2's fourth day. The first night was rough for him. The withdrawals hit him hard right about the time the pizza delivery showed up. I always order pizza on junkie-withdrawal days. It's the perfect food because if I don't finish the whole pie, I don't have to rush to the refrigerator to preserve it. I usually want another slice before bed, anyway.

Gary 2 always vomited in the blue bucket, which I appreciated because some of his predecessors acted like they were auditioning for *The Exorcist 4* (or did they already make that one?). Junkie puke is among the worst things I have smelled. Mom's body is still probably number one, but not by a lot. After I added the drain to the floor, it wasn't so bad, just hose 'em off like how Mom used to spray the cat turds off our driveway. They were strays. Mom said I couldn't be trusted with animals.

Gary 2 hadn't kept anything down for days, and the fog in his brain was beginning to lift. His body's primal needs surpassed the ache of withdrawal. He prodded his ribs and smacked his waxy lips, drank all the water I provided.

I enter the room, the tray wobbly as the bowl slides back and forth. The camera doesn't capture my face well, which is good, because I tend to bite my lip when concentrating, and it looks a little silly. In another view, Gary 2 sits up. He is no longer confused about my role in his captivity. He hides behind skeleton fingers, eyes swollen grapes held together by throbbing capillaries. I place the tray on the floor, nod, and walk away. Gary 2 watches the door for a minute. Then he worms across the bed, certain he won't have enough slack to reach the tray. He does reach it, however.

There are so many expressions on his face, eyebrows arching and collapsing, lips undulating, offering glimpses of gray gums and candy corn teeth. He looks toward the camera and back to the bowl, then places it on the floor, not with violence as some before. Confusion, maybe?

He might suspect I was attempting to poison him. What a waste of effort that would be, to kidnap someone, hold them hostage for days, only to poison their food.

Gary 2 stirs the spaghetti, which is just noodles and room temperature, extra-chunky pasta sauce. I used to put more effort into the meals, but the subjects were unreliable with their feedback, only telling me what I wanted to hear (if still able to speak). He twirls the tiniest bite and grazes his tongue past it, recoiling at once. Sigh, there goes my Michelin star. Hand on belly, he scrapes a bit off with his teeth. He chews, casts a sideways glance at the camera, and chews some more.

He licks his lips, twirls again, then takes a big bite. His cheeks swell like a water balloon. He chews. Once. Twice. Then he shudders, sits upright, glances at the camera. He opens his mouth, and pulverized noodles slide past his lips, the cartoon red of the sauce mingled with a darker crimson. He pinches a shard of glass, holds it under the lamp, then looks back at the bowl. He stirs, blood dangling from his lips in twisting ribbons.

What is that expression on your face, Gary 2? What do you feel? Betrayed? You didn't even know me. Sad? Angry? Help me understand. Gary 2 places the bowl on the tray, nudges it under the neighboring bed, then zombie-walks to the bathroom sink where he spits pink water until it turns clear.

"What do you mean she's dead, Avery?"

I held my nose as I peeked inside the bathroom. The water had drained from the tub, and I could only see a hemisphere of her shoulder. Still dead. Extra dead, actually. The skin looked like bread dough rolled in cigarette ash.

"She killed herself, Uncle Dale, just like she wanted. Remember how she always said that?"

"Avery, what? This doesn't make sense. What are you saying? Have you checked to make sure she's not breathing?"

"I checked the first day. She wasn't breathing then."
"What do you mean the first day? When did this—"
"Last week."
"She killed herself last week?"
Uncle Dale's concern was slipping into anger.
"Yeah, but she wanted to. She told me all the time and-"
"Avery, why are you...why are you just telling me now? I c-could've saved..."
I cleared my throat, "No, she did a really good job, went all the way to the bone. Not like the other times."
"But why didn't you call?" He sobbed.
"Well, um, Friday is tater tots day at school and..."

What did I feel watching Gary 2 eat room temperature spaghetti and glass shards? More importantly, what *should* I have felt? Uncle Dale was inconsolable when he arrived, though he and Mom were only birthday-phone-call-close. He punched holes in the walls and kept gripping me by the shoulders, tears in his eyes while asking me to tell him how it happened.

Mom died because she wanted to. Why punch holes in the wall over that? Gary 2 more than likely did not want to eat spaghetti with glass shards in it, but my reaction to witnessing it was the same.

It shouldn't have been. I know that, even if I don't understand it. Mom said I was incomplete. If I am today, it is not for lack of trying.

Back on the live feed, Gary 2 crouches to check beneath the unoccupied bed across from his. No, there is no food under the bed, Gary 2. This isn't an Easter egg hunt; it's a make-Avery-whole hunt. He sits on the bed, two hands on his stomach now, and watches the doggie door. Do you still call it a doggie door if it's only a cat using it?

Gary 2 hasn't had a roommate in a while. The last one nearly broke him, I think. I navigate to my Gary 2 and Rita file, skip past their first couple of days together. Gary 2 was so helpful pushing her through withdrawals. He held her hair when she puked, told her not to trust anything I fed her the first few days. In fact, Gary 2 shared his food with her, even inspected it for glass first.

They were becoming friends. I introduced television to the dynamic, one of those fatbacks the teachers used to wheel in to play *Bill Nye the Science Guy*. Gary 2 mostly let Rita pick. I improved the quality of the food, switched the toilet paper to three-ply. Things were going well for them. Rita sometimes watched TV from Gary 2's bed. He pretended to watch, to be interested in the small claims courtroom shows she favored, but mostly he looked at her. He sought moments for them to touch, picking lint off her top, counting and comparing track marks.

Gary 2 drapes an arm over Rita's shoulder when I enter. He is her protector now. I tell Rita to come with me and show her the remote to remind her she does not have a choice in the matter. She does. I provide enough slack for her to follow me through the door. There is no camera here, but I remember the interaction.

"What is this?" she asks, hands like little mallets at her side.

"Almond Joy. It's coconut with almonds. I buy all I can because it seems like one of those candies no one eats except for me, and I worry they're going to go out of business."

"No thank you," she sneers.

I show her the remote, and she puts out her hand.

"Don't tell Gary 2. I didn't bring one for him. Eat it and give me the wrapper."

She does. There was no expression on her face, but my guess is she doesn't prefer coconut in her chocolate. I take the wrapper and tell her, "Remember, Rita, don't tell Gary 2. I'm listening."

Gary 2 peppers her with questions, which she deflects, "He said not to tell you."

He reclaims the remote, spreads out on the bed so she can't join him. For dinner that evening (ham sandwiches with kettle chips) I include a stick of spearmint gum for each of them. Inside the wrapper of Gary 2's gum, I wrote:

Check toilet tank after Rita is asleep. Don't tell her. I'm listening.

I do dose their food and beverages occasionally. Just enough to keep them from waking if I enter the room. The night before, I hid a "junkie kit" inside the tank of the toilet. I included everything Gary 2 would need for his fix, except for the heroin. I also included a box cutter and another note.

Made Rita swallow sixteen baggies of heroin.

Gary 2 sits on the bed, back to Rita, who was asleep. He reads the note for maybe the fiftieth time, examines the supplies again. He doesn't look at the cameras, seems to have forgotten where he is. Remember what I said about a junkie's thoughts? It goes for recovering junkies as well.

"Hey!" he hisses.

She wakes after the seventh attempt.

He shows her the kit and the note.

"Just throw it up. W-we can use the bucket," Gary 2 says.

He's rubbing his hands together.

"Wh-what? No. He didn't give me heroin. He gave me a fucking nasty candy bar."

(I was right about the coconuts.)

"Don't lie to me. Why w-would he g-give you candy? That doesn't make sense."

"I don't know why! He made me eat it in front of him, then told me not to tell you."

"You're lying."

"Why would I lie about that?"

It's then, Rita notices the box cutter. Gary 2 has a death grip on it.

"Then throw up and prove it," Gary 2 says, leaning forward.

She refuses.

The argument persists for thirty minutes. At the end of it, Gary 2 is standing over an eviscerated corpse, sobbing, hands thick with Rita's blood. There is no heroin. He was very thorough in his search.

During her conversations with Gary 2, Rita mentioned she never wanted to be a mother, that she would be terrible at it. Well, bullet dodged on that one, but it was a hell of a way to find out.

• • •

Mr. Gray is asleep on Gary 2's bed. His belly is extra full. Gary 2 sniffs the tuna-scented air around the cat and cradles his stomach again. Mr. Gray is his only friend in the whole world, probably the sole reason he hasn't drowned himself in the toilet. But a thought has invaded Gary 2's mind. He eases off the bed, careful not to wake the sleeping puff ball. There are tears in his eyes as he shuffles to the toilet. He checks the tank.

No. Not this time. You have the right idea, though.

He sits next to Mr. Gray, pets him awake.

Come on Gary 2, home stretch now. I can almost feel the tears brimming in my eyes. Almost.

Mr. Gray stretches, presents his quivering belly.

I believe in you, Gary 2.

I believe in us.

"What would you do if I let you go?" I ask Gary 2.

He is not speaking to me, has the blanket pulled over his head. I flip the switch on the remote.

"Fuck!" Gary 2 screams, thrashing free of the blanket.

"Would you kill me?"

There is something darker than hate in his eyes. In the silence, I think I can hear the squeak of his enamel, flexing as he clenches his teeth.

"Would you kill me?" I ask, showing him the remote.

"No."

"What would you do?"

He only breathes through his mouth, probably to avoid the stench of the chaos on the floor.

"I would make you suffer. I would cut your mother's eyes out and feed them to you."

I hold up a hand, "She's passed, unfortunately."

Gary 2 is hyperventilating, "I would kill every member of your family in front of you. One by one. But I wouldn't kill you.

No. You would suffer. You would beg for me to kill you. I would destroy everything you loved. I would never stop. Never."

I take a breath. Something stirs in that place below my belly button.

"Promise?"

"Yes," he spits.

The collar unclasps and falls free of his neck. I place the remote on the nightstand and hop onto the neighboring bed. I fasten the collar around my own neck and secure the lock. (I practiced this all day. When the time came, I didn't want to look foolish.)

"My address book is on the kitchen counter," I say.

Gary 2 stands, grabs the remote and holds it to his chest. He slinks away, never turning his back to me.

I am incomplete, Mom. I know that now. I also know watching people suffer won't change it.

I hope Gary 2 keeps his word. It's the only way I'll learn.

Everyone's a Critic

By Greg Sisco

Forgive me, Father, for I have sinned. It has been two restaurant reviews since my last confession.

I ache. Every night, I drive home specked with tiny burns from droplets of grease, legs sore from standing, spirit worn from smiling. Every night I need a glass of whiskey to help me sit at the computer and check Yelp for new reviews.

These people, Father. You can't please them.

My parents and teachers prepared me for a world where you succeed to the level you're willing to work, but the world we have now isn't the one they grew up in. It isn't the one they promised. When I built Pasta Pronto, I told myself the harder I worked at perfecting my ingredients and my atmosphere, the higher the business would rise, but it's not that simple anymore.

We have the internet now.

It used to be the jobs picked the people, and it took skill to get started. You had to study, to pass tests, to be apprenticed by a master before you could work a trade. But the new generation, they just *decide*. They say, "I'm a novelist now," or "I'm a graphic designer," or "I'm a food critic," and then they just *are*, without having to learn a thing in order to get there.

The novelist self-publishes a sixty-page diaper rash with more typos than commas. The graphic designer opens an online T-shirt shop built entirely on infringed copyrights. And the critic...the critic says that *my* fettuccine with shrimp doesn't have enough shrimp.

He actually says that. And nobody cross-checks him either. Nobody holds his feet to the fire about the correct shrimp-to-pasta ratio and how he'd know better than I—I who spent four years in culinary school, scribbling through notebooks to make sure I took in everything. All that time spent working up to my profession. I didn't just give myself permission to start wherever I wanted the way these young people think they're entitled to.

No. He says not enough shrimp, and that's the end of it. Yelp lets him say it, and now it's there in print, forever. My fettuccine is short on shrimp. Case closed.

I'm sorry, Father, I'm getting sidetracked. I just want to fill you in, so you understand. My usual church is on the other side of town, but this couldn't wait. I needed to get this out tonight.

Father…

I am…bad…at taking criticism.

I noticed I had this in me a few years ago, before I bought Pasta Pronto. I was still studying the culinary arts at the time, and I was at home every night, reading, cooking, going over notes. I got exhausted one night and needed a break, so I went to a movie. I saw *Chef.* Did you see that one, Father? My classmates and professors had been raving all week. They were right. It was the first time I'd seen passion for food translated effectively into fiction.

I went home, wanting to share the experience and the love with the world, but then I looked at the movie's Facebook page. There were reviews there, and I made the mistake of reading them.

It would be one thing if these were professional movie critics who knew about subtext and shot composition and all those other things I don't know about, but these were just normal people. They used empty words like "boring" and "stupid" and complained that they didn't want to watch an overweight person on screen for a whole movie.

When I came across one of the angriest, most hateful, vitriolic reviews I'd ever seen for anything, I clicked on the profile of the person who'd posted it. There I was on his Facebook page. A page full of sarcasm and flippancy, the dismissive rantings of a sociopath who contributed nothing and sought to demoralize those who did. There was no profile picture, but there was a name and a city. And it was my city.

I tried to find an address. I didn't have a phone book, but I had the internet, and after an hour of Googling, I'd found two sets of phone numbers and addresses that matched his last name. I called the first one and asked the woman who answered if Robert was home. She shouted for him.

A moment later, it was a little boy's voice that answered. A child maybe twelve years old.

I hung up.

I stood there shaking. I'd wanted to confront him about the review, to ask what gave him the right to tear apart another person's labors like he did. Maybe I would have said something, but I knew his mother was next to him, and I had no idea, back then, whether such a call could be easily traced.

Still, I had a name, and now I had a phone number, which meant I also had an address.

The next morning, I cut letters out of magazines and glued them to a sheet of paper, the way I'd seen in movies. I left the letter in his mailbox, in an envelope with his name on it. It said, "Delete your review for *Chef* or I will come to your house and kill you."

I cannot tell you the rush I felt.

Of course I wouldn't have done it, Father. But it thrilled me to imagine an anonymous destroyer feeling the wrath of his own tactics turned against him.

If I'd been more introspective in those days, I suppose I would have known the danger of someone with my affliction owning a restaurant, working in a world where slanderous reviews come so freely and easily, but I was years into my schooling and deep in debt. And besides, what job in today's world is free from critique? This very church has a 3.8 on Yelp, Father. A church! Somebody gave you a two-star rating last month because she couldn't hear the sermon well enough from the back. She chose to sit in the back and then ridiculed your church because the laws of sound weren't to her liking. How do these people live with themselves?

Well, I don't know if that boy's parents saw the letter, or if they notified the police, or if there was an investigation. All I know is that nobody ever came to me, and when I looked at the Facebook page the next day, the review was gone.

I know I'm taking up your time, Father, but it's late and no one else is waiting. I hope you don't mind. It's just that I want you to hear my confession in context. I've had my own restaurant for a year now, and it's a battle to persuade contented people to remember to post reviews. Malicious people, meanwhile, are champing at the bit.

Do you know they use bad reviews as a threat to get discounts? It happens every day. They say thinly veiled things like, "We just want you to know we were unsatisfied. We'd seen a lot of great reviews for this place, and it seems like it's not deserving of such a high rating on Facebook." Then when you ask them what you can do to make their experience more pleasant, they say, "I don't know. Maybe if we got a free dessert or something…"

What can you do? You can't say, "Get the fuck out of my restaurant, you scheming piece of shit." You'd just be giving them fuel!

Sorry. I'm sorry, Father. I'm getting riled up. Forgive me. I think I've established that my control over my emotions isn't what it could be. But can you blame me?

Two weeks ago, this family is placing an order, and a little girl wants to try the chocolate cake, and her mom says, "I don't know, honey. Apparently, the cake is pretty dry here."

Can you believe that? Dry? My chocolate cake? I've seen you at the restaurant, Father. You've had my chocolate cake. Is it dry? Could anybody in their right mind describe my chocolate cake as dry? You get a slice every time you come in. Would you do that if it was dry?

It's the least dry chocolate cake in the city. It's *too* moist, if anything.

Well, no. It's not too moist either. It's perfect. And damn to Hell anyone who says differently.

But here's this woman making this claim, and I can't understand why. Then I realize her phone is open to Yelp, and I have to take a deep breath and make myself check for new reviews. And there it is. Somebody that morning has given me one star—*one* star!—because the cake is dry. My cake. Dry.

I checked the cameras. I studied the footage of everyone who ate chocolate cake for the last three days, trying to spot even one face that looked like the face of a person eating dry cake, but it wasn't there. Of course it wasn't there. How could it be there if the cake was never dry in the first place?

I might never have found that man if he hadn't made himself obvious in just one way. When I looked at his review history, he had given one-star ratings to every Italian restaurant in a ten-mile radius.

Every Italian restaurant except one.

Don't get so antsy, Father. I'm getting to the point.

Let me ask you this: do you ever read about serial killers? They say what usually happens is a gradual escalation. Harming animals as a child is an early sign. For years, maybe they stalk or threaten. They subsist on the fantasy without ever quite following through. But the fantasy only takes them so far. Eventually they cross a line, and once they cross it, almost none of them can ever go back.

I guess that's how a lot of things are.

This guy, Ralph, who had a restaurant in my area, maybe that's how he felt the first time he posted a negative review for a competitor. Maybe each time he saw somebody go into Pasta Pronto, or Rigatoni House, or even the goddamn Olive Garden, maybe he had to find somewhere private to pleasure himself to the fantasy of posting a bad review. Maybe he'd write up a flurry of blistering takedowns, complete with one-star ratings, coming as close to posting them as he could without doing it, just to feel that rush. Then one day, something pushed him over the edge and he just...*did* it.

Then once he'd done it, he had to do it again. Over and over. More and more. Rude waiters, dirty restrooms, dry cake. He pulled out all the stops. Every day, a new bad rating, dragging down all his peers, giving every one of us a shoddy reputation, trying to make his own restaurant stand out amidst the sludge.

I know how he felt. When I went into his restaurant that day and sat a table, when I looked him in the eye and ordered his chocolate cake, a moment passed between us where he knew that I knew. For the last two years, it had been enough to track critics to their houses, leave them threatening letters—it had been enough to indulge only the fantasy of revenge. But, looking into Ralph's eyes, I knew the fantasy wasn't enough anymore. This was the time to finally just…*do* it.

When he asked me how everything was, I said, "That was some chocolate cake, Ralph. I don't know how you do it. Mine always comes out dry."

Here's the thing, Father. Most of these critics, I don't understand. They have lives outside of food. They're teachers and firefighters and politicians and veterinarians. Shattering the dreams that we business owners have built is just a hobby for them, an afterthought. It's not even their livelihood.

Ralph, I understood. I didn't respect him, but I understood him. Maybe that was why I hated him that much more.

When I went into his house that weekend and waited for him to come home, I sat in his living room and thought about how we were really the same breed. If we had met in culinary school, we might have opened a restaurant together, instead of as rivals. But here we were. Our similar but opposing natures getting the better of us.

It wasn't hard to do, like I thought it might be. I didn't have second thoughts. I didn't gag. It felt right.

A chef's knife is a part of his body. A part of his soul, even. It guided me through it all. I built my business with that knife, and now I was protecting it. I hadn't butchered a hog since my teens, but some things never leave you.

I don't know that I have an interest in cannibalism. I didn't cook him, and I certainly didn't eat him. But the way I took him apart, I *could* have, and I left him in his freezer in case anyone else should want to.

It's like I said. For a while, you fantasize. Then eventually, you just do it. It's important to always have something to build to. So, maybe I'll cook the next one. Maybe I'll try a bite. For now, it's just a fantasy, but we'll see. If you'll pardon the pun, I'm not taking anything off the table.

Whew. It feels good to have that off my chest. I've been carrying that burden for over a week now.

After it was done, I went into his phone and deleted all his reviews. Not just for Pasta Pronto, but for all of us. It might have given me an edge to keep the others up, but it felt wrong. There are some sicknesses that go beyond even me.

Is that part a sin, Father? Deleting a dead man's fraudulent reviews? Or is that something Jesus might have done? The world has gotten so complicated in the internet age, it's hard to even tell sometimes.

One way or another, there is one more thing. One more thing I definitely need to confess.

As I said, it has been *two* reviews since my last confession. The chocolate cake was the first, and the fettuccine with shrimp was the second. "Too little shrimp," said that cowardly anonymous reviewer.

You tried my fettuccine with shrimp, didn't you, Father? I saw you at the restaurant last night. What did you think of your meal? Was there enough shrimp? Or did I go cheap on you?

Sit the fuck down, Father.

You know what you did.

Now tell me how many Hail Marys this will cost me.

Monster Misunderstood

By Catherine McCarthy

This story is dedicated to all the 'Callums' out there, of whom there are many…

The girl who sits opposite me in the waiting room wears a bright red coat and a wolfish grin that makes me think of Red Riding Hood. My favorite story, when I was five years old. I liked the wolf best, but only in the version where he ate grandma. Mind you, the woodcutter wasn't bad either, though he could have done far more damage with that axe. Split the bastard down the middle, that's what I'd have done.

I sniff the air, like a wolf. Dust, damp, and a faint smell of piss coming from the toilets. I slip my hand into my trouser pocket and give Mr. Tibbit a squeeze. The girl in the red coat bites her bottom lip and smirks. Holy shit! She thinks I'm playing with my dick. I pull out Mr. Tibbit and pretend to talk to him so that she can see he's just a stress ball with a zany face. "See you soon, amigo," I say, in my best Ricardo Diaz voice, and the girl sniggers and covers her mouth with her hand.

Mum elbows me and frowns. "Shh, Callum! Behave."

I hold Mr Tibbit up to Mum's face, real close. "You no like Mr. Tibbit?" I pretend he's crying. "Mr. Tibbit sad."

She swats Mr. Tibbit like he's a fly. "Cut it out."

Two office doors, both with names on them. The one on the left opens, and out steps a woman with big tits and a pretty face. "Cassandra Hope?" she says, smiling at the girl in the red coat.

"Hah!" I laugh. She doesn't look like a Cassandra, not posh enough. Her shoes are scuffed. Mum elbows me again, harder this time. The girl in the red coat stands; her mother does, too.

"Cold out there," the woman with big tits says, and I want to ask if the cold makes her nipples stick out. I put my hand over my mouth to stop the words from spilling out.

All three disappear into the office, and I'm left alone with Mum. "Am I seeing her?" I ask.

"No," she says, pointing at the name on the other door. Dr. J. Rawlings (DPsych), it says. "You're seeing him."

My heart sinks. "So, I get a man?"

She sighs. "Looks like it."

Typical. I walk over to the door and trace the name with my finger. "What's the psych bit stand for? Psycho? Hah!" Kids at school call me psycho. I laugh out loud, then run back and slap the plastic chair with both hands. Boom!

Mum points a finger in my face and is about to tell me off when the door opens, and out he comes. "Callum Winters?" He grins at me, and I think, holy shit, he's gonna wanna be my friend, or at least pretend to be. I can tell by his eyes and his cheesy grin. I hate those types. They pretend to like you, but they don't. Not really. No one does. Not even Mum. As if I give a shit.

I slip Mr. Tibbit back into my pocket. He's warm from being in my hand. He makes a big bulge, and I hide a smirk by chewing the sleeve of my sweater. It's got a wet patch and loose threads around the cuff because I suck it a lot.

He invites me to sit down. "Nice to see you," he says. "My name's James. How are we today?" I don't know if he means me, Mum, or himself, so I don't answer. The chair is made of hard plastic, gray, like everything else in this place. Except the girl in the red coat. My feet can't touch the ground, even though I'm ten, so I swing my legs back and forth, back and forth, until Mum puts a hand on my knees, which means stop. I hate being short. Mum's not, but I don't know how tall my father is because I've never seen him. I hope I grow soon. It pisses me off, being short, but I'm hard as nails. Don't have to be big to be tough.

"So," he says, drumming his fingers on a black file that sits on his desk. "You've been having a few issues at school, Callum. Is that right?"

I shrug and wipe my nose along my sleeve. "Dunno."

Mum side-eyes me and gives me one of her *you've been warned* looks. I grip the seat of the chair with both hands and swing my legs really hard until it rocks.

"Sit still," she says, and her mouth quivers like she's about to cry.

"It's okay," the man says. I've forgotten his name, but I remember the name of the girl in the red coat: Cassandra. I wonder what she's doing right now in the room next door. I hope she's not telling the big-titted woman too much. Mustn't let them get inside your head, see.

"So, Callum," he says, looking me in the eye. "The fire you lit in the school cloakroom...We need to talk about it, okay?"

No point denying it. You can bet he's got it all written down in that stupid black file of his. But I ain't gonna admit it, either. The sleeve of my sweater is in my mouth, and I slurp. Tastes nice, this wool. Makes my mouth water. "Mum, can I have McDonald's?"

She gives me a sharp look, no messing. "If you're good."

I fold my arms across my chest and pout. "Starving."

"Sorry," she says to the man. "We've come straight from school. He hasn't eaten."

He opens a drawer, pulls out a bag of Starburst, and winks at me. "Go on," he says, holding out the bag. "The red ones are my favorite."

I rummage in the bag until I find a red one, then look him in the eye while peeling the paper.

"Say thank you," Mum says.

I put the sweet in my mouth and chew. "Thanks," I say, showing him the sweet on my tongue.

"So, Callum. Tell me about the fire."

I take as long as I can to eat the sweet. He's clever, this guy. Starburst never last long in your mouth, so he knows I can't stay quiet for long. Mum elbows me. "Tell him what happened, Callum."

I dribble and suck the drool back up, really loud. "He knows. It's in there." I stab at the file.

He strokes the file, like he's in love with it. "In here I have the school report, Callum. Their version of events. That's why I'd like you to tell me what happened in your own words."

He waits for me to say something, but I'm silent.

"Don't you think it's fair that you get a chance to tell it from your side?"

Why are they making such a big deal of it? It's not like anyone burned to death. I slide off the chair real slow, and slump to the floor like I'm dead. Then I crawl, sniper-fashion, towards the far wall. Cassandra's through there. I press my ear against the wall and listen.

"Callum!" It's Mum. I ignore her. "Right, you can forget McDonald's."

I don't care. I've got my own money. Nicked a tenner out of her purse the other night. I'll buy my own McDonald's.

"Tell you what," I hear the man say to Mum. "Why don't you wait outside for a bit. I'll speak to Callum alone and call you in once we're finished."

Mum stands. She's shaking. "Callum," she says, looming over me. "Sit down and behave, for Christ's sake." Then she leaves the room, closing the door behind her.

To my surprise, the man comes over and squats on the floor beside me. He's invading my space, so I shuffle away and sit knees to chin and head tucked in. I might leave in a minute. Get up and run out. Mum won't catch me. I'm too fast.

"Sweet?" he says, stretching out his arm and shaking the bag. I can smell the Starburst from here. I really want an orange one. I don't like the red ones much. I try to resist, but I hear him peeling the wrapper off his sweet. It's orange. I can tell by the smell. Bastard. He must have guessed. He scoots the bag across the floor towards me. "So, are you going to give me your version of events?"

I stay where I am, sucking an orange sweet.

"How old are you, Callum?"

"Ten," I say, before I can stop myself. He already knows how old I am. Stupid me. I slap my forehead.

"Look mate, I want to help you, but you need to understand that you've reached the age of criminal responsibility. Do you know what that means?"

I nod. I've heard it all before. Does he think I'm stupid or something? I do a fake yawn and stretch like my cat, Ronin. "Bored," I say.

"Is that why you started the fire? Because you were bored?"

"Dunno."

"What is it you like about fires, Callum? This is not the first time you've lit one, is it?"

I steal a glance. He has a zit on his chin, so he can't be very old. "The color."

"And?"

"Oh, man! Do we have to talk about this?" I get to my feet and lean against the door, my back to him.

"We do, actually. Either you talk to me, or you talk to the police. Your choice."

"Already have."

"Yes, and it was agreed you should have counseling, otherwise they might prosecute. Do you understand what that means, Callum?"

I rub my face with the flat of my hand. I need to get out of here. I'll tell him what he wants to hear, then I can go. He's sitting at his desk now. I return to the chair and sit on the edge so my feet can touch the floor. "They all hate me. My teacher, everybody. They're always picking on me."

"And your friends?"

"Don't have any."

"Why do you think that is?"

"Dunno."

"You must have some idea."

"Cos I'm naughty."

"Do you think you're naughty? Or is that what others say about you?"

I think about this for a minute. "Both."

"And the fire, how would that have solved your problems?"

My fists are clenched. "Cos the fucking school would be gone, and the teachers, and the kids."

I'm in the waiting room. It's Mum's turn to be interrogated. I can hear her crying through the door. Martin, the man who comes to school to talk to me about my behavior, asked if I feel upset when Mum cries. I told him I do sometimes, but I don't. Not really. I like it. Makes me feel powerful. I grab Mr. Tibbit and squeeze the hell out of him. He takes it without complaining.

The door to the other office opens, and out steps Cassandra. She sees me on my own and freezes, but after a couple of seconds, she wanders over to the window and pretends to read a magazine. There's a pile of them on a coffee table. Women's magazines. Titles like *Take a Break* and *Woman's Own*. My nan used to read them, before she died. I liked my nan. She was my favorite. Sometimes she'd slip me a fiver behind Mum's back. Her teeth were always wrapped in a tissue, never in her mouth, till she threw the tissue out by mistake. The bin man came before she realized, and she couldn't afford a new set. I called her Gummy Bear after that, and she would cackle like a witch. She wasn't, though. A witch, I mean. Don't want to think about my nan cos it makes me sad.

"Cassandra the panda," I say, grinning.

She turns round and glares at me.

"What you here for?"

She sticks her tongue out. "Mind your own business."

"I'm Callum. I set my school on fire. Hah!"

She gasps and puts a hand over her mouth. She's grinning though, behind her hand. Her eyes are smiling, all wicked like. She's the same as me, I can tell. Psycho.

"So, what did you do?" I ask.

She puts down the magazine and steps closer. "Stabbed a girl with a compass." She whispers it because she doesn't want the adults to hear us talking. "Went right through." She holds up a hand and points at the skin between her finger and thumb.

"Wow! Nice one! Where do you live? You don't go to my school. I'd know if you did."

She shakes her head. "Nah. Top o' town. Park Primary, except I'm excluded now."

"Cool. Me too." That's a lie. I'm on a final warning. "Know The Inky?" The Inky's a field behind our street. You get to it from the back lane. No adults go there, only kids and weirdos. It's called The Inky cos it's where kids give each other tattoos with a needle and a permanent marker. I've got one on my ankle, except I did it to myself. It's supposed to be Tommy from

GTA, but I'm shit at art. I think about showing it to Cassandra, but I'm afraid she'll laugh.

"Course," she says. "Everyone knows The Inky."

"Wanna meet me there?"

"When?"

"Saturday? About six?"

She thinks about it for a minute. "Okay."

The office door opens, and Cassandra's mother steps into the waiting room, all red-faced. She flaps a leaflet around to cool herself down.

"See you next week," the big-titted woman says, and me and Cassandra grin at one another.

I'm desperate to find Cassandra on Instagram or Messenger, but Mum's taken my phone away as punishment for lighting the fire. I've searched the house but can't find it anywhere. Reckon she's given it to her friend, Zuz, to look after. She knows, see. She knows I'll nag, and she knows she'll be tempted to give in, just to shut me up. I try Mum's phone when she's in the shower, but it's password-protected. I'm grounded too, but I know that by Saturday, Mum will be so sick of me she'll let me out for a bit. I'm driving her nuts without my phone.

On Saturday morning, I offer to go to Aldi with her. She's so gobsmacked that she doesn't answer for a minute. I push the trolley, without bashing into anyone, and even help her pack the bags.

"Mum, can I go out later? Just for an hour?"

"No. You're grounded," she says, twirling spaghetti round her fork.

I let mine dangle, then slurp it up, real slow and loud. "Please. I've been good. I need some fresh air. Only for an hour. Please, Mum."

She looks at me, eyes narrowed. "Where do you want to go?"

"Just for a walk. Burn off some energy." I thrust my chair back and move my arms all wobbly, like I'm gonna burst. "Hah!"

She slaps her forehead and laughs, and I know I have her beat.

I get to The Inky by half five in case Cassandra's early. I'm wearing my new Nike Air Force 1 trainers, black with white soles. I think she'll like them. There's no one here but me. It's still light, see. The kids don't come here till it's dark. I'm glad no one's here because I don't want anyone to see me. I crouch low at the top of the field, next to the old horse trough, and wait.

And wait.

Without my phone, I have no idea how long I've been here, but it feels like ages. I keep looking. Sometimes I get up and walk along the ridge, but there's no sign of her. What if she doesn't turn up? Perhaps she's grounded too, but she didn't want to admit it. Yes, that's what's happened, I bet.

Still, I wait.

It's getting dark now. I must have been here at least an hour. My ass is freezing from sitting on the grass, and I'm so bored.

Gutted!

On the way home, I sing the words to *Floating Through Space*, quiet like, under my breath in case anyone hears me. I like the words, about making it through another day without breaking. Feels like Sia's inside my head, cos that's how I feel a lot of the time.

As I reach the lane, I hear them. Pooky and two of his mates. They're huddled together, laughing and sharing a doobie. I can smell it. Sometimes, Pooky gives me a few puffs. Depends what mood he's in. I don't want any today though.

"Look who it is!" Pooky says when he sees me. "Hey, shithead. I wanna word with you."

My heart's pounding, and I think about making a run for it. Thing is with Pooky, you never know what to expect. Better not run though. He'll probably catch me, and then I can look out.

I slow down, eyes fixed on the ground.

"You set my sister's school on fire, you dumb bastard. Could have killed her."

I freeze. *Like a rabbit in the headlights*, my nan used to say. Before I can think, they're on me. All three of them. Kicking the shit out of me: stomach, kidneys, nuts. I curl in a ball and cover my head with my arms.

"Grab his hands," Pooky shouts, and the skinny boy does as he says. I kick out and beg them to stop. "Feet, for fuck's sake," Pooky says to the other one.

I kick my hardest and land a good one on his temple, but it makes him madder. He kneels sideways across my legs, pinning me to the ground. I wriggle and squirm, but it's hard to breathe. I spit in Pooky's face. Watch it slide down his chin. His eyes glow red with anger as he wipes it away.

"You're dead," he says. And the blows from his fists come thick and fast. A cold wind blows across my stomach where my sweatshirt's ridden up, but apart from that, I'm sweating like a pig. The pain's unbearable; my strength is sapped. I smell his sweat and the sickly-sweet skunk on his breath. The other two are still holding me down. Pooky stomps on my face, and I hear my nose-bone crunch beneath his boot. Feel the spray of blood against my skin.

The other two sense I'm done for and let go. They stand, hands on knees, catching their breath. Although I'm free, I'm too weak to help myself.

"Kill the fucker," Pooky shouts. I close my eyes as the other two join in, shrieking and whooping with every blow. I spit blood. Teeth. Bits of bone. And all the time it gets darker and darker.

"Run! Someone's coming!" It's Pooky's voice, though it sounds as if he's in a cave. I think my eardrum's bust.

The sound of feet and wicked laughter. Then they're gone, and the world turns black.

• • •

I'm in a tunnel. No sound. Nothing to see or smell.

"Come on, Callum. For God's sake, wake up." It's nan, I'm sure. But it can't be, because she's dead. I try to tell her my teeth are gone, like hers, but I can't find my voice. It's buried in my bowels, and it ain't moving.

"I'll give you a fiver if you wake up. Tenner, even." She's crying. A whimper, like a young child.

I try my best to wake up. Not because of the money, but because it's Nan who's asking, but my eyes refuse to open.

I'm not afraid. Just tired. Tired of everything.

The Myth of Pasiphaë

By Andy Davidson

Our last night together, I dream of a rodeo in which steers rope cowboys and horses race cowgirls around barrels, and pigs run down greased children to rip at their ears with tiny, crooked teeth. In this dream, I am in a metal chute on all fours, naked. Arms and legs trembling, coarse rope cast around my belly and cutting into my balls, as two thousand pounds of Charbray bull settles onto my back. My spine snaps like a pine branch under ice, and mud and shit and piss fill my throat in a wet squelch as I open my mouth to scream, but then the buzzer sounds, the shoot opens, and I wake up.

Next to you.

In a tangle of quilts on a hardwood floor, by the light of dying embers, you and me, sheened with sweat. Outside, the snow is covering the pump house, the pool furniture, the barbwire fence, and pastures beyond. The long, humped shapes of Big Frank's chicken houses shine like twin alien spacecraft out there in the dark. The pens and arena glaze over white, a blank and formless void mounting, as in the barn, that mad, nameless bull paws at cold dirt beneath the straw. This familiar world, made foreign to us as we suss out the end of it. Outside, there is only the lonesome clank of pipe chimes, and you suddenly, are behind me at the window. Pressing warm, skin to skin. A bitten fingernail tracing the blade of my shoulder.

"What's wrong?" you ask.

Snow-thunder, out of clouds black and heavy.

"She's coming down."

You shift your hips, snake your arms around my belly. "Is she?" Hands roaming over pale skin, a long-busted hip, old pain that remembers youth, and on down to softer parts. I shut my eyes against the weight of it, this monstrous thing we will do. You and me and the bull in the barn, and the cold, blessed snow to bury us all.

A month back.

On the phone, Big Frank said he'd bought a monster no man could ride, needed me to talk to it, tell him its name. "Bastard thing won't say peep to me," he laughed. "But these bulls, they talk to you, don't they, Pete? That's what old Jasper says." A pause, and then, in a kind of mocking, breathy voice: "Oh, Bull Whisperer, come and whisper to me." He laughed again, then hung up.

My pickup rattled over the cattle guard at the turnout to Big Frank's property. I followed the long gravel road up to the house. It was a beautiful place, the sort of thirty-acre spread a man who lives in a trailer in the woods might covet. But every place—even the prettiest—has its own history of secrets and sorrows, is steeped in the unseen. You taught me that. How a spread of land can be a map of the human heart, byways and gates and rolling hills and, at the center of it all, a beating, throbbing pain you long to cease.

Others had driven out. A handful of cowboys come to cuss and drink and throw money down on who had the sack to go eight seconds on Frank's new bull. I parked away from them, in the shade of an oak, and got out and limped up to the fence to look at the cow, the goats, a donkey or two. Cloud shadows drifted across the pastures, leviathan-like, into the yard. Sunlight broke over the in-ground pool, blinding bright, and that was when I saw you, there among the potted palms, lying on your belly on a flattened lounger. You wore a black single piece, the straps off your shoulders, soles of your feet turned out like the petals of a new flower.

The cowboys gathered in the turnaround on the far side of the house. I joined them, but had to walk past you first, past the rock steps that rose up to where you lay, oblivious to the young bucks preening in shined boots, grins wide as hat brims, faded rings on their asses where Skoal cans bulged. Every so often, they took a can out and thumped it, pinched a bit, snapped it shut. The only man among them was Jasper Koontz, a sunken-cheeked drunk with a tremble in his hands. Also, on the regional circuit, a damn fine rodeo clown, daring and fearless.

Jasper said, "Reckon the bull ain't the only thing Big Frank wants to show off," and when he laughed, I saw what few teeth he had, yellowed and crooked and long in their sockets.

"Who is she?"

"Sue Wise's daughter."

I said, "Sue Wise." The name was a memory, fleeting, of an auburn-haired girl in a cheerleader's skirt. Smiling down at me. Blue sky behind her. I carried her books once. In the ninth grade.

The great wide door of the nearest chicken house swung open, and out of the heat and stink strode Big Frank Dudley. In truth, Big Frank was short, not much to look at. Coke-bottle glasses and a buzzed head, he wore the same tight white T-shirts he'd worn twenty years back in high school, only he'd swapped his motorcycle boots for shit-caked ropers. His sleeves were pushed up to his shoulders, a rolled pack of Red Man jammed beneath one like an epaulet. With that belly, it was hard to tell what was muscle, what was fat. Rumor back in school was he liked to fuck his daddy's cows. We used to take after him in the hallways, between bells. Mooing at him.

Big Frank led us into the barn, musty and gloomy, six stalls empty save the last, where the bull stood half in shadow. The cowboys all fell silent when it turned its head and shifted its massive bulk to face us. Nothing but boards and a peg latch between us. The air went still and charged. Coat the color of straw, it was a Brahman-Charolais, neck and shoulders passed down from Plummer stock.

Easily the size of Big Frank's Ford tractor.

"God damn a'mighty," Jasper Koontz said.

Big Frank tucked a handful of chew in his bottom lip. "Bought him at auction, East Texas, last month," he said. "Five years old. Man selling him said he done broke two legs, three hips, and a Mexican's neck." He grinned around at the lot of us. "How about that, Mr. Whisperer?" he said to me.

All eyes shifted my way.

I took a step toward the bull. Then another. Marveled at its wide, yellow anvil of a head. How it blew hot air like an ironworker's forge. A laundry stone of a nose, dripping wet. I put my hands on the uppermost stall board, a boot on the bottom. Peered over and saw legs thick as fresh-hewn fence posts, hooves like plow blades. Horns that curved inward above ears big as sycamore leaves. Its eyes were small and black and shining with years of pent-up hate. Hate for bootheels and flank straps and hot branding irons. For the breath of men who had cursed it into being. The bull's heart thrummed inside my head, and its spirit opened up like a hole in the deepest, darkest space, all gravity and light at its mercy.

It wanted no name.

I dropped down from the fence.

"Any man rides this bull is a man with a death wish," I said. "You should destroy this animal."

Big Frank's grin slipped. His bottom lip hung down like a drawer yanked out.

I walked away, looked back only once.

The bull had turned its face to the sunlight, was licking the air.

I shut myself up in the cab of my pickup, hands trembling, head buzzing with the hurt of it, phantom smells of earth and manure. I looked out my cracked windshield and saw you. In the window of an upstairs bedroom facing west, through the branches of the oak. Afternoon sun on its way out. You'd shed the one-piece like an old skin and stepped out of it new and raw, long black hair, narrow hips. Body warmed by the late-day light. You looked down and saw me too, and it was like a ring of steel struck by a hammer, the clarity of that moment: my shaking hands grew still, and the pain in my head steamed off, and we looked at each other, and neither one of us looked away.

Weeks later, after it turned cold.

Big Frank and his trailer trucked off to Oklahoma, ten hours away.

I knocked on your front door, Jasper shivering beside me. He was off the wagon, had made it six days this time. What we were about to see, he would not make seven. Clutched to his chest was his little black bag, the one he lost his license to carry a decade back for expired antibiotics on the practice shelves. His first offense, punishable by fines. Next came the discovery he was selling ketamine out the back door. He went to prison a doctor of veterinary medicine, came out a man willing to paint on a smile and throw himself between a pair of horns. You'd hesitated when I said his name over the phone, but the nearest true vet was forty miles, and the forecast said freezing rain. So, you answered the door in a heavy parka, jeans tucked into rubber boots, and led us out to the barn, skies the color of ash. The ground was frozen, the whole property wind-scoured.

"I think it's infected," you said, once the barn door was shut.

The bull lay with legs tucked under, its flank a ruin of charred flesh.

"What the blue fuck?" Jasper said.

"A branding iron. He was drunk when he did it."

If the tool was lousy, or the fire not hot enough, it could happen. But this was no mistake. It was meanness. Torture. I saw that right away. Big Frank raging at a stubborn beast for which he had paid good cash money.

"Wound like that, we won't get him into a chute," Jasper said.

Those black eyes watched us.

"Prep the needle," I said.

I slipped into the stall quietly, syringe of antibiotics in hand. I moved like a man feeling his way over a frozen lake. Heart walloping my breastbone. The bull struggled on its side. "Easy now," I said, but the eyes rolled white. So, I leapt at the flank. The needle went in. The bull cranked up. I slid the plunger home and danced back, but my old, busted hip gave way and I fell, and now it was coming at me, this living locomotive, and suddenly Jasper, the rodeo clown, hurled himself between us, arms splayed, jigging sideways. Seconds were bought, enough for me to clamber up and over the rail, even as the bull horned Jasper, who lit over into the next stall like Jack-be-Nimble, and the beast struck the wall and the whole barn shook.

"It won't be happy 'til it kills a man," Jasper spat, then went into a coughing fit.

Your hand gripping my arm as the bull shambled in a circle and kicked the air, and the needle flew out. Was crushed beneath those hooves.

Your hand tightening around my arm, your body pressed close.

The bull and you, breathing heavy.

In sync.

Saturday. Still no Frank. Not due back until Sunday, and even then, the weather could stall him. "Just checking in," I said, embarrassed to have braved icy county roads to stand on your porch, an old man with a limp. Hat in hand, like some beggar.

You stood in the crack of the door in a red sweater, jeans tucked into black wool socks. "The wound looks better."

I didn't move.

You said, "Come inside, Mr. Crane?"

"Pete," I said.

You brewed coffee and I watched you from the kitchen table, the way you moved from sink to stove, slump-shouldered and cold, craving warmth. Too young to seem so old. We sat and drank. The silence heavy between us. Until I said, "I used to ride, back in high school. Made it to the national semi-finals in Shawnee, Oklahoma, year I turned sixteen. 1986. It was a bull named Tourniquet. Threw me into a wall, broke my pelvis into seventeen pieces. Bone soup, the doctors called it."

It was more than I had said to a person in a long time.

"Frank said you talk to bulls."

"A bull is a lonely creature," I said. "They are captives of their own genes. You listen, more than talk. That's all."

You didn't say anything.

I listened.

Later, the coffee was dregs, the dark come on. You needed a fire lit so I went at it, pretending it was my fire and this was my house, and it was our warmth, and afterward, I said I had to be getting on and you took my hand to shake it but held it, and your skin was cold, so I closed both my hands over yours, and suddenly you pulled me, a rough jerk. Toward the stairs, up into a guest bedroom where Big Frank had never slept, and what happened that night was like a spark of fire in the darkest wood.

The days that followed numbered among the coldest of winter days. I huddled up over an electric heater in my trailer, which was parked on a ledge by the river. Once, on this spot, there was a cinder block church, erected by fishermen. But it all washed away in an April flood, years past. I'd bought the lot cheap. I ate beans on toast and sat wrapped in a blanket of my own farts, trying to read paperback westerns. But I thought of you between the paragraphs and forgot the words I'd read. Once, perhaps, it had been enough, to live out my days in this tin coffin, to know I would die here and be found too late. A comfort to be had, in such anonymity. A kind of lantern, lighting a clear path. But you, you blew that lantern dark, and now I'd built a fire in another man's hearth.

One day, weeks later, as my thoughts turned to desperate, darker things—a shotgun in the corner, taste of metal to plug the loneliness, the emptiness, the utter heartsickness of a lack of you—my phone rang. Your voice was choked with anger, pain. You parsed your words, said Frank was gone. Said you'd be outside, on the porch swing.

But when I got there, I found you in the pasture. Barefoot. Half naked. Your footprints in the new fallen snow like a tether to the farmhouse porch. You were shivering, blue. Bent over the frozen grass and scooping up handfuls of snow and hardpacked cow chips. When I spoke your name, you turned to me, madness in your eyes, and I saw it: a ragged *F* scorched deep into your thigh—the softer, inner part. Days old, the flesh still blistered red. You were pressing the snow, the cow shit, bits of brittle grass into it. Like some arcane poultice. Your eyes were wild, and you said through chattering teeth, "I'm going to kill Big Frank. Will you help me?"

I thought on it. I said, "Sure."

Deep night. After the rodeo dream, the snow.

It is now, and Big Frank is in Texarkana. You told him the truth: you'd screwed another man. Just lied about who. Said it was some cowboy in Texarkana, an old flame come back into your life. After the branding, you named an ex who had not been kind. Which was enough for Frank. If he and the patsy don't kill each other, he'll likely be back tomorrow. Tonight, we're at peace in each other's arms. The fire roars up in the living room. I've cleaned your wound in a warm bath, and the only scrap of cloth between us now is your dressing, and suddenly, you say, "It ain't knowing someone. Fucking them, I mean." You say it like a warning to me.

In the hallway, behind the stairs, an old grandfather clock chimes the hour. Ticks on toward the next.

"When did it start?" you ask. "This thing with you and bulls?"

A pine knot bursts in the fire.

It began a lifetime ago, the last time I rode, a few years after Shawnee. I was twenty, easing down onto a Brahman's back in a chute out at old John Wall's place, and suddenly, I felt it: this racing heart that was not mine, but the bull's, beating in my own breast, huge and warlike. No breath of peace between the notes, only terror and rage. And in my own heart, when I picked myself up from the dirt and the bull had gone trotting off to some far corner of the ring, I felt no thrill, just an emptiness. It's been with me ever since. "Whatever broke that day, it went to the heart of me," I tell you. "All feeling inside. Until now."

I wait, in the hopes that you, in turn, will confess the same, how you are mended by me, and in this our hearts will fuse and be drawn out of a forge and doused in the cold, clear water. Each the sharper, the deadlier for it. But you only touch my face, yawn, and roll over to sleep. I lie awake, listening to your pulse race the clock.

Big Frank's house creaks every now and then, the way old houses do.

Early next morning, Jasper brings the needles full of tranquilizer. He stands on the porch smelling of dark rum and hands everything over in a Ziploc bag, out of a fleece-lined coat pocket. He doesn't ask why. Just takes the hundred bucks I give him. I, shirtless, shoeless on Big Frank's porch, breath coming in clouds of cold. "Guess you know what you're doing," he says. I don't answer him. In the driveway, a pickup idles, whoever drove him here. A woman behind the wheel. Older. Hair done up. No one I know, but I hope she's good to him.

Big Frank comes through the door mid-afternoon, reeking of aftershave and that deep, un-scrubbable smell of chicken shit. Blood under his nails where he gave some scrawny-assed boy what for, back in Texarkana. He shuts the door, turns to the living room proper. Calls your name. I step out from behind the drapery and put the needle into his neck. Press the plunger as he jerks. His eyes go glassy, and he drops like a sack of bricks on the pine board floor.

• • •

The sky hangs heavy with more snow, but isn't ready to let go. The steel fence is cold beneath me, and I have to make sure my gloves are on before I touch it, lest my fingers freeze right to it. The pen's in back of Big Frank's barn, the arena itself an oval of white. I perch above the chute, wearing a flannel shirt and my crumpled high school Stetson, no coat. Lamb's wool chaps I wore back in Shawnee. My hip throbs with pain and pleasure, a stirring in my breast I have not felt for twenty years. I settle onto the bull, and it jolts beneath me. Clangs the metal and sends my nuts into my navel, and the fear is good. There are glories yet to reap, blood yet to spend.

Easy now, I think, and the bull seems to hear me, to sigh and shudder, as if it accepts this gift we've given it, upon its waking from a deep, drug-induced slumber. Here in this strange metal chute, held up by a harness, the securing of which dried up all saliva in our throats. How we suspended him here, a hammock beneath him so his belly could not touch the ground, then dragged Big Frank from the house, drugged likewise, and set to work beneath the bull, with ropes and straps. Afterward, we had coffee, watched the clock. Stood in the barn and spoke not a word to this or any mystery, there in the sweet-smelling hay, and upon the first, faint stirrings of the man, mutterings of "What the hell, the fuggiz this," we loosed the harness, and you stood your post at the gate.

And now: I ease down, off the rail. Nod. I'm ready.

The latch clicks and the gate swings open over snow-shoveled dirt, and the bull is loosed upon the arena.

I cling to the flank strap and feel it move beneath me and imagine this must be the thrill of men who swim with man-eating sharks, who climb high cliffs and cling by fingers to outcroppings over miles of air. This wild, exuberant stupidity, this proof of something we cannot name. All the while beneath us, we hear the screams of Big Frank Dudley, lashed naked to a bucking monster's belly, facedown and rear facing, the bull's hairy member walloping him, every third, fourth buck, as a plow-blade hoof cleaves some portion of Big Frank's skull, his body, and the bright, crystalline snow is spattered red.

I do not know how long we ride, how long we buck our fury.

Once, from the fence, you cry out in horror, in triumph.

Some eternity later, all sounds having ceased, I shut my eyes and thank the bull for this final grace, and the world heaves beneath me and I am flying—until my skull hits a sheet of galvanized metal along the fence, and I hear the crack of my neck, and I drop down into the cold, drifted snow.

And you, across that vast, white gulf.

And the bull, stock still and snorting cold.

Big Frank limp and undone. A smear.

You reach out, slowly. Not for me.

The bull steps free of its ropes, one last indignity visited upon Big Frank as it crunches his head into the snow. It comes to you. Lays its head between your hands, nose to your bosom, as you gaze into its eyes and know things I will never know. Hear things I will never hear.

"It's a good name," you say.

The bull follows you to the far gate, where you open the pen, and the two of you walk through and away, across the white pasture and into a curtain of falling snow that sweeps back from the tall dark pines like a wedding veil.

I see all of this crookedly.

Until it's cold and dark, and after that, it's not.

Into the Barn

By Stephanie Nelson

The world will end by fire on June 26, 1992.

That's today.

Pastor says fire purifies, and only the most holy of us will be caught up in the clouds for the feast. But first, the purification.

It's my job to take care of the chickens and put them to bed in the barn before church every night. I live on an orchard in Tonasket, Washington. Most people think of Seattle when they think of Washington, but Tonasket's in the middle and it's not green or rainy. Our orchard looks like someone poured dirt all over little treed hills, then plopped a single-wide trailer and an old barn on it. Dad grows apples, but it's just him and he can't keep up, so most of the fruit rots on its stem. He tries to sell the good ones in town, but it's never enough. Mom worries. Once I heard her crying, asking about food stamps, and Dad said, *Are you calling me lazy?* She never brought it up again.

Dad says you show God you're serious about serving Him by how often you attend church. Lukewarm Christians only come on Sundays, but the committed, the chosen of the Lord—that's us—we're there whenever the door is open.

I fill the chicken trays at the water pump inside the orchard. Between the orchard and the trailer sits the old barn. It leans away from us, like it wants to escape. The white paint curls back and comes off in long strips if you're careful. Sometimes I stand there and peel it when Dad's not looking. Underneath, the wood is gray and rotten.

When the water trays are full, the chicken-chasing starts. It's hard work because chickens don't listen. If I run, they run faster. If I yell, it's worse, so I sneak up on them until I can grab them from behind. If I go really slow, they don't even notice when I pick them up. All this effort with the chickens makes my belly go off in a big rumble, and I get dizzy when I bend over. I've got the last two chickens now, one under each arm, and they flap hard, twisting my long hair in their feathers. I cringe away and squeeze them tighter. We walk into the barn.

The wind sings between cracks in the old gray wood. After closing the barn door, I push my hands into worn-out pockets until my fingers find holes at the bottom. I walk toward the trailer, trying to ignore the twisting in my stomach. That's when I see Aunt Jane's car. It's a tiny speck in the driveway, and she's hefting grocery bags up the trailer's rickety steps. Mom tells her not to come anymore, but she does anyway. She brings us food. Peanut butter sandwiches do a little dance across my mind and my stomach jumps like I just made it a pinky promise. I run. I'm not even halfway there when a knock of fear hits my chest. It slows me down.

What if Dad gets mad at Aunt Jane again?

Last time they fought, Aunt Jane stopped coming, and we only had seven eggs from the hens and some applesauce Mom canned. *Seven is the number of perfection,* Dad said that time. *The Lord will provide.*

I can almost taste the macaroni and cheese, grapes, and fruit snacks. What if she brought strawberries this time? The thought of those berries makes my mouth water. Aunt Jane's brown bags never have enough to last until she comes again. Still, what's inside is all I can think about. Aunt Jane walks away from the trailer empty-handed. That means the bags are waiting for me on the kitchen table. I sprint the rest of the way; who cares if I get dizzy now?

Dad says Aunt Jane will pollute our minds if we talk to her, so I slip behind the trailer to hide. I wait for her to leave. Her big hair looks like it's trying to take flight off her head with every gust of wind, so I laugh. She hears.

"Jordan!" she shouts and walks toward me.

My throat goes dry, and I look around. What if Dad sees her coming at me? I should run, but I can't move. I stand there like some dummy until her face is right in front of mine. Black sunglasses sit on her head, buried in all that hair. She looks like a younger version of Mom, even though she's older. Mom doesn't do up her eyes, maybe that's why.

Aunt Jane bends at the waist to inspect me. She glances behind her, then all around. Is she afraid of getting caught? I look down and kick at the dirt. She sidesteps behind the trailer to join me. We're both hidden.

"Baby, how are you doin'?" She pushes my thick bangs back with long, hot pink fingertips.

I don't answer because I shouldn't talk to her. The Lord knows when we disobey. When was the last time I talked to Aunt Jane though? I was eight, maybe nine. So, three years ago.

"Do you have enough to eat?" she asks.

I shrug. "The Lord will provide for all our needs," I say, looking at her now.

Aunt Jane shakes her head and squeezes her lips together like she's mad. "Sweet girl, I know you love your parents, but that church you go to—it just ain't right."

Heat rises to my face. I can't believe she said that. I want to shout that she's wrong! I want to tell her what Pastor says about people like her. *Whose god is their belly...their mind is set on earthly things.* I know what that means because one time I asked Dad. He said it's when people care more about their next meal than they care about eternity.

"You got a few years yet, but as soon as you're old enough, you get the hell outta here," Aunt Jane continues.

I blink until the silence is uncomfortable. I should speak up and make the quiet better, but I can't. She cocks her head to the side, like she's wondering if I speak English. "You and your sisters both, you hear me? Grown-ups make their choices and maybe your mom made hers, but you got time. Get out before it's too late."

My legs wobble when I step back. She shouldn't say those things about Mom, about our church. Plus, what does it matter? Today's the end of the world anyway. Just as I have the gumption to run, I see tears bringing black makeup down her face in long drips. My heart pulls toward her. Why is she crying?

"If you ever need *anything*, you call me," she says. "Life's bigger than this." She motions with those pink fingers at the orchard, the trailer.

Life isn't bigger than God though. Not bigger than eternity. That's what I want to say, but the words won't go out of my mouth.

She pushes a scrap of paper into my hand, "That's my number. Best hide it from your parents." Aunt Jane holds my hand a minute too long, then gives it an I-love-you squeeze. A jolt goes through me as I remember how Mom used to squeeze my hand like that. Before she got sad. The memory makes my face all pinchy, but I can't cry in front of Aunt Jane.

She doesn't see anyway. Instead, she stands and wipes her eyes. She puts on her sunglasses and grabs her poofy hair into a side ponytail so the wind can't take it. She fusses with it all the way to the car.

It's night now. I can't sleep because something's bothering me. I thought the end of the world would come at church. But despite all our praying in the spirit, crying, and shouting, the service was no different than last night. But Pastor said the end of the world would be today and he's God's mouthpiece. Dad said it'd be today and he's my spiritual covering.

Yet, my alarm clock says it's almost midnight. Almost tomorrow.

What if the end of the world stuff is all just bull honky? If it isn't happening, neither is the feast in Heaven. Tears wet my pillow, and I add up how many more days of Aunt Jane's food we have.

Counting makes me light and floaty, and just as I'm about to find sleep, a flash of light moves across my closed eyelids. I open my eyes wide, and the walls are wiggling red and white. I make a quick move to stand on my bed and look out the little window up high. I can't believe what I see. I shake Mom and Dad awake.

"It's here! It's here! It's the end of the world!" I shout.

Dad feels around for his glasses and then looks out the window. He's moving too slow! I can't hear everything he whispers to Mom, but I hear "fire" and "the barn." In one motion they're up, and the metal door slaps its jamb behind them. They're gone.

Loud squawking breaks into the trailer when they open the door. The chickens! I can't help it; I think of those poor chickens stuck in the barn. But Dad's voice comes to me with one of my memory verses, *I shall come into Your house with burnt offerings.*

I wipe my nose. Maybe the chickens can be like our offering to the Lord. I stare out the window. Flames wash the barn around the ground, like they're eating that old gray wood because they're starving. Smoke curls up the sides where I used to stand and peel paint. It gathers at the roof and shoots up into the sky.

That's when I see the back of Mom and Dad as they run with shovels and buckets. Mom's nightdress kicks up behind her. They're running toward the end of the world.

The barn glows like a mountain of embers now. Like an altar pouring out the incense of worship into the Lord's nostrils. It's just like in Revelation.

My sisters are still asleep, but I worry. What if Mom and Dad are purified without us? What if the Lord doesn't know the chickens were a gift from me too? What if I miss the feast in Heaven? A new fear lays down on top of all the others and crushes them:

What if I'm not chosen at all?

Then, out of nowhere, something stands up inside me and I scrape the tears away. I know what to do.

Moriah's three, so she moans when I wake her. The baby goes right back to sleep in my arms. We step into the black night and the smoke smell hits me so hard, I want to cover my nose. Stars hang low, and it seems like I could reach up and touch one.

Where are Mom and Dad?

They must be inside already.

Every step is hotter than before.

What if this *isn't* the end of the world? I stop to dawdle over that thought. But thankfully, Dad's voice is there with another verse, *Why are you fearful, O you of little faith?*

I take up Moriah's dimpled hand. It's wet and sticky, like she just pulled her thumb out of her mouth. She looks at me. Her face throbs, reflecting close flames against the dark.

"Jordy, I scared," she says. She's in the Strawberry Shortcake nightgown Aunt Jane's daughter outgrew. Moriah's outgrown it too.

Moriah's words hang in my mind. They try to push me back to the trailer because I'm scared too. What does it feel like to burn? Will the Lord make it so it doesn't hurt?

Perfect love casts out fear.

Dad's voice reminds me there's no room for fear if I want to show God I'm serious about Him.

I give Moriah Aunt Jane's I-love-you squeeze and say, "Remember your verse: 'Be strong and courageous, for the Lord is with you wherever you go.'"

The barn door falls with a crash, and a smattering of sparks soar through the air. Moriah and I startle. She cries. My skin feels sunburned.

Moriah pulls away from me, back toward the trailer. I hold her hand tighter and say, "Mom and Dad are in there already. Think of the feast in Heaven. You'll never have a tummy growl again."

Moriah gives a slow nod.

Now the baby's awake, screaming because of the heat. I bring them both closer, and we step into the barn.

BodiBag

By Rebecca Jones-Howe

In the afternoon, Kelly always gets me to babysit the girls so she can film her Instagram reels. It's for her essential oils business. Normally I'd roll my eyes, but she let me stay in her basement after I lost my job. The least I can do is be a half-decent brother and uncle to her kids. Kelly sprays down all the surfaces in the kitchen with Young Living Thieves Household Cleaner while I take Sofia and Olivia to the playhouse in the backyard. We usually have tea parties. There is no actual tea to spill, just pretend tea that I spill whenever I take a too-eager sip out of my pink plastic cup, pinky finger out.

The girls laugh, and I wave my hand like the fucking Queen. Then they paint my face with their cheap glitter makeup for an hour. Kelly takes a picture of me holding a bottle of Young Living Orange Blossom Facial Wash and posts it to her feed, claiming how blessed she is to have such a wonderful little brother who can look after her "little princesses" while she "works her business." All this so I can live rent-free and figure out my next move.

I go back to my basement bedroom and order Five Guys.

The Grubhub driver who takes the order is that cute blonde again. She comes around the back of the house and knocks on the door three times, just like I specified.

She's got her back turned by the time I open the door. The glow of her phone illuminates her face. She swipes her thumb down the screen over and over, looking for a new order with a decent payout.

I give her five stars like always.

She smiles in her profile picture. The dark circles under her eyes make me feel less alone. She probably gets good tips from the people who can afford them, but she's also probably desperate as fuck, considering this is the third time this week that she's taken my tip-free order for a cheeseburger with a large fry and a Coke.

I eat in front of the TV in the basement. *The Office* theme song plays over the sound of Kelly arguing with Ted upstairs. They're fighting over the essential oils again. He says she's not making any money. She insists that she's so close to "hitting next rank" and that he needs to be a more supportive husband.

"The money will be pouring in soon enough!" she yells.

I take a bite out of the burger and pull my phone out of my pocket. I open up the BodiBag app and refresh the main page for any new listings.

The_D0CKt0r: *In need of a cute brunette millennial girl. Nice legs. Live.*

Every couple of weeks, he posts a new order.

Each one of the The_D0CKt0r's orders is worth $10,000 in Bitcoin, but the other hunters always get to them before I do. This order's been up for over an hour and no takers.

My heart starts thumping. This could finally be my chance. I think of my brunette sister and how she fits the description in the listing. I think about how I'd do it, how I'd get her to him. I've been a BodiBag hunter for three weeks now and I still haven't taken my first order. She could be my first. I'd be solving Ted's problems as well as my own.

Upstairs, Kelly tells Ted that she's "building up a community of women," whatever the fuck that means.

For a while, there were news stories of missing women popping up on my Twitter feed, but they always get buried under the barrage of coverage about the wildfires approaching the city again. I sometimes wonder what The_D0ckt0r does with all the women he orders. Maybe he's got his own little community of women. A harem. A slave ring. A human centipede. Maybe they all have their own little camgirl cells in his basement, creating adult content for men who like brunettes with nice legs. Utilizing gig workers to source his models is probably a decent business move. It's a bit gross to think about, really, but a part of me is curious about how much he must make.

I haven't worked a real job in months. I had to sell my gaming computer to pay Kelly for groceries, which she then used to buy more Young Living product that now takes up Ted's parking space in the garage.

Upstairs, Kelly accuses Ted of not supporting women.

"You're basically scamming them by roping them into this," Ted says.

"I'm not scamming them! I'm *helping* them!" Kelly says. "If they can't sell the products, it's because they're not committed to the business."

I refresh the page again, and The_D0ckt0r's order disappears. I take another bite from my Five Guys burger. Some of the ketchup slips off the bun and lands on my lap.

"Dammit," I say, wiping my index finger over the red.

The smell of smoke seeps through the closed windows the next morning. It descends into the valley from the hillside fires, but we get no evacuation orders and are thus forced to pretend like everything is okay. The sky only darkens as the day progresses. The girls cry, and I have to hold them and tell them that everything will go back to normal eventually.

"When?" they ask.

I don't have the heart to tell them that things have been pretty fucked up for a while now.

Kelly live streams the fire from the patio, nearly crying in front of her phone. "Everything just gets so overwhelming sometimes," she says, "so I created this oil blend that really helps me calm down."

"Your mom might have an oil," I say. Both girls just look at me.

"You're silly," Sofia says.
"You're *very* silly," Olivia says.
The day progresses like most days do. Kelly films. Then she scrolls. Then I scroll.

The_DOCKtOr: *In need of a cute brunette millennial girl. Nice legs. Live.*

My stomach growls, but then the girls come and grab me, wanting to have another tea party inside the playhouse. Instead, I queue up *Peppa Pig* on Netflix.

Ted comes home later than usual, his face sweaty and covered in smoke. The girls look up and scream, "Daddy!" Ted tells them not to hug him because he still has to wash the ash away.

"Kelly's in the bathroom," I say. "She's doing a live stream."

Ted sighs.

"She just started," I say, but Ted heads down the hallway anyway, his shoulders stiff.

I grab the remote and tell the girls that we should probably have another tea party. They both eagerly jump at the opportunity. I open the door and we step out into the red gloom.

"It smells like campfire," Olivia says.

The girls both talk in British accents now. They've watched so much *Peppa Pig* that I can't help but take them seriously.

"It's really not so bad when you *think positive*," I say in my best Daddy Pig voice.

"You sound like Mummy," Olivia laughs.

"Mummy's always positive," Sofia laughs.

"You have to think positive in a time like this," I say, forcing a laugh that doesn't sound convincing.

I cough. The girls cough. In the playhouse, however, we make more pretend tea and they both call me Earl Grey. Then the girls pull out some Younique makeup and brushes from Kelly's last business venture. Sofia sticks some plastic doll clips on my hair. Olivia pokes me in the eye with a loaded Q-Tip of glittery blue eyeshadow.

"Fuck!" I say, and they both wither back.

"*Fuck* is a bad word," Sofia says.

"Then don't say it," I say. "And don't tell your mom I said it."

"Mummy says you're a bad influence," Olivia says, coughing.

I wipe the blue off my eye. "Maybe you girls should go back inside."

Sofia shakes her head, and Olivia pushes the playhouse window shutters open. Inside the real house, Ted is still yelling. He's animated. His arms flail and his face is red with exasperation.

"Why do Mummy and Daddy fight so much?" Sofia asks.

"Because your mom's in a pyramid scheme," I say.

"What's a pyramid scheme?" Olivia asks.

"It's something moms do when they don't have real jobs," I say, balling up my shirt to wipe away the eyeshadow. Some of the glitter gets stuck under my eyelid, and I blink it out with a bunch of tears.

"Mummy says she's making *lots* of money," Sofia says.

I pull out the plastic hair clips one by one. "She'd probably make more money doing OnlyFans, to be honest."

"What's OnlyFans?" they both ask.

"It's a cry for attention," I say. "Hopefully your mom doesn't get that desperate."

"What does desperate mean?" Sofia asks. She's the younger one, the naive one. Even though I'm the younger one in our family, I try to take comfort in the fact that I was never that fucking naive.

"It means you need something really bad that you'll do anything to get it," I say.

"Is Mummy desperate for money?" Olivia asks. She stares out the window again, and I realize that I've probably said too much.

"I'll tell you what *I'm* desperate for," I start.

"Five Guys!" the girls scream.

"Exactly!" I say.

I crawl over to the playhouse door and wedge myself through, but my gangly knees catch in the threshold, knocking the entire house askew. All the teacups wobble off their saucers. The teapot slips off the pretend stove, and the girls scream and cry and point at me for spilling it.

I check the BodiBag app.

There's a new listing, just another copy of the last.

The_DOCKtOr: *In need of a cute brunette millennial girl. Nice legs. Live.*

My heart pounds again.

Upstairs, Kelly's cooking minestrone soup, probably putting a couple drops of basil oil in the broth.

I order Five Guys again. This time, a different driver shows up and forgets to bring my Coke with the order. I grit my teeth and give the Grubhub guy one star while *The Office* theme song plays.

The beer fridge is in the basement, and sometimes Ted comes down after his shower to interrupt my nostalgia with his forceful sigh of relief.

"Kelly only ever wants to watch *Friends* when we have a night together. *The Office* is better than *Friends*," he says, cracking open a can.

"I agree."

Ted takes a swig, then drinks half the can before nodding at the crossbow hanging over the bar. "You wanna shoot some hay bales this weekend?" he asks.

I shrug and refresh the Bodibag app. "I'm still kind of looking for job leads, honestly."

Upstairs, the girls scream in their British accents. Kelly pleads at them to stop.

Ted takes a seat on the opposite side of the couch just as Michael Scott yells at Toby: *"No, God, please no!"*

Ted laughs, but I laugh only because it feels obligatory. I've seen this episode so many fucking times. I refresh the page, but there's nothing new. No bratty little girls. No whipped husbands. No fucking brunettes.

Ted finishes his beer and goes back to the fridge. This time he takes out two cans.

"I'm good," I say, and his shoulders slump a bit. I smirk, watching him put the second beer back into the fridge.

Fucking Beta.

The girls mock Kelly, screaming, "Thieves Oil! Thieves Oil!" in their British accents.

"I'm kind of glad you're here," Ted says. "It's nice having another guy around for a change."

"Yeah," I say, refreshing again.

Ted points again at the crossbow. "You're a decent shot with that thing, man."

"I wasn't that great," I say.

"For a first time, though."

Refresh.

Refresh.

I glance up at the bow and then at Ted. "Thanks."

Somebody knocks on the basement entrance three times.

"Oh, you ordered food?" Ted asks.

I get up and look out the window. The Grubhub girl is already at the top of the steps, her back turned, the red bag on her shoulder, her thumb moving just like mine. I open the door and pick up my order, the drink included.

Five stars.

"Why don't *you* do Grubhub?" Ted asks.

"Are you kidding me?" I say. "I'm not that fucking desperate."

The girls watch *Peppa Pig* while Kelly films herself scrubbing the kitchen on her hands and knees.

"So sorry for the TV noise," she says to her screen. "I'm just about to take the girls for swimming lessons, but I can *still* make money while being a mom. I don't have to miss a thing!"

I find myself reaching for my phone.

The_DOCKtOr: *In need of a cute blonde millennial girl. Nice legs. Live.*

Blonde. A fucking blonde this time!

I order Five Guys and grip my phone in my shaking fist while Kelly rambles about which oils the girls love most. The blonde girl takes my order. She'll be here in twenty minutes.

"Holy shit," I say.

Kelly ends her video and immediately starts checking her DMs.

My limbs tighten. The adrenaline builds. Excitement makes my heart start throbbing. I get up from the couch. "You walk the girls to their swimming lessons, right? Since the pool's just down the street."

Even though the skies are still gray with ash, Kelly nods, her thumb scrolling like all is normal.

I swallow. I nearly choke. "Can I borrow the car?"

"For what?" Kelly doesn't even look up from her phone.

"I really need to borrow the car."

"He sounds *desperate*," Sofia says in her British voice.

"Sofia!" Kelly says. "We're helping your uncle, okay? He lost his job, and he needs our help."

"He's a *charity case*," Olivia says.

"He's not a charity case," Kelly says. "Go put your shoes on. We gotta go now if we're walking."

"But you said he was a charity case!" Sofia says.

"No, I didn't." Kelly looks at me and then at the girls. I clear my throat, and her lips purse. She clutches her phone, thumb scrolling, refreshing her DMs again.

Olivia pulls at my shirt. "Mom said you had no money and nowhere to live."

"She said you'd be homeless if we didn't let you stay here," Sofia says.

"Go and put your shoes on. Both of you!" Kelly finally breaks her gaze from her phone to stare down the girls. She points at the door. "Go! Now! You don't want to be late!"

I go back to the BodiBag app and accept The_D0CKt0r's order.

Before Denny's laid me off, the Grubhub drivers were the worst part of the day. They never came in at the right time, never knew where to pick the orders up. Sometimes they left without portions of the meal. But the blonde knows my order through and through, and she opens the gate to the backyard within thirty seconds of my estimated delivery time. She walks around the side of the house, with the red Grubhub bag bouncing against her knee.

She does have nice legs.

I raise Ted's crossbow and aim it through the open shutters of the girls' playhouse.

The blonde turns down the basement steps, putting herself in the crosshair: Head, shoulders, black and white striped shirt, the red Grubhub bag.

She knocks three times and I swallow before drawing a breath just like Ted told me to back when I was just being a good brother-in-law.

Head, shoulders, Grubhub bag.

I pull the trigger, and she doubles over. She takes a knee. Then her head goes down and she tumbles backward down the steps.

I pull another arrow from the quiver and raise myself to cock the bow. I pull at the bowstring but end up hitting the back of my head against the low ceiling of the playhouse. It shakes on its foundation. The teacups scatter across the plastic floor.

"Fuck!"

I shove the bow out the window and scramble my way through the narrow door. The delivery girl moans, and I crawl faster, wrestling my knees to escape. I drag the crossbow with me, lifting it up as I approach the steps. The blonde writhes on the landing, trying to sit up as the white stripes of her shirt turn red. She grips at the fletched end of the arrow, which pins the red Grubhub bag to her stomach.

"Oh shit," I say.

She starts to moan, her voice echoing against the side of the house. Her fist tightens around the shaft of the arrow. Her muscles clench as she pulls.

"No, don't—"

But she rips it out anyway. She climbs to her knees, and I jump down to stop her. The bag gets tangled between her legs and mine. I use the crossbow to pin her down before her cries can draw attention. The back of her head hits the Five Guys bag. The paper crinkles. The Coke spills over and drenches her shirt.

I grab her by the shoulders and slam her head back against the pavement. Her eyelids flutter. Her groan turns guttural, but her arms still flail. I lift her up and slam her down harder.

This time, she yelps and goes limp.

As I gather my breath, I pull the Five Guys bag away from the spreading pool of blood.

I drag the girl inside and find a tarp. It takes half an hour for me to find a YouTube video that shows me how to hogtie her right. I duct tape her mouth and wrap a towel around the arrow's puncture wound. Then I drag her up the basement steps and into the garage, where she comes to and starts to moan through the tape. Slamming her down a few more times keeps her quiet, but she never stays under for more than a few minutes at a time. Her cries don't sound so bad beneath the plastic tarp, though. I get some bungee cords and wrap them tight around her body. Then I wrap one several times around her neck so she's forced to focus more on breathing than on screaming.

Then I clean. I bleach the crime scene and hang the crossbow back on the wall. I pick up the Five Guys and throw it into the passenger seat. I get behind the wheel and drive to the highlighted route on the BodiBag app.

In the grand scheme of things, I've done worse.

My first job was at Whole Foods, where I once tried to tackle a shoplifter who shoved an entire honey-baked ham down his sweatpants. My manager pulled me into the office after the incident and reprimanded me. He read from the company manual about how my life was worth more than the merchandise, and never to tackle a shoplifter again.

Then I worked at Value Village, where I cleaned enough homeless-person shit out of the bathroom to realize that they weren't exactly the danger that everyone made them out to be. Then a crazy homeless dude held me up during my Chevron night shift with a used needle. I threw a can of Monster Energy at him, and he bolted. One of the local newspapers called me a hero, but the manager fired me for not following proper hold-up protocol.

The dishwashing job at Denny's paid so little that wasn't even worth keeping.

The delivery girl's cries screech like the metal utensils at the bottom of the sink. I cringe and turn on the stereo. Kelly's workout mix bursts from the speakers. I crank the volume to Cardi B, who likes nothing more than money.

$10,000 in Bitcoin, I think as my heart starts to pound.

The blonde cries harder until the bungee cord around her neck causes her to wheeze. I stop at the red light and the tarp starts crinkling. Blood seeps out all over the back of the SUV.

"Shit."

All I can imagine is Kelly trying to clean the stains out with Young Living Thieves Household Cleaner.

The girl moans against the duct tape. She begs me to let her go.

"You gotta stop," I say over the throb of the stereo's bass. "Maybe save your energy for when you're actually being tortured or whatever."

The light changes and the girl starts to sob. Through the tape, she asks if I'm a BodiBag hunter.

"I meant to shoot you in the leg, immobilize you a bit," I admit. "Hopefully The_D0CKt0r can fix you up, assuming of course that he is actually a doctor."

The BodiBag app tells me to turn left, and I drive past the crowds of eviction protesters gathered in front of city hall. Soon to be charity cases, all of them.

"Maybe he won't even be that bad," I say. "Maybe he'll treat you nice. And hey, *maybe* you'll even manage to escape. Maybe you'll get a bunch of press coverage and write a book about it. You'll get to do paid tours and exploit all your trauma. They'll make one of those shitty Lifetime movies about you that my sister can watch."

She sobs harder.

"Look, I'm just trying to help you out here, put you in a better frame of mind. Think *positive*, you know?"

The sobs turn into gasps of hyperventilation.

My grasp tightens around the wheel. I grit my teeth, wondering if The_D0CKtor will give me give five stars for a partially botched order. "Look," I say, "you gotta be alive when we get there. This is my first fucking order, and you're fucking it up."

Her groans turn into muffled words that beg against the lyrics of "Work Bitch" by Britney Spears.

"It's 10k in Bitcoin," I seethe. "It might not be a lot for a kidnapping but it's something to me. That's rent for almost a year in a shitty apartment! You took my Five Guys order for what, like twelve bucks?"

You better work, bitch.
You better work, bitch.
You better work, bitch.

Her crying eases. I get to the next light and firm my grip around the wheel. "We've all done shitty things for money," I say, glancing at the rear-view mirror. Her body shifts inside the tarp. "You'd do this, too, if you had the chance. Wouldn't you?"

She doesn't respond, so I look at myself. There's red in my eye, a burst blood vessel. I blink over it and draw a breath, reaching into the Five Guys bag. I take a bite out of my cheeseburger. Thankfully, it tastes just as good as it always does.

• • •

The route on the app takes me to a battered mid-century home at the end of a cul-de-sac in an older suburb, tucked behind some old trees. I glance at the cracked branches and the gray skies overhead.

The Grubhub girl has stopped crying, but the tarp behind me still crinkles.

"You still there?" I ask.

The pool of blood's soaked fully into the carpeted interior of the SUV. I pull up to The_D0CKt0r's house, and my phone chimes with a BodiBag notification.

ORDER CANCELED

"What?"

The phone chimes again with a text.

My bad, man. I meant to order a BRUNETTE, not a blonde. I always get a Blonde Roast at Starbucks and autofill must have fucked it up. Didn't even realize until now. Sorry for the trouble, lol.

I burp up the taste of my Five Guys burger. Onions. Ketchup. Overcooked beef.

I grab the phone off the cradle. "No, no, no, no!"

The phone chimes: *Don't bring her in. I'll report you if you bring her in.*

The girl stirs again. Starts to moan.

I refresh the BodiBag app over and over, but The_D0CKt0r's order is long gone.

Pull away from the house. You're going to draw attention.

I glance up at the window on the upper floor, at the crack in the blinds.

You wanna lose your BodiBag account, asshole?

"Fuck!" I scream, and the girl jerks back to life, her caterwauls sounding like British gibberish. My body tenses as I draw a breath. I check BodiBag's terms of service, which inform me that in the case of a canceled order that the body is mine to deal with. A rare circumstance, but one that I apparently signed up for when I clicked Approve without reading the contract.

BACK AWAY. NOW.

"Please," the girl mumbles. The tape must have shifted.

My heart throbs to the bass. I do as The_D0CKt0r orders, putting the car in reverse and going back the way that I came. I take another bite out of my cheeseburger, but it's already cold.

Britney's on repeat, telling me to *Work, work, work.*

I tap back to the list of open orders. Maybe there'll be another request.

Men always love blondes. Maybe even a dead blonde?

"Please, I'll do anything," the girl cries, her desperation a trigger, filling my nerves with adrenaline. My scrolling thumb goes into hyper-drive. All I see is red.

Refresh.

Refresh.

Refresh.

Everything You Want to Be, Everything You Are

By John F. D. Taff

Please don't squirm while I tell you this.

After three months, I didn't feel any different.

That's a small lie. I felt *something* fading, ebbing within. Like a drained battery.

It's a light. I just thought of that. A light.

It was dying.

Eye-roll emoji, right? Isn't that how you say it?

It lit the way for me, within me, during those three months. Walking the halls at school, faces staring at me. Not people, just faces. I realized they'd always been faces, nothing more. Just a herd of stupid faces. Their sympathy, their concern for his murder curdled on my skin, unnecessary and unwanted.

Every day I raced off the bus, jumped right into the shower to wash all their fake pity off. They had no idea how misplaced it was, how false.

I did. I knew.

After those three months, I realized the only way to bring that light back was to replace the batteries.

Here's the thing about batteries.

Some are, you know, alkaline or whatever.

But some…some are *rechargeable.*

Remember when roller skating was a thing? Those huge rinks where people strapped on rented skates and zoomed—or more likely flailed and fell—around a smooth, wooden oval. Rock music blaring, colored lights?

No?

It was 1982, and roller skating was a thing. I think there were at least six rinks within a fifteen-minute drive of where I lived.

Journey's *Escape* album came out in '81, and the music was inescapable. I know. I tried. They were everywhere. On the radio. On MTV, when that, too, was a thing.

It became the soundtrack of the year, even though I wasn't a particular fan. When I hear it now, it takes me right back to that period in my life.

Maybe I've finally become a fan after all these years.

I'd sat in my room at our house for months, rarely going out, rarely being *asked* out. I wore a pall of grief, that unseen, unsmelled but repulsive smear, marking me as a person difficult to be around.

What do you say? How do you act?

You do neither because it's easier. Just nod at the person as they pass, keep your eyes down, avoid any contact greater than some vague acknowledgment.

Death in America is awkward and lonely. Not for the dead, but for the survivors. It leaves its stain, like a skid mark in a pair of tighty-whities, and those stains are contagious.

Like death is a disease, spread through contact. You know, like Covid. The only way to avoid it is to hide behind masks, behind closed doors.

Anyway, roller skating was a thing, so I went skating. To get out of the house and spread my disease a little.

I was eighteen at the time. Tall, coulda used a few pounds, as Seger said. Looked a little older than I was. Could have passed for twenty, maybe. Not bad looking, just, well, you know. Average. Nothing particularly outstanding about my looks. No startling eyes or high cheekbones. No great hair or fantastic skin or awesome body.

Just a plain teenager. Because of that, I passed through. Passed through unseen, unacknowledged, unremembered. As I grew older, I realized this was a godsend, this was my charm.

To flit through it all as a ghost, unremarked, unremarkable.

The gravel parking lot of the Skate-Inn was brightly lit, packed. People hanging out near their cars, clustered around the entrance. The garish neon lights of the sign—a huge single skate, lifting its toe and sending a cascade of lightning bolts across the entrance—lit everyone in reds and yellows, like souls in Dante's *Inferno*, which I'd studied as a junior.

Damned souls, clinging to each other in lust, in desperation. When the sign flashed, their laughs became cries of pain, of despair, and I drank it in.

I'd chosen a place far from my house, far from my school, far from anyone who would know me, see the grief staining me.

What they *saw* as grief, right? Wink emoji.

No? Well, this place, packed with people I didn't know, offered a cool anonymity, a *no* to the *where* I needed. Not hide exactly, more like *skulk*. That's a word, right? *Skulk*. I like it. Makes me think of things in holes, waiting to come out, like those trapdoor spiders. Yeah, *skulk*.

I passed through the tangle of people in the parking lot. Guys clustered in groups, smoking and laughing, catcalling. A mellow skunk wafting on the air. Girls in little throngs, laughing nervously at the guys' attention, eyes narrowing at other girls drawing similar interest. Couples making out on the hoods of their cars.

Inside, the music blared. "Rosanna," by Toto. Couple's skate. Lights flared. A disco ball over the center of the floor, sparkling, pinkish lights washing over everything like a pulsing Valentine's Day card.

At the counter, I paid for one and a skate rental, size thirteen. I picked up my skates a little farther down, sat on the crowded bench to put them on. Once they were snug, I stood, tested them.

As "Rosanna" finished, "Heat of the Moment," by Asia. I took it as a cue, pushed through the couples coming off the floor to rest or share a soda and stale popcorn.

• • •

I can't tell this story if you're going to make so much noise. I can't concentrate. I've been taking those memory enhancing drugs. You know, the ones you see on television, supposedly made from stuff found in jellyfish.

I don't think they work. My memory seems normal, but I still can't concentrate, can't focus like I used to. Maybe old age. Maybe there's nothing to be done, as with so many other things.

You just have to live with it.

Let me continue the story.

Or, and I promise this, there are things I can do to *make* you quiet.

I skated a few rounds, through a John Cougar Mellencamp two-for, then "Come on Eileen." I sniggered through "Do You Really Want to Hurt Me," by Culture Club.

I skated off the floor, exhilarated. High. I bet I was higher than those guys outside smoking weed. I needed to catch my breath. It was so energizing to be among all these people, these empty faces, without being noticed, without being *seen*.

How could they not see me? How could they not know what I was, what I'd *done* just three months prior.

What I'd *do*.

I surveyed the crowd, noticed another sizing me up. For a brief moment, a sizzle ran up my spine, down my legs, to the tip of my dick. Contact, almost recognition between her and I, ignited.

But it wasn't. Not at all.

It was just...well, interest. Plain old teenage, hormonal interest.

She was cute in a plain sort of way. Kinda Mary Lou Retton-ish. Petite, with dark brown hair like the gymnast, and a ready smile

Didn't turn away as I caught her, which I found even more enticing.

I waited for the right song, like a cue from a soundtrack to a movie. I sat out for "Hold Me," by Fleetwood Mac and "The Look of Love," from a band whose name escapes me at the moment.

Went back onto the floor for Hall and Oates's "Maneater." The right track.

Out of the corner of my eye, I noticed she followed me onto the floor. The music blared, the lights flashed, and the crowd of teenage hormones circled, laughing and clutching and falling and laughing and circling and screeching.

It was like a fucking Bosch painting. You know the one? We learned about him in Art Appreciation. Dutch painter in the fifteenth century. Painted all sorts of strange, grotesque shit. I mean, really bizarre. Butts where faces should be. People with fish heads or multiple arms or spider eyes.

It was exhilarating but also harrowing.

Like before. Like three months before. When I'd…

Tsk, tsk, tsk. You almost got it out of me, didn't you? Almost got me to talk about it.

Nope. Not the right time or place.

I skated a few laps, watched little Mary Lou peripherally. Once or twice, I returned her stares, just enough for her to know I was watching her, too. That I appreciated she was doing the same.

Eddie Money came on. Not being a particular fan, and needing to catch my breath, I skated off the floor.

Mary Lou slowed as she passed where I sat on the bench, almost pouty. I wiped sweat from my forehead, my upper lip, as I watched her swing by. She seemed part of no group. No gaggle of girls. No guys trying to hit on her.

As she rounded the far turn, she slowed, almost jumped out of the rink and onto the floor outside. She pigeon-toed slowly to me, feigning a casualness I knew was anything but. Her interest pulsed from her. The pheromones of her sweat seeped into the air around her, like a corona of sex.

She turned, as if looking for something or someone else, then took notice of me.

"Hi," she said. "Having fun out there?"

"Sure," I replied, mimicking her demeanor, her tone. "Great time."

She nodded. This was almost as awkward as grief.

"You here with people?" I asked.

"I was just gonna ask you the same," she laughed, and it struck me.

Mary Lou wasn't sixteen or seventeen. She wasn't nineteen or even twenty-one. Mary Lou was at least thirty. The harsh lights revealed the slight creases of her skin, at the mouth, at the corners of her eyes. The subtle slackness of her chin and neck, her cheeks.

She was an adult. An adult who could pass for a teenager.

The opposite of me, my opposing trump.

I held my hand out, careful to dry it first on my jeans.

"I'm Jordan," I said. Why bother with fake names? No one knew me. No one was going to know me. That secret would stay with her.

"My name's Laura."

"Like Branigan," I said, and her face scrunched in confusion. I pointed into the air, to what was playing on the loudspeakers.

"Like the song," I said, but it was clear that the clue, "Gloria," confused her even more. Not a music buff, at least not my music. "By Laura Branigan."

"Oh," she laughed. "Duh."

"So, you want to skate a while?" I asked, standing so she could see my full height close up. I don't know what it is, but short girls dig tall guys. She was short, maybe just five-one, and the difference between us was dramatic.

"Sure," she said, relieved.

I ushered her onto the floor, took her hand, which she seemed pleasantly surprised by. We skated in silence for a lap and a half, while "Save a Prayer" played.

I loved the dance of the lights on her dark hair, in the reflection of her dark eyes. Her perfume was Love's Baby Soft, a fairly run-of-the-mill drugstore perfume thirteen-year-olds favored. It made her seem all the sadder and more pathetic, an older woman clinging to whatever fading youth she could.

Wearing a little girl's idea of a woman's cologne. Coming to a place a high schooler would find entertaining. It disgusted me, you know?

It began, just as it had before. The interest sours in my gut, colors my vision. Seeps into the rest of me, carried by my blood everywhere in my body. To my organs, brain, the marrow of my smallest bones.

Revulsion.

Even the feel of her hand in mine, at first so pleasant and soft, was reduced to the clamp of her meat, the pull of her sinews, the stalks of her bones.

She looked at me and smiled. What before would have been radiant, exulting, wonderful, was now in the null leaking from me, horrid, foul, ghastly.

It was so similar to how it had been three months ago. That overwhelming frisson of disgust that had rippled through me then, moved through me now. I thought back to that time, to what I'd done, who I'd done it to.

My friend.

It almost put me off, I can tell you. Almost made me stop what my very biology had set into motion. I loosened my grip, her hand moist in mine.

What got me back on track?

"Urgent," by Foreigner. Hah. Stupid, right? The things a simple song, some words and a melody, can do. Make you dance. Make you sad. Make you horny.

Make you kill.

I knew, as the pulse of those synthesizers flooded the rink, exactly how easy it would be with her. How willing she would be to take me home, to her bed. How easy every little thing following would be.

It was almost too easy, and that nearly put me off again.

What worth is there in the rabbit when the gazelle waits somewhere out there?

Journey again. "Who's Crying Now?"

We whirled around the turn, and I drew her closer. She fit neatly under my arm, like a puzzle piece. I could smell her shampoo, the kind with the kangaroo on the label. Her soap, Dove. I could smell the flecked enamel of her nail polish, the skin cream she wore, the laundry detergent she washed her clothes in.

I remembered how I could smell him, too, the cologne he wore. The Arm & Hammer detergent his mother washed his clothes in. His toothpaste. The smell of his sweat, his *loathing.*

Ultimately his fear.

Her face tucked in close to my body, I thought maybe she heard my heart, my inner voice. Maybe she knows exactly who she is to me, what she represents.

What I will do to her.

Maybe she accepts, appreciates what I will do to her. How I will worship her, elevate her. Raise her above all these other nameless, faceless blurs.

I lean in to kiss, our lips meeting. I can smell whatever she'd eaten for dinner, rotting in the crevices between her teeth. The milk that still coated her tongue. The metallic taste of her blood.

It was like kissing a wad of raw hamburger.

She enjoyed it, though, met my tentative kiss with a more assertive one of her own.

This one with tongues, and I gotta tell you, I almost gagged.

Like two eels wrestling in the cages of our mouths.

Not funny? No?

Against me, her pulse quickened, and waves of heat rolled off her body like a crashing surf. Her heat stoked my own, very different blaze.

The smell of her changed too. Ozone and muskier.

"You have a place? Or wanna go back to mine?" she breathed, coarse and rough and oh so sexy.

It fell into the seemingly bottomless, at least untouched, pit inside of me.

"Your place is cool," I said, into her ear, so close I could smell the yellowed wax curling inside.

"Let's ditch these skates and get out of here."

She led me off the floor to "Jessie's Girl," by Rick Springfield. I liked that song, but it wasn't the right time. We doffed our boots, giggling like those girls outside.

Once we'd donned our street shoes, she yanked me outside into the parking lot. It was maybe eight o'clock then. It was a school night, so curfews were about to kick in for most of the teens, and the parking lot was a lot clearer.

"We'll take my car. It'll be easier," she breathed, stepping up on her tiptoes to kiss me passionately. The slime of her kiss smeared across my mouth, my cheek, leaving a disgusting snail trail there.

"Let me grab something," I said. I fished out my keys as I ran. I popped the trunk open and grabbed the plain, green duffel I kept there. Hidden behind the upraised trunk, I wiped the stain of her kiss away.

I donned my smile as I closed the trunk.

"Got it," I said as I loped back to her.

"Prepared, eh?" she asked, eying the bag. "I like that, Mr. Boy Scout."

I laughed as she drew me down to her, grabbing the lapels of my shirt, kissing me again, filling me with her bloat, her death gases, already burbling up from the cauldron inside her.

I thought of the merit badges I would earn later.

Eww, right? I mean, she was thirty-something and I was only eighteen. Yuck, especially today in this world of teachers seducing students and priests molesting altar boys. Distasteful.

At least it is when the older person is a man. Not so much when it's a woman. Then it's more *well...still distasteful, sure, but when I was younger, it would've been wow!*

That small difference provided cover for me. Another place to insinuate myself, hide what I was.

What I was becoming.

I could rest in my larval stage, pupate beyond the watch of prying eyes, unfold my wings, moist with rebirth, without anyone knowing, thwarting me.

You just won't shut up, will you?

I mean, let me get a word in at least.

Here. How about…*huff*…this? That do it?

No?

Shit.

We got to her place. A cheap apartment complex behind a grotty strip mall. A 7-Eleven, a used bookstore, an insurance agency, and a Chinese restaurant. We turned in, looped around a bunch of streets lined with cars, parked near a building around back.

We kissed a little in the car. She was blatting out air now like an overworked bellows, fogging the car windows. I put my hands on her, leaned across, our mouths sliding over each other.

One hand tripped accidentally over the points of her nipples, and her sharp intake of breath as she raised her head to the car's ceiling rasped through the air.

She pulled away, ripped the keys from the ignition.

"Grab your stuff," she said, almost leaping from the car.

I fished my bag out of the back, slung it over my shoulder as I exited.

"Jeez," she said as what was inside clinked and rattled. "Got your golf clubs in there?"

I said, "Something like that." And we laughed and laughed.

Inside her apartment, I dropped the bag, and she pushed me against the door as she closed it, kissed me and kissed me and kissed me. She slid my shirt up, kissed my chest and stomach, down, down, down until I closed my eyes and didn't watch.

Zipper snarling, the slide of pants, the elastic snap of underwear.

Then more wet, smacky sounds, the feel of her teeth scraping me, her horrid tongue curling around me.

I kicked off my shoes, shimmied from my pants. Now my breath was labored, but not from that, no, not from that.

She released me, stood, and I fumbled with her blouse, fingers spasming against the catches of her tasteful bra. She sighed a little as she reached behind her, undid it. The sacks of her breasts slapped against her stomach.

More fumbling with her jeans. At least these were catches I understood. Soon, she was revealed, her clothes puddled on the beige carpet. I focused on the marks the vacuum cleaner had left.

"Do you have a roommate?" I asked as she drew me into her bedroom. There was one of those *Hang in There* corporate posters with a kitten, framed over her bed. All the sadder in this setting.

"Nope. Just you and me." She slid onto the bed, turned, scooted to the pillows. She lay there, I suppose she intended, sexy as hell and absolutely inviting.

My own body, so often not under my control, obliged. It raised before me like a flagless staff.

"Let me grab something," I said, ducking into the main room to check the lock on the door. I opened my bag, found the two things I sought.

I reentered the room, and she crawled to me as I came to the bed. I dropped the one thing, let her settle her mouth back on me.

I took her hands. She thought I was telling her to proceed without them. But I needed them, looped duct tape around their wrists, binding them behind her back.

I don't know if she didn't hear or feel the tape, or if she just went along with what she supposed was a kink.

Until I wrapped the tape around her head, stepping back so I could cover her mouth, pulling it tight, cinching her lovely dark hair around her head.

I bent and brought into the light the thing I'd dropped. When the screams came—and rest assured, they did—the tape muffled them, so they didn't drift through the walls.

• • •

After, I stripped, wiped down everything I might have touched before I donned latex gloves. I showered in her bathroom, left steamy clean and smelling of Dove. I took the towel, swiped it across the shower controls, the door.

I saw she had a washer and drier, so I dumped in the towel and washcloth, lots of bleach, set the cycle, and let the lid clang closed.

I found a plastic garbage bag under her sink, stuffed my old clothes inside. Not to carry away any trace of her blood—the shower had done that—but in case anyone noticed what I'd worn that night. I'd take this to a Goodwill, stuff it in—socks, shoes, belt, jeans, shirt. All of it.

From my trusty bag, I took out a fresh set of clothes, put them on.

I'd cleaned all my tools before I cleaned myself, like any good craftsman.

I peeked inside her room before I left. She looked so serene atop her bed, unconcerned, tranquil. No trace of the fear, the abject horror those same features had flashed just hours earlier.

I think she fled her body some point during the butterfly portion of the evening.

Letting it all remain as it was, I shouldered my bag, left the apartment unlocked, walked back to the skating rink.

It was about 4 a.m. when I got into my car, drove home.

I slipped into my room, aglow from the evening, engorged with something vital.

In the morning, after laying in bed fully clothed and ready to go, I raced downstairs, ate a piece of toast, downed a glass of orange juice, kissed my mom, and bounded out the door.

Full, almost crowing I could do what I did, and it had worked.

I was fully recharged.

Shhh…do you know "Night Moves?" By Bob Seeger and the Silver Bullet Band?

Nod one way or the other, or I can assure you, I'll make you.

There. Fine. Not quite in my wheelhouse, just a little before. When it starts, you think it's about teenage sex, kids getting it on here, there, and everywhere.

When the song ends, though, it's about a guy in middle age, looking back, seeing how it seems he doesn't have as much to lose.

Exactly how I felt, like I had nothing left in me.

Then, I remembered how it had recharged me, made me new again.

It's been so long. I found you, and it all came together.

Shhh, no more screaming or yelling. No one can hear you.

No one cares but me.

I care. Oh, I care deeply. About what you're about to become.

Don't worry, my love, my dearest, if I start humming a song from 1982.

Different decade, I know. But still so long ago.

It'll be fine. Don't worry about the mess.

I'll clean it. Always have, always will.

It's who I am.

With autumn closing in.

Drea's Sparkly Pink Kaboodle

By Dana Vickerson

Drea stares so hard at the car pulling into the McDonald's drive thru that the rusted edges of the bumper start to blur. From the vantage of Larson's parked Mitsubishi Spider, feet from the overflowing dumpsters, she's seen every car riding the strip tonight. She knew sooner or later the green Impala would show.

"Didn't y'all used to be friends?"

Her eyes fixate on the tires, so bald she wonders how the car manages to grip the road at all. Her mind spins scenarios where the Impala careens off in a fiery crash as she watches, delighted. "Yeah, when I was a little kid."

"They're such losers," Larson says, taking a drag of his cigarette and turning up *Rx Queen* on his neon red stereo. "Complete stoners."

"Says the guy who just asked me to make him ketamine."

Larson laughs and walks his long fingers across the glass vials and little plastic cups in Drea's sparkly pink kaboodle. "They really just left the chem closet open? What kind of summer camp was it? Walter White Academy?"

Drea shrugs, still fixated on the Impala as it makes its way to the second window. Her eyes burn, but she doesn't look away. This is her last night in town. Ignoring them would be too easy.

"Adults seem to think that *smart kid* means the same as *good kid*." Drea pulls a Parliament out of Larson's pack and lights it, letting her right hand float out the open window.

"How about this one?" Larson asks, but Drea's not looking. The Impala is leaving and heading for the strip. Its busted turn signal makes a sad attempt at blinking.

The windows are rolled up and tinted a deep purple, so she can't see inside, though a thin wisp of smoke curls out of a cracked gasket. Can they see her? Do they know she's in town?

Larson releases the stopper on a small, clear vial and a subtle tang, almost like licorice, snaps Drea back to attention. "Whoa, not that one. You'll wake up twelve hours later with a splitting headache and no memory of the dumb shit you did."

"Why don't you label these?" he says as he carefully puts it back.

"Because I don't need anyone knowing what's in them but me."

Drea stares out the window of the Spider as they make a loop through their desolate town.

Expensive trucks and cheap two-door sedans and everything in between follow an endless figure eight. McDonald's. Over the tracks. Turn at the courthouse. Pass the old, abandoned prison. Back onto the main strip. McDonald's. Do it again. Stop off at any number of cracked asphalt parking lots. Bum a smoke. Buy a joint.

They pass the hanging stoplight in front of the copper topped courthouse, and Drea sees the rusted Impala sitting in the closed bank parking lot, flanked by three other cars. AJ and Rick sit on the hood, paper bagged bottles in hand, Newports dangling from their leering mouths. Drea grips the kaboodle.

"This town is fucking dead," Larson says. "You're so lucky you're getting out."

"You could, you know, go to college too."

"With what money? I'm not smart. I have no talent, unless you count getting kicked out of band for giving Clark Atterton a blow-job in the practice room. Who's going to give me a scholarship?"

"There are loans," Drea says, but her heart's not in it. She can't imagine Larson leaving, even though the whole town hates him. They all hate her too, but fuck them. She's getting out. She's already gone.

They do another loop before Larson sighs and says he's ready to head home. Drea tries to act like bailing on her is no big deal, but she's not a good liar. Her face says everything, even when her words never do. As a consolation, he pulls through the McDonald's and orders her an Oreo McFlurry.

"Want me to drop you off?"

The Impala loops through the parking lot, coming so near her passenger window that she thinks she can see AJ in the driver's seat. Her body feels like a bow string ready to fire. The theme song to *Full House* plays in her head. Maybe the McFlurry will extinguish the bile rising in her throat.

"Naw, I'm gonna walk. It's not far."

Larson eyes her for a minute, then shrugs. "Okay, don't drop your meth lab."

She leans over and gives him a smoky kiss on the cheek. "I leave tomorrow. Come by early?"

He doesn't look at her. The car is alive with his tense energy. He takes the McFlurry from the gangly teenager at the window and hands it to her. "Sure."

Drea pulls open the door and flicks her cigarette into the metal halide glow of the parking lot. It's packed. Cars overflow with teenagers, the only entertainment in this podunk town in full swing. No one so much as glances at her.

She tosses the McFlurry into the nearest trash can.

Three blocks from her house, she hears the muffled sound of bald tires. She slows down, pulls her kaboodle against her hip, and lights a cigarette from the pack she filched off Larson.

The Impala rolls up, windows down, and a mix of menthol cigarettes and weed roll over her. She doesn't turn to look at them, just grips her kaboodle tighter.

"Drea, that you?" Rick says as he hangs out the passenger window. Inside, AJ is laughing, keeping the car at a crawl to match her stride. "Haven't seen you in a minute."

The sight of the two of them running up to the front door of her house used to bring her such joy, until one day it didn't. Until she started hiding behind the couch, hoping her mother wouldn't ask why she didn't want to go play, but they never came back. They knew what they'd done.

Hearing them speak makes her want to run, to dart through Mr. Rainer's lawn and hop the fence onto the next street, push until her lungs burn and the porch light of her tiny house turns on. She doesn't though. She's ignored them for years, and it eats her alive.

"Heard you were on that sale shit now. What you got?"

Rick is two years older than her. AJ four. They're both working the night shift at the chicken factory. Everyone here knows everyone's business, so whether she wants to or not, she knows theirs. Tomorrow she'll be gone, though she's been gone for most of the last three years. First to her dad's, then when her parents decided she had to spend summers in this shithole with her mother, she found every academic summer camp she could. Always got in. Always got scholarships. Her mother thinks she doesn't want to come back because of something she did wrong. Drea doesn't tell her it's because of the wrong thing that was done to her.

"Seriously, Drea. Can you stop for a minute? Elliot said you got that good shit. You want a ride home?"

The vials jingle in her kaboodle. They're so close to her house. She should tell them to fuck off. Instead, she turns to face them.

AJ barks something at Rick and the car stops. Rick pulls his huge body out, an imposing figure in an oversized Cowboys jersey. Drea wants to take a step back, but she won't give him the satisfaction. He doesn't grab her arm, doesn't need to, but leans in like he and Drea are in on a little secret. In this together.

"We'll drop you off. He just wants to see what you're holding."

She knows she should not get in the car.

Rick pulls his seat forward, and Drea hesitates, but the kaboodle grounds her, tethers her to the strength she's built in herself, so she ignores every warning signal firing in her brain and climbs in the back.

The last time she was alone with them, she was ten years old. The TV in AJ's room blaring so they wouldn't be heard. The opening credits telling her everywhere she looked, there was a hand to hold onto.

Rick's hand wet from her muffled screams.

The car door slams shut, and Drea clamps her teeth together. AJ revs the engine, and Drea pushes into her seat as the Impala shoots through a stop sign.

When they pass her house without slowing down, Drea tenses, and Rick looks over at AJ. She expects a conspiratorial smile, but he looks surprised.

AJ brings his glassy eyes to the rearview mirror, locking with hers. "Fucking relax. We'll smoke you out, we'll buy some shit, and we'll take you home."

Drea's neighborhood passes in a blur as tears smear her black eyeliner.

Drea's sparkly pink kaboodle rests between her knees. She got it for her eleventh birthday, filled with department store nail polish and makeup. Her mom went all out that year, not understanding what had changed in Drea but trying in her limited way to push away the dark clouds that had enveloped her daughter. First the makeup became her armor, then the vials.

The ten-minute drive from town to the river is agony. AJ pushes a tape into the deck and Deftones' *Knife Party* crawls to life. Drea hates that they listen to the same music.

By the time they pull onto the gravel road and the Impala climbs over the levee and parks, Rick has rolled a fat blunt.

The Mississippi rages in front of them. It's dark, but the moon is almost full, washing the scraggly trees and muddy ground in a milky haze.

AJ rolls the windows down, and Rick lights the blunt. He takes a huge drag and passes it to AJ, who lingers on it before giving it to Drea.

She puts it in her mouth and almost gags at the thought of tasting their saliva, but she pulls in the heady smoke and holds it.

For years, it had been just the three of them, her best friends in the whole world, playing Sega and eating junk. Being with them was so much better than being at home, where her mom was always upset or gone.

She remembers what it felt like the day AJ's brother walked through the living room and said, "Give it another year, and ya'll are gonna be trying to fuck that little fat girl."

Rick, chubbier than her, had said, "Ew, no way."

But AJ had looked at her like a hungry wolf who'd just noticed that their pack mate was a rabbit. She was too young to know she should be afraid.

"So, what? You make your own shit?" Rick says as he takes the blunt back from Drea.

She shrugs. "Some of it."

Drea hears the hiss of a can as AJ cracks open a beer. Rick opens one too. Always following AJ. Always doing what he says.

They don't offer her a beer, and she passes the next time the blunt comes around. Soon the car is silent as the three sit back in the haze. Chino Moreno's mournful voice sings about changing into a fly. Drea imagines floating out of this car and into her new life, leaving these assholes and this town behind forever.

AJ stretches out, his rangy body filling the front seat, like he owns the world, like he isn't just another burned-out loser in a dying town. "Well," he says, restarting their forgotten conversation, "give me some shit that will take me to the moon."

"Sure," she says, and clicks open her sparkly pink kaboodle.

She slips two tabs of blotter paper up front. "On me."

They look back at her, eyes bloodshot. The first hint of wrinkles crawl across the edges of their leathery faces, showing signs of a hard life they haven't even begun.

"Bet," AJ says, and puts the tab under his tongue. He swigs his beer and sits back. Rick watches her for a minute. She doesn't want to see the regret and mistrust swirling in his ugly face.

"You're not gonna take any?" he asks.

"Naw, too much to do tomorrow. I'll babysit."

Rick hesitates. She knows he wants to ask why she's doing this, why she's being nice to them, but he doesn't. He swallows his doubts behind his bravado and places the blotter under his tongue, swigging his beer just like AJ.

As Drea waits, she makes herself remember the day it happened. AJ telling them both he got a TV in his room.

They should hang in there. The feeling in her gut when she heard the pop of the door lock engage.

Later, after it was over, after she'd walked home crying, her wrists hurting, hiding in her room, she thought about the last thing AJ said before he told her to go home.

"Hope you don't get pregnant."

She knew what a period was, that she hadn't had hers, but her stomach stayed in knots for weeks, wondering how she would tell her mom about the baby.

The tape finishes, and the three of them sit in the car listening to static. Drea feels the mighty river rolling so near, only a few feet and a gravel embankment between them and the gripping undertow.

The words were on her lips so many times the days after it happened. Her mother never even asked why her friends stopped coming around, and Drea was thankful. She knew if pressed, she would have told, and in the early days, she didn't even understand what had happened. Did she let it? She felt like it was her fault. But if it was, why had she fought so hard?

Would her mother be mad at her if she knew?

When she was older, she understood that ten was far too young to give consent, that the moment it went from kids exploring bodies to her being held down on a bed while she cried and told them to stop, it was rape. She thought about telling her mother then, but to what end? She knew it would only burden her with guilt and heartbreak, and to Drea, her mother already carried enough of that.

Drea watches AJ and Rick take long sips of their beers and giggle uncontrollably, staring at their hands as if they're the most interesting things in the world. They're too fucked up to notice when she unstops the clear vial and pours the entire thing into their cans. Too high to notice the slight tang of licorice.

She thinks they've finally passed out when Rick says, "I'm so sorry, Drea. I'm so fucking sorry."

He mumbles his apologies to the dashboard, and Drea hears the sincerity in his voice, the pain and guilt he's likely carried for years. It's nothing like what she had to carry, and all it does is breathe oxygen into the growing fire in her chest.

When Rick's head slumps to the side and his snores mirror AJ's, she puts on her latex gloves and gets to work.

Drea stares at the moon as she sits on the trunk of the Impala, waiting. The air is thick with the sweltering heat of the end of summer, but the weed and adrenaline make her shiver.

A faint glow emanates from the tinted windows, and she hops off, taking ten careful steps away before turning to look at the car. The drug she gave them, her own mix of GHB and flavored synthetics, was powerful enough to knock them out cold for as long as she needed, but she wants them awake for the end. Screams from inside the car are muffled but growing louder.

The little plastic cups she left balancing in their laps have finally fallen over. The sodium hydroxide pellets, now dissolved, eat through their jeans and set the fabric alight, burning everything, filling the car with noxious smoke. Because of their inebriated condition, they can't figure out why they're hurting, why they're on fire, only that they are. Drea watches it all.

The car shakes as they try to pull the doors open, but she's sealed them. It's an easy trick, really. Just a few drops of her new favorite concoction, muriatic acid and a few accelerators. Eats metal in a flash. Doors so jammed they'll never open. She's really proud of that one.

She walks to the windshield and AJ slams on the glass, yelling, crying, snot running down his meth-lean face. Rick is no different. He's screaming at her, but she can't tell what he's saying. It's pleading and incoherent and as horrible as she'd hoped.

AJ and Rick flail in futility, and she's thankful that neither of them have shifted the car out of neutral. That would have proven more difficult. Her heels dig into the gravel, and she pushes against the rear bumper with all the hate she feels for these two men, the friends who stole her childhood, her sense of safety, and her relationship to her body. The wheels start to roll, and after that, it's all momentum. The car goes over the edge, and Drea digs her heels into the gravel so she doesn't go with it.

The Impala hits the water nose first and flips, rusty undercarriage up. She watches it float swiftly downstream before the hungry river sucks it in. Dredging here would be close to impossible, and who would go through the effort for a couple missing burnouts?

The moon keeps her company while she stands on the edge of the roaring Mississippi, soaking in the overwhelming relief that is left when her hate dissipates. Washes downriver. Gone forever. People say revenge doesn't take away the pain, but standing on the embankment under the cloudless sky, Drea feels euphoric.

She tucks her gloves into her sparkly pink kaboodle and pulls a cigarette from her back pocket. It's a long walk back to town, but the sun will rise tomorrow, and she'll leave this fucking town and never look back.

One and Done

By Stephen Graham Jones

What did Rhett's uncle used to tell him? If you don't sleep in the cab of your truck at least once a month, then how do you really even call it a marriage.

It applies to girlfriends too, Rhett's pretty sure. Or, Celine seems to know that old saying, anyway. Except she must have heard it with a different count. Rhett hasn't slept back at their place for three nights, now. As far as he knows, his records and his magazines are still out in the yard. His guns were too, but Doretta's fifteen-year-old kid, who works back on the dock—Doretta and the boy live next door to Rhett and Celine—shrugged his way into the break room at lunch, informed Rhett that the guns were under his bed now, because if the dew set on them they'd probably rust.

Rhett had just nodded, spit another sunflower seed shell into his Styrofoam cup then toasted the kid a grudging thanks for that, catching his eye just long enough to get across that he'd make it up to him. A case of beer, a carton of smokes, keys to the truck one Friday night.

For a few weeks in the fall, Celine had thought Doretta's son was for sure the one abducting college girls and doing who knew what with them—they'd just be gone, never to turn up again. But then Doretta's husband put the kid in the hospital, and while the kid was laid up, another girl poofed out of existence, so Celine had to start her investigation all over again, starting with talking up all the women down at the beauty salon, probably.

Who cares.

"What you need?" Rhett says across the counter to the dude, crusty brown from the waist down, flannel-colored the rest of the way up. But then the guy's smell catches up. Rhett reaches over for the smokes in the cash drawer, gets one going. Screw what the fancy new assistant manager might say, and says, even though it hardly needs to be said. "Septic?"

Mr. Septic's nod is so grim as to hardly be there at all.

Rhett rents him the shit he needs—like "shit" is what needs more of—takes the deposit, and says, like always, "We close at six-thirty, so be here by six, yeah? Don't want you paying for another day."

The guy dragasses out, back into what Rhett's guessing isn't exactly the day he had planned. Probably not the life, either.

Rhett blows smoke out, chuckles about the sad states other idiots find themselves in, then snubs the cherry off under the counter, saves the rest of the cigarette. As for the smoke, the shop vac sucks it right up, fills the air with that musty smell that means its plastic belly is roiling with rot. But the assistant manager doesn't ride Rhett's ass about that. Just the smoking.

Because there's nothing else to do but get caught sleeping, Rhett organizes the equipment more or less, at least until he senses another customer standing there.

"Bell there," Rhett says, nodding down to the silver clapper by the register.

The man looks down to it like he's stoned, then reaches forward, taps the clapper.

The sharp *ding* crawls up Rhett's spine. He turtles his hand over that ringing, looks up into this man's bloodshot eyes, takes the rest of his sorry self in as well: chin and jaw stubbly, the brim of his hat grimy and curled—and then Rhett clocks him, knows just what he's here at the hardware store for again.

"Excavator, twenty-four hours?" he asks, already hauling the Bobcat paperwork out.

Mr. Bobcat's dry lips crack into a grin.

"Like clockwork," Rhett says, shaking ink to the ball of the only pen he can find.

"Almost done," Mr. Bobcat says.

For the past four months, on his one day off a week, Mr. Bobcat's been working on some irrigation project or another. *Old* Rhett, shiny and new, would have asked all about the project, maybe even had some recommendations, or at least anecdotes about similar jobs he's been involved with.

Today's Rhett could give a rat's ass.

"We close at—"

"Six," Mr. Bobcat finishes.

Rhett flourishes up the key up that unlocks the trailer hitch the Bobcat's on. When you rent a little digger like that, you get the trailer too.

One jackhammer and two steam cleaners later, and one more microwave burrito from the gas station, Rhett's cruising slow by his and Celine's trailer.

Like he expected, the pages of his *Easy Riders* are flapping slow in the evening breeze, their pages already that kind of stiff they get when they've got wet and then dried in the sun.

Screw it.

They're old anyway. And, not like he's ever really going to get a bike. At some point you've got to cash your dreams, get some new ones. Why didn't Rhett's uncle ever bother to teach him *that*?

Still, Rhett's tempted to vault over the short little chain-link fence, scoop up his clothes, finally have a second shirt to wear, but the idea of Celine parting the thick drapes and grinning to see what he's been reduced to…no thanks.

Instead, Rhett stalks the aisles of the dollar store, leaves with four T-shirts, three pairs of bright-colored underwear—that's how they come, three to a pack—and two tubes of chips that sound mostly shattered in there, so he's going to have to drink them, probably.

The shirts all have the same three cartoon pineapples on them, and some beach or surf situation fizzing white behind them.

Whatever.

Gassing up at the place across town, mostly just for somewhere to go, Rhett finds himself studying the face of the last missing girl. Her flyer's taped to the side of the gas pump.

Seventeen? Twenty? Once upon a time, Rhett would have known, but, halfway through his thirties now, all that young stuff's getting so it looks the same, like he's looking at them through a crappy telescope. From a ship that's sailing farther and farther away.

"Five days, girlie," Rhett says, nudging her sharp cheekbone with the knuckle of his index finger, as if telling her to hang in there.

Not likely, he knows.

The four girls before have yet to turn up, either with a story or in a dumpster, so chances are this one's gone just the same.

Really, it's so useless that Rhett just pulls her flyer down.

Under it is the flyer for the girl before.

"Shit," Rhett says, hissing a laugh out, and pulls her down as well, only to find *another* face underneath.

It's some sick commentary on America, or the world, isn't it?

"Call me up," Rhett says to the comparatively clean space on the pump where the girls were. "I've got one for you."

But then he looks around to see if somebody caught that. Because you're not supposed to give these kinds of dudes ideas, are you? Even if you're just imagining doing it. Well—you're not supposed to let anybody hear you telling them to set their sights on your common-law sort-of wife, anyway.

The truck's tank sloshing full, Rhett aims back across town for the creek he's been parking by, because he can cross the bridge there, use the rest stop's dark bathroom. Once again, though, Celine's is on the way.

He's pretty sure she might be exactly at the midpoint between him and anywhere he could possibly ever go.

And she knows it, would have it no other way.

Rhett pushes his headlight knob in, walks his truck slow across the cattle guard into the trailer park, feeling each pipe under his tires.

If he's lucky, Doretta's kid will be playing with Rhett's .30/06 and jack a round in, let the trigger get pulled somehow, and that 180-grain slug of justice will blast through the wall of his bedroom, stab into a certain kitchen next door, where a woman with a French name is mixing another of her Irish coffees up.

Rhett won't even hold it against the kid, will just plug that hole in the wall up and move back in.

Accidents happen every day, don't they?

Rhett grins, spits a shell into the Dr Pepper can between his legs, and crunches through the gravel, the tall dry grass rasping against the underside of his truck, making him feel like a snake, slithering.

But, no, not a snake. He's the injured party here, isn't he? He's the one who's been wronged, anybody can see that. If Celine can't understand that she's never going to graduate him through her own personal charm school, turn him into someone whose ass Rhett would kick just on principle, then—

Rhett doesn't get to finish that thought.

Celine's parked on a saggy lawn chair on the porch.

And she's not alone.

He doesn't know who the guy sitting his ass on the metal cooler Rhett's been fishing with every summer for the past five years is, but he's pretty sure Celine must be saying something without moving her lips, because the guy looks up to this slow truck passing, its headlights off, making Rhett look like the whipped dog he is.

He sucks air in through his teeth, jams the heel of his right hand against the top of the steering wheel hard enough to shake the whole blamed dash, and, not because he wants to but because he can't help it—he *deserves* it—he drops into first, mashes the pedal down, and spits gravel and smoke and fan-belt screech up into the night, fishtailing so he has to pull his headlights on at last, else he might mow some grandma on her walker down, and that'd be a stupid thing to get sent up for.

Parked at the creek, his door open behind him, he pulls on the public trashcan until it finally breaks free from its pole. Then he kicks it, runs it down, kicks its side in some more. When that's not enough, he lifts it over his head, runs for the bank, slings the thing as high as he can, the trash gloriously spraying out, dirty diapers and fast-food bags and a dirty blouse hanging in the air for a moment before the creek sucks them away.

The trash can clangs against the few rocks on the bank then ducks under the water, never to rise again.

Good riddance.

Rhett blasts out onto the bridge, wanting to tear something else up, but there isn't anything.

Under him, the blouse, cleaner now, finally gets unsnagged from whatever'd grabbed it. It floats underneath the bridge, looks for all the world like a woman in the water on her back, drifting past.

Celine, maybe?

Yeah, Celine.

Rhett can believe that for a breath or two, anyway.

Sitting back in his truck, then, he finds himself trying to figure that blouse's backstory. Did the woman who chucked it have a spare with her, or'd she drive home in her bra? And since when is a shirt dirty enough to a woman that it's better not to have a shirt on at all?

Rhett sits up all at once when it occurs to him: maybe she *didn't* drive away, right? Maybe this was somebody throwing her shirt away *for* her. To hide the evidence. Spread it around, anyway.

Not like she's going to need it again, where she's going, right? Or, where she probably already is.

Frantic, sure he's going to lose the thread his thinking's got hold of, Rhett digs in the passenger side floorboard for the three flyers he balled up.

He pops his hood and unfolds each of them carefully under the hood, because the light under there works, unlike the one in his cab.

None of the three girls are wearing this blouse.

"Shit," Rhett says, pushing away from the truck.

He thought he was solving something.

Really, he was just being a hopeful idiot. Again. Like when Celine said it'd be cheaper for them to move in together. That nothing would change.

"Nothing except *everything*," Rhett says, whipping his cap off his head and wiping his forehead with his arm, then watching the hairs there slowly unpress themselves, the sweat letting them stand back up.

He shouldn't let Celine get him worked up like this, he knows. It's just what she wants. She's probably having a good chuckle back on the porch, tipping another one back with her gentleman caller.

Or, it's been an hour, hasn't it? *She's* probably the one getting tipped.

Until now, Rhett had had the idea that they were going to work it out, they were going to find a way through. That there were maybe going to be some good times again before too long.

Wrong.

Time to start looking for a room to rent, a place to crash.

But—for once, maybe the first time ever—he really liked that trailer. Something about it stayed cool all the time. Rhett doesn't know if it has to do with the insulation in the walls or the aluminum on the outside or with some crosswind seeping in past the fairing, underneath the floor, but he wasn't always sweating through his shirts, living there.

He can make it without Celine, no problem. The world's full of Celines.

A trailer that stays cool in summer, though, that's worth making a play for.

Some kind of play.

Maybe Rhett'll crack that mystery open tomorrow.

For tonight…it's the truck seat for a bed again.

He crosses back to the hood, is about to guide it shut—Chevy hoods are bad about folding in half—when one of those dead girls' faces stops him.

Well, not her face, exactly.

Her "last seen" date.

"Hunh," Rhett says, pulling the flyer closer up.

He gathers the other two as well, lays them out in chronological order, and considers them like the cop he isn't.

There's twenty-three days between the first and second, and then twenty-five between the second and third.

"Well well well," he says out loud, trying to kickstart some mental processes. He can feel some sort of dim, huge answer swirling around just under where he can grab it.

Three hours later, at two in the morning, it hits him.

He sits up fast, casing the darkness, worried like he always is that his thoughts are in a white balloon over his head for anyone to read.

It's just him at the creek, though. Him and the raccoons, it looks like. They're dredging that trash up from the water. Their eyes glow when Rhett turns his parking lights on, gentle-like.

"Go about your business," he tells them, then rolls both windows up, eases away.

To the hardware store.

He doesn't have a key, wouldn't want to be on that list when anything shows up missing, but getting in through the service dock just takes working a crowbar under that big metal door and jerking up a few times while pulling out on the knob, waiting for that moment when the little metal tongue isn't lined up.

He throws the crowbar back onto the dock behind him, the clatter making him wince. There's a reason he got a nine-to-five instead of becoming some sort of second-story man in a one-story town.

He does know enough not to announce his presence with the store's overhead lights, though. Instead, he gets the flashlight from the emergency kit in the breakroom, grabs a loaf of bread to snack on, and walks through the store, stepping in his puddle of light over and over, eating the bread a slice at a time, crumbs cartwheeling down the front of his shirt and then launching out into space.

At his register, he pulls down the logbook then sits backward under the counter—you never know who's going to be looking through the front glass—flattens the flyers around his feet, comparing them to the records.

"You son of a bitching genius," he finally has to say.

Mr. Bobcat isn't engineering some grand irrigation project. He's burying college girls where they'll never be found.

The dates line up perfect. If Rhett had the other two flyers from the first two girls, he bets those dates would line up even better, wouldn't they?

"Got you," Rhett says, tapping the logbook, and then after some creative pencil work, he leaves everything just as it was, even locks the door behind him.

Instead of sleeping at the creek, he just drives around until dawn, checking his plans for obvious holes. Then it's coffee and a honeybun and a new bag of sunflower seeds—dip's going to cancer him out sooner or later, he knows—a long visit to the men's side of the rest stop, and another forever day of renting tools, saying it over and over, until it's meaningless: "We close at six-thirty, be here by six."

Mr. Bobcat is there at a quarter of five, his right pants leg tucked into his work boot.

"Parked in three," he mumbles—the third slot.

Rhett nods, passes him the metal clipboard to sign off on, careful not to actually watch the guy's face. Just his fingers.

They're crusted with muck, are calloused, thick—a working man's hands.

Someone who can *do* work, that is.

They clench into a fast fist when Mr. Bobcat sees what's on the clipboard: this last girl's flyer.

"No, no, you're being smart," Rhett says, still not looking up, his voice hushed and controlled. "Were I doing a project like this, I'd do it just the same. Anybody would. Bury them deep, tamp it down, throw some Bermuda seed across, nobody'll ever have to know."

And now Rhett finally looks up.

Mr. Bobcat is staring right into his soul. Rhett wants to stagger backwards, sit on his ass like a kid, blubber an apology.

But he's been steeling himself for this all day.

"That's not the sound of sirens you're hearing," Rhett says, quietly.

"You're wrong," Mr. Bobcat says.

"About the sirens?"

"About this"—the flyer.

"Maybe I am," Rhett says, shrugging, leaning back real casual, like this is everyday, nothing big. Like the muscles near his bones aren't clenched so tight he wants to run for that bathroom. "But maybe I'm not, right? Maybe I should… maybe I should ask someone else how wrong I *am*, think? I mean, I only went through tenth grade, yeah?"

Mr. Bobcat's just glaring at Rhett, now.

This is a very calculated thing, Rhett knows. He's gambling Mr. Bobcat doesn't want a scene, won't want to out himself.

If he's packing, though, well, this could get ugly fast. And for someone like him, "packing" probably doesn't only mean a sidearm. There's knives, there's hammers. Hell, he could reach over into the bucket of rebar ends, do his damage with one of them, probably leave every soul in this store burbling blood.

But Rhett doesn't think it's going to come to that.

He holds Mr. Bobcat's eyes. It's not easy, but it's necessary.

Mr. Bobcat says, "I—"

"I know, I know," Rhett says. "This is the last time you're in here. You're leaving this town today. The address you've put in here"—the logbook—"is fake. I know, I know. And, know what?" Rhett leans forward, his hands two tall spiders on the counter. "I don't *care*, man."

"Then why this?" Mr. Bobcat says, about the flyer still between them.

Rhett looks down at it like just seeing it, then comes up again.

"Just, you know," he says. "*Thinking*."

"About?"

"You know," Rhett says, and, holding Mr. Bobcat's eyes the whole time, so there can be no miscommunication, unfolds the copy he made on the machine in the break room.

It's an enlargement of the one photo he had in his glovebox. Of Celine.

Her face is on a flyer, now.

"Don't know her," Mr. Bobcat says, pushing the flyer back across.

"Count yourself lucky," Rhett says, pushing the flyer *back*.

They don't say anything for the whole thirty seconds it takes a hardware customer to muddle past, lost in his phone.

"Just saying," Rhett finally says. "What's one more body down there, right? I mean, down wherever."

"Who is she?"

"Doesn't matter, does it?"

"I can't just— Even if—"

"Address on the back there," Rhett says, nodding down to it.

Mr. Bobcat studies the trailer park's address. The number for the slot still rented in Rhett's name.

"Free rental, too," Rhett throws in.

"And this is it?" Mr. Bobcat says.

"One and done, boss."

"I can't just—"

"Hey, I don't care about the when," Rhett says. "How doesn't make a damn either."

"You're serious?"

"As a heart attack. Look, I even messed the dates up in here, yeah?"

Rhett spins the logbook around on the counter to show where the dates no longer match up with the missing girls. Mr. Bobcat doesn't look down to confirm this.

"Who is she to you?" he asks.

"My underground wife, I hope," Rhett says, and closes the book on this, his eyes darting to the assistant manager vectoring in like he does any time a customer interaction threatens to go long. "Tick-tick," Rhett says, not using his lips to say it.

Mr. Bobcat hesitates, can hear the approaching footsteps.

Right before they're there, he scrunches Celine's flyer into his hand and pivots on his right heel, keeping his back to the assistant manager, and is already gone, turning to smoke in broad daylight, the way his kind can.

"Who's that?" the assistant manager asks.

"Returning the Bobcat," Rhett says, clapping the logbook shut.

"Those your sunflower shell husks in the break room?" the assistant manager asks, keeping his voice low so as not to alert the customers to any problem over here.

Rhett sucks the pale meat from the soggy one on the tip of his tongue, spits the wet shell down into his palm and considers it, then holds his hand out for the assistant manager, says, "I don't know. Want to do a little comparison?"

The assistant manager spins away in a huff, stalks away, probably to audit Rhett's time card or police his locker.

It doesn't matter.

All Rhett's problems, they're about to go away, aren't they?

Pretty soon he'll be back in his trailer, his shirt cool and dry, and every time he hears a tractor engine he'll raise his beer to toast it, he knows, saying inside to be sure to tamp that down *right*, son. You don't want anything down there turning up in five years, or ten. Or ever.

Some problems *do* just go away, right?

All they need's a nudge or two.

Scrying Eyes

By Laurel Hightower

Sasha could still smell her brother's blood when she opened the cellar door.

She'd kept it closed since the last time, when all the people had been there. Boom mikes and cameras, heat radiating out of too-bright lights. It was all wrong. The conditions hadn't been right for Alex to try a reading—he needed quiet, and darkness.

"You don't have to prove anything," she'd told him, standing behind his chair before the bedroom mirror while he combed his hair into a slick, even part. "People who believe, will believe. And people who don't never will."

He met her eyes in the mirror and raised a brow. "Like you, sis?" It was said without rancor, and it hadn't stung. Not then, but now it did.

"Was it for me?" she asked the darkness at the top of the stairs. Her voice was thin, breathless. Like Alex's had been. "Were you proving it to me?"

He wasn't going to answer her. Not up here. Where Alex had gone, voices couldn't reach just anywhere. The conditions had to be right, he always said that. For a long time, during the first decade of his gift, the cellar had been enough. He'd unbolt the heavy, solid-core door and thump down the stairs without pulling the string to turn on the lights. Sasha would wait to hear his feet hit the earthen floor, and he'd call to her.

"Okay, I'm good," he'd say, and Sasha would close the door and lock him in.

She hated that part. They'd always looked out for each other, even before being on their own. Growing up the way they had, they only had each other, and Sasha's greatest fear was losing him. Throwing the bolt with him down there, unable to get out on his own, felt like betrayal. And he *would* need to get out, usually in a hurry. While he was down communing with spirits or whatever, she would pull up a kitchen chair and sit close to the door, listening for a cry, a bellow, a scream, followed by thundering steps at high speed. She'd fling the door open, Alex would hurl himself across the threshold, and she'd slam it behind him, her heart thudding at what always felt like a near-miss.

Alex swore she didn't need to worry, that nothing in that cellar could follow him out, but Sasha, believer or no, refused to take chances. Sometimes in the middle of the night, when the house was silent and her brother moved through dreams, she heard things down there. Scraping and thumping, and once, the rattle of the cellar door. It was in these darkest hours that fear held her in place, but in the light of day, that fear receded, and it became easier to believe Alex's reassurances. After all, where would she go if she convinced him to leave? His money kept them afloat, let them stay in the old homestead, and if the sounds she heard *were* real, she doubted they'd be left behind so easily. Alex might believe it was the power of the location, but she wasn't so sure. Nothing had ever spoken to her in the deep dark of the underground room, back in the days before, and Heaven knew they'd both spent plenty of time locked down there. If there truly was something lurking in the shadows, it was because of Alex.

If. Sasha gave her arm a vicious pinch. She'd reluctantly accepted her brother's assurances about their safety, but refused to invest fully in belief of his talents. An ability to speak to the dead that came about after the accident that took their parents. He discovered it after three nights in a row of something calling him from down the cellar stairs. Sasha was sure they were dreams, but Alex went down to investigate and returned in a state of euphoria, his eyes wet with joyful tears.

"They're okay," he said, squeezing her tight enough to hurt. "Wherever they are, they're okay, and we don't have to worry anymore. Not ever again—that part is over."

Maybe it was jealousy that set her against him from the beginning. Maybe she felt it unfair that only he could receive messages from Mom and Dad, even if it was only through a spirit medium. After everything their parents put them through, why hadn't they spoken to her? Why hadn't they sent reassurances to their only daughter? It reinforced a lifetime of bitterness at being the lesser child, the least loved. But if she denied her brother's claims, she could turn away from the pain of rejection, pretend it wasn't still happening.

The other stuff was harder to explain. Once folks got word of Alex's talents, his connection to the other side, he was flooded with requests for readings. Down there in the silent dark, he communed, and then returned with answers that made their tears fall anew. Always grieving, always seeking that last connection, forgiveness, closure. It got worse when the murders started—violent deaths of people they knew, sometimes whole families, and whoever was left would come to Alex, seeking a beacon in the endless dark. Even the police sought him out, their desperation growing with each unsolved death.

Sasha didn't know how he did it. He was always closed off when the grieving imparted their information; he insisted on that. No one was allowed to speak until Alex was locked in, unable to see or hear. Then they would turn their eager eyes to Sasha and tell her how their loved one died, or about their life, and the questions they wanted answered. Most of them were open, trusting, and as honest as a confessional. Those types were easiest to deal with. Sasha was used to the skeptics too, the ones who stood over her the entire time, narrowed gazes searching for the trick, the cheat. She didn't like it, but she never complained. They could look all they wanted. If there was a trick, she wasn't in on it.

The one thing Alex never allowed was direct observation. Occasionally, he'd let someone come down and snoop after a session, look around with the lights blazing to see where the trapdoor was, the phone, the computer, whatever would explain how he knew the things he couldn't possibly know. These were just tests, anyway. Clients already knew that information, it was just a way to prove Alex's skill so he could help them accept and believe the answers he provided. He welcomed investigation and questions, but he remained adamant that no one was allowed to be down there with him. For many, it was enough, and they left satisfied and full of renewed joy. For some, his refusal to allow witnesses confirmed their suspicions that he was a fraud. And when Alex did what was asked of him by the police, when he sought clues to the spate of unsolved murders in his spirit sessions and came back with leads that panned out, skepticism grew.

That was why he finally said yes to the camera crew. A documentary team, they were there to record everything up to the actual scrying. They shot the whole cellar, explored every inch, testing for spaces that shouldn't be there or hidden technology humming away in the walls. There was nothing and no one. Even Sasha felt the same thrill of excitement that hummed through the film crew. This was real. Her brother was truly communing with the dead. The possibilities were endless, but here, today, he might finally put a stop to the killer who had terrorized their city for so long.

But they never heard the message. Cameras at the ready, mikes held close to the sealed door to his scrying chamber—his psychomanteum, he called it—that they'd built together when Alex decided the cellar alone was no longer enough. The crew had been perfectly poised to capture his screams. With the noise muffled by the soundproofing of the small room, they'd exchanged concerned looks, but it wasn't until an ooze of crimson blood flowed beneath the door that anyone realized something was terribly wrong.

There had been investigations of a different sort after that—police questioning Sasha, exploring every inch of Alex's private sanctum. She never objected, had given free reign to anyone who asked. She didn't care about keeping secrets. She only wanted the truth.

Despite their efforts and Sasha's cooperation, the police were unable to find any other way in or out of the psychomanteum, so they concluded Alex's wounds were self-inflicted.

Of course, she thought bitterly. Alex had entered the psychomanteum wearing nothing but his underwear, his skin still prickled with goose flesh after allowing the touch of strangers, assuring themselves he wasn't carrying anything in with him. The camera crew shot the inside of the little room, checked for hidden devices, and came up empty. Yet somehow, her brother managed to cut out his own eyes and asphyxiate by his own hand, despite there being no weapon found that day or any after. She fought the findings, refused to leave the detectives alone, intent on finding the truth for her brother.

Until she realized he'd gone from victim to murder suspect.

"A little convenient, wasn't it?" asked a thin-faced officer behind a desk heaped with old coffee cups and paperwork. "He comes up with all this stuff, things only the killer would know. Locations of bodies, clues no one else could find. That hat." The woman's eyebrow went up, her lips pursed, and Sasha's blood ran cold.

The hat, the black beanie with rams horns embroidered on the front, left behind at the scene of the second murder. The police found it only after Alex told them where to look. She never asked her brother about that hat, but it was impossible not to think of the matching beanie up in their parents' closet. The same one their father wore when he started losing his hair. Alex had worn it sometimes, in the early days after the accident, the same way Sasha had worn their dad's sweaters and her mother's perfume, resentment mixed with longing. But it couldn't be the same hat. That was impossible, so she never brought it up. Yet somehow, the detective knew.

"And just as he's about to solve the murders, become the hero, *boom*, he's gone."

Sasha turned on her heel and left, slamming through the doors of the station for what she swore would be the last time.

When the documentary aired as a three-episode miniseries, it was critical of the suicide conclusion. "We'll never know what happened to Alex Guyver," the narrator concluded in the show's haunting last lines. "Alone at the end but for the spirits that guided him."

The crew's tacit support gave Sasha new life, knocked her out of the loop of fury and grief she'd been trapped in since she lost Alex. She wouldn't let his legacy die like this. She needed to know the truth of what happened, so here she was, at the top of the stairs, watching the light's pull chain sway from side to side.

Today there was no camera crew. No grieving clients save for herself, an orphan who'd lost the only family she had left. An empty woman in an empty house, her mouth dry and her hands shaking. She hadn't believed her brother when it might have saved him. But she was prepared to believe him now.

She couldn't make herself leave the light off the way Alex always had. She wasn't made of the stuff that would let her step into his place of death in the darkness. It would be dark in the psychomanteum. Dark and haunted by whatever parts of her brother he'd left behind. And with any luck, she'd find an answer.

The sound of her steps became muffled when her shoes touched the earthen floor at the foot of the stairs. The naked bulb's circle of light only spread so far, stopping short of the little room where Alex had searched for his own answers.

Sasha stopped at the edge of the light, the toes of her sneakers nudged up to where darkness took over. Her breath came in erratic gasps, her heart thudding in her ears. It felt the same as all those nights she laid awake listening, knowing she'd heard things moving in the empty house. Daylight could no longer chase away the certainty that something was there—not now that she was alone.

Sasha drew a deep breath and made herself step over the line into blackness. It was only twenty or so steps from the lit staircase, but the darkness grew in the space of a few paces. She stopped, certain she'd heard something moving. She held her breath, listening, and the sound came again—a soft, stealthy scraping coming from behind the psychomanteum on her right.

Acid splashed the back of her throat and she swallowed painfully, her chest tightening.

"Hello?" she whispered.

The noise stopped. The silence felt heavy, oppressive, and she almost turned back then and there. Fuck this place. Fuck the homestead, and fuck seeking answers from things beyond this plane of existence. She could live with not knowing.

The door to the psychomanteum creaked open an inch or two, and Sasha froze. She couldn't leave if she wanted to—Alex wasn't going to let her.

Adrenaline shot her heart rate up and sweat gathered on her palms. *Go inside. Get it over with. See him one last time.*

"I don't want to," she said out loud.

Do it for the closure. A concept Alex had touted daily, but one Sasha never put much stock in, until now.

The iron smell of blood was overwhelming, spilling from the cold dark in invisible waves. She pulled the door open and stopped. What would her brother look like now? Would he look like himself? Would he be translucent? Angelic? Or would she have to see him as he looked when he died—nearly naked, a wide, open mouth of flesh splitting his throat in two, gouged meaty sockets where his blue eyes once sat?

What if he was angry?

"Sasha..."

She put her shoulders back and stepped into total darkness. The door eased shut behind her, the latch giving a muffled click as it settled in place. She wasn't going to turn and look—she knew he was here. If he could speak to her, why not close the door? She wouldn't make the mistake of disbelief again.

The thinnest glimmer of light from the bulb over the stairs trickled in from beneath the door, and Sasha caught sight of the mirror. It had always been draped in black cloth whenever Alex wasn't using it—he covered it just to be sure nothing came through. But the police had left the cloth crumpled in a corner, and now Sasha wondered what might have come creeping through its dark surface.

She stared into the glass for long seconds, squinting at shadows that gathered. But it was too dark for anything to cast a shadow, wasn't it?

Don't stand in front of it.

Alex's words—he'd warned her not to look at her own reflection in the scrying mirror.

"That's not where you want to see yourself, believe me," he'd said.

She moved to the side, at an angle where she could just make out the mirror's surface. She wondered what the point was—she could barely see its outline, and that was with the cellar light bleeding through. Alex would have been in total darkness, so what would he have seen?

She waited, her flesh growing steadily colder, her back and neck aching from tension. What was taking so long? He was here already—she'd heard him. Likely he'd never left, so why was he making her wait?

"If you don't get on with it, I'm going back upstairs," she said finally, teeth chattering. She winced against the way the soundproof walls swallowed her words. It was too easy to believe she'd never get out of here, that no one would hear her ever again.

More scraping, this time much closer, then the sound of earth shifting and wood sliding against wood.

"See meeeeeeeee," came the voice. *"Look upon the mirror and see meeeeeee."*

Sasha's breath came in small gasps, her heart thudding in her ears. Every nerve screamed at her to get out, to leave this place, but still she was drawn to the mirror. Two unsteady steps brought her in front of it, and she leaned forward, straining to see.

A shadow slowly rose behind her, the silhouette of someone's head just over her right shoulder. She couldn't breathe. Finally, it was happening for her—she would be the one to see into the beyond, to receive the messages of love and reassurance.

"Alex?" His name trembled on her lips.

Then, another smell overwhelmed the blood stink—a musty, sickening scent of unwashed flesh. Arms wrapped around her from behind and something soft tightened around her throat. A scarf. It slipped smooth against her skin, but as the figure drew it tighter, she choked, her airway closing.

"You shouldn't have come looking, Sasha." The whisper was hot in her ear, a rotten stench flooding her nostrils.

She clawed at the scarf, but its fabric slipped away from her fingers. There was something so familiar about the man who held her close—the way her head fit in the crook of his neck rang bells in her subconscious. Her head pounded and he lifted her off her feet, the pressure on her windpipe increasing.

Sasha pulled her legs in against her body, then kicked out with all her might. Her shoes hit the mirror and knocked it to the ground with a jarring crash. The man behind her cried out and let go, staggering backward. She hit the floor but didn't stop, crawling forward on hands and knees, ignoring the bite of broken glass cutting her flesh to ribbons.

An animal roar sounded behind her as she closed her hand over a long shard of mirror. Still on her knees, she spun and thrust upward, the jagged glass puncturing the man's flesh with a sickening plunge, his hot blood splashing Sasha's face. Her attacker screamed in pain, but she pushed harder until finally striking bone. Her own hand sliced open by the shard, she let it go and fell backward, breathing hard, scrambling for another weapon.

She didn't need it. A gurgling groan and the soft patter of blood was all she heard in the darkness. She scooted back to the door, shoving it open, letting in what little light there was.

Two wooden floor planks had been moved, revealing a spill of dirt and a deep hole in the earthen floor. Breathing hard, she looked back at her attacker, his eyes glazed and unfocused, the glass shard protruding from his throat, jammed all the way through to his spine. His hair was long and matted, beard thick and wild. The killer of Cardinal Hill, that was what they called him, what would end up in the headlines and on everyone's lips.

But as Sasha stared at the dead man, pieces clicked into place with numbing, dreadful certainty. Alex wasn't the murderer, and neither was he a medium. His "spirit guide" was flesh and blood, and it was no wonder he'd known what to whisper to her brother in the darkness. She couldn't understand all of it, her mind only firing in fitful bursts, but at least one thing made sense now: the message from their parents.

For though this man lying dead before her would come to be known by many names, for Sasha and Alex, he would always be Dad.

The Total Price of One Human Baby, Sales Tax Included

By Tim Meyer

"Cute baby," the woman said as she pushed her glasses up her nose. She had blonde hair and light freckles, which reminded Marlena a lot of her cousin, Elsie.

"Thanks," Marlena said, lightly *boop*ing Baby Stanley's button-sized nose. The infant cooed, the perfect sound to accentuate his cuteness.

"What a wonder." The woman clasped her hands together, prayer-like. "How old is he?"

"He's only four months."

"Four! Oh my, so perfect."

Marlena flashed a smile, trying to be cordial, but she preferred to resume shopping and avoid small-talk.

"You and your husband must be so happy," the woman said, her eyes changing. Marlena couldn't diagnose the woman's intent, her mood—not exactly—but she knew she didn't like it.

"It's just me, actually," she corrected, not knowing why she felt compelled to say so. Usually when someone assumed there was a man in this family picture, she would go along with it. Not that she was embarrassed by this—quite the opposite. She was glad Rob left when he had. And being a single mother had been rewarding—so far. Powerful. Meaningful. The best days of her life. She just didn't feel the need to announce this to strangers.

"Oh, so sorry to hear that." The woman's eyes sparkled with sympathy. "That must be tough."

Marlena shrugged. "Well, it was nice meeting you, but…I better get back to it." She held up an adorable outfit for the kid, a onesie designed like an old-school baseball uniform. Rob hated baseball with a passion, so she couldn't wait to post pics of Baby Stanley's new attire to her social media accounts.

"I have a question," the woman said, lowering her voice. She stepped closer, violating Marlena's margin of personal space. Close enough that she could smell the woman's breath—*hmm, we had a tuna salad sandwich with a splash of oil and vinegar for lunch, did we?* The woman clearly needed a lesson on boundaries and breath mints. "If you could have any amount of money in the world in exchange for your baby, what would he cost? Total price. Sales tax included."

Marlena snorted with laughter, then she looked around the store for the hidden cameras, the eccentric television host hiding behind the modeling mannequins, waiting to fire off his finger guns and say, "Gotcha!"

But there was no one. The store was pretty quiet. A few other customers wandered by, minding their own business.

Marlena was hoping someone else heard that. Her eyes fell on the woman's stare, and Marlena was disturbed when she saw the woman wasn't kidding around. If she was, she was doing a damn good job hiding it.

"I'm sorry, what?" Marlena put the clothes back on the rack, ready to split the scene at a moment's notice. She already felt she'd stayed too long, but a part of her was curious.

"You know," the woman said, smiling. "Hypothetically, of course! How much for the baby, total with tax?"

She had no idea why she wanted to answer, other than she thought the question was not hypothetical at all. "No amount of money."

"Are you sure about that? A billion dollars, you wouldn't do it?"

"I have to go. This has been a lovely conversation."

Marlena put everything from her cart on the nearest display and got out of the store as fast as she could, not looking back.

But she should have. *Looked back.*

Because the woman was following her into the parking lot.

• • •

"I'm really sorry to bother you," the woman said. "But my name is Tessa Honeycutt, and I work for…for someone who's very rich, very powerful."

Marlena wasn't finished strapping Baby Stanley into the car seat, but she turned around anyway. She resisted the urge to pop the woman in the mouth. Instead, she put up two pleading hands. "Please leave me alone. I'm begging you. Please?"

"I know it sounds weird, but he's willing to pay you—cash transaction preferably—for your human baby. He's…" Her eyes roamed toward the car seat. "He's perfect."

Marlena stepped in front of her, blocking Tessa's view. Felt wrong to let the woman stare in his direction. "Listen, I don't know what your problem is, but I think you're sick and you need some fucking help. You better scram, lady. I'm calling the cops as soon as I'm on the road."

"Oh, please don't do that. Don't." It was her turn to plead. "This is serious business. I know it sounds…golly, *messed up.* But my boss can't make children, and you can. You can just pop out another one. Right?"

Marlena snarled. Leaned in. "Why don't you go fuck yourself and then *you* can pop out another one? Hmm?"

At this, the woman bristled. "Very naughty language. As a Christian, I don't appreciate your behavior, but I understand. Listen, maybe we got off on the wrong foot. If I told you why he wants your baby, maybe that will help ease your mind. Yeah? Okay?"

"Get. The. Fuck. Out of here."

"He just wants to save the world!" Tessa shouted loud enough so anyone nearby could have heard, but there was no one nearby.

Marlena turned around, hating that she had to put herself in such a vulnerable position to finish strapping in the baby, but what choice did she have? If the woman had a weapon and was determined enough, she could easily knock her out cold, take the baby, and leave Marlena bleeding to death in the parking lot.

Marlena worked the straps, adjusted the harness, and clicked the locks into place in record time. When she turned around and faced Tessa again, she was surprised to see the woman hadn't moved an inch. Her arms were folded across her chest.

"Did you not hear me?" Marlena asked.

"He could take him, you know."

Marlena's heart fell like a hammer.

"He could snatch him up when you're asleep, or he could send a whole crew into your home, break-in, have them rape you, then take your pukey baby." Tessa's upper lip twitched with a hatred she hadn't displayed before.

Christian my ass.

Marlena felt the threat justified a punch to the woman's jaw, but she wasn't the violent type, had never hit another human being in her thirty-three years of living, and she wasn't starting now.

Unless she had no other choice.

She slammed the back door of her SUV and locked the doors.

"I'm leaving, then calling the cops." Marlena scurried around her vehicle, unlocked the driver's door, climbed behind the wheel, and struggled with the keys and the ignition. But only because she was trying to keep her eyes on the strange woman. She wasn't moving, and when Marlena realized there was no more fight in Tessa Honeycutt, that she'd said what she'd wanted to say, Marlena got the car started.

She was halfway out of the parking lot in a blink.

"Yes, her name was Tessa Honeycutt," Marlena told the officer over the phone. He appeased her by assuring her he'd look into it, poke around, knock on some doors, but when Marlena hung up, she didn't feel settled. She spent that afternoon in Baby Stanley's room, watching him nap. When he woke up, she didn't let him out of her sight. Not for a second. The only time she left him alone was later that night at bedtime. And even then, she felt guilty. Scared. Vulnerable.

She went to bed furious with Tessa Honeycutt. She'd robbed her of an afternoon, an evening, and probably a full night's sleep.

Miraculously, she did find sleep. And dreams. Of course, she dreamed of Tessa. It was dark in her bedroom, and Marlena was looking up, frozen still, and Tessa Honeycutt was on top of her, straddling her, pinning her to the mattress. Tessa leaned over her, grinning, the shape of her human mouth almost *in*-human. Moving in waves, distorted, the dreamy filter at work. The darkness of the room rippled like a heat shimmer. She could do nothing but lie and watch.

"Told you he'd take him," Tessa said, in the dream, where no one could take Baby Stanley. Where no one could touch him.

Then the room faded to black like the final frame of her favorite movies.

When she woke up, she was groggy. Like she'd spent the evening doing shots of tequila and not dreaming about Tessa Honeycutt. She stumbled to the bathroom and threw up, having enough resolve to make it to the toilet.

Then she listened to the noise. There was none. She glanced over her shoulder at the alarm clock and saw it was 10:30 a.m., which made no goddamn sense considering that would mean she was an hour-and-a-half late logging into work. She quickly checked her phone, saw six missed calls from her boss.

Fuck.

The silence of the morning was too eerie, and it was then she knew something was gravely wrong.

She rushed down the hall, barreling into Baby Stanley's room.

He was gone.

Two weeks later, the police still had no leads, no trail, and not a single clue as to where Tessa Honeycutt had taken Baby Stanley. Worse yet, Tessa Honeycutt had Casper'd right off the face of the earth. In the police's eyes, Tessa was truly a phantom. The only thing that kept Marlena out of hot water was the security footage from the clothing store. The footage from inside the store and the parking lot proved she wasn't crazy.

It was the home invasion situation that stumped the detectives. Would have been easier if Marlena or one of her neighbors had one of those video doorbells. And—get this—there had been no evidence of a break-in that night. It was like she had a key to the place.

It was like she knew which rock in the garden had been hiding the emergency key underneath it. It was like Tessa Honeycutt had done her research. Planned the whole thing.

Marlena decided she'd sink her next few paychecks into security cameras and home alarm systems and doorbells that alerted her phone every time so much as a mouse ran past, but only if she got Baby Stanley back alive, because if she didn't...well, the pain of losing him was already too much, and she didn't know if her body and mind would survive if she never saw him again.

Another week passed, and she couldn't take it anymore. She was losing her mind. Little by little, these subtractions were adding up in a big way, and she started not taking care of herself. It started with forgetting to brush her teeth Monday night, but come Friday, she was forgetting to feed herself. Wear deodorant. It became too much to get out of bed. And even though she'd told her boss she would call out every day until she felt like working again, she stopped doing that too. She ignored phone calls from friends and loved ones. Didn't answer the door. Didn't pay her bills. Didn't even care when the cable company shut off her internet service.

But a week after that, she found new life. If the police weren't going to help, weren't going to find her son, then she'd have to. It was the only way. And she knew where to start.

But first, she needed a weapon.

She needed a fucking gun.

• • •

"Not giving you a gun, Lena," Rob said over the phone. "What're...what are you doing? You haven't answered your phone in weeks. Your parents are hounding me, by the way. Asking me where you are, like I'd fucking know."

She sighed. Gritted her teeth. It wasn't going to be easy. "Get me a fucking gun, Robert. I know you can."

"I know I can too, but I won't do it, because you sound like a fucking psycho. And whatever you're planning on doing, I don't want to be involved."

"It's for..." *Lie, lie, lie,* she thought. She'd lied to Rob a lot during their relationship, all the *I love you*s she hadn't meant, plus so much more, that a lie here should have come so naturally. But it was hard. She never had to lie like this. "It's for protection, okay? The police aren't doing anything." The last part wasn't so much a fib, but the first part very much was.

Rob sighed. "Okay, fine. Fuck it. Whatever."

She waited in the parking lot of the clothing store for three whole days. It was her only clue, her only lead, and even though she doubted the woman would return to the scene of the crime, she had no other option but to see how this played out. She spent the days combing blogs and social media sites, searching for stories about other people who'd had their children abducted. The number of similar stories surprised her. At least three separate articles mentioned the victims' parents being offered a cash exchange before the abduction. Two of them happened in other states, but one of them...

One of them also happened in Jersey, forty-five minutes away. The story was exactly the same, down to the language the abductor used. *"How much for the baby, total with tax?"* The name of the woman was different. Instead of Tessa Honeycutt, it was Adeline Jacobs. But...

It was too weird, too exact to be a coincidence.

As she read, something caught her eye. She glanced up from her research and...

It was her.

Tessa Honeycutt.

She had dyed her hair raven black, but the freckles and glasses remained. But it was her, no question. She was harassing another woman, leaning in and getting close, and Marlena could smell the tuna sandwich from here, inside her car. The woman was holding a baby away from Tessa, looking frightened, too scared to do anything but shield her newborn.

Marlena got out of the car, gun in hand. She lowered the safety like Rob had taught her. Then she marched over there.

The mother was the first one to turn and face her, grimacing with terror. "Can you help me, this woman is asking—" Then she noticed the gun and shouted, "Oh *shiiiiiiit!*"

Marlena pointed the gun at Tessa, who wasn't moving. "Run," she said to the mother. "Get in the car and get out of here. Tell no one."

The mother needed no second command. She never bothered with the car seat and drove off with the baby on her lap.

Marlena kept the gun trained on Tessa and said, "Get in my car. The driver's seat."

Tessa eyed the near-empty lot, looking like she might bolt.

"I'll kill you, I swear," Marlena said. "Don't make me."

"You won't." Tessa shook her head. "Because then you'll never see your son again."

"Is he alive?" The emerging tears burned like a bad rash.

Tessa nodded.

"Take me to him."

Tessa didn't look like she was willing to listen, so Marlena stomped over and smashed the gun against Tessa's nose, hoping to inspire the woman to move a little faster.

"If I have to ask again," Marlena said, "I put a bullet through your eye."

• • •

The woman drove Marlena's car, and Marlena rode in the backseat, pressing the barrel of the gun against the headrest. They had been on the road for about thirty minutes. Marlena didn't watch the road, didn't dare take her eyes off the woman and *her* movements. There were two outcomes Marlena feared in all of this: 1) Tessa would drive head-on into oncoming traffic; or 2) she would drive her somewhere far away from Baby Stanley and attempt to flee. She feared the former more, mostly because she believed the bitch was crazy enough to do it. But also, that would in all likelihood signal the end of her renegade rescue mission.

"Don't try anything funny," Marlena warned, for like the fifth time. "I swear to God I'll kill you. I swear to *God*."

This last bit of information seemed to irk the woman. In the rearview, Marlena watched Tessa's upper lip writhe. "What do you know about God?"

It was a confusing question, and one she couldn't easily answer.

"What?"

Slightly, the woman's head turned, but not far enough to unstick her eyes from the road. "What do you know about God? Do you believe in Him?"

An agnostic all her life, Marlena couldn't answer. Didn't want to. "Keep driving. Take me to my son. And you'll live through this. Then we can go our separate ways, and I won't turn you into the fucking police. Okay?"

"He came to me," she whispered. "He came to me and said He needed my help."

"That's great. Really. Keep fucking driving."

Her heart was kicking up something fierce. As the woman pulled into a church parking lot, Marlena ran through all the lessons Rob had taught her—how to aim, how to shoot, how to "defend" herself.

• • •

The woman parked around back, the closest spot to the entrance. Marlena glanced around the area. The lot was empty save for one car. Behind her, a line of trees stood watch over a stockade fence, and behind them, was a residential area—the backs of several houses could be seen through the branches and greenery the trees provided.

"What is this, why are we here?" Marlena asked, not understanding.

Tessa craned her neck. "You wanted to see your child again. Your child is with God now."

"You said he's alive." Marlena jammed the gun into her cheek. The woman recoiled, covering her head, clearly expecting the shot that would paint the windshield with her brains. "You said he was ALIVE!"

"He is!" The woman continued to cower. "He is! I swear it!"

Rattled, Marlena thought about ending her right then and there. She'd be doing the world a favor, and come to think of it, she'd be saving a lot of taxpayer money, not to mention, saving police officers, detectives, lawyers, and judges loads of time and energy.

She almost did it.

"Get out," she said to the woman. "Take me to him. And if he's hurt, if there's one hair on his body missing, so help me GOD, I'll kill you and stuff you in the confessional booth."

The woman uncovered her head, went for the door slowly. Then she got out.

Then she got running.

"HELP ME!" she screamed, running for the trees, the fence. "HELP ME, SOMEONE!"

She got halfway across the lot when Marlena lined up the shot. She sunk a bullet into the woman's backside on the first attempt, which she thought was pretty good. Then again, after Rob's lesson, she had been deadly accurate against his empty Coors cans. Hitting the meaty woman in the hip came easy-peasy. Surprisingly, there was no spray of blood like in the movies. A red mark like a ketchup stain appeared where the bullet got lost inside her.

But the woman kept running, the shot barely slowing her down.

Two more shots—one miss, one hit. The miss got lost somewhere in the trees and probably struck the house behind the fence. The hit ripped through the woman's back. That one took her to the ground. Marlena jogged up to her unmoving body and peered down. A considerable spill of red was pooling beneath her. She looked…dead.

"Fuck," she muttered, glancing around. There was no one traveling along the side streets, but certainly someone in the neighborhood heard the shots.

She turned and looked at the church. Her mother's intuition urged her to head inside.

The church was quiet. She expected to see someone inside, running toward the gunshots (or away from them), but she saw no one. In the small foyer, she had two choices: head into the nave, or take the stairs into the basement. She heard a faint noise coming from below, an incessant whisper. After a quick peek inside the church itself, she decided the basement was her best option.

She's hiding him down there. I know it!

But she didn't know it, not really. She knew nothing, and for all she *did* know, this was a dead end, or worse, a trap.

She descended into the darkness. Once down there, the main hallway was lit by a few wall sconces. The old stucco walls were peeling in spots and everything smelled moldy and potentially hazardous, but she ignored her own health. Laser-focused, she only wanted one thing.

Baby Stanley.

She rushed down the hall, following the sound of the white fuzz that reminded her of an old television, losing reception. Sprinting, she reached the door, peeked inside.

A strange miasma, bitter and biting, filled her nostrils. She covered her nose and pressed on into the room, where a projector was displaying images on a screen that took up the entire far wall. Flashing by rapidly, the footage showed stills of Jesus and his disciples, the latter bowing before their messiah. Then Jesus was on the cross, suffering, bleeding from His crown of thorns. Then the Holy Lance poked His belly. A photo of a fiery lake in the pit of Hell, demons rising from the magma. Pictures of the Black Death. The Holocaust. The worst of humanity on display. Between the awful imagery, hypnotic images of spinning spirals—sometimes black and white, sometimes colored in groovy neon—flashed up on the screen, giving Marlena an instant headache. Then the parade of paintings and real-life photographs started over. Jesus again. Hypnotic spirals. It was on a loop. The static hissed consistently throughout.

Marlena noticed several highchairs facing the screen, could see the tops of several fuzzy heads. Four of the dozen seats were occupied.

"My..." She almost whispered the word *God*, but even in this holy place, no evidence of God existed.

She moved around, found the four infants in the highchairs alive and doing reasonably well. Two of them were eating yogurt melts. One of them was staring at the screen, absorbed by the images.

Baby Stanley cooed when he saw his momma. Marlena cried as she kissed the top of his perfect head. She checked him for injuries and found none. Not a bruise, not a scratch. As she unstrapped him from the highchair, her foot slipped in something wet. Looking down, she saw a man on the floor, spread out in a pool of black blood. Above his black and white collar, his throat had been opened, and the murder weapon—a serrated shard of glass—lay near his head.

"Father Rodrigo did not agree with my methods," Tessa said from the doorway. She was covered in her own blood now, and her complexion was milky white. Her colorless lips trembled. "Jesus spoke to me," she said, "and He needed an army of soldiers to stop..." She retched. Nothing came out, but she wiped her lips anyway. “To stop the apocalypse, to save the world. I had to show them…show them all. Start them young. He wanted me to pay for them. He promised me riches, to afford his army.” A nearby table was covered in spent scratch-off tickets, thousands-of-dollars-worth.

Marlena lifted Baby Stanley, then grabbed the infant closest to her. She bundled them into her arms and eased her way toward the door, toward Tessa Honeycutt. She did this while aiming the gun, ready to pull the trigger if the woman tried anything.

“Kill me,” Tessa begged. “No one will understand this, so please, just kill me.”

Marlena thought about it. Thought the world could use one less monster. Instead, she slid by, exited into the hallway, and didn’t look back. Not even when Tessa howled, begging for God to forgive her failures.

Between The Crosses, Row On Row

By Venezia Castro

After the death of her husband, Inés' mom packed a single bag, told each of her four children to put on all the clothes they owned, and took them to live with her brother in Las Ventanas. It was a week-long journey, most of it on horseback. During the day, the sun was charring. The nights were wet and cold. There were no roads, just narrow mountain trails of stifling fog and weeds that threatened to catch on the animals' hooves. They had to move slowly. Many skulls had been shattered against the rocky walls of those mountain ridges. Yet Inés remembers the trip almost fondly, with a sense of adventure. Amidst the murky greenery, she felt for the last time in her life like she could live within a story.

At the time, her mom was pregnant with her fifth child, although no one knew yet and very few would ever know. The thing in her womb that would've become a baby did not survive the journey. She bled into the thick wool blankets they used instead of saddles. She sobbed the pain away at night, when the children were asleep next to the horses for warmth. She walked further into the forest alone, so they wouldn't hear her, and fell to the ground and dug her fingers into the dirt as she convulsed in tears. The sounds she made, like those of a wounded animal, far from moaning and close to growls, kept away the man she hired to take them across the mountains. She was lucky.

Inés's family was, in a way, escaping. The death of her father had not been an accident, or as many said, a coincidence. He sold portable radios from town to town. It was not unusual for him to be gone for days, so when Inés first heard she would never see her dad again, they were already settled in Las Ventanas. She was told a stranger shot her daddy in an attempt to steal the radios. Inés did not care to hear the story, so she stopped listening. She should have held onto the doorway that morning when she asked to not to leave for work that day, should have blocked his exit. She often tried to stop him, but every time, he just tickled her, kissed her head, and left anyway. She did not need to know more. The truth came to her in fragments over the years.

Inés is ten years old. She is the oldest. The big sister. The second mother. She can change diapers. She can cook eggs. Except there are no eggs here. Her uncle's house is not really a house, it is a large room with a curtain in one corner, a cot behind it where he sleeps, and floors of pressed dirt where for several days the children nested in blankets still smelling of horse sweat. There is nothing to eat. The babies cry all day.

It makes Inés angry to think about it. They don't even understand. They don't understand that Dad is gone, that Mom is dying, that they will never again live in their big house with the crops of corn and their two cows and the chickens. They only cry because they're hungry. Well, she's hungry too, and she's not crying.

She looks at the mist clearing off the poppy fields. White and purple flowers, thousands of them, peek through the veil of haze as far as she can see. The breeze blows through them and helps them shake the condensation off of their petals.

Next to Inés, Isaac is playing with the small knife he's been given. He cuts off sticks from the bushes nearby and sharpens them to picks, which he uses to draw figures in the dirt. He is testing the blade; that is the whole game. He is restless. Inés has to gesture at her brother to stay close and keep quiet. They are waiting for the sign that lets them know it is safe to go back to work.

She thinks she hears footsteps and freezes for a minute, crouching under the cover of a pomegranate tree and holding on to her own knife, but the soldiers either go away or were never there. She is yet to see any of them, but uncle Vicente warned her they would be around. There are many sounds this deep into the furrows of the mountains that could pass for the march of armed men, and it is part of Inés' job to listen.

Vicente calls them guachos. In a recurrent nightmare, Inés dreams that when they finally come, they make no noise. They slip with the mist through the crack under the door while she is sleeping and draw slits in her stomach like it is the head of a poppy. In these dreams, no blood comes out, just the sticky milk that turns thick and brown overnight; she lays there until morning, waiting for the men to harvest the opium gum off of her belly. Her mother spanks her when she wets the bedroll, so she must get up before sunrise to rinse the *petate* of woven palm leaves before anyone notices the smell. Dry pee and the discharge of the flowers have a similar scent.

Now what she hears is unequivocal. A long whistle, soft like a sigh. The echo rolls down the hillside. It is impossible to tell where it comes from, and in a couple of seconds it is gone like it never happened. Isaac looks at her, and she nods. It is Memo's sign the mist has cleared enough and there are no guachos in sight. Isaac practically runs to the closest poppy plant and gets to work.

Deshijar. That is the word they use. To unchild; more specifically, to undaughter. They cut the smaller buds, the thinner limbs of each plant, leaving only one tall stalk crowned by a flower. The job itself is not difficult. Even the stems of the poppies are soft, and Inés likes to run her fingers through the downy leaves. But she cannot linger, she must move on to the next plant, and then to the one after.

At least for now, the weather is mild. It does not matter if it rains or if the cold gets so bad the skin on their fingers cracks open. They are only allowed to stop when the threat of soldiers grows too close.

Some days, their task is to thin out the plants. Sometimes they are taken to another side of the field, or to a different one entirely, and they have to cover the roots in the guano Uncle Vicente gathers from the caves nearby; other times they collect the rattling buds remaining from the harvest, cut them open and fill a few sacks with the tiny seeds they find inside. Those are good days. When they finish their work after ten or twelve hours, Inés and Isaac receive two handfuls of seeds each, to eat on the way home. Those nights feel less cold, and the hunger ache feels less sharp. The anticipation makes Inés almost eager to go back to work.

Ahead of her, Isaac is passionately hacking weeds away. She pretends she doesn't see him pause to wipe his face with the back of the hand that holds the knife. He sometimes cries when they are out in the fields, but it is a quiet emotion; he keeps working, and they never talk about it. She stays behind to give him space and to stop the spread of the contagious sadness.

There are other kids—some older and some, like Memo, as young as Isaac—but they rarely see them, and even when they see each other, they do not speak. Memo´s job is to hide somewhere up the mountain where he can see the entire field. He has good eyes and he can whistle. He is too small for anything else.

"Niña," someone says. "Do you know what you're doing?"

Inés looks up from her work to see two men sitting on the roots of a tree only a couple of meters away from her. They face her like they have been watching her, partly concealed by the overgrowth around the edges of the field.

They are not wearing a uniform, but their heads are shaved and they are carrying guns on their shoulders. The ends of the weapons touch the ground. Then one of them stands. He is short and stocky, dark-skinned like her daddy, and with a belly like a pregnant woman. The man drags his words like uncle Vicente, in a sierra accent. Singsongy.

"Answer me."

She cannot speak. She has forgotten how to speak. She opens her mouth to say something for the first time in months, but she has lost all her words.

He smiles. "I think you do."She knows. She knows. Her mother explained the guachos want the sap for themselves, but they don't work for it, they just steal it. They don't care for the earth unless it smears on their boots. They would kill an innocent man for selling it without giving them some of the profit, her mother said. Inés and her family have to protect the fields, to take care of the fields. They live only as long as they harvest the blood of the poppy.

"You shouldn't be here, a muchachita like you. So pretty. *Tan bien formadita, pues.* You're nice to look at, niña. I say you know that too."

Inés takes a quick glance in the direction where she last saw Isaac and finds nothing but the rows and rows of flowers and the quiet tendrils of mist coming back. Looking away is a mistake. The man uses the opportunity to move a little closer. When he speaks next, his voice is gentle.

"Do you like it here, niña?" he asks. "I can take you away. I'll make you a wedding. Do you like babies? I can give you *chamacos*, and you don't have to work."

Inés looks down and shakes her head. No. No, thank you. Please. She stares at her hands, brown and slimy with sweat and mud. He stands in front of her with his legs spread apart like he wants to take up the entire world. He wears huaraches, not boots, and his blackened toes peek through the grass like crickets. He strokes the gun on his side, up and down.

"Are you stupid?" He asks like a father would ask his daughter if she is hungry, his son if he is sleepy. "*Niña, te van a chingar si te agarran.* They'll screw you if they catch you. You want that? Let the men do the work. What are you doing here, *pues?* If not the soldiers, someone else is going to grab you."

She shakes her head again.

The second man mumbles something she cannot hear, and both men laugh. It sounds deafening and alien. In the fields one must be quiet, but these men do not fear being loud.

"I think you want to be stolen, *verdad*?" says the one closer to her. "I can make you my little wife but I don't want you to scream. I know you girls like to scream when you find a man that likes you. Like you don't want them to take you away. *Pinches chamaquitas,* you wouldn't be out here if you weren't looking for a husband."

He sounds almost weary by the burden of having to do what he is about to do. The man behind him gets up and takes the gun off of his shoulder. He walks around Inés to block the path down the rows of flowers, holding the weapon with both hands.

Another long whistle billows down the hillside. This time it travels with urgency, there is nothing soft about it, as if it knows it might be too late.

Isaac hears it from far away but pays no attention to it.

It means nothing under the sound of his heaving. With one eye, he tries to find his way through the undergrowth, careful not to trip again. The other eye is shut tight and covered in blood.

When he heard a strange voice behind him as he worked the poppy plant, he cowered. When he saw a strange man step out of the shrubbery and move towards his sister, he ran. At first, he did not know where he was going, he just bolted downhill. It took him a minute to realize he was running to his mother and that he would never reach her on time. The fields are at least an hour away from town.

Before he could change directions, his feet got tangled in the bejuco roots and he fell face first into the shrubs. Something pointy slid over his brow bone and caught on his upper eyelid. He does not know what it was, and for a few seconds after, he did not even feel pain. He got up and kept running. Now the blood dripping down his cheek is thickening, and the entire left side of his face is throbbing. He does not know where he is anymore.

If they had chosen to fire, she would be dead. Hunted like a hare while hopelessly scurrying away. But they missed their chance, or they did not consider her worth the bullets. A dead girl is of no use to them anyway.

She was able to escape because Memo's whistle distracted the men for long enough, but now she has nowhere to go. The fog crawled back into the forest. It swings from the branches and glows green through the rogue rays of sunlight. Everywhere around her looks the same. She cannot be far from the fields, but even if she knew the right way, going back is not an option.

She is afraid to move in either direction. She curls up like a fist on the ground. The side of her face, her hair, her clothes are all covered in mud. If she still believed in stories, she would imagine herself as a plant. Untouched and inconspicuous. She would know no hunger. She would know no loss.

She does not imagine anything. She just lies in the forest and waits for the dark.

Inés and Isaac's mom looks like the Jesus on the crucifix over her head: her cheeks are sunken and her chin is always resting on her chest. Her baby boy is nursing. His eyes are open, wild and angry at the short supply. She apologizes in a murmur, that is all she can do. The baby does not care.

Her other daughter is somewhere around the house, looking for mushrooms or berries or wild onions. Whatever she finds, they will eat raw, and they will be thankful for it, at least until the money of the poppy harvest comes in and they can afford to buy tortillas and, if they are lucky, some meat for the week.

The afternoon is ending, and she is beginning to drift into sleep when she hears Vicente's voice outside.

"Get in the house. *Que te metas, chingao.*"

The little girl, who looks just like Inés and much like her father, comes inside running before her uncle. Still holding the stem of a radish, she finds shelter under her mother's arm.

"Get up, we have to leave," says Vicente as he swings open his privacy curtain and starts packing the few things he owns into plastic bags.

"Where are my children?"

"They're gone. They ran away or they were caught. Now hurry the fuck up. I'm not waiting for you."

The woman clutches her baby like she is trying to force him into her chest.

"No."

"Yes. One of the kids saw the guachos in the field. If the soldiers found it, they're going to burn the entire crop. Be glad your children aren't there."

"Where are they?"

"I told you I don´t know. They´ll be fine, but I'm not going to risk them talking and having the soldiers find me here. Now you get up or I´ll make you get up. I don't know why you want so many children anyway, when you can't even feed them."

That is the last thing she hears him say before she storms out of the house with the boy's mouth still pressed to her skin and the girl's hand held tight inside her own. She does not get far before she starts to scream her children's names: all four plus the one she lost on the trail up the mountain. She yells her husband's name. After a while, she yells her own.

She stops only when she hears the boots approaching. Stomping without order all around her, the men in uniform point their guns at her. Another daughter of the poppy, they think. Another one not to be missed.

I Swear I Didn't Kill the Others

By Kelsea Yu

When the first box arrives, you don't think much of it. Nondescript black, sealed with a glossy logo sticker. *Dark Deeds: Midnight Reads for Horror Fans.* You set it aside to deal with later. After all, surgeons are busy people. Your practice has been thriving. You don't have time to look up what to read—that's why you're trying a book subscription.

It's not until several nights later, after a full day of surgery, that you remember the box. It's 11 p.m., and you know if you close your eyes now, your mind will fill with the frantic beep of a heart rate monitor, the convulsing of the man on the table, his blood spilling out and staining the bedsheets red, red, red…

Better to soothe your mind with invented horrors. Since residency, it has become the only genre you consume; it takes your mind off the real-life horrors you witness in the operating room and the other thing that haunts you. That time you—

No. Best not to think about that.

You flick open a box cutter and slice through the sticker; a motion familiar after two decades of cutting into skin. This blade is duller and less precise than your trusty scalpel, but it does the job.

The first thing you see is the printed note, obscuring whatever is packed in the nest of shredded paper beneath.

Dear Horror Reader,

Welcome to the Dark Deeds family! Each month, we send a handpicked horror book and a wrapped item labeled with a page number. When you reach that page in the book, you'll be prompted to open your gift.

You'll also find a scratch-off ticket in every box. Check yours for the chance to win your next month of Dark Deeds FREE! Concerns? Contact us at darkdeedsbox@gmail.com.

This month, our theme is FRIENDSHIP. If that doesn't sound like a horror theme to you, it will once you've read the book.

Enjoy the nightmares,
Team Dark Deeds

You toss the note aside and dig in. The cover is black with a double-exposed image in the center. Two different faces fight to occupy the same space: one staring straight ahead with a wicked grin, the other looking up and screaming. You flip to the back to read the blurbs.

"Full of dark humor and shudder-inducing imagery, *If You Say Kill* will make you consider how far you'd be willing to go for your best friend...and just how far they'd go for you."

Your thoughts turn to your former best friend. Nadine would have loved this box. The first week of college, she invited you to her dorm to watch *Saw*, her favorite movie. You were a shy, sheltered boy who had never seen anything scarier than *Hocus Pocus*, but you were lonely enough to say yes. As your friendship grew, so did your love for horror movies.

She hasn't spoken to you in a year. You miss her.

You bring *If You Say Kill* to your room, turn on your lamp, and begin reading. It's exactly your style—fast paced, engaging, and full of morbid humor—but the friendship in the book reminds you so much of Nadine that it hurts. After reading a few chapters, you go to bed.

It takes you two weeks—you work long, unpredictable hours, and sometimes you're too tired to read—but at last, you reach the page paired with the surprise gift. Out of pettiness, you finish the chapter before fetching it. You're used to being the one in charge; no note is going to tell you what to do.

You tear through the black wrapping paper, revealing a book bound in tanned leather. Inside, each page is blank, made of thick, hand cut paper. There's no brand name anywhere. It looks like one of those handmade $200 journals people sell on Etsy.

In *If You Say Kill*, what begins as a dare from one friend to the other escalates until they kill one of their teachers and skin him. From his skin, they craft covers for a matching set of journals.

It was clever of Dark Deeds to include an item that feels like it was pulled straight out of the story. You run your fingers along the leather surface, wondering what animal it was made from. How human skin would feel.

You're excited when the second box arrives. Despite your initial hesitance about the first book, the ending was decent. And while you don't use journals, you'll save it for your mom's birthday. You won't tell her it was free—that would make it feel less special. A little white lie never hurt anyone.

News plays in the background, distracting you. Some solemn-faced reporter goes on about a budding serial killer who's claimed two victims. They were found laid out on picnic tables at different parks, covered by sheets. Both were stabbed with thin, sharp blades, and various body parts are missing. For this quirk, the killer has been dubbed The Harvester.

You're not worried; men like you are rarely the target of these kinds of attacks. Still, you turn off the television and return your attention to the box.

It's hard to believe you won another month of Dark Deeds, especially since the first box was a free trial. But you've always been lucky, and secretly, you feel you deserve every good thing that happens to you. You cut through the sticker.

Dear Horror Reader,

We're pleased you decided to stick with us and promise you won't regret it! This month, we picked a theme everyone can relate to: ENVY. Whether it's at work, in your friend group, or in your love life, surely, you've experienced that soul-crushing, frustrating-as-all-hell emotion. It could drive anyone to the darkest of deeds.

As always, we're at darkdeedsbox@gmail.com if you have any concerns.

Enjoy the nightmares,
Team Dark Deeds

Intrigued, you check out the book. Below the title, *To Dine with You Every Night*, is a bird's eye view of a place setting. The white plate in the center holds a human heart and the matching white mug is full of blood. One corner of the book features a silver award medallion.

Looks interesting enough. You put it on your nightstand.

The next night, after getting paged six times, you need a few minutes to wind down before trying to fall asleep yet again. You pour yourself a glass of sparkling water and start reading.

Several chapters in, you're not sure you'll enjoy this book as much as the previous one. The writing is crude, and the main character feels like a caricature. He's in love with his neighbor, a woman who clearly has no romantic interest in him. As she begins dating someone else—a man who seems a little too perfect to be real—the main character starts stalking her and growing more obsessive.

You feel your irritation grow with each scene. You hate when books are reductive. You know exactly what it's like to be that guy, and it doesn't always happen this way. Sometimes, the girl really does end up with the wrong guy.

This damned subscription box keeps making you think of Nadine. You picture her in a sleek black dress and red lipstick, the way she looked the last time you spoke. That night, a year ago, when you went to her house for drinks, hopeful that it was the start of something. Instead, your friendship ended. You still don't know why. All you know is the next day, you woke with a pounding headache and no memory beyond those first few cocktails.

Despite your annoyance, you continue reading throughout the next few weeks. As much as you hate to admit it, the story is addictive. You watch the main character's obsession turn full blown, ramping up until he attempts to kill his neighbor's boyfriend.

As you read the climax, a chill runs through you. You try to stay focused on the page, but your mind flips back to Nadine, crying. Asking you to recommend a colleague you trust. Her husband, Nathan—even his stupid name matched hers—had been diagnosed with pancreatic cancer. As a surgical oncologist, you were perfectly positioned to help find him the best doctor.

So, you did. You offered to treat Nathan yourself.

You force yourself to focus on *To Dine with You Every Night*, pushing away thoughts of the past as you finish the book. In trying to kill the boyfriend, the pathetic main character accidentally kills his love interest instead. In a wildly implausible turn of events, he manages to sneak into the morgue and steal one of her bones, which he then cleans, grinds up, and mixes into clay. He turns the clay into a dinnerware set so he can have dinner with her every night for the rest of his life.

You'll admit it is fun when the meaning behind a title only becomes clear at the end of the story, but it's not enough to save the rest of the book. You're still annoyed by the main character, and the ending leaves you unsettled in a bad way.

Prompted by the book's last page, you open your gift to reveal a huge, white mug signed "Ash Ceramics" at the bottom. While it matches the mug on the book cover, there's nothing special about it other than its size. After long nights on call, you need lots of coffee to stay alert enough to operate, so it'll come in handy, but you're disappointed by its plainness. If this box hadn't been free, you'd be really pissed.

While it's on your mind, you email darkdeedsbox@gmail.com to cancel your subscription, adding a strongly worded suggestion to source better items.

An hour later, you receive a reply. They're apologetic. They've canceled your subscription; you won't be charged for any boxes. They'll take your thoughtful feedback into consideration. And if you ever decide to resubscribe, you can use a special discount code to get twenty percent off your next box.

You roll your eyes. You're not going to resubscribe. Ever. You stick the latest book into your bin of items to donate and think no more of Dark Deeds.

When the third box arrives, you're outraged. You canceled. You *know* you did. You pull up your last email exchange to confirm, and it's all there. Evidence. Annoyed, you log into your credit card account and scroll through the transactions, searching for the Dark Deeds charge to dispute.

There's no charge.

Both confused and angry now, you send Dark Deeds another email. The response is immediate. It must be a warehouse mistake. They'll make sure their system is updated. But, since it was their error, you're welcome to keep the box.

With mixed feelings, you decide to see what their system error has brought you.

Dear Horror Reader,

We hope you enjoyed last month's selection! This month's theme is one of our favorites: MURDER. The book is about someone seemingly normal who ends up doing worse and worse things. Anyone can be driven to commit murder, don't you think? In fact, we bet you've committed murder. You can lie to us (and everyone else!), but you can't lie to yourself.

As always, we're at darkdeedsbox@gmail.com if you need us.

Enjoy the nightmares,
Team Dark Deeds

You reread the note. What the fuck? If this is their idea of a joke, it doesn't land. Who would find this funny?

It occurs to you that you don't know anything about the team behind Dark Deeds. You only gave the box a try because you were getting ads for it, increasing in frequency until you finally grew curious enough to click. (Funny, how easy it is to narrow down your advertising pool when you know your target audience well. Really well.) And then they offered the free trial box, and you won the next one free…

You hop in the shower to clear your head. By the time you're out again, you're back to being your regular, non-paranoid self. The note isn't personal. It's a horror subscription. Of course they'd try to spook their fans. You pop a frozen dinner in the microwave and dig the book out of the box.

The cover of *Cadmium Crimson* resembles a canvas splattered with red paint. Below the title, a disembodied hand holds a paintbrush with a knife's handle, blood dripping from its bristles. According to the back cover, it's about an artist who finds herself in a rut. Nothing feels fresh, and her work isn't selling. Then she cuts herself, accidentally bleeding onto the canvas. The piece becomes an instant hit, and suddenly, galleries everywhere want her inventive new paintings. She begins drawing her own blood to keep up with the demand. Soon, her body can't produce enough blood, so she looks for supplies elsewhere…

Finally! A book with a premise that carries no personal baggage for you. You take your meal out of the microwave and sit down to read while you eat. It's so good that you end up reading until you're ready for bed.

Later that week, you're in line for lunch at the hospital cafeteria when you hear two orderlies talking about The Harvester. One of them mentions that she doesn't leave her house after dark anymore, lest she end up "dead on a picnic table like those three other women."

Someone else in line chimes in. "The *Times* released info about the third victim yesterday. Lorilee Sorenson, mother of two young kids. Cancer survivor."

Clucks of sympathy sound around you, but you stop paying attention. Why does that name sound familiar?

Lorilee Sorenson. Cancer.

Could she have been one of your patients?

The Harvester doesn't seem like a distant figure anymore.

As the cashier rings up your meal, you remind yourself that all three targets have been women. He—it's a safe assumption since serial killers are usually men—seems to have a penchant for killing women. He's not going to come after you.

Still, you look up articles over lunch. The internet is abuzz with speculation on how he's choosing his victims. The first two had kids in the same school district. The second and third were cancer survivors.

You picture The Harvester at work. Stabbing women with a sharp blade, then slicing them open and removing something, possibly while they're still alive. It's not unlike the surgeries you perform, ridding patients of unwanted parts. Organs riddled with cancerous growths. Tumors heavier than a newborn baby. You're always taking things out of people. But you operate to help others, not hurt them.

Except for that one time.

That night, you can't sleep. Images of murdered women keep running through your mind. *Cadmium Crimson* promises to be a good distraction, so you continue reading. This time, you're prompted to open the gift around the halfway mark, when the artist, compelled by guilt, uses blood to paint her first victim, "a young girl lying on her back in a field of wildflowers, viscera spilling out from a hole in her chest."

You rip open the black paper to discover an unstretched canvas, furled up like a scroll. You unroll it. As you do, your fingertips brush the canvas, feeling the raised texture of paint on its surface. Based on the other gifts, you expect a painting like the one described in the book. You let the rest of the piece drop open.

Instead, it's a man lying on an operating table, skin splayed open, organs exposed. Hovering over him is a surgeon in scrubs, looking furtive as his gloved hand touches the patient's IV pole. The three other people in the painting are busy, attention focused elsewhere. The entire tableau is rendered in monochrome, every detail a shade of reddish brown—the color of old bricks.

Or dried blood.

You stare. The thing you've been suppressing for a year and a half forces its way to the forefront of your mind.

Your best friend's husband lies unconscious on your operating table. As you open him up with your scalpel, you remind yourself that Nadine loves him. That you became a surgeon to save lives. Soon enough, you slip into the zone, and he becomes just another patient. You'll do your best for him the way you do for everyone you operate on.

You mean to. You really do.

But the Whipple procedure is long and complicated. You have too much time to think. You start to wonder—to hope, even. Maybe you'll open him up and the cancer will be too widespread. Maybe it'll be impossible to get a negative margin, and you'll have no choice but to close him back up and give them the bad news.

But it doesn't happen that way. It's operable. You'll be able to save him.

You took an oath, so you do. But before you close him back up, you think of Nadine. You imagine giving her the good news—you've saved her husband!—only to have Nathan sicken, in subsequent weeks, from an infection he could've gotten anywhere in the hospital.

Maybe after Nathan dies, she'll turn to you—her best friend, who did everything he possibly could for her and Nathan—for comfort.

When the anesthesiologist, circulating nurse, and scrub tech are all busy looking elsewhere, you reach out and touch Nathan's IV pole, breaking sterile technique. Your heart hammers as you look around to confirm that no one saw you. Then you continue operating, wearing your contaminated gloves. Introducing bacteria into Nathan's exposed body.

It was a momentary lapse in judgment. You regret what you did, but it's too late now. No one should lose their entire career over one split-second decision. Your chest tightens, breaths growing shallow as you remember those guilt-ridden months after Nathan's death.

You thought no one knew what you'd done. But someone does, and there's only one person you know who would go through all this trouble to toy with you. You understand, now, what Dark Deeds is.

A threat.

You drop the scroll, pick up your keys, and head to your car.

It's near midnight when you arrive on my doorstep.

Up until now, every scene has been composed in my mind, perfected, played on repeat. My imagination does not match reality precisely, but it's close enough. I know you better than anyone does—and time spent peering at you through a telescope or following you in disguise filled in the rest.

I let you in, and we stand in my living room, facing off.

You speak first. "Why the elaborate scheme, Nadine? Inventing an entire subscription box? You always were a drama queen."

"Better than what you are." I clench my fist. "When you operated on Nathan, you infected him." I fight to keep my rage tamped down—I've struggled to keep it under control this past year. Ever since that night you came over for drinks. You'd been acting strange, and I had a suspicion. Drunk and drugged, you confessed.

"I swear it was an accident." You sound so sincere when you lie. "By the time I realized his infection might have originated in the OR, it was too late. You were there with me through college, med school, residency. You know how hard I've worked, how many lives I've saved. Why should my future patients suffer over one mistake?"

"But there have been other mistakes too."

You look confused.

I press on. "My husband isn't the only one you've killed. You covered it well, but I pieced it together and contacted others. Patients whose operations you botched, then lied when their recovery was slower than it should be. Or, in the case of the unluckiest ones, family members of patients who died because of your *mistakes*. I've gathered all the evidence I need."

"I never killed anyone but Nathan."

At your admission, I smirk.

Your eyes narrow, tone changing as you drop the contrite, nice guy act. "You've obviously grown unhinged this past year. No one's going to believe you."

I flick my eyes over to a corner of the room and back again, as if by accident. Your gaze follows, landing on the camera's red light—recording.

In an instant, you cross the room and tear the camera from its spot on a shelf, throwing it against the wall. I flinch.

"What the fuck, Nadine?" You notice the other items on the shelf. A Ziploc bag containing a stained surgical sponge. Notes in your handwriting, printed from patient records. A rusty scalpel. You pick it up. In the yellow glow of the overhead light, its blade glints a sickly hue. You step toward me.

"I'm going to expose you for the instruments you left in patients. The surgeries you botched," I say.

"But I didn't do those things." You're closer now. I don't shrink away.

"It won't matter. Everyone will believe you did. I found former patients of yours who suffered difficult recoveries. A woman whose sister died on your operating table. I convinced them there's a pattern. That you've been covering up your mistakes."

You're an armlength away. The veins on your neck pulse as your anger builds.

I talk faster. "I'm going to destroy you for murdering my husband. No one would believe just me, but they'll believe all of us, together. We'll file a malpractice suit. We'll testify, and you'll lose your reputation, your practice, your license. Everything. You'll—"

Your hand wraps around my neck, squeezing, cutting off my air. Your face is a mask of rage as you lose the tight control you usually keep. "Why, Nadine? Why are you making me do this?" You release your hold for a minute, and I gasp.

"You deserve it. You're a murderer and—"

I cry out as you plunge the blade into my throat, precise as a surgeon. It's a sound I've grown familiar with these past few months. Each time I killed one of your former patients.

"It didn't have to be this way," you say as my blood spills onto your hands.

I collapse forward. As I lay dying in your arms, I smile up at you. "Human leather, bone ceramic, blood painting."

"What?" You lean closer, certain you must have misheard.

"Doctors make good harvesters." My words come out garbled.

"You're in shock. You're speaking nonsense." You sound panicked.

"I swear I didn't kill the others," I whisper, mimicking your voice. Savoring the look of confusion on your face as you try to understand. You'll see soon enough. They're your words to keep.

I close my eyes, letting myself imagine one last time. When the police arrive, summoned by my pre-recorded, frantic call, they'll find the evidence I gathered in my amateur hunt for The Harvester. How I suspected my former best friend. The victim profiles I've built; all former patients of yours—or their loved ones.

You never hurt any of them, of course. You've always been a genuinely good surgeon. Except for the one time.

Good thing none of them can contradict my story. Not since The Harvester silenced them and turned pieces of their body into souvenirs that now grace your home.

I didn't want to die, but it would've been too easy for your lawyers to poke holes in my evidence otherwise. This way, I'm impossible to ignore. The world will think you went on a murder spree to silence us all and save your career.

Eventually, you'll own up to killing me. You'll claim an argument between friends, gone wrong. My death will stop bothering you.

But you'll never get over the death of your reputation.

You'll try to save it. Prove you were a good surgeon if not a good friend. Convince everyone I'm the only woman you killed. I hope, then, that you remember my last words. *I swear I didn't kill the others.*

You'll be repeating them until the day you die.

Grave Bait

By Chad Lutzke

It started as a dare.

Liza sat in the passenger seat of her friend's car, brushing lint off her skirt. "The least you can do is wait for me."

"No way. I know you. You'll head inside, take a peek, and if he doesn't look like Jason Momoa, you'll turn right around before you even get a chance to know him. You've gotta break that superficiality, girl. Or you're gonna wake up one day in a rundown trailer, totally alone, with a dozen cats pissing in your laundry. Now get in there and give him a chance."

"Just two minutes. That's all I'm asking."

"Liza, I love you, but no. Matter of fact…" Michelle reached in her purse, grabbed her cellphone. "I'm turning my phone off so you have no choice but to have an actual discussion with him."

"You bitch."

"I'll turn it on in an hour. If you're suffering, I'll come get you."

"I never should have agreed to this. Blind dates are bullshit."

"Not true. That's how Kelly and Jay met."

"Jay's a drunk. Not a great example."

Michelle rolled her eyes. "He doesn't drink any more than you do."

"Well, I don't drink and drive."

"It was one time." Michelle stuffed her phone back into her purse.

"That's all it takes."

"Listen…worst case scenario, you don't call him again. Best case, you're not alone anymore. Aren't you tired of being the…" Michelle bit her tongue.

Liza swung her head around, her eyes slits. "Say it."

"Sorry."

"Say it...the fifth wheel. That's what you were gonna say."

"Hey, it doesn't bother me, but I know it does you. I want to see you happy again. And if one of us doesn't push you into the pool, you're just gonna cling to the side, alone. At the very least, you need to get laid. When's the last time that happened?"

It hadn't been that long. Just last week, actually, when she'd gotten drunk at a party and woke up with Michelle's boyfriend, John. She remembered none of it—not even the first kiss—and snuck out before he woke. No way was she about to share that with Michelle.

Liza looked at the restaurant, sighed. "I hate you." She opened the car door, got out.

"No you don't," Michelle said through a smile. As she drove away, she yelled out the window. "No peek and dash!"

Liza rolled her eyes and checked her hair in the reflection of the restaurant's windows.

The date had been set up through Michelle. Kenneth Spruill was one of John's friends. Michelle claimed he was at last week's party, but for Liza, that night was a blur. She could have met Brad Pitt and wouldn't have remembered it.

"I dare you," Michelle had said. "Don't be a bitch. Just one date. You're gonna love him."

She didn't feel comfortable having a complete stranger know where she lived, especially considering she'd premeditated a potential ghosting. So, reluctantly, Liza accepted the challenge, with the caveat they meet at Hong Kong Foo-Eat—a restaurant Liza was familiar with, a place where she knew exactly what to order.

And now, she stood outside the restaurant with half a mind to ditch the guy, call a cab, and come up with some half-assed story to tell Michelle. With her hand on the door, Liza was already dreaming up her story. *He was rude and talked about his ex for an hour. It was awful!*

The restaurant was split in two—one side filled with tables, the other with booths. A family and two couples occupied three of the tables, and a lone figure sat at one of the booths, his back to her. Kenneth. She remembered the name because it bothered her. *Why not just call yourself Ken? Kenneth sounds so pretentious.*

She stalled, contemplating. And then he turned, looked at the waitress who was handing him a small cup of sake. Not only did he not look like Jason Momoa, he was a close resemblance to Ron Howard. Richie Fucking Cunningham. Opie! And the way he looked at the waitress, the emptiness in his eyes, the stone lips. This was someone who wore a smile only when it pleased him.

"Nope," Liza whispered, then crept back outside. "Nope, no way. Personality can't fix that." She reached for her phone, dialed Michelle's number.

The phone rang four times, then went to voicemail. "Ohhh… you bitch. I can't believe you actually turned your phone off. Call me when you get this." She hung up with an aggressive punch of her thumb.

Liza peeked through the window, saw Kenneth tip back his sake and wave the waitress over. "Really, dude? Getting drunk on a first date?"

She watched him look at his watch, then swing his head around toward the window. Toward her. She ducked, then hustled to the side of the building and tried Michelle once more. Again, the voicemail. "I'm not fucking around, 'Chelle. This guy's a drunk, and he looks like fucking Howdy Doody. Call me!"

Liza searched her purse for cash, knowing full well the only money she had was a two-dollar bill she refused to spend. The bill *used* to be lucky. Now it's just a reminder of a past she couldn't let go of: Tim and his cheating ass—the one guy she still compared others to. "And no cab fare. Great."

Her eyes scanned the dark parking lot, as though the answer lay there, and played a quick game of guess-his-car, settling on the rusted Mustang, giving the minivan to the family of four.

Choosing this restaurant was a horrible idea. Familiar or not, it was in the middle of nowhere, just off the freeway, with the nearest business at least another mile or two down the road. It was a wonder the place got business at all.

She dialed Melissa once more, cussing with each unanswered ring. Left a third message: "Are you fucking serious? I'm supposed to wait here until you decide I learned a lesson on dating etiquette?"

Liza pulled a pack of cigarettes from her purse that'd been sitting in there for at least six months. They were nothing more than a security blanket. She sparked a lighter and inhaled, tried not to cough, and failed. The flame left a bright orange ghost in her vision that slowly faded as her eyes adjusted back to the dark.

With her lungs on fire and cigarette in hand, she crossed the parking lot, taking a seat on a curb in one of the empty spots, where she searched through her apps and considered downloading the one her friends spent far too much time on. It annoyed her, that app. She'd vowed to never use it.

But...desperate times call for desperate measures when your best friend has fed you to the wolves.

Liza tapped the app to download it out of spite, drew on her smoke, managed to stave off another cough. She watched the smoke disappear, reaching for the sea of stars overhead. It made her feel small and insignificant. Couldn't wait to get back to the city, where the lights were inviting and the noise a warm embrace, reminding her she wasn't alone. But this. This was tortuous. The still, black sky, with its bullshit quiet, forced her to think too much.

She went back to the phone.

Twenty minutes passed, scrolling through video after video on the app, before Liza tore away from its hypnotic loop. She checked the time and rubbed her eyes, then tried calling Michelle again, this time not bothering to leave a voicemail.

She wondered just how long Howdy Doody was willing to wait for his no-show date, when the squeak of the restaurant door seemed to answer the query. Startled, she stood and ran behind the van as a man's shadow stretched across the parking lot. It was him. Red hair like fire as it passed under the lot's light.

Mustang. Go for the Mustang.

But he didn't. He was headed for the minivan. On drunken legs, he walked toward her.

She ducked, knocking into the yellow cement post behind her. Listened to the clank of keys as they hit the car door, unlocking it. Her heart raced—a fluttering of bird wings caught in her chest. The door opened, the van shifted. The door closed. The next sixty seconds were an eternity while the threat of confrontation plagued her.

I could tell him I'm waiting for a friend.

Okay, so why are you crouched behind his van?

I had to pee.

Then why didn't you use the restaurant? It's right there.

Dammit.

The vehicle turned over, and the exhaust coughed in her face. She coughed back.

Brake-light red splashed across her. And before she had time to regret her hiding spot, the vehicle rolled back. Flesh tore.

Immediately after she screamed, the van stopped. The door opened, a scuffle of footsteps.

"Oh shit oh shit oh shit. Fuck…fuck!" Kenneth's hands went to his head, pulled at his hair.

Liza's leg was pinned between the van and the cement post, the van's exhaust driven into her thigh. Droplets of blood slowly poured from the wound—a leaky faucet filled with scarlet rust.

The man covered his ears. The screaming wouldn't stop. "Okay…hold on. Just calm down. Shit shit shit." He cupped his hand in front of his mouth and breathed, smelling for alcohol on his breath. "I'm screwed, I'm screwed, I am so screwed. I'm fucked."

The screams gave way to guttural moans as Liza grabbed her leg.

"Shhh…" The man put a timid hand on her shoulder, carefully, as if she were made of eggshells and tissue paper. "Be quiet."

The moaning grew louder as Liza tried to speak.

"Shut the fuck up!" Kenneth balled his fist and punched her in the eye.

Her head rocked back, and spittle flew. She found another scream and filled the black sky with it.

"Shut up!" He swung again, this time at the side of her head. Her eyes rolled back, and she went limp against the van.

Liza woke. It was very dark and took all of ten seconds before every unsettling aspect of that moment came to light. The excruciating pain in her leg, the strange chemical smell, the pounding head. But something else was wrong, something that struck her with unsurmountable panic. Her eyes refused to open. She reached for them, feeling along her lids. They were sealed, her fake lashes fluttering against the ends of her fingers like centipedes.

"Help!" she screamed, her mouth stretched impossibly wide.

"Don't yell," a man's voice said.

She stopped. Listened. She recalled the van pinning her, but nothing after. "What happened?"

"We fucked up is what happened."

"I can't open my eyes! Am I…am I blind?"

"For now."

"Is this the emergency room? What's wrong with my eyes?" She reached her hands out, feeling for the man. "Who are you?"

"Kenneth."

The name didn't register at first. She played it through her mind, flipping the files. It was familiar somehow.

"We had a date tonight."

Ken!

Howdy Doody!

"But you were standing me up, huh? Hiding in the parking lot because you didn't want to sit there and look at me over dinner. Well…now you don't have to."

She kept silent, putting the pieces together. This wasn't an emergency room. There was no overbearing scent of bleached linens and antiseptic. No echoing of her voice off barren walls.

She felt around her. Rough, fuzzy carpet. The kind found atop the floorboard of vehicles. She was in Kenneth's van. And by the sound of it, he was in no rush to get her help.

Trying to keep a calm demeanor, she said, "You hit me with your van, Kenneth."

"Yeah. I'm sorry about that."

She felt her thigh, the unnatural splitting of skin that formed a half circle—a wet chasm that burned like hell.

She tried to make sense of the situation, but nothing pointed toward anything rational. This wasn't right. Her false calm gave way to panic as she finally lost control. "Help! Help! Help!" Her voice cracking through each scream.

"Yell one more time, and I'm gluing your mouth shut too," Kenneth said.

She felt her eyes again. A thin layer of crust lingered at the seam between the lids. That's what she smelled. The intense chemical odor found in the strongest of glues. She'd used that same glue to fix her glasses, the handle of her favorite mug, and even the gash she'd gotten on her thumb while chopping an onion, helping keep the skin closed.

Just like it was doing now.

"Why are you doing this?" she cried.

"Good question. I'm trying to figure that out myself. It wasn't supposed to go down like this, but I can't exactly call the police. That sake hits harder than you might think. The last thing I need is to lose my license and spend the night in jail."

"You're gonna spend a lot more than one night, asshole!"

Kenneth shifted in his seat, sighed. "You're a piece of ass, Liza. That's all. I figured you were worth the price of dinner. But now—"

"Fuck you."

"If I were you, I'd bite that tongue."

Liza's face scrunched, her chin quivered. "You're right. I'm sorry. I'm just scared. I'm really scared, Kenneth." Tears formed in the corner of her eyes, seeping around the glued flesh. "I promise I won't say a word to the police. They don't need to know about any of this. I'll just get stitched up, and if anyone asks what happened, I'll say I fell."

"Your eyes are glued shut, Liza. How are you going to explain that?"

Liza tried opening her eyes. The skin stretched but wouldn't give. She tried with her fingers, pulling at each lid, struggling to separate them. The corner of one eye gave, and light poured in. If she turned her head and spun her eyeball to the right, she could make out Kenneth's silhouette.

"Stop!" he said.

"Help me fix this, Kenneth. You can let me go, and I'll go home and clean up, and nobody will ever know. You didn't mean to back into me, right?"

"No."

"See? It was just an accident."

"You expect me to believe you're not going to tell anyone?"

"All we need to do..." Liza put her fingers back to her lids and pulled, grunting through the next few words. "...is fix this." The lid gave, tearing. Her bottom lid now held a thin layer of skin from the top, as well as the strip of fake lashes which poked her eyeball whenever she blinked. Blood seeped into her eye.

"Stop!" Kenneth's face was covered in disgust. He jumped from his seat and grabbed Liza's hands. "Just stop it!"

The sound of the van's rear door opening turned both their heads. There stood Michelle, both hands filled with objects.

"You sick piece of shit!" Michelle raised an arm and something shot from it, hitting Kenneth. Kenneth's eyes went wide, his teeth clamped shut, body stiffened. After a moment of seizure-like spasms, he collapsed on the floor of the van, wires from a taser jutting out from his chest.

Before Liza was even able to offer a sigh of relief, Michelle jumped in the van and swung a hammer at Kenneth. The hammer met skull. A dull crack. Then she wrapped a garbage bag around the man's head, cinching it tight.

Too shocked to move, Liza watched, with one bloody eye, as her friend murdered the man. There was no more movement from him, other than the subtle suck and blow of the bag as it molested his open mouth.

Then his breathing stopped.

Michelle lunged for her friend, arms around her in a tight hug. "I'm so sorry, Liza."

Liza stared single-eyed and emotionless at Kenneth's shiny, plastic face. Michelle scooted back, grabbed her friend's arms, looked at her. Liza resembled a broken doll left on a basement shelf, the one eye swimming behind its broken lash. Michelle brought a gentle hand to her face, caressed it. "What did he do to you?"

Liza trembled. "Glued my eyes shut."

"I can't believe I let this happen."

"It's not your fault."

"Yes, it is. I knew he was a bad person. Not *this* bad, but I knew."

Liza's eye zeroed in on Michelle. "What do you mean, you knew?"

"Last week...at the party...he raped me. He put that date-rape shit in my drink. Then I found out that wasn't the first time he's done it. Him *and* his friends."

"Then why the hell would you try and get me to go out with him?"

"This was never going to be a date, Liza. It was me planning my revenge."

"I was bait?" Liza scowled.

"No...well...sort of. I don't know. But I was parked right down the street the whole time, waiting for his van to pull out so I could follow him. I knew he'd bring you out here in the woods. It's what he does. And I was prepared. I even brought a gun." Michelle reached behind her back and pulled out a pistol. "I just didn't expect him to do *this* to you. I'm so sorry."

"So, you didn't see him hit me? With his *van*?"

"What? No, of course not. I would have come running. I couldn't see his van from where I parked, only when he pulled out." Michelle looked Liza over, saw the wound on her leg. She winced. "I'm so sorry, honey. I never even turned my phone off. I was just gonna follow you, then we'd take care of him together."

"And you thought I'd agree to kill him?"

"I wasn't sure, but I knew you'd have my back. And like I said, I knew he'd bring you out here, where no one's around. It was stupid. I'm sorry. I didn't know how else to deal with it. He needed putting down, Liza. His dad's rich. His friends are rich. He'd never get caught and would keep doing this." Michelle grabbed Liza's hand. "I couldn't do this alone."

Liza looked back at Kenneth. "Umm…I think you handled it just fine on your own."

Michelle swallowed hard. "We're not done yet."

After agreeing that a hospital visit would have to wait, Michelle made Liza sit in the van while she pulled her car up and grabbed two shovels out of the trunk. Then, fueled by adrenaline, Liza helped dig the hole for the first twenty minutes, then had to rest.

As she sat with her back to a tree, watching her friend dig a grave, she wondered if Kenneth drugged her that night too. She'd been drunk plenty of times, but never blackout drunk. Not like this. This was like having amnesia, as though the night in question never existed.

Him and *his friends.*

Or maybe John did it, notching his belt and bragging to friends about his conquest after divvying up the roofies.

"'Chelle…I have to tell you something."

Michelle stopped shoveling and wiped sweat from her eyes. Mascara smeared like old roadkill across her cheek. "What?"

"I…" Liza lightly touched her still-sealed eye, gathering the nerve to spill the secret. "I think I slept with John."

Michelle smiled and got back to work. "I know. He's in the trunk."

Five Ways to Kill Your Rapist on a Farm

By Emma Alice Johnson

The first time she killed her rapist, she used a hay bale hook.

Her rapist's arrival interrupted her as she sternly lectured a woodchuck that hid in the cracked foundation of the danger barn. She called it the danger barn because it had partially collapsed and looked like it could topple at any moment. Shards of glass littered the floor. Coils of rusty barbed wire dangled from the support beams. A woodchuck glowered at her from the concrete.

On summer Sundays like these, she enjoyed following critters as they went on their little errands. This one's errands had involved chewing up the bottom of her car, so she'd chased it to its current hiding spot to admonish it about respecting other people's property.

The sound of tires on her gravel driveway forced her to stop before she was certain the furball understood. She didn't know the car belonged to her rapist, not at first. Most days, she got to exist free of interactions with other humans, and she preferred it that way. Not that she was antisocial. She was plenty social, mostly with bumblebees and wildflowers. Occasionally, a delivery person came with a package, or some teenagers pulled in to beg to hunt on her land, and she'd chat with them.

She peeked out of the danger barn. A car with Minneapolis plates parked by the house. She didn't recognize it as belonging to one of her friends from back home, and people from the cities usually didn't stray so far into Wisconsin. Her immediate instinct was, it's him, it's the man who raped me.

She chastised herself for thinking this. She'd spent the last couple of years training herself to shove such thoughts aside. In the days following the sexual assault, she'd seen his face on every man she passed. She'd broken down screaming at the grocery store when she turned into an aisle and saw him, fled her doctor's office because he sat in the clinic's waiting room. Her therapist had assured her that this was normal, her brain stuck on survival mode.

It had never been him on those occasions, and surely it wasn't him now. It had been more than two years. The trial long over, he'd been convicted, put on probation, and gotten on with his life. The restraining order was still active. And how would he even know where she lived? Only a few of her friends had her address. She'd moved far from the city to make sure she never saw him again.

But when the car door opened, her rapist got out. She panicked, ducked back into the danger barn, glanced at the crack in the concrete where the groundhog hid, and wished she could join. Why would he come here?

After the trial, his friends had taken to social media to convince people that he'd been the victim of a travesty of justice, that she'd made a mistake, misremembered. He even did a fundraiser to pay his mortgage because he lost his job. A big boo-hoo that so many people fell for. Even with her word, even with all the evidence, even with a jury convicting him of felony sexual assault, so many people refused to believe a woman. Maybe he'd come to kill her, to finish what he'd started. If everyone refused to believe he was a rapist, maybe they'd refuse to believe he was a murderer too.

From in the barn, she heard him knocking on the front door of her house. She considered waiting him out, hiding here until he left. For a moment, that plan seemed reasonable, until she realized that if he had found her now, he could find her later, tonight, anytime. She'd never not be thinking about when he'd come back. That's when she picked up the bale hook.

When she bought the farm, she'd had so much fun digging through everything the previous owner, and each owner before that, had left behind. Some of the tools she found had likely been here since the house was first built in 1893. Jagged, bladed things, dinged from years of use and oranged with rust. The bale hook had immediately piqued her curiosity. A half-foot long metal hook attached to a U-shaped piece of metal, with a handle running across its prongs. Not being from a farming background, she hadn't known what it was. At first, she thought it was a meat hook. Meat hooks were usually S-shaped though, one side to impale the meat on, and the other side to hang it. A neighbor corrected her, told her that farmers used the bale hook to grab bales of hay, pull them off a trailer and toss them into the barn.

She gave the shush finger to the woodchuck, who wedged deeper into the crack. She liked the way the tool felt in her hand, light, natural. She kept a loose grip as she emerged from the danger barn. She rarely wore shoes unless she was going deep into the woods, so her bare feet made little noise as she stepped through the lush green grass toward the house.

Her rapist stood facing the door, knocking occasionally. How very city of him to come to this farm in the woods, on a day when the sun kissed the world to life, and assume she was sitting inside. In moments, she was behind him. He didn't notice. She stood there for a beat, enough to take a deep breath. Then she swung the hook and sunk the blade into the side of his neck, right below the spot where his jawbone met his ear.

Before he could turn around, she pulled, using both hands now, dragging him off his feet. She yanked again. He flailed at the tool as it dug deeper into his neck. She thought about farmers sticking the hooks into bales of hay and wondered, once they had moved the bale where they wanted it, how did they get the hook free? She tried wiggling it. Eventually it came loose. He didn't put up much of a fight, just pushed awkwardly at the hole and grunted. Blood spurted from between his fingers.

Standing above him, she wasn't certain she'd done enough to kill him. She wanted to, she realized. She'd wanted to since that night, since she'd woken up to his weight on top of her, to her dress pushed up and tights pulled down.

She kneeled beside him and drove the bloody bale hook into his ear, but couldn't get it in very far. He slapped at her now, writhed and kicked, flopped around on the grass. She lost her grip on the tool for a second.

When she got hold of it again, she sat on her bottom. She straightened her legs and pressed her heels against the side of his face opposite the ear she had hooked. Pushing his head away from her with her feet and pulling the bale hook toward her with her arms, she drove the hook in deeper and deeper. She strained her hamstrings.

When she thought she couldn't do anymore, she gripped the tool's handle even harder and stomped her feet against his head, impaling him further onto the hook. He soon stopped moving. When she had pulled so hard her forearms felt likely to combust, she released her grip and lay flat on her back. She thrashed out with her feet, driving the body away from her.

A sound under her car drew her attention, teeth on metal. She glanced over and saw the woodchuck, gnawing at some wires dangling from the vehicle's undercarriage. The critter looked at her. She held her pointer finger to her lips, shushing.

The second time she killed her rapist was the cutest.

Can you even imagine the sort of hunger pigs must feel, after humans have spent centuries breeding them into insatiable eating machines so they will grow as big as possible as quickly as possible? She thinks about that a lot when she feeds her four pigs. When dinner time comes, they thrash and roar in anticipation. How they must ache. How hollow they must feel inside. But then she feeds them buttered potatoes and their eyes gleam at her with such sweet gratitude.

She fed them much more than buttered potatoes today. She'd spotted her rapist on her way back from the feed store. He was changing his tire on the shoulder of 64. Different car this time, but definitely him, and obviously on the way to her place. She hadn't thought about it, just the gentlest little nudge of the steering wheel and she grazed him with the side of her car, enough to knock him out, bloody him up and make it easy to drag him into her backseat.

At first, the pigs wouldn't eat him. They were used to pellets, plus the odd fruit or veggie. The only time they'd eaten meat was when she'd found one of her chickens with its head ripped off and fed them the remains. Maybe this body seemed too much like her, so they didn't want to eat it. That thought disgusted her, because she was nothing like him. She understood how her pigs might make the mistake though, even though he was tied up, lying in the slop with his mouth taped shut. Or maybe his contortions threw them off.

She ran into the house and scoured her cupboards until she found just the thing. Back out in the pen, she smeared a handful of peanut butter on his face, used her pointer finger to get nice globs of it in his nostrils and ears. His incessant blinking made it hard for her to pack it around his eyes. Before she could, the pigs started digging in. His body went still pretty soon after that.

Her oldest pig, a 400-pound Yorkshire sow, pulled away, crunching on a chunk of her rapist's skull. Excited, the pig spun in circles so fast it fell down into the slop beside the body. The other three pigs, still gilts, barely 200 pounds, were more focused. They rooted into the bowl of red mush her rapist's face had become, slurping, their coiled tails whirling with joy. She'd watched those pigs use their snouts to flip cinder blocks like they were nothing in order to get at the centipedes and other bugs hiding underneath. Human bones were no obstacle for them.

As the pigs ate, they pushed the man's head so he looked like he was nodding, the same way he'd nodded while she testified against him, as if agreeing with everything she said. She'd wanted to stand up and scream, "Why are you nodding? Why are you making me go through this if you know what I'm saying is true?" But then he'd taken the stand and told the jury that she'd remembered wrong, that she'd consented, and that she'd been awake the whole time.

For a moment, she worried the pigs would only eat the head and leave the rest for her to deal with. To entice them, she smeared peanut butter on her rapist's fingers and toes. She noticed he didn't have tattoos anymore. Maybe he'd gotten them removed. Could tattoos be removed so quickly?

Before she could finish with the peanut butter, the sow got back to business. She was surprised to see her rapist pull his hand away. Was it a mere death twitch, or was he still alive in there? One of the gilts looked up at her, a piece of the man's brain hanging from its dazzlingly long chin whiskers, so she figured it was unlikely that he was still living.

Every once in a while, the pigs pulled their mouth away from their meal, lifted their heads to the sky and smiled, oinking their celebratory oinks. "I love you, my sweet girls," she said, petting their muscley pink rumps and booping their blood-soaked snoots. Just the cutest thing in the whole world.

The third time she killed her rapist, she tried stoning him. This was a mistake. Do not try to kill your rapist by throwing rocks at him.

She caught him hiking in the woods near her farm, his skinny body all decked out with a backpack and a shiny canteen. When they crossed paths, he acted as though he was lost, as if he hadn't come to hurt her again. She knew the truth though. She picked up a stone and hurled it at him. It thunked on his shoulder, which didn't damage him so much as anger him.

She bolted, weaving through the trees. She'd walked these woods every day since she moved here, so she knew her way around. Keeping a steady pace, she did her best not to lose him without giving him the idea that she was leading him somewhere. Which, of course, she was.

She cut across her neighbor's cornfield to the old silo on the edge of her property. A sturdy tube of concrete, walls at least a foot thick. It hadn't been used in decades. Inside, the bottom dropped out, a twenty-foot fall to a pool of stagnant water. Mosquitos swarmed the entrance. She ignored them and ducked inside. There, next to the entrance, a steel ladder was built into the wall. It went up, but not down. She clung to it, waiting for her rapist to follow her.

As expected, the man stuck his head inside the door, cursing at her about the thrown rock. With her feet firmly on the bottom rung of the ladder and one hand gripping another, she used her free hand to snatch the man's collar. With a quick pull, she flung him into the water below. He splashed toward the wall, screaming, slapping at the concrete as if he could scrabble up it.

She thought about how, upon waking up to find him on top of her, she'd kicked away from him, crawled backwards from that couch. All the while, he'd just stood there in the shadows, watching as she screamed, savoring her panic, as if this was the moment he had been waiting for, not the act itself. He'd lost weight since then, she noticed. A lot of weight. He seemed younger too. Not fair. She'd aged a decade in the two years since he raped her.

She swung herself out of the silo and grabbed one of the cinder blocks stacked outside the entrance. This time, her aim was true. The block fell onto the man's bald head, collapsing it. Almost instantaneously, he and the block disappeared beneath the surface, leaving a little dab of red to delight the skeeters.

The fourth time she killed her rapist, she got creative.

She enjoyed tinkering with the old machines she found in the barn, the smaller ones at least, or the larger ones she could figure out how to disassemble. Not that she was mechanically inclined. She didn't know what half of them were, but most had a screw or a bolt somewhere that she could undo, and the next thing she knew, she'd have a bunch of rusty metal parts spread out in front of her in the grass. She'd clean them, maybe oil them, and put them back together, replacing any screws or bolts that broke. She'd been proud when she got an old weed whipper to work again that way, and she'd gotten a kick out of cutting down tall grass as the machine roared. It felt powerful.

Her rapist began popping up again, driving by, pretending to be the mailman. Naturally, the idea crossed her mind to use the weed whipper on him. But she didn't think the orange string could do as much damage to him as she'd require. It had been foiled by a few saplings she'd tried to cut down, so it didn't stand much of a chance against bone.

She loved the concept though, of whipping him down to bits, so she started tinkering. The first thing she tried was attaching a chain to the head of the weed whipper. A chain would definitely do the trick, and she found a big one in the danger barn. She duct-taped it onto the head of the weed whipper, but the tape got gummed in the works, and the machine wasn't powerful enough to spin the weight of the chain.

After a lot of daydreaming, she decided to dissect her riding lawnmower. She excavated the spinning parts out of the housing, inverted them, punched holes in the blades, and threaded the chains through. She mounted it on a wagon, along with the engine and battery. It didn't exactly work like a charm. She had to hopscotch away fast after she started it, to get clear of the chain before it picked up momentum. For a brief moment, it spun perfectly, before it worked itself into a frenzy, tipped over, and whipped up a cloud of dirt until it choked to a stop. Good enough, she thought.

The next day, she wheeled her little death robot out and hid with it behind some brush on the side of the street opposite her mailbox. As she waited, she thought about how, in court, her rapist's lawyer had asked her how many times she'd kissed him before she passed out. How many kisses, she wondered, would have made what that man did to her okay?

When her rapist came by, she waited till he reached out to open her mailbox and shove some letters in, then she started the death robot and kicked it out at his car. One of the wagon's wheels flopped off along the way. The machine leapt and sparked on the blacktop, throwing an epic hissy fit. In the process, it managed to smash her rapist's side mirror before sputtering out with a loud *chunka chunka chunka* noise.

Not what she had hoped for, but it distracted her rapist enough that she was able to open his door and smash his face with a hammer before he could even take his eyes off the smoking machine.

The fifth and final time she killed her rapist was a real barn burner.

He hung limp from a ceiling joist in the danger barn, wrapped snuggly in rusted barbed wire. She'd been careful not to get any of the wire around his neck, not wanting him to strangle. Instead, she wrapped it under his arms. She also coiled some around his face, piercing one of his eyes in the process. That's when he passed out, his cornea gobbed up on the barb as she pulled the wire taut and snipped off the excess. That had made it easy for her to hoist him up to where he hung.

Now, she stood near the inside wall of the barn, peering through a crack to see her house, where a group of police officers gathered at the door, knocking. They'd been there a minute already. Soon enough, they'd give up and start snooping around the outbuildings, and the danger barn was the closest to the house. She'd have to move quickly.

She splashed gasoline on her rapist. He bled pretty bad now from all his puncture wounds. The blood trailed down his body, disappeared into his shoes, and dripped from the toes, where it had soaked through. His body quivered as he wormed his way back into consciousness.

"You look different," she told him. He was missing the thumb and pinky on his left hand. She wondered when that had happened. Her neighbor at the adjacent farm had a similar layout, she remembered. He'd told her he'd gotten messy with his dad's circular saw as a teen. Maybe her rapist had tried to hurt someone else, and they'd gotten at him with a saw. Well, there'd be no more of that, thanks to her.

She lit a match and flicked it at him. He caught fire fast. He fully regained consciousness in time to scream as his face melted off his skull.

She'd been sloppy with the gas, and soon the whole barn was aflame. The police came running, but stood a safe distance outside the entrance, staring in at her. She saw that they weren't police at all. Each one was her rapist, costumed in black, even outfitted with a badge and a gun. She couldn't believe the lengths he'd go to so he could keep hurting her.

"Come out, now!" they shouted.

They raised their guns at her. As the air heated up, she thought the threat funny. Did they intend to shoot her if she didn't come out? Would they fill her with bullets before she could catch fire? They couldn't stand to give up control of her.

She turned back to her rapist, the one suspended inside her burning barn. The fire had no itinerary, no rhyme or reason. In some spots, it burned through to her rapist's bones, while patches of his shirt collar and underwear still remained. His legs had blackened and looked bizarrely thin as the meat dissolved from them. Fluid leaked from tiny fissures in one femur, fizzling and popping.

Flaming hunks of rafters fell around her and a spark caught her hair on fire. She braced herself for pain, feeling an odd sense of ease knowing that at least he wouldn't be able to come after her anymore. Gazing out at the men standing outside her barn with guns pointed, she wished she could burn them too. She wished she could burn every last one of them.

Victim 6

By Belicia Rhea

The casting call advertised the role as a breakout chance, maybe working alongside some A-listers. Silvia drove the four hundred or so miles up from Phoenix to audition at a dingy warehouse in the hell of Southern California. The money was terrible, but she could afford a motel for a little while. Besides, all of her actor friends lived in their cars in the city, and she'd never been afraid of sacrifice. Ever since she was a girl, she wanted to be a big name in Hollywood, and for that, she'd do anything.

Silvia took a deep breath and looked around the lobby of the warehouse. There was an old patterned carpet that looked like it had seen many decades, like maybe this place was once a pizzeria or an arcade, with a long past of spills and feet trudging across it, and even if it had been cleaned, who knows if they really vacuumed all that gunk up, if they used actual detergent or just smeared around the filth and pushed it to the corners of the baseboards. Everything looked like you could run your fingers along it and find grease. The yellow tint of the walls suggested the building had seen incidents of fire damage, or was once the smoking section of a Denny's.

The girl at the front desk popped her gum while trying not to make it too obvious that she was texting. She barely looked up, waving Silvia towards the direction of the chairs, most of them already filled. Silvia signed in and stared at the packed room. She was nervous, almost enough to turn around and walk out, until a girl moved her purse onto her lap and motioned for Silvia to sit down, patting at the empty seat beside her.

"You here for auditions too? For the victim role?" the girl asked. "I'm Danielle."

"Yes, thank you. I'm Silvia." Silvia sat down, too shy to say much else.

Danielle had a commanding presence, one fit for the lead girl, but she was too young for the part, maybe eighteen, barely out of high school, maybe here because someone who knew someone wrote her name on a list.

Silvia looked around the room at the rest of the women waiting. They looked like they had it all together, like each of them would be a perfect face for a twenty-second, possibly even a five-minute role, and Silvia wondered how she could compete with them, how she could look as fascinating, trying to sell ordinary and unassuming—the look of a background victim, with the glitz of a star. She opened her compact mirror and checked her reflection, misted her makeup with a setting spray, and swiped another layer of mauve shimmer on her already glossed lips.

Danielle's name was called first. She got up and smiled at Silvia. "Well, let's see how this goes. I hope you get it."

"You too," Silvia said, and meant it.

Silvia was the second-to-last to audition. She could see the producers and assistant directors off to the side, nearly arguing, looking at headshots of some of the women. She felt strange reading out her lines, acting out her suffocating and choking gasps, forcing a smile afterward, like a professional, trying to hide her nervousness.

The casting director looked dirty, like he lived in this warehouse and was the reason it wasn't clean. His stringy combover lay smeared to his scalp, and he smelled cheap, likely doused in half a bottle of something from a drugstore that had been rolling around the back seat of a car.

"We want to give fear, to invent it. We don't want to glorify violence, or violence against women, of course." The casting director seemed surprised at what was coming out of his mouth. "We want to make people sick, remind them why clowns are their worst nightmare. Get them to realize a fear they never knew they had."

"Like John Wayne Gacy?" Silvia suggested, eager to demonstrate her understanding, her deservedness of the role.

"Worse," he said, as spit shot out of his mouth and nearly landed on her. His knuckle hair was so long it suffocated his wedding ring. Silvia couldn't imagine who would marry this man.

"So, what do you say, sweetheart? You think you can do that? Give us afraid?"

Silvia smiled.

Silvia landed a small role which didn't have a name, just VICTIM 6, but that was fine with her. She practiced in the mirror of her cheap motel, her terror-filled eyes scrunching into the black fog of her clumping lashes. She thought about what the casting director had said, how he wanted her to feel the way a woman was meant to feel when she's being hunted, when she knows it's too late, when someone's got her in his grasp. She didn't want to acknowledge how hearing this made her uneasy, so she started looking at pictures of John Wayne Gacy, but that only made her sick, and he was dead, and she didn't want to think of every horrible thing he'd done to those boys.

She was happy to learn Danielle also got a role as VICTIM 5— and that Isaac Patel was cast as the lead, the killer, Malachi the Clown. Isaac was well known for his role in a high-grossing slasher, and she felt heat in her cheeks as she imagined being in the same room with him, the reflection of her face glowing in his eyes, the two of them sharing the same air, the same shot on screen, his hands all over her. He was a man she could hang posters of in her apartment and not be ashamed. She'd loved him since she first saw him in a few low-budget horror shows, watched his rise to fame, and he became her near-obsession, a dream she never imagined could be real.

She wondered how many actresses or models he'd been dating, if she would even be able to manage conversation with him. She had to be perfect, couldn't ruin her chance.

But that first day, they were shooting in Death Valley, in some boiler room—it was hot, she could feel her foundation slick on her nose, nearly melting off her face, and the actors had to change wardrobes quickly and get into their bathing suits for the pool scene, for which she was grateful. Still, she was nervous for Isaac to see her in that suit. It was boring, an athletic looking one piece.

She wanted him to notice her in it, even though he was just supposed to be drowning her. Silvia imagined that maybe he would become enamored with her, that she'd feel his heart pounding as he grabbed her, and when he held her, he'd really mean it. Maybe it could be something romantic, even affectionate, his want showing through the character, cutting deeper than the on-set violence, their unscripted chemistry obvious—people thinking to themselves how things are really heating up, that these two aren't acting—this is something much more than a clown holding a woman's head underwater. She daydreamed about him falling in love with her, them making headlines together, their high-profile coupling, their sex life, their stardom.

The dreaminess escaped her quickly when she saw him in person for the first time. He was trudging around set, practicing his walk. Pacing, with a menacing grimace, his shoulders hunched up to his ears. He kept them glued there in a weird swagger, him jerking around with that awful protruding prosthetic ridge over his brow, those fake teeth in points, a gouge in his cheek that looked like he survived a morning star to the head. The mask of his ragged skin shook, like it might fall off his face, but at the same time appeared to be glued on permanently, like maybe it could never come off. He kept repeating over and over in his low growl, "Hey, come here! Come here!" to each actress as she passed, never acting like a regular person, never once straying from that horrible rasp, his cigarette voice barking out like an animal.

"The trick is, you never ever break character," he'd famously said in a magazine interview which explained much of his behavior on set. There were rumors of how ridiculous he was to work with, and Silvia wasn't sure how to handle it when he spoke to her for the first time. She didn't want to be rude or unprofessional, didn't want to ruin a first impression, wasn't entirely sure if he was joking.

So when she walked past him, and he shouted at her like he did the others, "Hey, come here!" and she shrieked, she felt embarrassed. She wanted to smile or introduce herself, but instead she froze, unsure whether to extend her hand or run away.

For a moment, she looked into the pupils that got lost behind the slits in his mask, and before she knew what to do, he had already turned and strode toward the hall, shouting again at Danielle who was passing just behind Silvia.

Danielle rolled her eyes at him and nodded over to Silvia, "You ready for makeup?"

Silvia smiled a smile that meant yes. She was afraid to look at Isaac again, to see the gray in his eyes with those contact lenses, his slicked-back waves shiny with pomade. His hair wasn't red or green or any obnoxious colors like usual clowns, but a deep, rich brown that made him look like a businessman, if you only saw the back of his head. But when he turned around, with all they'd done to him, he looked straight out of Hell.

The girls' makeup went quick, just a natural look with some gloss and false eyelashes. The actors gathered on set. Isaac was in the pool, looking menacing as Malachi. The stylists and special effects makeup artists glared at him, with eyes that said, *don't you dare*, making sure he remembered not to do anything too crazy that could mess with the hair and mask and latex that had taken them three hours that morning to assemble.

When a voice yelled for places, it was time for Danielle to get in the pool. At this point in the film's story, Malachi had just barely started killing. Four women dead. Now was Danielle's turn. Victim Five. Just before, Malachi ditched the dead girls in the desert and decided to follow another to this pool resort. After he knocked out the girl's boyfriend in the pool bathroom, he slipped into the water toward VICTIM 5. Remember, she wasn't given a name.

But Danielle had a name. Before she could scream her full scream, he pulled her head underwater.

Too soon, Silvia thought, as she let out a little gasp. He didn't even give Danielle time to hold her breath. A shocked *ssss* sound came from an inhale from someone in the back of the set. Silvia wasn't the only one who noticed how he threw her down early.

Silvia turned to watch the monitor. The look on Malachi's face was merciless. He scowled, his eyes pried open wide like Alex in *A Clockwork Orange*, staring at his victim with sick delight. Enjoying very much how Danielle was supposed to be drowning.

And she was. Drowning. Sucking up all the water. The shot zoomed in as Malachi kept pulling the chain around Danielle's collarbone, one hand yanking it like he was starting up a chainsaw, and the other hand gripping her throat with all his might, really wringing her neck, her eyes bulging with her shocked open mouth making bubbles everywhere. She started gasping underwater, flailing her arms, looking desperate through the liquid blur, fighting him with her pathetic attempts at survival. The crew just stood around in the longest silence Silvia ever heard, letting it go too long, as if they knew he was too good, this was too real, and the show must go on. Silvia scanned expressions for anyone else seeing what she was seeing. *Surely, she's fine*, their inaction said. *Danielle's an amazing actress,* they all silently agreed. By the time Gerard Monet, the Director, finally yelled, "Cut!" Danielle had stopped moving.

Isaac, still Malachi the Clown even after the cameras stopped rolling, pulled her head up out of the water enough for only her face to barely surface. He didn't make any attempts to revive her, like he was too in shock. Or still in character. Malachi didn't care about dead women.

It took a moment until a sound guy finally dragged Danielle out onto the pool deck, started CPR. They were lucky—she started coughing, shot a ton of water out of her mouth, wheezing and heaving, snot leaking out of her nose, until they turned her over and she ejected even more water. She touched her delicate manicured fingers to her necklace, her throat already blue and bruising all the way down to her clavicle. Paramedics took her away.

Shooting was called off for the remainder of the day. Silvia shook her head, thinking to herself, *I can't do that. I can't do that,* under her breath, teary and worried for Danielle, astonished by what she had just seen. She worried for Isaac, too, thinking surely he must be so upset, couldn't know what to do with himself, would never have meant for that. Isaac remained in full makeup and costume, didn't adjust his posture and his walk, even with everyone obviously uncomfortable by his lack of remorse—his lack of humanity.

After most of the actresses had already left, crying and worried, on their cell phones and carefully wiping tears from their made-up faces, Silvia wandered to further examine the set, unsure what to do. She walked toward the pool, looked into the depths, then followed the path past the outdoor bar that was closed due to filming, and walked back inside the resort, heading toward the hallway that would lead out the main entrance to her car.

"Hey," Isaac, still Malachi said, and grabbed Silvia's arm. She jumped, averted her gaze.

"Want to rehearse? You can come back to my trailer."

He was still doing the horrible clown voice, but he looked serious, sincere, and tilted his head in the direction of outside, nudging her to come with him. A cigarette hung from his mouth and he lit it inside like he knew he was untouchable, because killers and movie stars do what they want.

Silvia wasn't sure what to do. She wanted to go with him. This was a dream for her—being anywhere with Isaac Patel. But everything felt different now.

She glanced over her shoulder as she overheard a crew guy speaking low to someone in the back corner of the hallway.

"You know what they say. If she dies, the film goes cult classic. Shit, Monet probably wanted him to kill her, probably told him to hold her down there a little too long." The man laughed. Then the other one smiled. Silvia felt nauseous.

Isaac opened the trailer door, gestured for Silvia to walk in first, chivalry that didn't belong. There were a few things on the wall, hooks all over where he was to hang his various masks and costumes. The makeup artists had already left. They must have forgotten about Isaac, figured he could handle getting the costume off by himself. Maybe they couldn't look at him either. Silvia noticed that nothing in the trailer felt personal. Just a shell with cabinets and mirrors lined in bright vanity lights.

"Want to get on the bed?" Malachi asked, in a way that felt like more than a suggestion. "Here, have some of this."

Malachi dug in his pocket for a flask, swished around a liquid inside. Silvia didn't want the drink, she didn't know what it was. She took it out of his hand, set it on the fold-out table, and told him that she just wanted water. He brought her a plastic bottle, but she only stared at it and set it down.

"Is this okay?" he asked, then gripped her neck and squeezed until her breath escaped in scrapes. He took his hand away and waited. She lay back on the bed, trying to hide her tears, and he pulled her up to a sitting position.

"We need to rehearse."

Silvia nodded. "Okay." She sniffled, couldn't meet his eyes. She wanted him to take off that mask but knew he wouldn't.

After a few seconds, he rushed at her again, brought his hands to her throat, fingers lacing around the back of her nape, pushing hard enough to crush her windpipe had he wanted.

"Is this okay?"

She shook her head, *no*.

He let go. They remained in silence. Silvia took a sip from the plastic water bottle. Malachi went into the bathroom, started to fill up the tub.

"Now let's try it with the water," he said.

Silvia felt little bumps crawling up her arms. "No, that's okay. Let's just wait."

He said nothing, took a swig from a bottle of whiskey on the counter.

Silvia didn't speak for a long time. There wasn't much to say. But she was surprised to finally hear Isaac's voice, his real voice—as Malachi's wore down.

"How long you been doing this?" he asked her.

"Oh, not long. I hope to make it, you know. Like you."

He smiled, eyes glossy. "You will," he said. "I can tell. Got the look to you. Something special."

She smiled, couldn't believe her ears, and felt weightless all over, almost forgot everything terrible about the pool, about Danielle.

"Come help me get this off," he told her.

She got up and helped him with the prosthetics, grabbed a product off the counter to soften the adhesive, and took off each piece with care, delicately setting them down. He peeled Malachi off of him, hung up the mask on the wall. It sagged and flopped like some life of its own, perched and waiting to be brought back for death. She looked at it a moment, hollow in the open air, and was glad it was off of his face. She could actually talk to him now. Get to know him. Maybe find out if he was okay after what happened. But the liquor caught up with him and made his eyes look heavy, maybe even sad.

"*Now, as I was saying, let's try it with the water.*" Malachi's voice had suddenly returned. Silvia flinched when she heard it, but when Isaac turned to look at her, and she looked at his handsome face only a foot away from hers, she knew she had to impress him. She knew this may be her only chance.

She started inching toward the door. When Malachi leapt up to grab her, she ran.

He chased after her, calling out to her across the set. Then she heard his awful clown laugh as she ran to the pool fence, where she shook the gate in a dramatic performance, trying for the locked gate door. He caught up with her and gripped at her hair, pulled her head back, and whispered into the side of her neck, and she could smell the whiskey.

"Come on Silvia, give us afraid."

Silvia blushed. She didn't realize Isaac knew her name. She screamed a blood-curdling scream that in normal circumstances could startle an entire block, but this was a horror set. It would take more than screams to scare anyone here. Besides, they would barely blink at Isaac's antics, his method acting.

Just then, Silvia heard footsteps as someone approached them, and Isaac's slurring voice, "What the fuck?"

A masked man stood in front of them. Silvia froze, then screamed again as a pistol pointed at Isaac's chest and fired three times. The shooter yelled, "You fucking killed her!" before disappearing into the dark.

"Isaac! Oh my god." Silvia knelt over Isaac, blood pooling around him.

Her shaking hands fumbled around her bag, looking for her phone, but when she found it she kept dropping it, trembling and pressing the wrong buttons. Finally, she got through.

"911. What is the location of your emergency?"

"I need an ambulance. We're at some resort somewhere in the desert. I don't know, I'm not from California. He's an actor. It's Isaac Patel. Please hurry. He's bleeding out! Someone shot him. What do I do? We're near his trailer on set, by the pool. It's . . ."

The dispatcher started speaking but Silvia couldn't understand anything he was saying.

"It's okay, just hold on a little longer," she sobbed to Isaac. "Just hold on."

She tried to put pressure on his wounds, but she was shaking and had no strength. Isaac couldn't speak. His mouth was leaking red.

Again the paramedics came, maybe even the same ones from earlier who took Danielle, and they picked Isaac up, one pushing compressions over his chest. Through the small trailer window, that mask stared down at them from a high hook on the wall. Isaac's mouth looked just like the mask's, its gaping maw hanging open, those ominous empty eye holes where Isaac's used to be. Isaac gurgled out blood, and it spread to the side of his cheek and earlobe.

The ambulance spilled out figures in uniforms with their obscure gadgets, with shouting and lights flashing and horns and sounds and beeps of the other lit up vehicles. They wheeled Isaac off on a stretcher and took him away. The sirens blared like a sad carnival song, and the last few on set watched with their shocked faces, still awake from partying all night, breaths easing out of their white-caked nostrils, their worried eyes pleading for Isaac, that surely he's going to be fine. This is show business after all. Of course he's going to be fine.

Silvia squinted and looked around, still in shock when a reporter arrived and shoved a camera in her face. She kept shaking her head no. Tears drizzled in little lines down her cheeks. There was so much she was saying to the interviewers in her mind, but the right words wouldn't come out of her mouth. More questions, more microphones, bright lights in her eyes.

The incident flooded the media and soon received international attention. Silvia had been crying all night. Finally free from interviews and talking to police, she opened the door to her motel room, threw herself onto her bed, forgot the TV was on. The morning news crawl read:

TWO KILLED ON FILM SET–ISAAC PATEL SHOT DEAD.

A mug shot flashed across the screen of a tearful face: a young man, maybe eighteen, barely out of high school.

"Shooter has been identified as James Linden, allegedly dating the first deceased victim, Danielle Schwartz. Witness interviews at the scene describe the terror of these grisly deaths."

Gazing at herself on the screen, she froze. The blur in her eyes cleared, and she smiled, then laughed a laugh that can only be born out of a sob. She noticed how nicely her blush accentuated her cheeks, how her peachy lip gloss glowed as it caught the camera light. The tear dragging out of the corner of her left eye mixed just right with her highlighter as she spoke, and it glistened on screen, accentuated her bone structure, drew out a sparkle in her. The crimson of her nail polish popped as she wiped the tear away. Her V-neck hung low, revealing more than just the godawful bruising all over her neck from rehearsing with Isaac, dark marks staining her like a collar from his now-dead fingers, on camera and recorded forever as a permanent part of her.

The reporter nodded while he spoke, looking thin and sallow and disgusting, and Silvia noticed how she shined standing next to him, how she absolutely beamed, her face plastered there for all of Los Angeles to see.

Ambush Predator

By C. S. Humble

At a distance, Marie Evans appears to be a woman sitting on a park bench. From no more than ten feet away, she seems blissful, serenity itself, admiring the sun which, tipping like a bowl, pours light through the downy green of an alder tree. Her eyes are blue and wide. A gaze of remembrance, suggesting there is a smile beneath the surgical mask looped around her ears. This mask for pandemic fears indicates that she is both careful with her health and considerate of the health of others. Photographers dream of catching this moment in the wild. Painters hope to capture, with strokes of oil or swirls of acrylic, the feeling they are sure Marie is feeling: that moment of simple satisfaction on her smooth brow that is so elusive to others in a world anxious with many, many wrinkled cares.

At a distance, neither the politics of our time nor the economic uncertainty present in every age can penetrate the peaceable shield haloing the long silver-white hair. Ribbons gently rustled by the wind yet undisturbed by distant wars or the always-in-our-heart fear of societal collapse. These things exist in the world around Marie Evans. But they cannot touch her. These very real, very tangible threats plaguing every other participant in our modern life are, like any observers of the calmly sitting Marie, distanced from her.

But this is at a distance.

Closer inspection of Marie's life reveals that she was once as lucky and satisfied as she currently appears. She has a loving wife. Three marvelous children: two adopted, the youngest birthed from her own womb. Marie loves them all the same, and any intimate examination of her life proves an expert witness to the fact that she is filled with love and passion. She enjoys orchestra concerts and film—*The Sound of Music* is everything to her.

It was also the last thing to her.

Nine hours prior to this moment, Marie Evans spent her evening visiting the Dauphin Theater. Her favorite theater, featuring her favorite movie. Julie Andrews was a perfect ray of light. Christopher Plummer, an old indelible crush, remains her champion.

The film ends. Everyone applauds.

Marie Evans then leaves the theater at 10 p.m. She calls home, responsible and considerate, telling Jessica, her wife of two and a half decades, that she is on her way. This phone call takes exactly seven minutes and twenty-nine seconds. It is just enough time for Marie to reach her car, which is parked just out of reach of a singular lamp in the lonely parking lot, and long enough for the few other nostalgia-driven moviegoers to miss what happens to her.

She opens the driver-side door of her recently purchased sedan—a congratulatory purchase Jessica insisted upon—and just as she straightens one leg to slide onto the leather seats, still perfumed in brand-new-car smell, a big calf-skin-smooth hand slides over her mouth. The other hand, just as swift, moves with brutal effect.

Marie's vision flashes black to white. Her vision then comes back to her, where she sees her shoes, ankles and calves sliding across the ground as she is pulled away from the safety of the vehicle. She mumbles, confused. Her world flashes white to black.

Two months after this night, the media will, for the first time and not the last, use the phrase, "The Black Wells Annihilator."

Seventeen people after this night will see what Marie Evans wakes to see:

A large, round man with no aspect of athleticism or strength. His lumpy bulk, stuffed into white scrubs, hides completely the metal folding chair supporting him. Eyes large and bulbous, the shade of moonstone. "I've injected you with a paralytic agent" he says, his voice soft, almost fragile. "It'll keep you from doing what you're about to do."

Those cold stone eyes do not blink when Marie screams for help.

The fibrous cloth crammed into Marie's mouth, jammed deep in her throat, muffles the sound of the most violent, harrowing noise she will ever make. Only the two people inside the cramped confines of the modified storage truck will ever hear the sound. The muscles of Marie's abdominal wall squeeze into action, trying to curl her weight forward and rise. The leather straps across her breasts and thighs, along with the downy, lambswool-lined cuffs around her wrists and ankles, squeak against her straining. So new, the straps do not yet bear the wrinkles they will earn over the coming years. This is their first test. It is also the first proving ground of fantasy-driven exploits for the man looking silently at Marie. Like the straps and cuffs, the man will, over time, develop creases as his methods become well practiced. The procedure more nuanced.

This is also Marie's first time.

There will never be another time.

"Don't strain," the man says. "You'll hurt yourself."

Marie's heart climbs into her throat, trying to get out. Her mind gropes deep down into the dark strength of the reptilian-simple instincts crouching behind her human reason. It begins to kick and thrash, to doubt and deny the reality of her situation.

The man shoots out of the chair to full attention. With two blue, sausage-like fingers forked with varicose veins, he pinches Marie's nose shut.

"Stop," he says. "You're ruining it."

Marie twists her head violently. The straps hold her tighter than a lover. The man's clamped fingers simply ride out her wild struggle. She tries to breathe through the impacted gauze, which only serves to pull the fibrous loose ends against her gag reflex. Added to the fear of her abduction comes Marie's greatest fear made manifest without her captor even knowing it.

She is choking to death.

Pulling the cloth out of her mouth and throat would be easy were she not manacled to the bed bolted to the truck's floor. Her fingers, already growing numb at the tips, curl into claws, biceps knotting tight as she tries and tries to reach for the mass inside her mouth. Marie's stomach convulses. Saliva and bile fill her mouth, soaking the gauze. Making it heavier. Heavy enough so that the slickness of her throat mixed with angle of her neck allows the gravity of the world beneath her to pull the gauze past the cliff of her tongue, tickles her tonsils, and dangles in the aperture of her convulsing windpipe. For the briefest heart-racing moment, she hopes the man notices, simultaneously disbelieving that she's even thinking this. That her own captor will save her.

The man says nothing. He only waits, knowing that Marie will come to understand the simple unspoken pact between them.

Stop struggling and I will let you breathe.

Marie lays herself flat against the bed, believing that if she lies still, the man will release her. The numbness from her fingers crawls into her arms. Her complaining gag reflex makes the unmistakable, involuntary human gurgle of panicked asphyxiation.

The man tilts his head to one side, chiding her as he releases her nose. "You did that to yourself."

Though her nasal passage is clear, Marie can still feel the mucus-soaked gauze threatening to block her airway again. She breathes slow, shallow. Her heart beats so hard that every palpitation ticks a filament of cloth fiber against the roof of her throat, like a clock's steadily ticking hand. A warm sensation steals the strength of her arms and thighs, tingles beneath the flesh of her knees, makes her shoulders go slack.

Tears roll from Marie's wet eyes, so dense that she feels them pool in the folds of her ear.

"It's okay," the man says with the kindness of a mother soothing her child. Marie has spoken in this voice before, many, many times over. Has said a hundred times over the very words the lumbering giant says to her then. "You don't have to be afraid."

What he adds to those words sends a serpent of ice slithering through her brain.

"You don't have to be afraid of anything ever again."

The man turns. The scrubs pinched between the folds of his abdomen rustle, the sound muted against the white padded walls of the converted truck. "Science has given us the cure for fear and sorrow, pain and remorse."

She hears the hard, smooth sound of metal instruments sliding together. Eyes scanning her surroundings to find some possibility of escape, her ears prick up at the distinct sucking murmur of a small, empty vessel drawing liquid into itself.

The man spins around with a gleeful flourish, happiness on his face. A syringe, beaded wet at the needle's invisible terminus, looks small, almost inconsequential, in his pudgy hand. "And the best part," he says, delicately turning the dripping needle tip toward Marie's eye. "Is that you don't have to feel a thing."

Before she can twist her gaze away, the man makes a band of his strong hand, clamping it across her forehead. Thumb and middle finger mash into Marie's temples, the strength greater than a vise.

The needle pierces above her eyebrow, puncturing her sinus. The plunger sinks at the pressure of his thumb, and the liquid rush of its contents chills Marie to the skull. The relief of the needle sliding out is the second-to-last ecstasy she will ever feel. The last ecstasy comes just after the last tear her left eye will ever produce. This happens when the needle slides into her tear duct, spraying a numbing agent into the reservoir. Marie's eye rolls slack inside its socket.

Her tongue slides against her cheek, dormant in her mouth.

Now it is Marie, experiencing both complete relaxation and child-like terror, who sees things at a distance.

Feels, as if from a distance inside herself, the pressure of the slender icepick-like tool sliding coldly into the imperceptible gap between the ball of her eye and the bone of her nasal cavity. Feels, from so far away, the claw-hammer strike the end of the pick. She hears, wanting to scream louder and louder, the autumn-leaves crunch of the pick perforating a place inside her that has never once been touched.

Inside the imaginary mental place where Marie hides her secrets, her loves, and her deep passion for her wife, children, and musical films, she is screaming a prayer to any and every listening deity with the power to intervene.

A loud, booming sound breaks the silence. A hand, heavy on the bay door of the truck.

The man lording over Marie snaps his moonstone gaze to the sound's origin. Though his placid demeanor remains, from somewhere deep inside this creature comes the bestial growl of the predator inside him.

In silence, he waits.

Marie screams her prayer louder, saying the names of her children over and over in supplicant plea.

Again, the door booms with the hand of someone who has taken interest in this storage truck that must be, Marie thinks, sitting in the parking lot next to the Dauphin Theater. A police officer or a concerned passerby. Someone, Marie hopes—anyone—willing to be everything she needs them to be right now.

Right here.

The man releases his grip on the pick, leaving it jutting upthrust from Marie's eye socket as he walks toward the back of the storage truck. Marie, motionless, listens.

An old lever lifts.

The door groans.

"What is it," her captor says.

The words that follow are colder than the steel against her skull.

"Is it over yet?" A woman's voice. There is concern there, none of it for Marie.

"Not much longer. She's ready now."

"I don't want to rush you, but—"

"Five more minutes."

The door groans.

An old lever falls.

The man returns to supine Marie. With a deep sigh, he takes hold of the pick handle and draws it the metal—warm, red, and wet.

"Now," the man says, turning one last time back to the little bench behind him.

Marie does not see the little barbed hook in his hand. Feels, from an impossibly wide mental distance, the long invasive hook slide into the gap beneath flesh and bone.

Marie's head bumps up and down, up and down as the man's arm pumps in quick, short strokes. Then, turning the hook, he leans himself forward, pushing his tremendous weight into the final strokes that shear away Marie Evans.

Strokes that steal who she was, who she is, and who she might have become in the sweet, golden years she had been so ready to explore.

The husk of Marie Evans is settled on a park bench, surgical mask looped back around her ears. She hears, unable to listen, the storage truck rumbling into the night.

Time passes. The sun rises, shining gold and bright on Marie's vacant face, unable to comprehend its color or beauty. Unable to connect with the heart-lifting majesty as it rises like a celestial king between the blue, white-capped mountain spires so gloriously crowning the horizon.

At a distance, Marie Evans is sitting on a park bench.

But that is at a distance.

There was a time before when she enjoyed the park. The bench. The sunlight.

But she is not that woman anymore.

She will never be that woman again.

A Sunny Disposition

By Josh Malerman

The old, dying living room smelled of butterscotch candies because Grandma Meryl always had a bowl of them out, unwrapped, to scent the space, an air-freshener before such things were invented, a custom kept until her death. Having died only a month ago, the candies were a custom unchanged by Grandpa Ray, who hadn't swapped out the butterscotch cubes she'd left behind. Grandpa, who at this very moment, sat erect and still in his long lived-in easy chair. It was a chair his grandson Benji didn't like the smell of, an admission that angered Benji's mother and caused Benji's father to snicker, the way the boy complained of the smell of that chair and the eeriness of sitting alone with Grandpa Ray, as if the old man was a monster.

Benji sat alone with him now.

Grandpa wore a sleep mask like a signature blindfold, a thing he'd worn since having his eye trouble about the same exact time Grandma Meryl passed. Grandpa Ray didn't die, no—no lover's broken-heart to kill him—but eye trouble plagued him all the same, as if he could no longer stand to see the world without his wife of fifty-five years beside him. Both eyes did die, and as much as Benji didn't like the mask, at least Grandpa wasn't sitting in the easy chair with two huge holes in his face as the radiator whirred and trucks passed on Dillon Street here in Chaps, Michigan, in the year 2022.

Benji sat on the couch. The couch didn't smell much better than Grandpa's chair, but at least it smacked more of Grandma, that sweet, smiling woman, who to Benji, always seemed like the living color blue—Grandpa was like a deep brown or dark green. Grandma was always the daytime sky above Grandpa's dark woods.

Grandpa hadn't moved since Mom and Dad left for the afternoon movie and he hadn't said farewell to them when they left. Benji was used to this. He'd spent many afternoons and evenings at his grandparents' house when Mom and Dad went to a movie or to the store or, as Grandpa one time joked but also maybe didn't joke, to a hotel. But any good cheer in this house had died with Grandma, even a kid like Benji could sense that much, and staying put with Grandpa didn't mean what Grandpa-visits meant to other kids at school—those who spoke of puzzles, and playing catch in the yard, and long, interesting stories. These days, Benji just sat on the couch and waited for Mom and Dad to return, just like he waited now.

Benji sat quiet and still, inert on the couch, his shoes not quite reaching the carpeted floor, while Grandpa remained erect in his flannel shirt and dark jeans, his body seemingly melded to that easy chair, his shirt and pants sunken into the folds and shadows of the seat, Grandpa Ray's head set atop those shadows and cloth like a bust, the sockets of his eyes hidden behind the black sleep mask with the tiny lettering at the bottom corner:

LUCILLE CHAPS HOSPITAL

Benji tried not to look at him. But how? It was either the old man in the mask, or the chipped doorway that led in and out of this living room, or the radiator. The old man might as well have been a statue, as stoic as the ones at the foot of the Cyril Museum steps downtown. Best not to check the shadows for Grandpa Ray's breathing. Better to eye the old, boxy television on the floor across the carpeted living room. Benji knew how to turn the thing on, how to turn the volume quiet enough so as not to disturb Grandpa Ray. The set was old, ancient for modern sensibilities, but Benji had seen Grandma work the device, and he had since worked it himself many times.

He slid off the couch, felt the soft cushion of the carpet, crossed the space, and got on his knees before the black screen, all the while begin as quiet as he knew how to be, which was both considerable and also prone to mistakes. He was a kid, after all.

His finger upon the button, he saw himself reflected in the glass. Saw Grandpa Ray lean forward in the reflection too.

"Benji, grandson. You wanna see something?"

Benji turned quick to face him.

"I thought..."

"I'll show you something," Grandpa Ray said. "Because if I don't show someone, I'll go mad."

Benji had seen Grandpa get mad before. There used to be some yelling in this house.

"Sure, Grandpa Ray."

"Alright. But don't scream or cry when I show you," Grandpa said. His hand rose quick then from those ink-like shadows, and his big, discolored fingers removed the sleep mask from his face.

Instinctively, Benji closed his eyes.

"Look!" Grandpa Ray said.

Benji looked.

There were no empty sockets bored into Grandpa Ray's face.

"What do you think?" Grandpa said.

Benji couldn't bring himself to think. For a confusing second, he almost smiled. Almost said, *Grandpa! You can still see!* But something was off. As if Benji wasn't looking at Grandpa Ray, exactly. It was more like a living cartoon sitting in that smelly old easy chair. With wrinkles too deep to be real. And eyes too big—

"They aren't mine," Grandpa Ray said, his voice suddenly too loud, too creaky, too close. "And they're a little too big, aren't they?"

Benji only nodded, despite being unsure if Grandpa could see him or not. *Too big* was the right way to say it. Yes. The eyes were too big for Grandpa Ray's face. Too big and too blue.

"You're not saying anything," Grandpa Ray said, his ear cocked, as if listening for Benji. And that's when Benji understood that these eyes could not see.

"It's just as well," Grandpa said. He tilted his head, and the eyes remained unblinking, fixed, like the eyes of a statue, or a drawing, unchanging. Thick folds of skin circled the eyes, looking as if the eyes had been forced into those sockets. "I think it's the preservation method. The lamination was too thick. Still…they're mine now." Then, "Come on, Benji. Sit on the couch. Let me tell you a story."

Benji was too afraid to move. Grandpa Ray turned his face from side to side, and those big, blue orbs acted like headlights, unused, unilluminating.

"*Do it*," Grandpa said, his voice stern, rigid.

Benji, hot and embarrassed, got up and crossed the space, giving Grandpa Ray a wide berth on his way past the easy chair. He had to climb up the couch to get to sitting again.

Grandpa Ray turned his face Benji's way.

"You can't tell your father what I'm about to say. And you sure as hell can't tell your mother. Do you understand, Benji? Answer me or you're gonna make Grandpa mad."

"Yeah," Benji said.

"Yeah what?"

"Yeah."

"Yeah what, Benji?"

"I won't tell."

Grandpa nodded, and those big, lifeless eyes moved in step with his head.

"That's good, because I'm too old to go to prison. I wouldn't survive the drive there, I don't think." He brought those fingers to his face and Benji saw the mask still hung from them by the thin string strap. "I spent time in prison before. Did you know that Benji?"

"No."

"Well, you should. There's a lot you should know about your grandparents, because it's this kind of stuff that leaks out and becomes mystery, and when mysteries can't be solved, when the main players aren't alive anymore to tell you the answers, those mysteries start to haunt you. You ever feel haunted, Benji?"

Those blue eyes. Unblinking. Aimed at the carpet at the base of the couch now.

Benji moved his legs a little further away.

"No," Benji said.

"That's good. But that won't last. You'll come to be haunted by a lot of things the older you get. Each year brings another haunting, until you got forty, fifty, sixty, seventy, a hundred things you try not to think about." He leaned forward and more of him emerged from the easy chair shadows. More of that easy chair smell emerged, too. "But it's never a ghost that haunts you, Benji. It's other people, and your relationship to them, and how they see the world and how you don't. You know anything about perception?"

Benji only shook his head no. The word was too big for him.

"Do you?" Grandpa asked, anger in the two syllables.

Benji imagined Grandpa, as he was now, but in prison. Imagined those eyes behind bars.

"No, I don't," Benji said.

"That's the fault of your short-sighted parents. I'd expect as much from Steve, but not my own daughter. Your mother should know better. Perception is king. Your worldview and how you think about yourself is how your life goes. You ever think about yourself?"

Grandpa tilted his head at an up-angle, waiting for an answer.

"No."

"Come again?"

"Yes."

"Well, which is it."

"I don't know."

Grandpa Ray grunted and Benji knew he hadn't answered correctly. But the truth was, he *did* think about himself, all the time.

"Yes," he said. "I think about myself all the time."

"'Course you do. Everybody does. And if you're the kind of person who likes what he sees, if you like yourself, if you give yourself the benefit of the doubt, you're less likely to get angry at the world around you. You're less likely to cast blame."

A noisy truck rumbled by on Dillon Street, striking the uneven concrete Benji knew well from coming and going to Grandpa and Grandma's house (only Grandpa's house now) throughout the years.

"I've never liked myself," Grandpa Ray said. The words made Benji uneasy. What did this mean? "From back when I was your age, I liked nothing about myself, because I saw I didn't have anything special to offer. Now...there are friends and family who will tell a person like me that he is wrong in coming to this conclusion, that he is being hard on himself, that he *is* special. But I knew then and I know now that if there are going to be extraordinary people in this world, there must be ordinary people too. Lots of them. Are you special, Benji?"

Grandpa Ray turned his face toward Benji in full, but the dead eyes seemed to be looking at the windows beyond and the lowered blinds, as if he was finally reacting to the truck of moments ago.

"I don't know," Benji said.

"Your Grandma. Meryl. *She* was extraordinary."

Grandpa Ray looked toward the entrance to the living room, almost as if expecting someone to enter. The radiator purred and the street outside was quiet.

Grandpa Ray smiled and it made Benji shiver.

"It's the reason I fell in love with her. Her optimism. Her sunny side, which was all sides. It sounds like a fairy tale now, but I met your grandmother on the side of the road. My car had broken down and I was under the hood fixing it, and she pulled up in her old Buick, all alone, and she asked me if I needed any help. I told her I knew how to fix my car, and she smiled and drove off. But not far. This was all out on the Chaps-Samhattan exchange before it was called that. I figured her for a Samhattanite heading into Chaps for some shopping, and I didn't think much more on it till she pulled back up, seconds later, and said, 'You may not need help fixing the car, but everybody could use some conversation.' She parked ahead of me on the side of the road and got out and came and leaned on the side of my Chevy and just started... talking. And do you know what she talked about, Benji?"

"Perception?" Benji asked.

Grandpa turned to face him now. One of the eyes had gone a little uneven and Benji thought of a poorly made stuffed rabbit.

"That's right. That's exactly right," Grandpa Ray said. "Goddammit, if kids don't say the smartest things. *Perception*, indeed. Your grandmother started talking about how everything's in the mind. How your entire day is shaped by how you react to the events of the day. She asked me to imagine that everything was all right, that every worry I had wasn't as much trouble as I thought it was. I told her I didn't know if I knew how to do that, and she asked me to pretend. So, I pretended. And I saw things as she wanted me to see them. And she asked, 'Did you feel it?' 'Feel what?' I asked back. And she said, 'You know exactly what. You felt it. I saw it in your posture. You felt good. You felt light.' And she was right. I *had* felt light. For those two seconds, I felt weightless and like the problems that so consumed me were all fixable. Now, you might've got a taste of this in your time with her, but believe me when I tell you this is a *rare* trait in a person. But Meryl was like that from the start. And so, we got to dating, we fell in love, and through it all, Meryl spoke endlessly of how to solve problems and how, two years from now, two years from any day, when you look back, whatever you thought your problems were, would be problems no more. That was Meryl's 'Two Year Rule.' Two years ago, you thought your mistakes would ruin you. But they didn't. Two years ago, you thought you had lost it all, but you hadn't. Two years ago, all of life and living was hell, and here now, you got a whole new version of Hell, and that old Hell has been forgotten. And so why wouldn't this current version be one day forgotten too? Oh, Benji. She went *on* with this. Over time, through the years, even as we had children, as we had your mother, even after your Uncle Gary died."

Benji recalled the look in his mom's eyes when she told him about Uncle Gary.

"I know your mother told you about your uncle dying when he was a child no older than you. I also know she couldn't possibly have conveyed the true horror of such a thing. She's never experienced the loss of a child, so she can't know how to describe it. But let me tell you, it was a hell much wider and more barren than any I knew before. A landscape bereft of all hope and happiness. It'd be a terrible experience for anyone, but most certainly for the parents. Right?"

Benji nodded even though Grandpa Ray couldn't see him.

"Right?" he asked again.

"Right."

"Well, one would think, Benji. *One would think.* But Meryl… she cried for a couple days and then reacted no worse than if we'd been too late for a play and weren't granted entrance because of it. She turned sunny on me, Benji, at a time when I knew no sun existed. Your grandmother talked of time and timing and how bad things are part of this cycle of life and how even parents have to be prepared to continue, not only for the remaining child—your mother—but for each other—Meryl and me. She smiled as she spoke, and I detected zero bullshit in her face. That woman had moved on, Benji. That woman had assimilated this horror the same way she had every other nasty event we'd lived through, as if her Two Year Rule had been reduced to two days. And forever after, whenever Gary's name came up, Meryl would just smile sympathetically and wink at me, as if to silently say, *We made a good one with Gary. We had a victory there.*"

"Where did you get your eyes?" Benji asked.

He hadn't meant to blurt it out, but the words had been rising in him for some time.

Grandpa Ray waited a minute before responding, but when he did, he didn't totally answer the question.

"You know where I got 'em. You just don't know how yet." He cleared his throat and Benji nearly jumped at the sound.

"Fifty-five years this continued," Grandpa Ray said. "If we fell behind on bills, she said *don't worry.* When the crime went up in our neighborhood, she said *don't worry.* When your mother struggled with her grades, *don't worry.* When money was tight, things broke down, the house was falling apart, *don't worry.* When I worried? *Don't worry.* When I got sick with pneumonia? *Don't worry.* When the world seemed to be falling apart, what with wars and lunatic politicians, terrible horror stories from across the globe, global warming, *don't worry*. And mind you, Meryl didn't fake this. Understand, Benji, she spoke from as real a place as any cynic you'll ever meet, and you're sure to meet many. And the more I came to realize that this wasn't a façade, the more I determined that her optimism wasn't coming from an insecure place, and that it wasn't hiding some deep, dark truth—that this was her true nature!—the more envious I became. Do you understand what I mean by that?"

"You wanted to be like her."

Grandpa Ray laughed.

"*Yes.* I wanted to be like your Grandma Meryl. I wanted so badly to be just like her, to react to things the way she reacted, to say the things she said, to mean the things she meant, and to see the world the way she saw it."

Benji looked to the carpet and when he looked back up, Grandpa Ray's big blue eyes were fixed on his own.

Benji stifled a gasp.

"We got sick about the same time," Grandpa Ray said. "You know this. I'm sure your mother and father were all abuzz with it. I got sick with my eyes, and Meryl got something worse. And even as her time was coming up, even as she lay upon her deathbed—just a floor above where you sit right now, Benji—she spoke of our accomplishments, our victories, the goodness in our lives. She was optimistic even then." He waited a beat, then added, "It drove me mad, Benji. Do you know what I mean by that?"

Benji couldn't speak. Those eyes. Unblinking.

"And do you know what fifty-five years of envy can do to a person?" Grandpa Ray asked. "I'm telling you this because if I don't tell *somebody*, I might lose my mind entirely, and you're the perfect person to confess to. You're just a kid. Nobody will believe you when you tell them that your Grandpa took your Grandma's eyes and jammed them into his own face."

"I gotta go to the bathroom," Benji said.

Grandpa Ray smiled. "No you don't," he said. "You need to stay seated. Right there. And you need to listen to what I have to say. What good would her eyes do for me if I got them after she died? What good would dead eyes do me? Do you get it, Benji? I needed to see the world through Meryl's eyes. I needed to see the colors she saw. I needed to see how war and pestilence and famine and murder looked to *her*, not to some long dead objects on a hospital tray."

Benji was crying. No way to stop it.

"She'd already purchased for me a set of glass eyes," Grandpa Ray said, "because of what was happening with me. Because she was exactly the kind of person to tell a man who was about to lose both eyes that he need not worry, two more were on the way. But once those glass eyes arrived, I knew exactly what needed to be done." He paused to stare, it seemed, at Benji. "She was awake when I took hers. There was no smile then, Benji. She didn't tell me not to worry *then*, Benji. She cried out as I tore 'em from her face, and she died as I jammed the glass replacements into the bloody holes in her head."

The front door opened, and Benji jumped at the sound.

Mom and Dad were back from the movie.

Benji jumped down from the couch and ran to the living room entrance, arriving just as his parents got there.

"Benji!" Dad exclaimed. "Christ! You look like you just ran a marathon."

"Did Grandpa Ray wear you out?" Mom asked.

She looked over Benji's head to Grandpa Ray on the old easy chair.

The old man sat still as a statue, the sleep mask squarely over his eyes.

"Hi, Dad," she said.

"How was the movie?" Grandpa Ray asked.

"It was whatever," Dad said.

"I liked it," Mom said. "You hungry, Dad?"

"Yes. Benji and I did nothing but talk. This kid, I tell you, he says the craziest things. Wish I could tell stories like he does."

"Mom..." Benji said.

Mom smiled down at him. "Let's make some lunch together," she said.

Dad was already in the kitchen, opening the refrigerator, when Mom joined him.

Benji looked back to Grandpa Ray in the chair. From the shadows that pooled at the old man's right arm came the old man's right hand, and in that hand, two blue eyes, both aimed, it seemed, directly at Benji.

Grandma's blue eyes. Preserved.

"You two want sandwiches?" Dad called from the kitchen.

On further inspection, it appeared to Benji that the eyes his Grandpa held were aimed at a spot just below Benji's nose, as if Grandpa Ray were staring at Benji's mouth.

"*Mom!*" Benji called, his voice trembling. He ran to be with his parents, leaving the blind old man behind.

"Easy," Dad said, as Benji crashed up against his legs near the kitchen table.

From the living room, came Grandpa Ray's voice, speaking just loud enough for those in the kitchen to hear. "There's no greater gift than a sunny disposition. And for those who it was not given, it's taken."

"Jeez, Dad," Mom called over her shoulder from the kitchen counter. "You sound like Mom."

Down the Road You Might Change Your Mind

By S. P. Miskowski

These angels were made of fire, and they swirled up in the air like they were dancing, like they were crazy from the heat all the way across the red rock face of the canyon. Their wings flared as high and wide as clouds at sunset...

When I was little, I used to see things sideways. My mom took me to have my eyes tested, but my vision was fine. The doctor winked and said my eyesight was two steps behind my imagination. Mom said I made things up.

My imagination made these leaps without trying. A saguaro casting its shadow across a moonlit road was a Skinwalker. A runaway German Shepherd sneaking through our neighborhood at dawn was a werewolf looking for a place to hide, to shed its fur and return to human form. Nearly every day, I'd spot a thing that became something else in my mind.

Dad called me a natural storyteller. I said I took after him, but he said he was a gambler, and I'd better not ever take after a gambler.

He was always looking for fun, but he didn't like to hang around with his co-workers from the shop. He only had one friend, and that friend's nickname was Slick. The thing was, Slick was really a bunch of different guys, one after the other. He was a tall ginger-haired man my dad met while doing some drywall installation for cash. Then he was a ranch hand Dad met at the Rusty Spur, where fistfights broke out from time to time over old grudges and older girlfriends. Later, Slick was the skinny convenience store clerk with shaky hands who never stopped by without a carton of Pall Mall Golds under one arm, as a gift.

There were others, over the years. Some of these men were smart. Some were lazy. Some were funny. Some were wise. All were called Slick and never answered to any other name, as far as I can remember. Each one appeared out of the blue, and when he left, he never came back.

On weekends, Dad and Slick would "make a run" somewhere. The way they talked, they could've been Butch and Sundance riding off to buy supplies and hole up in a cave for the winter.

Almost every barbecue at our house prompted one of these adventures. It was here that a dozen or so adults sat slouched in folding chairs on the patio, where they smoked and talked. Mom set the picnic table while Dad poked a barbecue fork at a row of burgers sizzling on the grill.

The men stood around drinking Coors. The metal clack of crushed aluminum sounded every time an empty can hit the others piled high inside a nearby trash bag.

Me and Melody and Fran Dixon from across the street practiced cartwheels on a patch of dry grass between the concrete and the withered mulberry tree Dad was supposed to cut down every year.

At some point, Slick would take a drag on his cigarette, exhale a long strand of smoke, and say, "Hey, Roy. What say we make a run up to The Vegas tonight?"

The suggestion wasn't as glamorous as it might sound. In 1978, old people went to Vegas to gamble their last fifty bucks and die between hotel sheets. People went for the booze, the slot machines, the bright lights, and naked women.

This was Vegas before its facelift in the 1980s, before it was transformed into a twenty-first century caricature of itself. Back when I'm talking about, nobody took their wife and kid on vacation there. Guys like my dad and Slick would camp out in the truck when they weren't gambling or drinking. Dad hated motels.

I was fried after a long day of work and just about to nod off when I heard that sh-sh-sh sound under the bed and then all around it. Cockroaches! That's the first time I'd thought of it in weeks, that broken-apart thing we found by the side of the road in Kingman, crawling, leaving a blood trail in the dust...

There was never a doubt about whether Dad and Slick would take that drive. Once they mentioned it, we knew they'd be gone before we woke up next morning. Mom would remind Dad how he promised to fix the radiator in her car, or the swamp cooler, or the gate to the alley, while knowing he would never make it back before the weekend was over. Whatever chores he left unfinished would have to wait another week, and maybe another.

While the neighbors ate their burgers and wandered to the edges of the yard to gossip, my dad would promise again to repair everything as soon as he got back. Then Dad and Slick would talk about this side job or that, some house painter or a bricklayer they'd never work with again, or some rich lady, a singer up on Camelback who wanted her high-maintenance lawn dug up and replaced with gravel.

After a while, with nods and side glances, they'd settle on an excuse: they had a friend named Dewey or Donny who lived just outside Vegas and needed their help. The more cans of Coors they drank, the more a "quick trip" seemed like it was necessary, maybe even a matter of grave urgency.

My mom always ended up handling the grill on her own after the first six pack was finished, a metal spatula in one fist and the other hand free to flick her long ponytail over her shoulder each time it slid loose.

"Violet," my dad would say to her. "You know me, Vi. You know good and well I can't leave an old friend like—uh."

"Dewey Grainger," Slick would chime in.

"Good old Dewey!" Dad would shout, eyes pink as a rabbit's, blinking against the late afternoon sun. "I can't leave old Donny twisting in the wind, like. He's got to fill in that irrigation ditch before his boy comes for a—you know—custody visit. It's… dangerous. Could be a life-or-death situation for a small child!"

Mr. and Mrs. Clark from next door would nod thoughtfully. The Dixons would smile awkwardly, satiated with grilled beef and free beer.

By nightfall, the neighbors were gone. Mom cleaned the grill and went to bed after agreeing to let Melody sleep over. Fran was too silly and too young for pajama parties, her mother said. We finished off our sodas and chips in our T-shirts and underwear, watching *The Bionic Woman* on the portable TV in my room.

Dad sat out back in his lawn chair, arms and legs flung wide, head back, snoring like a jackhammer while Slick finished off the beer and, I guess, kept watch. This was the cheaper tail-end of Scottsdale, between the reservation on Pima Road and the Motorola plant on McDowell—technically speaking, the suburbs. No wild animals were likely to come drag my dad away, but Slick kept an eye out just in case.

We were leaving Cottonwood, and the gray-purple clouds hung low over Mingus Mountain. Giant shadows climbed over the peak and then down, down that mountainside towards the main road, towards us...

Back when I was little, just barely walking and talking, me and my dad were pals. Mom, camera shy and not easily talked into stuff she didn't want to do, was the family photographer. Her photo album is proof. In one photo, we're in the backyard together. Dad is loading a six shooter while three-year-old me is taking refuge behind a palm tree and peeking out. Both of us are wearing cowboy hats and belts with holsters.

He signed the back of that picture with our names and the date. I only discovered that a while back when I took it out of the album for the first time.

We had our own language back then. Our own signals and private jokes. Some of it was inspired by cartoon characters like Yosemite Sam, and some was just the way my dad talked. I don't remember all of it.

The first time he brought Slick home, I was in kindergarten. Mom wore her nurse's uniform because her shift ended right before dinner, and she didn't have time to change. She set out enough beans and pork to make burritos for an army. But it was all for Slick, who must've eaten five by the time he noticed me giving him the dirtiest look I could manage.

"I don't think your youngster there approves of my table manners," said Slick. He picked up the paper napkin next to his plate and passed it from one hand to the other, delicately dabbing his fingers clean.

"She takes after her mom," Dad told him. "Kind of shy. Just ignore it."

This was the first time he talked that way in front of me. But it wasn't the last. Whenever we were alone together, Dad and I shared all kinds of stories and jokes. We would even pull pranks on Mom, like hiding her uniform in the freezer until she yelled at us to give it back. But the minute Slick showed up, he commanded all my dad's attention.

There were gaps between some of the versions of Slick. Maybe a few weeks or a month would go by, and Dad would drink less and fill his spare time with little jobs around the house. He put up new blinds in the bedrooms, replaced the cranky swamp cooler with a newer model, and painted the garage door.

If Mom could get another nurse to fill in for one of her shifts, we would take a day trip. One time, we three took a tour of Arcosanti, which is a village built by an Italian architect. Artists go there to live and study and make pottery.

Dad bought Mom a set of the bells Arcosanti was famous for. He could've picked them up at a department store closer to home but buying a set right out of the artist's hands made it more special, Mom said.

"Special lady, special gift," Dad said. Mom smiled and said nothing.

He always had a trinket for me when he came back from his trips: a lock of hair braided with a strand of red silk; a gambling chip; a tiny cactus garden; a hand-tooled leather change purse. As I got older, the gifts became more expensive, more like the stuff I'd seen in roadside souvenir shops. And the trips with Slick took longer and longer.

A wino living in Tucson claimed he witnessed a man that walked on his knuckles, ambling across a dark road one night.

He caught a glimpse of this thing in his headlights. It had arms about eight feet long, and itty-bitty legs. It froze there on the road and stared for a whole minute at the wino and his wife. Then the wind picked up. The wino said you could smell the tang of mesquite all around, and that creature, it jumped up in the air and flew off into the desert...

Things got bad with Mom when Dad and Slick started taking longer trips. She worked her shift at the hospital and got home at dawn. She'd sit out on the patio, smoking. Sometimes the next-door neighbors would turn on their outdoor lights until she went inside and crawled into bed. But if Mrs. Clark ever asked where Dad was, or how things were going, it made Mom angry.

"Damn nosy bitch," Mom would mutter while packing my lunch for school.

"She's trying to be nice," I'd say.

"You don't know what nice is," she told me.

I thought about that for a long time. Melody would often say my dad's friends were dumpy, they didn't dress nice. I'd stopped hanging around with Melody at this point, partly for comments like this, and partly because she was sucking up to Chastity van Fleet, who lived next door to her and whose parents owned the only swimming pool on our street.

There were early-morning phone conversations between my parents. Mom would ask Dad when he was coming home. He would answer, and she would yell at him and tell him he was going to lose his job, which he finally did. After that, he had to beg favors for the side jobs he hated so much. We stopped having barbecues, stopped traveling as a family.

By now I was starting middle school. I'll never forget the last adventure I went on with Dad. It was going to be exactly what I'd hoped for. The trip of a lifetime.

"We don't need a tent," he had told me. "Your mom's the one that likes all the fancy equipment. Hell, we can sleep in the truck bed on some blankets and watch the stars all night. We'll drive straight up to Utah. There's nothing more beautiful than

Monument Valley; not in the whole world, not anywhere. It's better than the Grand Canyon! You'll see."

I knew he'd had a few drinks already. He used to stow these tiny bottles of vodka in his pockets and the glove compartment of his truck. Any time he needed a pick-me-up and didn't have time to guzzle a beer, he'd hit one of those bottles and swallow it in one gulp.

Mom was working a day shift at the time. She would never have let me go if she had been around.

Dad and I tossed a few shirts, a basket full of fruit, and a couple sandwiches in the cab, climbed in, and were off down the road. It felt like we were a couple of bandits. The desert belonged to us.

By the time we reached Cottonwood, we had stopped at least six times. One time was to pee. One time was for Dad to make a phone call at a rest stop. Then we started pulling over at every Motor Inn or Denny's we saw.

During these stops, I waited in the truck. I figured he was calling Mom to update her on where we were and how long we would be gone. But I was wrong.

"There's been a slight change of plans." He stood next to the truck, hitching his saggy jeans up, smiling for the first time all day.

He reached into his shirt pocket and pulled out a tiny bottle, didn't try to hide it when he took a swig. I sat there, window down, taking in the smoky blue of a mountain ridge in the distance. Taking in all I could.

"How long is it to the Utah border?" I asked, denying the obvious for as long as possible.

"Well, now," he said, and swayed a bit. He rested one elbow on the window frame and thought for a second. "See, what just came up is what you might call a sort of emergency. Old friend of mine by the name of Donny..."

I didn't hear the rest. I knew it was a lie, just like I knew he wasn't calling Mom every time we pulled over. All those rest stops and diner parking lots, where I sat in the warm midday air, with trucks and cars speeding by, kicking up gravel. People going places.

"Your mom's sister, Gloria, lives two miles away. I can take you there." He didn't look at me when he said this.

"You're not driving me home?" I asked. I noticed my voice was flat and dry, the way Mom sounded every time she hung up after one of their phone calls. I think one day she decided she was done, and never looked back. I don't know how she did that.

Sullen and hungry, I sat with my arms crossed over my chest. I watched dry batches of quail bush flash by. I listened to the radio. Willie Nelson was singing, "You'll Never Know." Some preacher talked about saving the children. I didn't care about any of it.

Dad dropped me off at Aunt Gloria's house, a pretty cottage decorated with wildflowers. She gave me a hug and said we were going to have fun. Then she handed me a coloring book and a box of Crayola crayons. Her miniature poodle danced at my feet like I was the only visitor he'd ever seen.

"Good riddance," she mumbled as she closed the door and Dad burned rubber getting out of there and back on the road. "Never mind. Violet's coming to pick you up tomorrow."

I colored all the cartoon characters purple. I sat beside my aunt on the sofa while she watched Julia Child bake a souffle on TV. Her poodle wriggled around beside me and tried to stick its tongue in my ear.

On Sunday, Mom arrived. We ate breakfast and then headed back south. She kept asking what I was thinking, going off like that. Asked if Dad was out of his mind. Asked where the hell were we going, and how could I forget to let her know where I was. On and on. I fell asleep.

That night, in bed, I imagined the wonders of Monument Valley. Giant red rocks, rising on all sides of me. I imagined myself in the bed of my dad's truck, gazing up at constellations that sparkled above in the cold night sky.

We didn't hear from Dad for three weeks. When he finally called, he said he wasn't coming back. Somehow knowing I might not see him again brought back memories of all the stupid little things I'd taken for granted. The stubble on his chin turning gray. The softened felt of his cowboy hat—a relic from his youth as a ranch hand. The deep rumble of his voice on the two occasions

I'd heard him sing along to the radio. The clink of the tiny bottles in his pockets.

Late at night, while waiting for Mom to come home from work, I'd lie awake and listen to the scratch of a creosote bush against the windowsill. Dad always said it would bring us luck and make me strong against allergies. Like everything else, it was just a stupid lie.

I kept the portable TV going for company. I'd doze off and then wake up to a movie about a mad scientist being torn apart by his monsters, or to a news report about a bunch of children who had been abducted and tortured, or to a late-night ad for the newest horror flick. (I begged Mom to let me go with Melody and her parents to see *The Hills Have Eyes* at the local drive-in. She said I wasn't allowed to see "that awful thing," and the Dixons were crazy to let their daughter see it. "It's going to scar that girl for life.") Mostly I drifted, half-asleep, floating above the desert, dreams soundtracked by the quiet hiss of white noise from my TV after the networks signed off.

One of my chores was raking the yard where the Clarks' bougainvillea fell on our side of the fence. I was doing just that the day that Mrs. Clark pushed open our unlocked gate and walked into our yard. It was this kind of behavior that made my mom avoid her. But Mom wasn't home.

"You're such a big help to your mother," she told me. There was a sick sweetness in her voice, like the tone you might use to praise a dog. "I bet she's glad she has a daughter."

"Why?" I asked. I remembered the time my dad had said I was almost as good as a son. Remembered how he'd forgotten my way of seeing things sideways.

Mrs. Clark blinked like a friendly owl, peeking around the yard with her glassy eyes.

"A boy your age wouldn't do all the things you do," she said. "Now that your mother's on her own."

"She's not," I blurted, reminded of how much my mother hated Mrs. Clark's nosiness.

"Oh?" She stepped closer and stuck out her chest, more curious than she wanted to let on. "You've seen your father?"

"Last night," I lied. A bright fire came alive in my heart.

"Oh, my goodness," she said, getting close, examining me with her owl eyes.

Something fluttered nearby. I imagined Mrs. Clark taking flight, soaring over the back fence, scanning the weeds around our trash dumpster. Maybe seeing her that way made the next thing easier.

I opened my mouth and words just flew out. I told her how Dad drove me out to the desert late at night. I told her about the man that had pulled up alongside us, the bed of his truck loaded with children. There were seven in all, crying, begging to go home. Dad built a fire. The other man tied one of the kids to a metal spit, and they made me watch while they roasted him alive.

Mrs. Clark's contorted features urged me to keep going. She was a grownup. She could have called me a liar. But she didn't. So, I kept going.

I told her about giant bats hidden in the canyon, and how they turned into monstrous demons. I told her about a drunk lady with bat wings who carved her name into children's faces, and the demons who tied us up and ran their tongues all over us. And how Dad helped a demon sacrifice a cow, and they all danced in the moonlight with blood smeared on their faces. And the demons dragged us one by one into a dark tent, our screams climbing into the night sky.

I still don't know where it all came from, but I did feel better after telling the story. This turned out to be a good thing, because I had to tell it again to a psychologist named Mary Frobisher. Mom was mad as hell when she found out our neighbor had taken it upon herself to call social services and the police. Mom said I was lying, but nobody listened to her.

Every adult I met paid attention to every detail I made up and seemed hungry for more. As time went on, especially after the cops located Dad in Cave Creek and dragged him to jail to await trial, I added things to my story. UFOs. Cattle mutilations. Old men in red gowns with pointy silk hats. Blood rituals with names from a Dr. Seuss book.

It didn't matter if there were no children missing who fit the descriptions I gave. It didn't matter if I had no marks of any kind to prove my ordeal. Everyone who heard my story wanted to believe me. My tale of abduction and torture fit with the nightly news reports across the country, the bestselling books about satanic rituals and repressed memories written by psychologists who were later revealed to be con artists, and the false claims made by other children who sent adults to prison.

Many of those children would eventually recant, but I never did. I listened to the defense lawyer who said, "Down the road you might change your mind. When you're grown up, you might remember things a different way." I said no at the sentencing hearing and no at the parole hearing, and I never said otherwise.

The prison where Dad ended up had a reputation for being rundown, dirty, and dangerous. Mom wouldn't go there alone, and she wouldn't let me go with anyone else. By the time I was old enough to make my own decisions, Dad was gone. Pancreatic cancer.

So, this collection is a souvenir, you might say. Here's the photo of us playing cowboys, outdoors, when I was little. On the back, Dad wrote, "Me and Slick hiding from the outlaws, 1974."

I keep the picture next to his ashes, and I keep those in a silver jar on the living room table. If I glance sideways, I almost catch him smiling in the polished surface. Besides, it feels good to know where he is.

The Other Wives

By Architа Mittra

The first thing that Lola noticed when she stepped inside Leonard's countryside mansion were the portraits of his ex-wives lining the hallway. The oil paintings were rendered in lush, provocative strokes, and glimmered as though alive. It unsettled Lola that nearly a half-dozen faces watched her with their poised expressions as if they were waiting for her to make a mistake or say something incredibly stupid. Above them, the chandeliers glared, their lights dancing off the walls and glass windows.

"Do you kill them like Bluebeard?" she asked Leonard, who had his arm possessively draped around her. She laughed weakly to indicate it was a joke.

Leonard smirked, cradling his champagne glass. "Don't worry, love," he replied. "I promise you'll meet most of them at our wedding."

Leonard made good on his promise.

At their lavish wedding, Lola wore a designer gown hand-stitched with crystals and semi-precious stones that made her feel less of a person and more of a work of art to be gawked at. And like intrepid visitors at a museum, all the ex-wives gawked at her, touched her bare arms, and caressed the crystalline embellishments that she wore.

They all introduced themselves with long, lovely names. *Esmerelda. Estella. Anamika. Helene. Sharmila. Katerina.*

Amongst their shimmering beauty, and her husband's guests of honor—guests that included several doctors and lawyers—Lola felt puny. As an orphan, Lola was raised by a distant uncle who turned her out as soon as she had come of age, so she had no close family or friends whom she could invite to the wedding. She nodded as the guests all effusively greeted her, afraid to say anything in case she mixed up their names.

Soon enough, the sea of guests parted, and Leonard was there with his customary swagger. His booming laughter filled the room, filled her ears, filled her heart with hope and adoration. He grabbed her wrist and pulled her out onto the ballroom floor for a waltz.

The venue was alive with the smell of roses, and it all made Lola's head spin. She laughed and drank and smiled and kissed Leonard, who looked at her like she was the most important work of art in his prized collection.

It made her feel very proud of herself.

Before her marriage, Lola worked in a tailor's shop. She sewed garments, measured suits, and stitched brassy buttons onto old coats. During a snowstorm, Leonard had stumbled in, seeking shelter. He'd surveyed the room with distaste, and she responded by making some pointed comments about his frayed Armani suit. For a few moments, Lola wondered if she would be the subject of this gentleman's wrath, but instead of the snobbery that was a hallmark of his class, she heard only his laughter.

"I wasn't trying to be funny," she said, now hiding behind the sewing machine.

"You amuse me," he replied, grinning. He asked her if she liked going to the movies. She nodded, then continued to thread a garment. He asked her what kind of movies she enjoyed—the science fiction types, or the sappy love stories.

"Bit of both," she said, smiling softly.

He smiled back at her. His gaze was confident and kind.

They went to all kinds of movies, and afterward, they sat in the park to discuss them while sipping milkshakes. They held hands as he walked her to her tiny apartment in the seedy part of the town. She learned that he was a medical student with grand ideas about the evolution of the human race, and she listened intently as he talked about his laboratory experiments.

When he asked her to marry him, she was utterly surprised.

"Why?" she kept asking him. "I'm a nobody. Your family will never approve of me."

He laughed. "Lucky we don't have to worry about them then. They're dead."

She looked at him with consternation. Unperturbed, he leaned in close and kissed her on the mouth.

Following their wedding and a whirlwind honeymoon across Europe, Lola's life settled down until it was a humdrum routine. As the lady of the manor, she had to oversee a small army of servants who cooked, cleaned the house, tended the gardens, and cared for their three Alsatian puppies, and took them for their daily walks. Lola tried being friendly with the maids, but they only looked at her dumbly when she talked about something other than housekeeping. She found their behavior to be rather robotic, but she was prudent enough to keep such harsh judgments to herself.

On the nights he was home, Leonard made tender love to her and told her she was very, very beautiful. But he wasn't home often. He was always off at some conference abroad, and when he did come back, he spent hours holed up in his study, talking in hushed tones to friends and colleagues who would often stop by.

"These are medical things," he told her kindly, after he found her eavesdropping. "You won't understand anything, so no use worrying your pretty head over it."

Although he trusted Lola with the house keys, there were several rooms in the mansion for which the windows were shuttered and to which the keys did not work. When Lola asked Leonard about the odd rooms, he brushed her off. "Just guest rooms that we have no use for."

"Why don't we rent them out?" she replied, gently folding his pants so that he could pack them for another trip.

Leonard was incredulous. "Love, why on Earth for?"

"For extra income, of course."

He laughed. "Darling, we have all the money in the world."

They didn't have all the money in the world. Leonard did. He brought her gifts from all the countries he visited: silk scarves, antique curios, first edition publications by some of the greatest dead thinkers, an assortment of necklaces, even strange serums in glass vials with an ouroboros symbol stamped on the labels—serums that he promised to be the latest in "anti-aging" technology.

"Say goodbye to wrinkles," he'd tell her, kissing her cheeks.

They were still very young, she thought. Too young to be worrying about wrinkles.

Not long after first using the serum, she began to hear voices in the walls. Without Leonard there to share the four-poster bed with her, or to ease her fears, she slept terribly and often woke in a cold sweat, convinced she had heard the voices screaming. Sometimes she would walk the empty house, the place alive with soft sounds, and creaks, and reverberations. At times, she was almost convinced she could hear her husband and his friends talking in hushed whispers behind the locked doors.

She mentioned her experience one time over breakfast, but instead of his usual laugh, Leonard became concerned and called in a doctor to check on her and treat her for possible hallucinations. The doctor jabbed her with a number of different needles, took a few pints of blood, and gave her a bottle of large pills that made her feel all loopy within minutes of taking them.

"I wasn't hallucinating, I swear," she protested.

The doctor and Leonard exchanged glances. "Your mind is playing tricks on you," one of them said.

That night, Leonard invited Esmerelda and Helene over for dinner. The two ex-wives were gay and flirty, and they continued to chit-chat with Leonard long after Lola had left the table, complaining of a headache.

A few days later, when Leonard asked her if she would like to go shopping with Anamika, Lola lost it. "I don't like any of them!"

"That's a pity. They quite like you, and I thought you were feeling lonely."

"I am lonely! I am your wife, but you barely spend time with me!"

"That's not fair, my love. You know how important my work is to me—"

"Yes, so important. So important, in fact, that you can't even talk to me about it."

He sighed. "You wouldn't understand, my dear. The science is just too complicated."

"Try me!" she cried.

He shook his head, saddened, and got up to leave.

"Is that why you divorced them? All your other wives. Because they asked you too many questions?"

Leonard paused, then turned to her somberly and said, "Why don't you ask them yourself?"

A few days later, Lola invited each one of Leonard's ex-wives over to the house, either for tea, or for an evening stroll in the gardens. She asked them all about Leonard.

They all had nice things to say about the man, but none knew anything about the work he did. So, Lola changed tactics and asked them about their lives instead. Once she got them comfortable and talking, she asked them why the marriage failed. Estella said they broke up because he wanted kids and she didn't. Sharmila had slept with another man. Anamika was bored of being a housewife and wanted to start her own business.

"You could still do that while being married!"

Anamika twiddled her curls nervously. Her answers were beginning to feel rehearsed. "I could…but I like my independence more."

"Then why did you marry him?"

"I was young and in love." She looked at Lola with a newfound intensity. "Rather like you."

Lola learned nothing about Leonard's work. She debated selling the expensive silverware and running away to a cottage far away.

Meanwhile, the voices in the walls grew louder.

Curiosity would not let Lola sleep. From the garden shed, she took a large axe and kept it hidden beneath her bed. She noted the license plates of the black vans sometimes parked in the driveway that Leonard said made necessary deliveries for his research. She searched into Leonard's friends online and learned they were leading scientists in their fields, all related to genetics. She even hired a locksmith to change the locks on the sealed doors, but the locksmith canceled at the last minute under mysterious circumstances.

Whenever she tried to leave the mansion, she found herself unable to do so. The servants would quickly surround her and prevent her from exiting. They would insist that with Leonard gone, it was Lola's duty to stay home and take care of things.

When Leonard returned from his business trip, she promptly asked for a divorce.

"Why?" he asked. His voice was tired and ragged from travel.

"Because all you do is lie to me. Either you tell me what I want to know, or I leave."

He stared at her for a long time. "Okay," he said.

"What do you mean, okay? I gave you two options."

"I heard you. I'll speak to my lawyer. We'll have the divorce finalized within a month."

He took leave of the bedroom without a backward glance at Lola's tear-stricken face.

• • •

That night, Lola once again stalked the darkened halls. With her ears pressed against the filigreed wallpaper, she followed the faint sound of voices all the way to the west wing, near where her husband's locked study was located.

She spotted a shadow creeping towards her and she screamed.

"Lola? What the hell are you doing out here?"

The voice belonged to Leonard's friend, Benny. He was dressed in a white lab coat, and amid the surprise, he had dropped his clipboard to the floor. The top paper contained words like "patient" and "experiment."

Even in the dark, it was apparent that something was tucked in Benny's elbow.

It was an arm! A human arm, she was certain. It appeared to be freshly amputated despite there being no sign of blood.

Lola blinked and the arm was gone.

Stranger yet, Leonard had suddenly appeared at the end of the hall, and was now rushing toward his wife.

Lola screamed at her approaching husband. "What is Benny doing here? And in the middle of the night!"

Leonard was now beside Lola and talking softly in an effort to comfort her. "He had a nasty row with his wife," he explained. "So, I let him stay over."

"And you didn't think to tell me?"

Benny just stood there, looking confused and embarrassed. Leonard walked Lola back to their room and locked her in. He apologized profusely for not informing her about Benny's situation and begged her forgiveness.

"You're lying to me again. You're both lying. You're hiding something. I can tell." She was now speaking through clenched teeth.

Leonard had filled a glass of water and was coaxing her to drink.

"Stop it!" she cried, smashing the glass to the floor. She was certain it contained a sedative.

But the glass was merely a distraction. Suddenly, she felt the sharp pinch of the syringe in her arm and saw her husband's expressionless face grow dark with the world around her.

She woke the next morning feeling sick. She recalled the strange appearance of Benny and the amputated arm, and wondered if it was all a dream. One of the maids informed her that her husband had to leave urgently for a conference, but that a lawyer would be arriving sometime in the afternoon with the divorce papers.

She knew she couldn't wait that long.

Once the maid had left, Lola retrieved her axe from beneath the bed and marched with it in trembling hands towards the west wing where the voices were always the loudest. Once at the door of her husband's study, she raised the axe and brought it down upon the locked oak barrier. She struck the door again and again, until finally, the destroyed wood fell away and Leonard's secret was revealed to her.

The wives, whose portraits all hung so pristinely in the main hallway, stood naked in glass cages looking older, thinner, and more frail than was possible. Their bodies were scarred and some were even mutilated. Two wives were awake (Lola recognized the open eyes of Anamika and Helene) but the others appeared to be asleep, even though they were standing, almost as if being held in a state of suspended animation.

"What…what is this?" she whispered.

The living corpse of Anamika was closest to her. "Why did you come here?" she cried. "Now he will never let you leave!" The sleeping wives stirred at the sound of Anamika's shrill voice.

Lola gaped in horror. "But…but I saw you…a few days back. You came over for tea. You said you're starting a business to help young women find jobs!"

"Rubbish! I've never seen you before in my life, and I'd rather never see you again! Run away! Run away as fast as you can!"

"Looks like you discovered our secret," said a familiar voice from behind Lola. It was Benny.

Lola tightened her grip on the axe.

She thought of the servants, all dead-eyed and mindless, following every instruction without complaint. She thought of the wives she'd met, and how their responses felt so rehearsed, as if they had memorized a script. She thought of Leonard and their early conversations back when they'd just begun dating, all his grand talks about evolving the human race.

Then she looked at the real wives in their cages, vulnerable and afraid. Leonard was harvesting their tissue for his experiments. He was using their bodies to make clones.

Benny took a step closer. Lola raised her axe.

"Now before you do something foolish, take a moment to appreciate all that we have achieved. All the lives we will save with organ donation. Cloning is the future, and—"

"RUN!" Anamika cried from her cage. "RUN before they turn you into one of us!"

She turned to run, but Leonard was now standing in the busted doorway.

Lola fought back her tears. "I loved you," she whispered.

"I did too," he answered. "In a way. How do you think I choose my subjects for cloning? You all are the best the world has to offer, I would know. And now the world shall have more of you."

"You monster!"

The bodies in the glass cages shivered, and the two men drew their concealed tasers. The axe in Lola's hand suddenly felt very heavy, but she wouldn't let go.

And for the first time in his life, Leonard looked at her with fear in his eyes.

Jubilee Juncture

By Nat Cassidy

The dummy sat in the corner of the room, slumped forward on its stool like a sentry asleep at its post.

The room, which stood just off the front foyer, was murky, lit only by a single floor lamp next to a small dinner table. Everything inside the room was fastidiously neat. A couch covered in plastic. An easy chair covered in plastic. Two small end tables covered by doilies.

There was one other light fixture, but it served only to underlight a single object: the large crucifix hanging on the rear wall. An enamel Christ pitched in agony over the crossbeam, and the lighting gave his martyrdom an eerie, campfire-ghost-story glow.

The shadows were heavy in this room. That's why it took Robby a few minutes to really notice the dummy after Marvin dragged him in.

"Please," Marv had pleaded on the front porch, "just let me show you; you've gotta let me show you."

"Now, come on, Marvin!" Robby wanted none of this. If he'd had his way, he would have been long gone by now. He'd dreaded coming here, and the confrontation hadn't gone any better than he'd anticipated. "I told you, I've got to go—!"

But Marvin finally grabbed Robby by the arm and pulled him through, into the foyer.

Robby hadn't liked this one bit. Now he was *inside* Marvin's house. Arguing over the threshold had been unpleasant enough, but at least that felt safer than this uncanny expanse of shadows.

Robby yanked his arm away. "Now, that's enough! Man!" Slang never suited Robby well, but what he lacked in authentic cool he made up for in sincerity. He rubbed above his elbow where Marvin's fingers had gripped. "Gee dee, Marvin, I don't want to be having this argument!"

Marvin looked legitimately cowed. "I'm sorry, I didn't mean to get physical. I just—"

"Well, you did! You *did* get physical, and now I'm upset and I don't want to be here!" Robby's face flushed from ear to ear. He checked that his soft blue linen shirt was still tucked into his pleated khakis. He was a slender man, easing into middle age, handsome in that second-tenor-in-the-choir kind of way. He was used to being an object of attention in their church's contained community, but not when it came to confrontation. He hated anger and yelling. As such, he avoided Marvin's eyes while he reprimanded him. "I told you. Begging like this isn't gonna change my mind, okay? I wish it could, but—"

Marvin, as if unable to keep from grabbing onto something, clamped his hands together this time and held them toward Robby. He was larger, with thinning hair and large wire-rimmed glasses. He wore a red plaid shirt tucked into shapeless jeans.

"Just, please. Hear me out. Please. I'm gonna put some water on for tea, and I just want us to sit and talk and figure things out. Please."

"No, Marvin."

"Please. *Please.*"

"No, Marvin!"

"Please! Pleasepleasepleasepleasepleasepleaseplease—!"

"Argh! FINE!"

"Yay!" Marvin waved his fists in the air in tight little circles. "Do you want some chicken, too? I made chicken."

"No, Marvin, I don't want your chicken!" Robby snapped. Then, because there was no excuse for rudeness, he added begrudgingly: "But thank you for offering. Ugh, I shouldn't even be here—"

"Sure you should! Sure you should! You're giving me a chance. That's what we're taught to do, right? I mean: 'Better a patient man than a warrior.' Proverbs—"

"Proverbs 16:32, yeah, yeah. What I should be doing is turning you in."

Marvin's face—normally smooth as milk and now dusted with several days' stubble—pulled down into a pout.

"Aw, man, that's really…that's really uncool, Robby. I told you—" Robby tried to speak and Marvin raised his voice over him. "*I told you my side of the story and you're not even listening to*— Look—" He exhaled, a clumsy parody of yogic breathing. "Okay. Ha. I almost forgot what I was *dragging* you in here for. Come and sit down. Is your arm okay?"

Marvin gently ushered Robby further into the sitting room—

"Yes, my arm is okay, you're not that stronGOHMYLORD! What is that?"

—and that was when Robby finally noticed it.

The shape of it, at least. From this distance, and in this murk, at first all Robby could make out was a figure sitting on a stool. The dummy had long straight hair which, in its current slumped position, covered its face like a dark curtain.

It was also huge. If you stood it upright, it'd be four feet tall at least. It was dressed in pink ruffled pajamas that looked like they'd been bought off the rack at a children's department store.

Robby's guts ran with ice water and, as he tried to make sense of what he was seeing, Marvin began to cry.

"You can't kick me off the show, Robby. I pour my heart into the show—*our* show. And you know that. Don't you? Tell me you know that."

"Yeah, I know," Robby said distantly, still staring at the figure across the room. "What's going on here? Is that a…a person?"

Marvin ignored the question. Instead, he took Robby by the shoulder and turned him so they were face-to-face.

"And you *also* know there's no one who can do what I do."

That brought Robby back a little. "Pride goeth—"

"Name one person!" Marvin's eyes sparkled with avid intensity as his damp hands crawled over Robby's shoulders. "Try it!"

But Robby couldn't. Marvin's puppetry segments on their local broadcast Christian-edutainment show *Jubilee Juncture* were beloved. They both knew it. That was part of what made this situation so difficult.

"Yeah," Marvin said smugly, after giving Robby a moment to twist in the wind. "And I've been working on a new bit! That's what I wanted to show you. I've got a new bit for the show, and it's gonna be super."

He let go of Robby and ran over to the slumped figure in the corner.

Robby couldn't help but follow a few steps.

"Wait, that's a...puppet?"

"You betcha!"

"Lord, it's pretty...uh."

Marvin bent down next to it. He lovingly moved some of its hair out of the way and now Robby was able to see the face.

It was featureless and smooth, with two round pink circles painted on its cheeks beneath two sunken black chasms for eyes. Its jaw hung slightly ajar, separated from its chin by two sharp, vertical lines.

"Pretty great, right?" Marvin cooed. "Cost me a whole heckuva lot, I'll tell you. But I don't mind. Because I put a lot into this job. I *love* it. I love the joy on their faces, I love finally feeling in control of something for once in my life. So, you can't just kick me off the show."

Robby swallowed a lump. "I was gonna say it's pretty creepy."

Marvin blinked, then looked at his doll as if for the first time. "It's creepy?"

"Yeah."

"How so?" He turned his eyes back to Robby. Again, they shone with a bizarre intensity that should have been impossible in this murky darkness.

Robby hemmed, uncomfortable. "I don't know—"

"Oh, you know what it is? It's the hair. It's got real hair." Marvin ran an appreciative hand through the long straight locks. "You don't see that so often. That's part of what makes it so special. Plus, the lighting, I'm sure that doesn't help, huh?" He gave a nervous, fluty giggle.

"Yeah, why is it so dark in here?"

"Photophobia, Robby. Light sensitivity. I can't have it too bright."

"Oh." Robby thought for a beat. "Wait, since when did y—?"

"Let me do the new act for you."

Robby curled in discomfort. "Oh, jeeeeez, Marv! You're putting me in a really rough position here! I mean, I'm doing you a favor already. I came here, as a friend, just to tell you we're not pursuing anything criminal; we're just *asking* you to, y'know, step down—"

"Listen to the act." Marvin's voice was clear and calm. Steady. No longer pleading. "It's the least you can do, Robby. Literally. It's the least. *You.* Can do."

Again, those eyes. He glared at Robby from the corner. His intent was obvious. He was playing *that* card.

Robby was stunned, although even in the moment a part of his mind reprimanded himself for not better preparing for this eventuality. Of course Marvin would bring this up. He was desperate…and he had leverage.

Robby tried to match calm for calm, hoping the dim lighting meant Marvin couldn't see his hands begin to tremble. To be safe, he rubbed them against his khakis.

"Luke 6:37, Marvin. And that was fifteen years ago. You do not get to bring that up—"

"You owe me."

"Proverbs 20:22!" Robby shot back. "Okay? I'm leav—"

"Matthew 18:21 through 35, Robby! Matthew 18:21… through 35."

The verse landed with an almost reverberant thud. Robby groaned, knowing he was beaten. He couldn't argue with Matthew 18:21 through 35.

Marvin smiled. "You'll listen to the act? Pretty please? With all sorts of confectionery on top?"

Robby seethed his assent and Marvin gave another little joyful fist shake.

"Oh! And here—!" He exclaimed, running out of the room.

Robby tried to protest but it was too late, he was suddenly alone.

No. Not alone.

That doll…

"Marvin!" Robby called, hoping his voice didn't betray how uneasy he'd become.

"Be right there, fussypants!" Marvin called. Robby heard the sound of activity in the kitchen.

He glanced at the crucifix, but he couldn't keep his eyes off the huge, slumped doll for long. There was just something so…wrong about it.

Robby inched closer, squinting.

Did…did its jaw just move slightly?

No, that was ridiculous. That'd be—

"Tada!"

Robby jumped and whipped around. Marvin was suddenly back again, standing by the table, holding a plate piled high with loose slivers of meat.

"You said you wanted chicken, right?"

He put the tray on the table.

"No, Marvin, I—"

"It's delicious. And I put water on for tea."

It did not look delicious. The meat was erratically cut and had a strange consistency. It was a darker shade than Robby usually associated with poultry, too. Or maybe that was just the lighting again? He hated eating food he couldn't see; he'd left restaurants for as much.

But Marvin wouldn't stop staring at him, so Robby sat down and picked up some thin meat with his fingers. "Why am I still here?" he muttered and popped it in his mouth.

"Because you're a good friend," Marvin said. "Really. I just appreciate it so much."

While Robby chewed (and, he was surprised to find, the chicken was sweet and tender, more like veal or pork), Marvin hurried back to the dummy. He dragged a chair over with him so he could sit alongside it.

"Why is that thing so big?" Robby asked around another mouthful of meat.

Marvin chuckled. "I could make a filthy joke there. I won't. But I could. Remember how we used to joke like that?"

He busied himself getting the puppet ready for a performance, moving it, and its stool, away from the corner, keeping one hand on its chest to steady it.

"Anyways, yeah. It's this new thing now, making 'em more life-sized. For the children. I think it makes 'em feel like they're listening to, like, a peer? I guess? Anything to get the blessed rugrats to pay attention! 'For we shall rescue them from the dominion of darkness and bring them into the kingdom of the Son,' am I right?"

"This apartment is the gee dee dominion of darkness," Robby muttered and ate another sliver of meat.

Once he and his dummy were in place, Marvin exclaimed, "Okay! So, the controls are a little tricky, but you tell me this won't be perfect for the show. Heeeeere we go!"

He waggled his fingers and then stuck them into the dummy's back.

Robby, who at that moment was rolling his eyes and eating another bit of chicken, had the sound of chewing and swallowing in his ears and so he missed the noise made when Marvin stuck his hand inside the doll. It was an unpleasant, wet *sfflllpptttt*. It sounded almost like a man jamming his hand into a Ziploc full of Vaseline.

Robby was spared that. But what happened next wasn't much less upsetting.

The dummy's head jerked up in a short, spastic movement. Its dark, bottomless eyes stared out from its plastic face, at nothing, at everything.

"Well, good morning, Marigold!" Marvin exclaimed in his cheery puppet-time voice.

From out of the side of his mouth, in a higher register, he answered himself back: "Mornin', Marvin!"

Marvin had never been a great ventriloquist, but that was part of his charm. He was indisputably talented at the physical work, moving the dolls and making it seem like their bodies were alive—in a way, his imprecision with their voices made the performances that much more endearing. You could appreciate his talents more by seeing the one area they fell short.

Not this time, though. This doll—this long-haired, unsettlingly large doll—moved in too herky-jerky a fashion. Its jaw, its neck, all its movements were wrong. Too sharp, too abrupt, too…Robby couldn't put any other word on it but *wrong*.

"Say," Marvin continued, "I wonder if we could get a volunteer from the audience. Anyone out there? Don't be shy!" He sang the tagline from their show's opening jingle: "I'm askin'. I'm seekin'. I'm knockin'!"

Robby begrudgingly raised his hand. The chicken was sitting like a rock in his gut.

"Yay!" Marvin cried. "And what's your name, little man?"

"Marv…" Robby grumbled.

"'That's a great name!'" Marvin-as-Marigold chirped, the doll's awful jaw chewing up and down. "'I love that name!'"

Then, as himself: "Naaah, I don't think that's your name, little man."

Robby gritted his teeth. "Lord…it's Robby."

"Robby!" Marigold proclaimed, head rocking back and forth on its neck. "Yay!"

Marvin broke character and leaned forward with a stage whisper: "Keep eating the chicken, Robby, I don't want it to go to waste." He leaned back. "Anyway, here's where Marigold gets sad, you know, like, 'Wah.'"

The dummy's shoulders fell forward in a dejected slump.

"What's wrong, Marigold?" Marvin asked, before proceeding to dialogue with the puppet.

"Gosh, I wish I could be a real person, like Robby."

"Well, Marigold, being a real person is a very special thing. Do you know the story of Pinocchio?"

"No."

Marvin faced his audience. "Robby, do *you*—"

"Yes," Robby growled.

Marvin turned back to his dummy. "And lemme ask something else, Marigold. Do you know what the word 'transubstantiation' means?"

"Trans…sub…"

"It's a tough one, I know. Well, basically, Pinocchio was a little puppet like you."

"Aw!"

"And Geppetto was his maker. Like God."

"Wow!"

"And Pinocchio wanted nothing more than to be real. So finally, one day, God performed a miracle...and gave Pinocchio flesh."

"Like skin?"

"Exactly! He turned *something*...into flesh and blood. It's a miracle He performs every day...because, well, flesh is a sacred thing. So sacred that God gives us his own flesh. To eat."

"To *eat*?" Marigold's head rocked on her neck again.

"I know how it sounds, little one, but yes. It's one of the holiest things we can do. It is to be made pure again, even if only for a moment."

"Wow," Marigold mused, "so if I become real, that's really special?"

"That's really special, Marigold!"

"Yay!"

"But—" Marvin's voice became low and serious, "you have to be careful, Marigold. Because your flesh is *pure* and *sacred* and there are people who want to take *pictures* of your flesh. *All* your flesh. Even your secret parts. They want to debase your sacred purit—"

Robby was on his feet without even knowing it, red faced and shaking.

"Marvin! You can't say that crap! I've had it!"

"What—" Marvin stammered. "What'd I say?"

"This is the whole reason we can't have you on the show anymore! Okay? Every *time*!"

"You're being hurtful."

"Every frigging time we give you the stage now, you're talking about gee dee pornography! It's sick!"

"It is sick! I agree!"

"*You're the one who keeps bringing it up!* A few weeks ago, you fit it into the story of Noah!"

Marvin shifted in his seat. He hand was still inside the doll, which sat with its mouth wide open, a blasé expression of shock on its neutral, empty face.

"Our children today, Robby, they can just open up their computer—heck, even their friggin' phones—and look at the filthiest, most depraved garbage imaginable. And if they're not careful, they'll wind up doing it themselves! They'll—"

"YEAH, WE ALL SAW THE DANG PHOTOS YOU SAVED ON THE STUDIO COMPUTER, MARVIN!" Robby had never yelled so loudly in his life. His throat burned. Spittle flew. And yet…it felt good. When he spoke again, his voice was raspy, deeper than normal. "How old were they? Ten? Were they even that old? Eight? Nine?"

Marvin was stammering again. "Come on, Robby. Come on. Y-you've gotta stop bringing this up."

"Stop bringing it up? Stop br—? I can't even look at you. I told you, I should be turning you in."

"You're not perfect either, you know!" Marvin seemed to have recovered his equilibrium. He cocked his head back in a haughty gesture and the lamplight caught his glasses, making his eyes the inverse of the doll's sunken shadows. "I know it was 'fifteen years ago,' but do you even remember that poor girl's name? Or how you called me up, crying? 'What do I do, Marv? What does this mean? Why couldn't I stop myself?'"

"Shut up, Marvin. Shut up."

"I think about that night a lot. You and I, we *know* things, important things, about the nature of man—"

"MARVIN. YOU SHUT. THE *FUCK*. UP!"

The curse word hit them both like a slap.

In the kitchen, the tea kettle began to whistle.

Both men stood there.

The whistle turned into a scream.

Then, Marvin made Marigold's head turn slightly in that spasmodic, uncanny way.

"Whatever happened to Luke 6:37, Robby?" the puppet asked with Marvin's voice.

Robby was preparing himself to respond when he noticed the doll's arms beginning to twitch. Pulse. Its legs shook a little. Its torso, too.

"Why are you making it move like that?"

Marvin put his hand on Marigold's shoulder. His other hand was still buried inside. His lenses shot golden daggers at Robby.

"Look, my hand is just stuck, okay? I'm trying to get it out." The kettle continued to scream. "Can you go get that, please?"

Robby puffed his chest. "That doll is a piece of crap," he proclaimed. "It's creepy and it doesn't work and"—as he stormed out of the room, he shot over his shoulder—"and I'm sorry you spent money on it!"

"I told you before," Marvin shot back. "Those photos were just research!"

"Research!" Robby scoffed from the kitchen. "Right."

Marvin ignored the sarcasm. He had other things to attend to.

His hand came quite easily out of the puppet with another wet *slllppptt.*

From the tips of his fingers to halfway past his wrist, he was coated in blood. A thick, clotty patina, so red it was almost black in spots.

The dummy continued to twitch and spasm.

The tea kettle ceased screaming with a defeated sigh.

"We're crusaders, Robert," Marvin whispered, holding his gore-soaked hand out. "We have to know what we're fighting against. No matter how it taints us. It gives us purpose."

A weak moan began to emanate from the dummy. Its limbs started to flail. It managed to stand uneasily on its feet, swaying, while Marvin searched about the room with his clean hand.

From the kitchen, Robby whined: "Where's your dang tea? Dang it, Marvin, your house is a mess! There are textbooks *all over* the counter! What is this, *Principles of Anesthesiology*? *Spinal Anatomy*? For Pete's sake! You really need help."

The dummy managed to bring one hand up and swat at its face. The smooth, plastic, rosy-cheeked façade fell away (except for the lower jaw, which had been secured by glue, not string).

Underneath was a different face. Far less smooth. Far less rosy. Ugly, raw wounds crisscrossed the cheeks and forehead where skin and muscle had been carved away. A few smaller tags hung errantly, loosened by time and movement. There were similar wounds all over the dummy's body—deeper wounds—but thankfully those were invisible for now.

Madness was beginning to resolve itself in the dummy's increasingly aware eyes.

Despite all that, the youth in its face was obvious.

Marvin watched this as he continued his search around the room.

"And flesh is a sacred thing," he said quietly to the dummy, though he knew it likely wasn't listening. Children were so easily distracted. "That's why we're told to consume it. It makes us pure again. No matter what we've done. It's a miracle."

Robby, who heard the sound of Marvin's voice, called back, "Whatever, Marvin, I can't even hear what you're saying." A cabinet opened. A small box rattled. "Finally. You want chamomile?"

Marvin also found what he was looking for: a semi-filled syringe. Just in time. The dummy had moved a hand to its backside and discovered the grisly opening there. Dig deep enough and it would find its spinal column, as well as exposed nerves waiting for expert hands to play them like marionette strings.

Those nerves must have begun transmitting pain again. The dummy's moans were turning into screams.

Marvin put a stop to all that with an injection into the dummy's neck.

The dummy's limbs went limp. Marvin eased it to the floor.

Then he checked its pulse.

"Dangit," he sighed. "Another one."

He shouted to the kitchen. "You're not going to see the reveal of my act now!"

"Oh well!" Robby shouted back over the clink of mugs. Then he gave a mock growl in frustration. "Ugh! Look, I don't wanna be this jerky guy with you, Marv. We're gonna have this tea together, but then…we're gonna call it quits. I know we've been through a lot, but…"

It was Marvin's turn not to listen. An idea had come to him. The next live taping of *Jubilee Junction* was tomorrow at 10 a.m. Could he be ready in time?

He looked at the underlit figure on the cross hanging on his wall.

Yes. He could do this. For the children.

This puppet would be a little bigger. Maybe not a Marigold. Maybe…the Good Lord Himself. Yes! He could use a wig and dress it in a white robe. It was "eat of *my* flesh," after all.

It should still fit in his steamer trunk. He'd just have to show up right before airtime so no one could get an early glimpse of the act. No spoilers.

And there was just enough left in this syringe to get started.

Without ceremony, Marvin turned and started for the kitchen, holding the syringe before him.

"Don't be upset, Marvin," Robby was saying. "I told you. I'm not gonna turn you in. And I still love you like a brother. A confused brother who needs help, but still. You were absolutely right. Luke 6:37. I take those words to heart. 'Judge not and ye shall not be—'"

Robby interrupted himself with a scream…and then, but for the sound of Marvin getting to work, the house was silent.

Meanwhile, in an empty room, the ceramic figure on the cross presided over nothing, its agony never abating.

The Better Man

By Jena Brown

The bitter promise of freshly brewed coffee pulls me from the soft cocoon of cotton sheets and Linda's arms. A chill clings to the air, but the desert heat builds as the morning sun stretches across the Las Vegas valley.

It's quiet, and I stifle a yawn, relishing these few moments alone before I open myself to the chaos of the day. The kitchen is orderly with everything in its place. Except for a single dish.

The plate sits next to the sink with eight slivers of crust neatly stacked in an obedient pile. Too neat for discarded remnants. There's only one man who is that meticulous when he eats. And he's dead.

I dump the crust in the garbage disposal and flip the switch. My heart drums a relentless beat, drowned out in the grinding churn of metallic teeth.

The scent of buttered toast still lingers, coats my tongue with the aftertaste of a nightmare I thought I buried. A scream rises in my chest. I want to wake up. But then soft lips press in the tender spot beneath my ear, and I know I'm awake.

"Good morning."

Linda. I close my eyes and wrap my arms around hers with a shaky exhale.

"Dave," she pouts. She untangles her arms from mine, eyes on the plate and the crumbs in the sink. "I thought we were having breakfast together."

I piece together the fragments of my scattered mind. But breakfast is no longer my priority, and I couldn't eat if I wanted to right now. Except I can't tell her why. I can't tell her a dead man ate the toast. My hand grabs hers before she lets go completely, and I turn to her with a guilty smile. That part isn't difficult to muster. Every second of that night is a brick, stacked on my shoulders and getting heavier with each passing day. But I'd do it again. Over and over if I had to.

"Sorry, babe." I kiss the corner of her mouth, work along her jaw to bury myself in the crook of her neck. "Had a bit of an upset stomach. Work is more stressful than I thought." I breathe her in. Jasmine and orange. A touch of mint. I pull away, putting my forehead to hers so she can't avoid my gaze. "Forgive me?"

Her mouth twists to the side, mischief brewing in her eyes. "Only if you bring home SushiSamba tonight."

She shouldn't be eating raw fish, but that's a fight for another day. My lips press against hers. "Deal."

Her body doesn't fit against mine like it used to. But the growing bump in her belly brings us closer, shifting everything and erasing unnecessary space. They're the reason I risked everything, and I won't let anything, or anyone, take them from me.

I move through my morning with mechanical efficiency as I poke and prod my memories for anything I might have missed. There's nothing. I was careful. I was thorough. But that doesn't explain the toast.

The light on my office phone blinks, and as the voicemail plays, a woman's voice fills the room.

"Yeah, hi. This is Veronica Harris again. I'm calling for David King. I'm hoping you can help me track down some information on a mutual acquaintance, Paul Ruxford. Please give me a call at your earliest convenience."

She leaves her number, but I don't write it down before I delete the message. It's the second call this month. It has to be a coincidence. But I only made it this far by refusing to believe in those.

Someone knows Paul's dead. Now I have to find out who.

• • •

The drive home usually calms me. Miles of empty desert unfurls beneath me, leaving the tarnished glitz of the Las Vegas Strip behind. Desolation may seem bleak to some, but years of working with Paul taught me that isolation equals safety.

Except tonight. Every shrub is a threat. Every shadow a secret. Hours of trying to find Veronica Harris have left me frustrated and hollow. Paul is who I would turn to in situations like this. I didn't think I'd feel his absence. Miss how he made problems go away. I didn't realize he'd leave this void that plagues me with sleepless nights. I can almost hear his laugh, taunting me with my own ineptitude. When I get home, I'm twisted in knots.

I loosen my tie, slip my shoes off. My business clothes are armor, as effective as the hardhat I wear on site. But I'm not supposed to need protection here. I want answers, but patience is key. Another lesson I learned from Paul. If you wait long enough, people will always tell you what they want.

Easier said than done. But there's nothing anyone can find. Nothing but my treacherous conscience. And I won't let anyone pry that away from me.

Linda is rifling through the fridge when I find her in the kitchen. "I'm glad you're home. I'm starving." She pauses, a strange expression on her face. "Where's SushiSamba?"

"Shit." I run my hand through my hair. "Shit, Linda. I'm so sorry. I'll go pick up whatever you want, right now."

She lets loose a sigh. It isn't meant as an accusation, but I welcome the spike of pain her disappointment brings. Emotions are a series of boxes stacked and welded shut, containing all the things I dare not let myself feel. I add her sigh to one of my boxes and hope I can carry the weight.

"It's okay," she says. "I know you're busy."

Linda turns back to the fridge, pulling out a carton of lettuce and various vegetables. I should start washing and chopping to help her with the dinner she wasn't planning on making. Instead, I open the liquor cabinet and pour myself a hefty glass of bourbon.

I swallow the contents in a single gulp and fill the glass again. It's been ages since I've drank like this. The liquor stings, then numbs the lacerations of a thousand memories.

"Is everything okay?" she asks.

I watch her chop the celery in slow, methodical chunks as I sort through my standard answers. *Work is a frenzy, contracts are snagging, I haven't been sleeping.* All true to various degrees, but it's getting harder to hide the truths she doesn't want to hear.

I sip the bourbon and lean back against the counter. "Yeah, babe. It's just work is crazy—"

"No. I mean..." She shakes her head, chews her lip, a gesture that normally makes my lips ache for hers. But in this moment, it only makes me more tense.

"I got a call..."

I set the glass down, harder than I intend, and I curse when she jumps. My nerves buzz, and I hold the glass tighter to keep my hands from shaking.

"From who?" I ask, each word constricted and blunt.

She shakes her head. "I don't know. Veronica something. She...she wanted to know about Paul."

"What did you tell her?"

Another shake of her head, this time punctuated with a shrug. She rubs her belly. Part of me longs to wrap my arms around her, comfort her, reassure her that everything is fine. But I don't. I need to know how fucked this situation really is.

"David, I told her the truth." Exasperation tints her words. "How he was upset, started drinking a lot. That he spun out of control and disappeared, and we haven't heard from him in months."

Her words should calm me down, but there's worry tangled inside them. My lies are the foundation of our future. Doubt threatens that stability. And if she learns the truth, it will all collapse.

I stride around the island to take her hands in mine. Her body is rigid with tension. This kind of stress isn't good for her. Or the baby.

"Hey." I cradle her chin in the crook of my finger and tip her head up. "Tell me why you're so upset."

I should have started the conversation like this, but memories of the dead have thrown me off balance. I need to find Veronica Harris, find who was in my home. But Linda comes first. She always comes first. Even when she first belonged to Paul.

"It's..." She swallows. I know this isn't easy for her. To remember all the things she'd rather forget. "What if he's dead? What if it's my fault?"

A tear spills down her cheek. I kiss it away and fold her into my arms.

"Linda, babe. Whatever choices Paul made are his own. No matter where he is or what he's doing, he did it to himself."

It's mostly the truth. The phone calls, the constant harassment, the emotional manipulation. I knew it would never stop unless I stopped it.

"If you knew something...you'd tell me, right?"

Her words are soft, tentative, but they send shrapnel through my core. Does she know? Is she the one who left the toast? But her eyes are open and honest. Scared.

I kiss her words and my doubts away. "Babe, we've been over this. We got in a fight. Things got heated. That was the last time I saw him."

The memory of the fight lingers. His accusations still sting: that I was a terrible friend, that I stole Linda. As if she didn't come willingly. As if he didn't play a role in pushing her away. It wasn't my fault I was better to her. Better for her. Better than him.

"Come on." I lead her out of the kitchen and into our bathroom. "Why don't you take a bath. Relax. I'll finish dinner."

I start the bath and add Epsom salt to the running water. As Linda eases herself down, I sprinkle a few drops of oil and watch the warm water fill around her. Already, she's relaxing, her worries melting away.

Mine are only beginning.

The torn vinyl seat squeals beneath my weight as I slide into the booth. The diner is quiet, a small building on the outskirts of Pahrump. Far enough away from the Strip that I shouldn't run into anyone I know. Another set of prying eyes is the last thing I need.

I don't look up from the plastic menu when Rachel slides in across from me. She's a sun-kissed brunette dressed in a gray suit.

Rachel gets right to business, picking up the menu and keeping her voice low. The consummate professional. "Veronica Harris is one of Paul's ex-girlfriends. A side piece."

"How did she know to contact me?"

Paul and I worked together, but not in the traditional sense. To anyone on the outside, we were acquaintances. That's how it works in our line of business. Carefully constructed illusions hiding complicated truths. I make clean money appear. He made people vanish. The only thing that tied us together was Linda.

"She's a journalist at some no-nothing paper in a dying town."

I weigh the information as the waitress interrupts. "Ready to order?"

My eyes flicker to her name tag, flash up to her tired face. All she needs is a half-smoked cigarette hanging from her lips to complete our clichéd gathering.

"Just coffee for me, Irene."

"How's your pastrami?" Rachel asks.

Irene lifts an eyebrow. "How's your stomach?"

Rachel barks a laugh, tucking her menu back in the rack. "Sounds like a challenge. I'll take the pastrami on rye."

Irene walks behind the counter, spins our ticket to the kitchen on a stainless-steel rack. Within seconds, she's back at our table with a half-full coffee pot. She fills our mugs and leaves before we can ask more of her. It's an efficiency I respect.

"It's obvious Paul talked to Veronica about you, but how much is hard to say." Rachel pulls a notebook out of her jacket pocket. "Here's what I know. They must have met when she was a cocktail waitress at Caesar's. She left Vegas about two years ago. Nine months later, a kid pops out. Paul's name isn't on the birth certificate, but I'd bet dollars to donuts it's his. They must have maintained some kind of contact. My guess?

She's looking for money. Tell her he split and you haven't heard from him. She'll eventually go away."

The coffee is as bitter as my mood, little more than sludge I can barely swallow. The information sounds solid, but it doesn't explain the goddamned toast.

Rachel senses my hesitation. "If you want, I can do the whole thing. Wires. Trackers. Maybe pay her a visit and have a girl-to-girl chat."

Irene sets a plate in front of Rachel. "You two need anything else?"

I shake my head and wave her away.

"No chatting…yet. Find out if she still has ties to anyone here. I can't find anything on her, and if she knows more than she should, I need to know."

"You got it," she says around the pastrami.

"You have that security consultant I asked about?" I lean forward to extract my wallet from my back pocket.

Rachel wipes her mouth and pulls a business card out of her notebook. She slides it across the table. "Mitch Thomas. Ex-military. Good guy. Pay him well, and he'll make your house more secure than the Bellagio."

I tuck the card into my wallet.

Rachel runs her tongue across her teeth and cocks her head. "You think this Veronica is that big of a threat?"

"Probably not." I peel away a twenty and put my coffee cup on top. "But if there's one thing I've learned about pests, it's that there's never just one."

The toast was a tactic straight from Paul's handbook. Disarm, disorient, destroy. But I'm better at that game than he was. I already beat him. Used his strengths and made them weaknesses. I won't let anyone do the same to me.

"Call me when you know something."

Linda's in the nursery when I get home. She's at the changing table, fingers dancing along the rim of a crystal glass.

"Linda..." But my voice trails off when I notice the bottle of scotch—*his* scotch. Bile climbs in my throat, sharp and smoky.

Her face crumbles, and I barely catch her words as she sobs.

"It's Paul," she sputters. "He was here."

Black spots explode behind my eyes and I'm suddenly next to her, glass in one hand, her arm in the other.

"Did you see him? Who was here? Who did you see? Tell me!"

Every word tightens the vice around my throat until I'm choking.

"David! Stop it! Let me go!"

Her scream breaks me from my trance. She fights against my grip and falls backward into the wall when I let her go.

"Did you see him? Did you see Paul?"

Five angry marks stain her skin as she tries to rub them away. Face white, body trembling, she shakes her head.

"Who else would do that?" she cries. "Who else would leave that bottle here?"

I lift the bottle. My thumb absently runs along the raised label. The texture of each letter is familiar, and a memory tugs at a distant part of my brain. But the bottle is a violation. An insult. With a snarl, I punch the scotch into the wall. I ignore Linda's screams. Ignore the shards of glass lodged deep in my flesh.

"I'll fix this," I say to Linda, to myself, to no one.

I startle awake, still in my chair. Sleeping pills are scattered across my desk next to an empty bottle of bourbon. It's strange, the sensation of waking with no recollection of falling asleep. But these last days have tested the limits of my body and mind. Linda is still upset, scared and skittish and crying more than ever before. I promised her a stable life. One far away from the volatile moods Paul displayed, worlds apart from the violence my other life demands. He showed her more of that world than I do. With me, she can pretend it doesn't exist.

Until now.

I rub the sleep from my eyes and log into the camera system I installed. They didn't record. Again. I stand up to check the wiring, but something crunches into the soles of my bare feet. Sand.

With stiff legs, I follow the barely visible trail out of my office to the front porch, where a shovel I don't own is leaning against the stucco. There's only one reason someone would leave a shovel on my porch.

I'm in the car and driving down the I-15 before I can think. I need to make sure Paul is still buried. My heartbeat riots in my chest as a cascade of action and reaction and the very real threat of consequences I'm not ready to face swirl in my mind.

It's true that Linda came to me, that she chose me. But when she told me she was pregnant, I knew there was only one way to keep her. To prove I'd never leave her. To show her that I was the better man. All I had to do was give Paul a drugged bottle of scotch.

Forty miles later, I turn off the highway. The dirt road kicks up a cacophony of rocks against the undercarriage. It's a tedious drive, but the place is easy to find. I drove this path a hundred times to make sure I could find it no matter the circumstances. I could probably find this spot in my sleep.

Digging in the desert isn't as easy as the movies make it seem. Difficult, but not impossible. The trick is knowing where to dig. Most of the ground is sunbaked sand crusted over layers of hard caliche clay. But in between the hills, where flash floods carve dried riverbeds, you can find pockets of silt. It isn't the best place to bury something you don't want found. Those waters come hard and fast and take everything with it. But if you follow the floods, you can find pockets where secrets stay hidden.

It took days before I found a place where flood water pooled to evaporate into dust after every monsoon. Here, nothing gets carried away, and secrets sink deeper every season. Here, the dead should stay buried.

Small mounds are visible from the car. But it's the ravenous flock circling above that sends me panicked onto the sand.

Most of the holes are shallow, but only one matters. The one with the blue lip of the plastic barrel jutting from the dirt, exposing the evidence of my crime.

There shouldn't be anything left of Paul. The sodium hydroxide should have melted his flesh and disintegrated his bones. It was supposed to eat through his limbs and slowly dissolve until nothing was left. But it's obvious I made a mistake.

Paul's torso is gruesomely intact, sitting upright in a gelatinous sludge that was once his legs. I could leave it for the vultures, but I can't risk it. Not now.

I go back to the car, the list of tools I need cycling in my head, a plan formulating. I kick the sand off my shoes only to frown at the piles on the floorboards. But then Linda calls. I answer on the first ring.

"David. He was here. Again. I don't know. I don't know why he would do this." She's crying so hard I can barely make out her words.

I slam the car in gear and peel down the road. "Linda, baby, calm down. What's wrong? What happened?"

"Why would he threaten us. Me. How does he know?"

I press the phone harder against my ear, as if that will sort her words into sense. "Linda. I don't understand."

"You told me he left. That he would leave us alone. That we would be okay. But we're not. We're not okay. He's back. He knows. I won't let him take my baby. I won't. I'm leaving. I can't stay. I—"

"No!" I bark into the phone. "No, please Linda. I'm on my way home. I'll make sure you're safe. Please don't leave."

Her voice cracks. "I can't, David. I can't. I know I've ignored it. Pretended like everything was fine. I didn't want to see… didn't want to *know*…but I can't do this anymore. I have to protect my baby. I'm sorry."

The phone goes dead, and for all her calls earlier, she sends me to voicemail now. I won't lose her. I can't. Not after everything I've risked. Everything I've done. For her. For us. For the baby that has to be mine.

Paul never knew she was pregnant. Never knew the genetic odds were the same as choosing red or black on roulette.

His.

Mine.

My future circling around Linda's wavering, uncertain loyalty. But I changed the odds. I rigged the game. I should have won.

The house is empty when I get home. Her clothes are strewn around our bedroom. The lingering remnants of the life we built. Everything else is pristine. Except the nursery. It's torn apart. Cushions destroyed. Linens ripped. The word "MINE" carved in the wall above the crib.

I find the card Rachel gave me and call the security consultant. It's time to show whoever this is that in Vegas, the house—my house—always wins. *I* always win.

I blink. My head pounds, and my throat is raw. Sunlight yawns across the floor in gentle rays, but Linda didn't set the coffee.

Another blink and it's night.

My wrist aches. My shoulder hurts. I shift my weight to cradle my arm and ease the pain.

Another blink, and it's day.

My trap is set.

Paul taught me how to turn any room into a prison, and Mitch—ex-military, good guy—brought my plans to life. Thick steel bars hide inside the walls. Pressure plates tucked underneath the carpet. The blue barrel with Paul's remains sits in the middle of the room.

One step into the nursery and the trap is sprung.

I know my tormenter will come. All I have to do is wait.

• • •

Night. Day. Time is a blur.

The sharp tang of urine and the meaty stench of sweat make my eyes water. A hoarse scream wakes me.

I lift my hand, bang against metal bars, wincing as pain shoots up my arm.

The screaming stops.

My throat is as dry as the desert outside. As if I haven't drank water in days.

The screaming starts again as I drift back to sleep.

I jolt awake. My cell phone rings, but it's in another room. One I can't reach, though I stretch and twist and try to escape the steel bars.

I scream for Linda.

But there's no one in the nursery. Just me and the remnants of Paul, surrounded by bars meant to catch someone else.

Guilt is a strange beast. A roaring, beating drum that follows me in my sleep. I dream of toast. And scotch. Of cameras I turned off, and linens I destroyed, and a body I dug up.

Veronica's call woke something in me. Something that came alive while I slept. Maybe she wanted money, but she didn't taunt me. Didn't threaten me. I did that to myself.

Maybe I deserve this. To die dehydrated and alone, hunger carving my body hollow.

I wanted to win. To live the perfect life. To be the better man. I thought killing Paul would give me all of that. I hear his laugh, taunting me with my own ineptitude. I laugh with him, sobbing, screaming, louder and louder, but it never silences the monster beating in my hideous heart.

One Man's Trash

By Samantha Kolesnik

Benny knew the value of a dollar.

He could tell you the value in dollars of all sorts of things. Three used tampons, vacuum-sealed to preserve odor? Twenty bucks.

Discarded condoms? Less valuable, five for a dozen.

Used pantyhose? Depending on what was left on the crotch pad, old hose could get Benny as much as forty a pop. Panties, the same.

It was all what the market demanded, and there was a growing market for trash. Some countries sold the shit in sex club vending machines, or so Benny was told. He'd never had the dough to travel much. The states—eh, they weren't as open-minded in the states. *Burn the witch* shit. Clients had to rely on expert divers like Benny to get them what they needed to get off.

As far as Benny could see, he wasn't hurting anyone. The shit was clogging up landfills, and most of the weirdos he sold to—they needed an outlet.

Better they jack off to used toilet paper than go fuck with someone.

Benny was on the lookout tonight for adult diapers. He had a client who was willing to pay top dollar for a bundle. The hard part was finding someone who fit the profile. Benny liked to hit up low-rent apartment complexes because those were the types that didn't keep the dumpsters locked. A lot of the trade was *take a guess, look and see.*

He'd spotted a few grandmas in building five, a crumbling tenement house with the name *Wintergreen* on a rusted metal plate attached to its brick facade. Benny waited until the night before trash collection to make his dive. That's when the dumpsters would be full, and also when they would most likely include trash from all tenants. As the night wore on, people came and went from Wintergreen. Men looking listless sat on the stoop and lit up cigarettes, only to put them out and go separate ways in loud cars with tinted windows.

At about three in the morning, Benny felt the place was quiet enough to make his dive. He grabbed the handle of his car door to exit, but then stopped when he saw a man walk out the front entrance of Wintergreen. Benny hadn't remembered seeing him before, but it was hard to get a good look in the dull yellow lamplight of the Wintergreen parking lot.

From what he could see at a distance, the man was of average height, receding hairline, dated-looking glasses, brown khaki slacks. He carried a black garbage bag, tied off in a large knot.

Must've forgotten to take his trash out earlier.

The man started to walk to the dumpster, taking a measured pace. Halfway there, he stopped and looked behind him. His head swiveled as he scanned the entire parking lot.

Benny's heart jumped.

Jesus, why am I scared? I don't have a reason to be scared of this chump.

The man locked eyes with Benny from across the parking lot. Benny was sure he could see more of the man than the man could see of him.

Move along, my dude. Move along.

But he didn't move along. He started walking straight toward Benny's car, black bag still in hand.

Benny could have gotten out of dodge, but he also had a good feeling the dumpsters had a big pile of diaper gold, and he needed to get the coin for it, or else he'd be eating hot dogs all week.

Just play it cool, Benny.

Benny rolled down his window enough to talk.

"You uh—you live around here?" the man asked.

"My grandma lives here."

The man smiled and adjusted his glasses. They were old-looking, thick-lensed, and square-rimmed.

"So does mine."

Benny nodded and put his hand on the wheel. He tried to look distracted, busy—*uninterested.*

"Well, is there something I can help you with or what?"

The man shook his head. He leaned down close to the window opening and peered inside Benny's car. Benny caught the man's eyes searching the interior, almost as if he were looking for something in particular.

"Sorry to bother you. We've had a few break-ins at other buildings, and I..." The man met Benny's eyes through the gap in the window. "...I try to look out for trouble. But you're not trouble." The man smiled at Benny again, and Benny got the sense he was being warned more than he was being small-talked.

Benny shook his head, "Just trying to get fresh air. My grandma keeps the heat on way too high."

The man laughed. "Well, if you're headed inside, I can walk you in."

Benny's neck broke out in goosebumps.

"I'm gonna stick it out here a little longer, but thanks."

"Don't be a stranger."

The man walked away from Benny's car door, black bag swinging in hand. He stopped and put his hand on the hood of Benny's car, as if he were contemplating turning back around. Benny opened his glovebox and grabbed a hunting knife just in case, but the dude finally walked over to the dumpsters. He disappeared behind the fenced enclosure that hid the dumpsters from view, and then came back out, hands empty. Stopping at the building entrance, Mr. Nighttime gave Benny one last wave before stepping through the door to Wintergreen.

Still time to split, find another dumpster. It doesn't have to be this one.

No. It had to be this one. He'd wasted a whole week scouting this place, and Benny wasn't going to let some creep scare him off from his paycheck.

I'll just make it quick. Lightning quick. In and out, no extras.

Benny stepped out of his car and opened the trunk to get his gear. With his empty loot sack strung over his shoulder, it was finally time to head for the dumpsters.

Fenced enclosures like this one were great for diving. They kept out prying eyes.

Once behind the wooden fence, Benny popped open the first of the trash containers. He grabbed the slimy metal rim and hoisted himself up until he was perched at the edge, precariously balanced on a pile of trash and the metal container. It reeked to high hell, but Benny was used to it.

He pulled out his pocket light and shone it into the pile. He had a system. His first round was to try to gauge contents by looking through the stretched white bags. It was easier and less suspicious if he could spot some diaper gold without having to slice everything open.

Fuck me. It's all groceries, plastic wrap, paper towels, and odds and ends.

The only yield Benny saw was a small vibrator resting at the top of one bag, just under the plastic tie-off. Benny reached in bare-handed and grabbed it. He gave it a sniff, but it smelled clean.

Goddamnit.

He'd have to add some flavor before he could sell it for anything, but he tossed it in his sack nonetheless and hopped down from the dumpster. The shock of hitting the pavement hurt his knees, reminding him that he was feeling a little worse for the wear lately.

There were two more dumpsters to check, but time wasn't on Benny's side. He'd have to slice and dice the next one to get what he needed, or the whole job would be a waste.

He flipped open the lid on the second dumpster. A ripe aroma gusted in his face as he swung over the side. He didn't bother balancing this time; Benny dove right in, feet first. He sank into the bags—they gave way until they didn't, and he was able to find his balance again. He took out his knife and sliced through one bag after the other, letting the trash flow out in putrid piles.

Onion peels, moldy casserole, balled-up tissues, a gigantic red lace bra (eh, worth taking for any case), empty beer cans…

Benny's internal inventorying halted when he set eyes on a bag in the corner of the heap. It was black and tied off at the top.

Mr. Nighttime's bag.

The thought of the man and his inscrutable, bespectacled face made Benny feel slimed out, and it took a lot to make Benny feel that way. Nonetheless, weird men threw out weird trash, and the night's haul was looking skimpy as fuck.

Damn those old grandmas and their healthy bladders. Couldn't even give me one lousy diaper grab. Nada.

Benny grabbed the black bag and shoved it into his loot sack. He'd take the whole thing with him and look inside later. He had to scram.

By the time Benny was on the freeway headed home, it was almost 5 a.m. and the sun would be poking its head out soon. He was dog tired and pissed-off. He had nothing for his client, and only a few odds and ends that would be tough to sell on the open market.

He had been counting on Wintergreen. It was supposed to score him enough for the month. Now he had to scavenge for the next few weeks to make do.

Unless…

Benny thought of the black bag he'd grabbed.

Whatever's inside, it had better be damned good, or I'll have to shove that vibrator up my own ass, I'm so fucked.

The parking lot was full again, so Benny had to take a spot on the corner. The asshole street cleaners were coming later today, so he was sure he'd get another damn ticket. Forty-five a pop, and it's not like the cleaners left the city smelling any better.

Garbage in hand, Benny walked quickly—but not too quickly—over to his building. The usual gang of moths and gnats circled around the stairwell light. Benny scouted the stairs for anything of interest in an efficient once-over, but they were surprisingly clean.

Just my luck.

He walked down to the below-ground floor, swung a left and was finally home, sweet home. *Apartment 2B.*

There was some leftover lo mein in the fridge, and Benny went for it immediately. He shoved forkful after forkful into his mouth until the carton was empty, nothing but a grease stain at the bottom. He tossed the empty carton and the fork into his sink and turned his body toward the loot. He pulled the whole sack from the table and gently emptied it onto the kitchen floor in case anything in Mr. Nighttime's black bag was fragile.

Benny took off his shirt in case the situation got messy and pushed all of the other garbage out of the way.

Maybe don't open this one. Maybe just bring it back to Wintergreen.

No. He had to see what was inside. It was his only chance at avoiding a total bust. Benny first tried untying the knot, but the garbage bag seemed to be layered—double—no, triple—bagged, and it was that thick, black plastic, the kind usually used for yard work.

Undeterred, Benny took out his knife and got to work. He first punctured the black plastic at the top, close to the knot. He sliced slowly so as to not damage the contents, and once a hole was made, he carefully slipped his hand inside. He dug around and felt…

That's…

That's someone's fucking hair.

As Benny pulled harder, he realized the hair was attached to something hard and round.

But hair would only be attached to…

The realization of what was in the bag hit Benny like a ton of bricks.

A head. A fucking head?

No. It couldn't be. It was probably a Halloween prop.

But when Benny sliced the bag open all the way, he could see this was no cheap prop. This was a very real head that was once attached to a very real woman. Blonde, from the looks of it. Looked like shit now, but maybe was pretty once. Hard to say.

Oh, fuck me sideways.

A million thoughts ran through Benny's head, but his main concern was that his fingerprints were now all over the head of a corpse. His first instinct was to panic, but after the panic subsided, he realized this rare find could turn around his luck. Sure, tampons and pantyhose sold fine enough—*reliable staples and all*—but this shit? This was next-level.

Selling the head would be nearly impossible. That he had to get rid of somehow. But souvenirs? Those would make him a fortune. Anything Mr. Nighttime wore, used, or threw out over at Wintergreen would one day sell for big bucks on the serial killer collector's market.

The bespectacled freak would have to throw out regular trash in addition to corpse bits, and when he did, Benny would be waiting for it.

He'd have to wait a few days to go back, maybe switch cars if he could, or scout on foot. He didn't want the people of Wintergreen to get too used to seeing him, though the grandma cover was decent enough.

In the meantime, what to do with the head? Benny forced himself to look at it straight-on. It was kind of like watching a horror movie—he felt that the more he looked at the scary thing, the more comfortable he'd get with it.

Dead now, anyway. No different than a chicken head, or a leg of lamb.

"Hey, hot stuff," he said to it, and he laughed for an uncomfortably long time just to hear any sound at all—just to pretend for a moment that he wasn't alone.

Hiding in the mess of hair was something shiny, and it caught Benny's eye. He parted the blonde strands to reveal one of those cheap drugstore barrettes. It was tangled and hard to pry loose, but Benny managed. That barrette was a true exclusive, and it was going to be worth a lot one day.

Well, hot stuff, into the freezer now.

It was just one man's trash.

But for Benny, it was treasure.

The Protest

By Jeremy Robert Johnson

Benjamin ran his hand over the rigid thermoset plastic of the packaging, feeling how hard and permanent the creation was, knowing that all he wanted were the pills inside the bottles beneath the anti-theft packaging. The day had been ruinous enough. Melody's resigned voice echoed beneath the flickering aura and throb of his oncoming migraine.

"If there's no future," she'd asked, "then *what is this*? What the fuck are we building?"

He'd wanted to tell her, "Nothing." He'd wanted to say, "We're running down the clock. Rearranging deck chairs. It's pretend, all of it. We're playing house until the other shoe drops." But he knew she'd heard enough of it, his obsession with the scarcity and all that was coming. If he spoke again, they'd end up running in the same circles, her unreasoning hope scraping against the variable and awful ends he knew were waiting for both of them. They'd end up talking about children again, and his refusal to create new life, not when he *knew* what was coming, and her anger would be replaced by tears. So, he said nothing, grabbed his car keys from the small wicker bowl in the entryway, and left her to her anger. Better, he thought, to remember her with her face filled with spite than to hear her weep again.

The knob of the front door felt too small in his hand, and he'd dizzied at the realization of what he was doing. Still, he took a deep breath and opened the door.

"I won't be here when you get back," she said.

He'd believed her. It was another thing he'd known from the moment he secretly scheduled his vasectomy. That decision had ended their relationship long before the fight, long before he quietly closed the door to his house behind him and realized a migraine was crawling its way across his cortex and sending his left eye snow-blind.

Of course his prescription meds were back in the house. But he'd heard Melody lock the door behind him and knew he shouldn't return until he saw that she and her car were gone. Instead, he raced to the closest store, knowing that if the migraine continued unchecked he'd be headed for twenty-four hours of nausea and wobbly legs and fumbling speech and the sensation of a hot iron strap being slowly tightened around the top of his head.

He'd normally avoided the beige behemoth that was the PriceCo store, but he knew they had his meds, and by the time he found a spot in their sprawling parking lot the aura of his migraine was already crawling across the right side of his vision. There was no choice. He'd flashed his membership card, shivered against the thrumming air-conditioned breeze blowing through the store, and stumbled across cold concrete to the maze of discount medicine that would save him.

And so it was there, cycling through memories of Melody in the pharmaceutical section of the massive store, that he laid his hands on the too-permanent plastic protecting the assets within, and he looked from the object he held to the hundreds just like it stacked on pallets beyond, and his eyes rose forever to the ceiling of the store where terribly bright fluorescents flickered off black security plastic and clear packaging stacked like pyramids, like objects to be revered, and the sound around him was one of pleasant chatter and satisfaction, and he tried to breathe deeply, but suddenly there was no air, only the sensation of greasy atomized fats from sausage samples filling his lungs, and he felt faint, his hands tingling, and even before he managed to brace himself against the perfectly-placed cube of over-packaged meds, he was vomiting that afternoon's re-heated Chinese across the shiny concrete floor of the super-store and feeling nothing so much as the desire that the end he saw coming would finally arrive.

With Melody truly gone from his life there was no one to wake Benjamin, and he quickly reverted to the nocturnal schedule he'd preferred before they met. His dog, Chewie, a sleepy old Labrador mutt, made the adjustment with him, seeming just as pleased with their long, nightly walks.

"You want a walk, Chewie? Go outside?" Chewie wagged in confirmation as Benjamin leashed him. The night air and smells of dog and fresh cut grass and waning BBQ sometimes served to save Benjamin from thoughts of Melody, of his stupid nostalgia for how they'd begun: meeting at the gallery, her realizing he was one of the artists, the way they'd fallen into bed together that night, laughing. The joy of those early years, the beautiful ignorance and purity of how they loved each other. The way he used to get her going, laughing till her face hurt. But that was before he'd learned so many terrible things and saw where the world was headed. Before laughing all the time started to feel like sacrilege.

Chewie stopped to sniff at the base of a rose bush, some animal message left there stealing his focus.

"You find something good, buddy?"

Benjamin preferred it when they walked fast. When they stopped, he had more time to think.

Should I take down her pictures?

There were photographs of Melody that she'd left behind, framed memories of Vegas and Times Square and the mountain-top at Whistler, all from the time before Benjamin decided he would no longer travel by airplane. She'd tolerated that change as well as anyone, and even helped him finance his electric car. And when he'd demanded they take on a vegan diet, she'd hesitated at first, only accepting the change after he showed her a video of baby pigs collapsing from heat death and engorged mama pigs swinging on hooks until they bled out.

Chewie tugged at his leash, satisfied and ready to leave the rose bush behind. They carried on, Benjamin barely registering the walk through the haze of his memory.

Benjamin felt that Melody, like anybody else, had to *see* the reality of what humans were doing to believe it. He had learned that from the Antagonist Movement, back when he was still a Promising Young Artist. People responded to wild, nasty imagery. It seared itself into the brain, made concepts real and undeniable, and doubly so if the image was shocking. That knowledge had allowed Benjamin to thrive as an enfant terrible in the conceptual art scene for a stretch and had continued to secure him the grants that barely kept him afloat. And though working in ugly truth had started to wear on his mind, he saw how wonderfully those images of war and poverty *worked*. In Melody's case, she knew she was eating pigs—*of course she did*—but until her mind was branded with the consequences of that truth—that swaying, screaming animal spraying red gouts of hot blood into the slaughterhouse sluice below—it wasn't quite real.

"That's the thing, Chewie. Like, she knows what's happening. Everybody knows, deep down." The dog offered no response aside from tugging in the direction of the park, hoping for an off-leash runaround. They both stepped over a ruptured white trash bag, its contents spilling loose where it'd been torn open by raccoons, the smell of rotting, liquefied rotisserie chicken seeping out.

Benjamin wondered why Melody wouldn't accept what was coming next for humanity. They scrolled the same sites, didn't they? She had to have seen the same bad mojo coming their way. But after a while together, *he'd* become their own little prophet of doom. Dinner conversation had skewed religiously dismal, running down the latest ecological tragedies while his carefully seasoned chickpeas went cold. He talked fast fashion, and fracking, and mass-pollinator die-offs, and nitrogen fertilizer overload, and factory farming, and the dirty diesel shipping corridor, and the oceanic plastic gyre, and overpopulation, and bleached-coral dead zones, and waves of crows falling dead from the sky by the fucking hundreds, and he watched her grow more and more annoyed until she started acknowledging him only in simple nods and "Hmms" while scrolling her Instagram feed.

One night, when they'd split a bottle of red and the evening air was warm and perfect on their skin, she'd asked him how he felt about having a child together and he'd thought she was joking, and he'd said, "What? Another version of us that'll have to suffer through what's coming?" He'd laughed and had expected the same from her. He'd believed her to be his partner, someone to enjoy the absurdity of human existence with, secretly envisioning them living as ethically as they could for as long as they could before scarcity drove the world into chaos, and then maybe they'd sail off together on another bottle of red and a fistful of painkillers.

But that wasn't true. He'd invented that version of Melody.

The real Melody had watched his art grow ever angrier and turned against it. "It's not even provocative anymore. It's just... *mean*." The real Melody had pictured a different future, one where they kept laughing despite it all.

But now both of their imaginary futures had unraveled, and he was alone with Chewie, and back from their walk, and it hadn't done enough to clear his mind. He threw a treat to the dog and sighed at the realization that another migraine was coming.

How many days in a row is it? Five? Six?

He kept the house dark, popped another migraine med, and began slowly taking down all the photographs of others he had loved, hiding them away in the dust-bunny-riddled space beneath his bed.

The walls were soon empty. Anyone could have lived there. Or no one.

Benjamin appraised his work and slowly walked to the living room.

"It's just us, Chewie." Having the dog was fine—that attachment didn't hurt in the same way as the idea of having a child. Chewie could revert to old behaviors when it all went bad and feel the joy of running through the night in pursuit of prey.

Unless we broke that too. Unless we took the wolf and turned it into something that would wait, simpering, for humans to pour the next bowl of food, and starve there in that trust and expectation.

Benjamin lumped himself, oddly exhausted, into the La-Z-Boy in his living room. The smell of Melody's perfume wafted up from the fabric. Something about the scent made his head hurt worse, and he wondered if this was the status quo now: an unending series of migraines striking him blind, bending him small, curling away from the light behind his blackout blinds. Chewie trotted over and laid his head on Benjamin's leg. Benjamin petted Chewie, feeling the fatty tumors under his fur, knowing he'd have to wash his hands to get rid of the old dog smell.

Still, the dog was good. The dog helped. He hurt less, for now.

Benjamin told himself that loving Chewie was okay. The dog was old and he'd be gone before it all happened, before the ice caps melted, and the rising oceans drove everyone to high land, and the land that remained turned to non-arable dust, and the weather was only extreme events, and food was whatever you could find, and the daily cataclysm unraveled what remained of civilized society, and the humans finalized their sixth great extinction by eating each other alive while tiny pockets of uber-rich assholes survived in New Zealand enclaves, munching on lab-grown meat and inbreeding their way into madness.

Benjamin pictured Chewie roaming those wastelands, scaring away crows to dine alone on the entrails of human corpses.

Chewie tilted his head, signaling to Benjamin that he wanted the area behind his ears scratched. Benjamin honored the request, and the dog closed his eyes.

"Hey, boy—that's good pets, huh? Hey...I want you to know something. If I die before you, you can eat whatever's left of me. I won't be mad. I promise I won't even care."

Benjamin's voice was alien to his own ears—a stranger in his house speaking from a darkened corner. Benjamin shivered. He thought he should cry, or laugh, but neither proved possible.

He rose from his bed, still haunted by the corona of another marathon migraine, to find messages waiting on his phone. He turned the volume down and held the device away from his head so the sound might become tolerable.

"Hello, Benjamin. This is Mark Araby with the Central Arts Commission. I was hoping to communicate with you about this in person, but I haven't seen any responses to my scheduling requests, and this communication is timely, so...the basics of it is that your grant payment from last August is going to be your final one from CAC. As you know, our funding has tightened up in recent years, and with everything else that's going on in the world, we're not sure, based on your last proposal, if your work is the right fit for a public institution. You know I love what you do, and I think the anger in your project proposal comes from the right place. It's urgent, and it's what we need, but...you know. We're publicly funded. People want to be comforted right now, not brutalized. Obviously, if the tenor shifts, we'd love to see another application from you, but for now—"

Benjamin pressed seven to delete the message and pulled his blanket up to his neck.

Cold. Why can't I feel my hands?

"This is Bethany from Auto Services making another call about your extended warranty. Time is almost up—"

He pressed seven.

"Bud, it's Dad. Give me a call when you can. Mom saw online that you and Melody split, and I just hope you're doing all right. Melody would barely message us, but she said your headaches were getting a lot more frequent, so if you need a little financial help with your prescription again, just let us know, okay? You can text me, Mom, whatever. Send a message. It'd be good to hear your voice. Also, don't know if you saw the game last Sunday, but oh man—"

He pressed seven. No more messages. Benjamin looked at the bright blue light coming from his screen. It stung the surface of his eyes. He powered down the phone and felt, for the smallest moment, a sense of relief.

There are a shocking number of self-immolation videos available on the internet. It's a very visual form of protest. People notice it—people *feel* it—even if all the flames and screaming and the final charred husk collapsing to the ground don't yield much more than a mess of ashes and melted fat.

Still—hunched there in the dark, lit only by the digital image of another man burning to death—Benjamin noted that all these incinerated bodies, all of these scholars and monks and activists and ex-soldiers, they never really moved the needle for their cause. Their suffering was immense, but it was short, a signal flare in the night, a big bright fuck you that, best case scenario, turned into a heavy metal album cover. Besides, the scarcity was coming, no matter what he did. That ship had sailed, and humans wouldn't change their behavior in time to do anything but turn "abject tragedy" into "abject tragedy with a couple of wind-powered turbines running in the background."

When Benjamin was twenty, he felt a zealous certainty that art mattered, but in his worst moments it felt like an abstraction—an evolutionary side effect that lost its value the moment it reached beyond showing you how to hunt a deer.

"Still," he thought as he scrolled through pictures of modern-day martyrs burning for their respective causes, "people know that these guys meant what they said." He pictured humanity as a boiling mass, a soup of consumptive desire seething over itself, unable to be reasoned with, unable to stop swallowing everything it touched. Inside that terrible miasma, he saw the self-immolators burning bright in the dark, each spark, for at least a moment, seen and known before it faded into beautiful nothingness.

Benjamin returned from an empty mailbox to find the bright orange Final Notice of Eviction on his door.

The neon ink in the paper shone surreal and artificial in the dusk light. It felt toxic just to look at the thing. Benjamin tore the notice down, crumpled it, and threw it to the ground.

That doesn't negate anything. You know that.

This is happening. Soon your home will be gone.

What will they take next?

What do you have left to give?

The very next day, Benjamin began his project.

• • •

It was hard work, all of it, and without grant funds or help from his parents, he was stuck taking mediocre OTC meds for his migraines, now a constant companion. Awful visions set upon him with great frequency, blocking out his sight, laying him low, showing him variations on a theme: cattle consuming feed made from cattle, humans waiting at the bottom of a pyramid for warm fresh hearts to be thrown down, a massive simian figure with a hundred hungry mouths pulsing on its suppurating skin. After each of these visitations, his nose ran, his sight suffered, and light was an enemy.

He pressed on.

He sold off most of his possessions online, feeling a freeness at the finality of it all, at the strength of his conviction and the determined reversal of his own consumption.

All the money he earned was portioned out and redirected into the project, first staving off his impending eviction for just long enough, then purchasing the parts for a hand-built computer that could safely access the darker corners of the web and further provide the supplies which would make his piece possible.

He traveled, phone-free, to the kinds of places where a person could anonymously acquire any kind of medical supplies.

He bought welded-steel plates to secure his property, and quietly covered the interior of his windows with plywood.

He believed his broadcast would be difficult to trace, but it was also best if it was hard for anyone to physically reach him while his message was being sent.

The longer people were able to watch, the better.

The hardest thing was setting Chewie free, but the dog was his final attachment. The piece could only be completed if Benjamin was untethered. So, he placed the kenneled dog, along with his favorite toys and a handful of treats, on the concrete pad in front of Melody's new apartment. He stuck his fingers through the grate and touched Chewie's soft snout and stroked his fur for a moment before something welled up inside him, something soft and needy that threatened all he'd set out to do. Chewie's whining tore at him as he walked away, and there was a moment when Benjamin almost lost his resolve, wanting to rush back to Chewie and embrace him, to fall prostrate at Melody's door and beg her for help, to save him from what he'd seen and what he was about to do, and then he'd call Mom and Dad and tell them yes, he needed medication and probably more, and then he would find a way to conquer his fear and his anger and live for whatever was coming, no matter how awful, and try to be the best of what he knew a human could be.

He stopped in the parking lot of the apartment, knowing the next step was over a precipice. He felt the air, warm on his skin, and even managed to take a deep breath without shuddering, but then that moment's calm was broken as a massive truck rounded the corner into Melody's lot and filled Benjamin's chest and ears with its bone-rattling thrum and his nose with the scent of burning fuel and reminded him of the true nature of the world.

The moment was only a moment. Just a *feeling*. Childish whimsy.

Benjamin returned to his rental car, purchased with a fake ID, and remembered his visions, and what he was meant to do. He looked to the back seat where a small, battery-driven heat lamp shone down on the box he'd received from Uruguay.

I have to keep them warm until it's time.

He was alone there, strapped to the table, starving to death in front of the carefully mounted cameras. And then, at last, the larvae began to emerge.

For days, he had felt his skin tightening against his bones, his stomach clenching and cramping on nothing. But more than that, he'd felt the itch and ache and animal violation of something *other* growing inside of him.

So now it was almost a relief when the larvae finally pushed their way free, pulsing and twisting against the black spiny barbs that rimmed their pale white bodies until they fell loose from the hundreds of bright red pustules on his body.

His art, ascendant.

All of this exactly as he had planned.

He had studied the life cycle of *Dermatobia hominis* carefully and vectored the botfly eggs himself, weeks ago, planting them by syringe, his body fertile ground for each tiny, precious seed. Botfly eggs were buried along each of his chakra points, tucked in next to his tear ducts, mapping his skeleton.

The visual symmetry of their emergence would be appealing.

He had automated the dextrose and saline IV drips to sustain him and his progeny.

He had blindfolded himself with gauze to erase identity and reduce the possibility that he would be quickly discovered. "I am you," he thought. "I am what you will become."

He had set a timer for the activation of the auto-restraints at his wrists and ankles. He was fearful he would weaken once the piece had begun, but the straps that held him made the outcomes of his choice inexorable.

He had covered the floor in precisely the soil the larvae would require and had nurtured one cycle to pupate before the project began to ensure breeding would be possible. The consumption had to continue for as long as it could. And no one would interrupt—his house appeared abandoned and boarded against squatters, and anyone who cared to find him had received this text: Driving to the East Coast for a job opportunity. Will text when I'm settled. Love always, Benjamin.

He had timed the cameras to activate and broadcast on the projected birthing day. A soft chime sounded the moment the cameras went live. He felt the wriggling bodies of the larvae intensify their movements, almost as if they knew it was show time, their jet-black mouthparts and wet, translucent bodies pushing excitedly up into the air.

It was perfect.

The increasing notification sounds from his shadow accounts told him that the broadcast was gaining an audience. When he faded into the now, he imagined the footage rapidly growing from a "what the fuck" oddity to an "is this real/please tell me this isn't real" viral sensation.

Every twenty minutes, a digitally manipulated recording of Benjamin's voice spoke to the audience:

There will be no comfort.

There will be no safety.

We did not deserve it.

What you see is what you've earned.

Every one of you, to the last soul, will feed the flies. And only in that rebirth will we at last be cleansed of what we've done.

And then, aside from the occasional moan, or the soft sound of fresh, fattened larvae falling to the dark soil below, silence.

Benjamin lost time. Visions and reality became the same. At one point his ego had returned and he had borne hot tears from his swollen, fly-pregnant eyes. He'd even cried out his mother's name and said, "Help me! Please!" But it was too late, always too late, for everything had been set in motion long ago and no help was coming.

So time became delirium, and prayers for death, and the sensation of matter changing shape—growing, itching, swelling and squirming in everything that used to be poor, precious Benjamin and all his wants and worries, becoming something vital and honest, wings buzzing in a room filled with new life.

His truth was now everyone's, across millions of screens. He'd shown them what he thought, what he knew. What they really were. And when he felt the next wave of flies land in the raw red craters that pocked what remained of his oozing, agonized flesh, he knew that no other protest had ever burned so bright, or for so long.

No one who was witness to what he'd done would sleep without seeing what he'd become, or wake without knowing that soon enough they'd be just like him.

Eggshell

By Gemma Amor

Mike Vasa came to me on a Monday morning with a special request. He came in person to my cottage, which was unusual, and found me in my workshop at the bottom of the garden, poring over a new selection of skin-tone paints I'd had delivered. He knocked, but I didn't hear. I had the music of John Tavener on as usual, turned up full blast. That was the wonderful thing about the nearest neighbors living a mile away. I could play whatever I liked, as loudly as I liked. Music was meant to be listened to at top volume, I always thought. It was a waste otherwise.

He knocked again, to no avail. Eventually, he let himself in, blocking out the sunlight with his bulk. I started, thinking it was Rhonda with a cup of tea. Instead, I saw Mike.

"Hello, Aggie," he said warmly, and I almost dropped the paint pot I was holding.

"Mike!" To say I was surprised to see him in the flesh was an understatement. Ninety percent of our interactions throughout the course of our careers had been by telephone or email. I was nevertheless happy to see him standing there, head almost brushing the ceiling joist. Mike had always been one of my favorite people. Colleague, friend, partner in crime, quite literally, on several occasions. I cut the music. We hugged. I marveled at how tall he still was. I had shrunk a good inch in the space between meetings.

"You look well, Aggie. Country life suits you." He gestured to the garden behind him, which was alive with bees, butterflies, the looping cries of birds. The lavender was in full bloom. Apple trees swayed in a warm breeze. My dog lay in a patch of sunlight, ears twitching lazily. It was an idyllic scene, and it did suit me, very well indeed. I'd moved out of the city with my wife a year ago, no regrets. I commuted to the lab three times a week, worked out of my custom-built studio the rest of the time. It was a peaceful existence and it had been doing wonders for my health. My blood pressure was the lowest it had been in years and my cholesterol had tipped back over into the healthy zone. No more horrible fried canteen food. I also slept better, or as well as could be expected for a woman who has seen some of the things I have seen.

"I need your expertise," Mike said, getting straight to the point. "Specifically, your craniofacial expertise."

Skull reconstruction skills, he meant. I didn't do it often anymore, partly because of my workload (skull and facial reconstruction is a laborious, time-consuming process), and partly because there were plenty of more qualified folks out there who could do a far quicker job, with the help of computers and modern software. Times had changed, physical models were no longer as fashionable as computerized reconstructions. Still, Mike was old school like me, and adamant. He wanted me to build a face from the remains of an old skull, part of a cold case, with the hope of identifying the victim.

He wanted me to bring a faceless ghost back to life.

"Why not get one of the young'uns to do it? They'd be much quicker, I'm sure," I said, not without a slight measure of salt.

"Because I want a forensic sculptor, is why. I want 3D facial approximation with clay. This one…it's a special case, Aggie."

"Must be if you can afford my rates. I raised them deliberately because I'm tired of working all the bloody time." I chuckled. "It's been a very effective deterrent, I might add."

"The cost is worth it to me. There aren't many forensic anthropologists who double as facial reconstruction experts on my books, as I'm sure you're well aware." Mike gave me a lopsided grin.

"Oh stop flattering me. And you had better have a more compelling incentive than just money. I'm on the cusp of retirement. I have absolutely no room for your particular brand of nonsense anymore," I admonished, smiling.

He sobered, his grin falling by the wayside.

"I'm working the Eggshell case, Aggie."

I nodded. "Is that so?"

The Eggshell case was a grim one. Notorious, thanks to a popular true crime podcast that specialized in unsolved cases. This one had all the ingredients of a story that could, and had, captured the public's imagination: an unapprehended, unidentified serial killer, a string of young, vulnerable victims, a horrendous M.O. A first-hand abduction account from a survivor. Conspiracy theories abounded. The internet was obsessed with the case. After a while, calls for reopening the investigation became so vociferous that the Somerset and Avon constabulary caved to the demands and agreed to allocate fresh resources to the case. I knew this, I just didn't know Mike had been placed in charge. But it made sense. Cold cases in our neck of the woods were revisited by specialist teams, headed up by people just like Mike Vasa: career detectives, with years of experience under their belts, who were, like me, knocking on retirement's door, eminently better suited for desk work. Cold cases were largely about desk work. There was also a specialist cold case unit at the local university. This unit was mostly students and professors who worked in conjunction with the police to revisit unsolved crimes. That was where I came in. I was a self-employed forensic anthropologist and reconstruction artist, with ties to both the police and the university, so it made sense that Mike was here, looking for my help. Still, I had the uncomfortable feeling that I didn't fully belong. I felt rusty, a little out of the loop. Science was advancing more rapidly than I could keep up with, and the speed at which forensic techniques had improved over the past few years staggering.

"What are the details?" I asked, with a degree of caution. I didn't want to get his hopes up until I knew more.

"Decapitated skull of a Jane Doe, found in Stockhill wood some years ago. Remains were never identified, or interred properly as a result. Now we have money, resources. People like you."

I sidestepped the flattery, thinking.

There are many reasons to dismember a body. The most common is to stop identification of remains should the corpse be discovered. This is called defensive dismemberment, and it often leads to a body being divided into six parts: the head, torso, arms, and legs. Sometimes teeth are removed. The head and face are almost always damaged. Our perpetrator was textbook in that respect. He liked to abduct teenagers from the streets in broad daylight, often in a red car, remove their heads from their bodies post-mortem, and smash the face and skull to tiny, eggshell pieces, with the hope of obscuring the identity of the victim as much as humanly possible. The other body parts were never recovered, only the heads. God knows what he did with the rest. I used the word 'he,' because I made assumptions on the physical strength required to do what he had been done over an estimated fifteen- to twenty-year period. After that, the heads stopped appearing in random places around Somerset.

"You're sure it's one of his?"

"I am. We found her in a shallow grave, same area of the woods as three of the others. Head smashed in like an eggshell. They managed to recover most of it at the time, but you'll appreciate that over the years...well...I think there's still enough for you to work with."

"Her? How can you tell?"

"We made assumptions. But I'd like to know for sure."

"I might be able to help. But it'll depend on how complete a reconstruction I can enact, just to warn you."

"Understood. But I have faith in you. If anyone can piece her back together, you can. I need an idea of her identity. I need a face I can release to the public. Posters. See if we can link her to other known victims. Encourage anyone to come forward who might recognize her face. We have some theories as to who the perpetrator is. Even have a few suspects. This will help us tighten the noose, so to speak."

"And you definitely want to trust me with this?"

Mike stared me dead in the eyes. "Sure as day and night," he said.

I couldn't refuse.

• • •

I took delivery of the skull fragments at my home studio. I could have had them sent to the lab, but home was where I had my tools, materials, and most importantly, my music, coffee pot, and dog. If I was going to make a good job of this, I wanted to be comfortable.

As if the poor body hadn't suffered enough indignity, the remains arrived on the back of a moped. I apologized to them profusely for this while unwrapping them. Later, I lit a candle. It burned every night for a week before snuffing out.

There are two types of identification when it comes to mysterious human remains. Circumstantial, where the bones and biological profile fit that of a suspected victim, and positive identification, when the unique biological markers of a known individual are matched up with skeletal remains. Sometimes, DNA can be extracted from the bone and cross-referenced with a DNA database, like the Guthrie card database, but in this instance, by the time DNA sampling had become commonplace, it was too late. Mike had given me a list of young girls who had gone missing in the region during the time the killer was active. The list included headshots, but I had chosen not to look at any of them yet. I did not want to be influenced before embarking on my own artistry. Forensic facial reconstruction requires a neutral, mind. Contrarily, at times it also requires imagination. With lips, for example. Lips decompose quickly. No matter how accurately I remodeled the structure of the girl's jaw, I could never fully recreate the shape of her lips, not without some prior idea of the shape. In these instances, I have to use a little creative license.

But first, I had a jigsaw puzzle to assemble.

It took me three weeks to piece together the skull fragments. I used a soft clay base, upon which I gently pressed every tiny sliver and chunk of skull, each neatly numbered, with a pair of tweezers. It was not an easy task. There were many missing pieces. Fragments often crumbled as I placed them. I ended up drawing around each shard and splinter first, so I had a template to use if the bone gave way. I replaced fragments that broke with hard wax, to keep the integrity of the skull. There was a lot of guesswork and an awful lot of matching fragment edges beneath a microscope. This did nothing for my eyesight.

Every skull is different. There are twenty-two bones that make up the whole. The cranium is responsible for eight of those, and the face the other fourteen. I tried not to make square pegs fit into round holes, but found this harder than I would have liked. I misplaced and replaced many fragments during the reconstruction.

Eventually though, I began to build up a picture.

The most noticeable thing about this particular skull as it took shape was the evidence of a prior frontal injury. Healing had occurred at the edges of an indentation on the forehead, and the wound was not as sharply demarcated as a newer fracture would have been, prior to death. I could see evidence of secondary bone healing around the site of the injury. This meant the victim likely had a scar on their forehead and quite possibly would have been admitted to hospital at some point for stitches. I had a similar scar on my own forehead. As a teen-ager, I'd fallen out of a tree and headbutted a branch on the way down. It took ten stitches to close the wound, which bled like Billy-Oh, scaring my mother to death. Information like this was important for identification purposes. The injury would have been a memorable event. Perhaps there were hospital records, or anecdotal recollections of injuries. This would all help paint a portrait of the person beyond their remains.

On completion of the skull, I sent Mike an email, with attached photographs of the head, which now rested on the stand I had made. Rather than speak on the phone, he visited me at home again. I was beginning to suspect he liked the drive out to the countryside and the face-to-face contact more than he let on. So did I. We were old school, after all.

He turned up with a bottle of wine, which I appreciated.

"Are you trying to turn this into a hot date?" I teased, accepting the wine eagerly. Rhonda and I would drink it later at sundown on our patio, which overlooked rolling green hills and fields of ripening wheat.

"A room full of heads on sticks," he said by way of reply, looking around and shuddering. "You're a strange fish, Aggie. Don't they creep you out?"

"Of course not," I laughed, looking at my career-long collection of over thirty reconstructed heads placed on their stands. I mounted all my reconstructions on stands to make it easier to move them around when I worked on them. It always looked a bit macabre, like heads on pikes, but then, that was the job.

Photographs of other heads in progress hung on the walls above my collection. Mike peered at them, fascinated.

"Why do you put the eyes in first?" he asked, taking off his glasses and wiping a smudge from the left lens. "I've always wondered that. Why you want them looking at you while you work."

"All the other muscles are laid over and around the eyes, so I can't put them in afterwards."

"Makes sense. So, what do we have?"

"I think it's an Eggshell murder. It fits his usual type. Caucasian female, petite. I would say around fifteen years of age, or thereabouts."

Mike made a note.

"The lower jaw tells me this is someone who went through puberty, evidenced by the position of the mental foramen here. It occupies the same position it does in an adult jaw, but the jaw length and position of the dental canal tells me she was not yet adult. The lower jaw also displays a certain asymmetry, which I am sure will come out in reconstruction." I caught myself before saying, "I know how she feels," for I'd always had a bit of a wonky jaw, but I stopped at the last moment. It was never good to see too much of yourself in your work, and I knew it would color my reconstruction efforts.

"Anything else?"

"Well, most of the teeth had been crudely smashed and removed, as you know, but I found fragments of a few roots and four whole, permanent teeth, including a wisdom tooth from the upper jaw, and a canine and two incisors from the lower. Again, from this I can tell we're looking at a young adolescent. Old enough to have a second set of teeth, not old enough to have experienced wear, tear, or decay. The lack of other teeth is going to be an issue with the reconstruction." I sighed and gestured to the appropriate spot on the skull with the tip of a pencil. "I need to figure out how the upper lip might have sat over the teeth here. The shape of her mouth is already beginning to bother me. But we'll see."

We stared at the girl's head for a while, the enormity of what rested before us sinking in anew. A young life, cut short. A brutal, painful end. An undignified journey for her remains.

This case had lit a fire in me that I had not felt the warmth of for some time. I needed to give Jane Doe her face back.

I wasted no time continuing the reconstruction. I had been feeling a mounting sense of urgency to give the girl an identity as soon as possible. She'd been lying in storage for so long, cold and unnamed. A lost child. I'd never had children of my own, not by choice. I could not imagine how the girl's mother had felt when she'd vanished all those years ago. It would be too late to give her any answers, for she was likely long-deceased, but I could give her daughter a name, and a face. Maybe.

I organized my tools like a surgeon does prior to an operation: clay tools, a chronometer, a flexible ruler to wrap around the skull, leather and sandpaper for skin texturing, turps, pins, a Dremel tool. There were, as I'd pointed out to Mike, people who do this job with computers—talented graphic artists using algorithms that automate the process—but I prefer to use my hands because it brings me closer to the person I'm trying to reconstruct. It helps being able to touch the face as I rebuild. It's a sensory connection with the dead, even if it's only a replica.

I made a mold and casting of the original skull so I could work on a replica, which I placed on a stand, as usual. Another head on a pike. Once it was mounted, I arranged the skull into the Frankfort plane position—the natural position the head would be held at during life—using a spirit level, the flexible ruler, and some soft clay at the base of the skull to hold things steady.

Then I started with what I affectionately call the 'pinhead' method. I figured out the likely depth of flesh that covered the skull, using the flesh depth charts and matrices forensic artists commonly use. I hammered in a series of pins at key points around the skull, which I covered in small lengths of rubber tubing that turned the pins into anchored scaffolding. Matchsticks also worked, but I preferred pins because 'matchstick head' didn't sound as good.

I sculpted muscles over the top of the scaffolding with clay, molding every single element of the face down to the minute details. I started with the major muscles, including the temporalis, but before that, I did what Mike hated so much: I put the eyes into the skull first. Artificial eyes come in a range of sizes and colors, so to keep it simple I went with gray, because blue felt too obvious, brown too assumptive, and green too close to my own. Gray eyes felt like neutral territory, although I am sure my peculiar internal logic would have been frowned upon by many.

I paid particular attention to the shape of the pyriform aperture at the base of the nose. The nasal spine, a tiny sharp spur of bone that runs behind the nose, deviated off to one side, indicating that the septum would follow the same path. This gave me a good idea of where the nostrils sat in relation to the base of the nose. Her nasal spine was elevated, indicating a snub nose, which somehow made the whole thing worse. An innocent young girl with a snub nose: what had she ever done to deserve any of this?

The muscles around the mouth did present issues, thanks to the lack of a full set of teeth. Having a canine was a bonus; it helped me figure out where the midline of the mouth was to be drawn, which was usually, according to *Gray's Anatomy*, was just below the canine. I did the best with what little I had to work with, aware that I was using creative license and trying not to beat myself up about that too badly. It was the same with the victim's ears. Ears are cartilage, and hers were long rotted away, so there were no indications of how they would have looked, including whether her earlobes were attached or separate. I made an educated guess and settled for partially detached.

When it came to hair, I was luckier. Usually, I choose a light mousy shade, which can be interpreted as either dark blonde or light brown. I didn't need to guess this time, however. A clump of red hair had been found at the burial site, and because hair is durable, it had survived storage rather well. Another anthropologist had kindly measured the strands of hair for me, so I knew enough to create something straight and shoulder length. My friend, who is a hairdresser, consulted long and hard with me about the hairstyle our Jane Doe likely wore, based on the girl's age and what was fashionable or commonplace the year she disappeared. Parted straight down the middle, bangs cut in, but nothing too flashy. She was only fifteen, after all.

The final piece of the puzzle was depicting the dent in her skull, or more importantly, the scar on her forehead. It was crescent moon shaped. In real life, it would most likely have been puckered, with a noticeable indentation beneath, even after it had healed. As if someone had pressed their thumb into the soft clay of her, and so that is exactly what I did.

And then, suddenly, she was complete.

I rang Mike. "She's ready," I said, and hung up immediately after. I was feeling too many emotions and was in no mood for idle chatter.

Mike was with me within the hour. He must have blue-lighted it the whole way to my cottage. "Show me," he said on arrival. There was no bottle of wine this time.

I uncovered the head, which I had draped a soft cloth over. The lively, soft face of a young teenage girl stared back at us, red synthetic hair glinting in a shaft of sunlight that poured into my workshop. We looked at her, and tears gathered in my eyes.

Mike cleared his throat, pressed a hand to his face. "She's beautiful," he said, eventually.

The next day, Mike released a video of the reconstructed face. In the video, we talked about the victim's age, the painful manner of her death, the history of her scar. The video went viral within hours. The case was still very much the internet's darling.

Three weeks later, we had a name. A relative had seen the video, then compared it to a series of old photos that had been kept in a shoe box and stashed in a cupboard under the stairs in an unassuming terraced house in nearby Bristol. The photographs were in color and faded in the way that all things from the seventies are faded. When I saw the first batch Mike emailed me, I was glad I was already sitting down.

Turns out, all my assumptions had been correct. The face I'd reconstructed was almost the spitting image of the face that grinned from the photograph on my computer screen. I was almost frightened of myself, when I saw it.

Frightened, but that paled in significance to the fact that we finally, finally had a name.

Lucy Harper. Fifteen and a half when she disappeared. Her mother would go out looking for her every day for years, never giving up hope. She died in 1997, never knowing what had happened to her only child.

A week later, Mike rang me, weary, triumphant. "We got him," he said. Dots had been connected. Witnesses interrogated. An attic ransacked, and then searched with a fine-toothed comb. In the attic, a trunk rusted shut. Inside, a murder kit. Rotten ropes, a hammer, a rubber mallet, a bone saw, an axe. A portable camera and twenty-three undeveloped film canisters.

"We found a diary," Mike said. I knew what was coming next. "The scale of it, Aggie. The scale." I knew. I had listened to the podcast updates. I had seen the news reports, read the articles. The Eggshell murderer was dead. He had died in prison, of a heart attack, aged eighty-seven.

He was dead, but his case wasn't.

"Fifteen more heads so far." Mike was full of emotion.

"You know I'm retiring soon, right?" I made the joke a gentle one.

"It has to be you, Aggie," he replied. "It just has to."

I didn't argue this time.

The next batch of remains did not arrive on the back of a moped. They arrived in the back of a van, and it took an hour to fully transfer them all to my workshop.

I lit a lot of candles that night.

Prototype

By Leah Ning

Your first prototype is nothing more than parted lips and the end of a nose, printed from thin, soft silicone. You lick your own lips as you take it from the 3D printer.

You look around your bedroom at the surfaces piled high with musty laundry and empty soda cans before deciding the floor is the easiest way. You sweep aside once-white socks and place the prototype on the floor. Had its eyes existed, it would have stared up at you. You were afraid the prototype would shrink away from you if you gave it eyes. No one has wanted to see you, much less touch you, since the day you were born. No one except your mother, and even she has shrunk away from you now.

On your hands and knees, you lean down and touch your lips to the ones made of soft silicone. They are too soft, the silicone too thin. It folds, then collapses beneath your lips like flayed skin, only without the rotting smell, and your hopeful mouth hits the rough fuzz of the carpet. You sit up, unsatisfied, and watch the distorted half-face pop back into shape like those old hollow baby dolls you used to squash beneath your thumbs.

You pick up the prototype and, using your fingers behind the lips like a sock puppet, hold it up to your face. The pink of your skin behind the hole in the silicone almost looks like the inside of a mouth if you don't think about it too hard.

You picture your crush as you lean in for another kiss, eyes closing. The mask doesn't buckle this time, and you can use your hand to move the mouth like real lips. But you're still unsatisfied. The lips no longer yield with your fingers behind them. You know they should, because yours do when you close your eyes and press your bare fingers to them before you go to sleep, aching, pretending it's someone kissing you good night. And even if you could make the lips yield under yours, the prototype still smells like warm rubber. You know it shouldn't, because your mother didn't in those shattered, fleeting memories you have from when your age was still a single-digit number. You're sure that before she was a haze of sour sweat and cigarette smoke, she smelled like warm salt musk and the flour she used to bake with. She is the only person you can remember getting close enough to smell who didn't also want to hurt you.

Still, your first prototype is what you have, and if you keep your eyes closed, it's not so bad.

You sneak another glance at your crush from the opposite side of the cafeteria and wonder what it would really be like to kiss her. You can almost feel the warmth and weight of her cheeks in your palms, the soft give of her lips under yours. You wonder about this because you already know what it feels like to hold her hand. You were friends with her when you were young enough for your mother to still love you.

On your first day of school, your crush ran screaming when you walked into the classroom. Sometimes you still see the look of horror on her face, smell the crayon wax and citrus surface cleaner of your second-grade classroom. None of them would touch you. Not even the teacher. Your chest ached. Your eyes were hot and damp.

God, you just wanted someone to tell you it would be okay.

Across the cafeteria, your crush laughs and touches someone's forearm. You put your hand on your own forearm as if it will feel the same.

Your second prototype is a disaster. It doesn't collapse under the pressure of your desperate mouth, but it's too rigid, as if the whole face were made of forehead and cheekbones. You can't move the lips against yours like you could with the first prototype. It feels less real that way, less of a person. Still, it has some real weight to it since you printed it with stiffer filaments and made it a full mask instead of just the bottom. Almost enough to imagine you're cupping someone's cheek in your palm while they look down from above. You know this because you've tried it with the boys who straddle your prone form to rain fists down on your malformed face. After a while even their knuckles begin to feel like relief.

You didn't paint the eyes because you're still afraid that the prototype will see you. The eyes are just smooth convex curves the same color as the skin. They stare up past you as you kiss its forehead, its cheeks, the bridge of its nose.

As a last-ditch effort to save the second prototype, you put the first prototype over its bottom half and lean in to kiss the hybrid. You can make the hybrid's lips move using yours, or by using your hands on the sides, but they still don't yield quite right. It's worse than your fingers behind the mask.

And it still smells like warm rubber. You're not sure how to fix that yet.

Even as you peel the first prototype back up and toss the second into a dirty closet, you wonder if you're onto something with the layered approach.

You watch from the middle of the cafeteria as the shape of your crush's mouth expands and contracts around white teeth. As you watch, you remember the feeling of your fingers pushing your lips into your own crooked, yellowed teeth at night. You think that might feel more real than just lips, and you make a mental note to buy ceramic for your 3D printer.

When you get home, your mother, from her place on the couch, gives you the same casual look that isn't quite guilt. On your good days, you almost don't hate her for her for shrinking from you. Your bad days are when someone hates the look of you enough to make you bleed. Her bad days are when she has to stay late at work.

Today is one of your good days, but you still hate her while you climb the stairs to order more materials.

Your third prototype has ceramic teeth behind the neat rolls of gauze you've glued to the backs of its thin, flexible lips. You've started mining cryptocurrency to pay for the materials you need because you're determined to get this perfect. You would have sold your body online, but that would have involved someone loving you. You haven't heard the words "I love you" since you last smelled your mother's baking.

This time, you sit up to try your kiss, cupping perfectly sculpted cheeks that are still too stiff in your palms. The hidden rolls of gauze lend enough softness to be close to what you think is real. The feeling of those false lips mashing against the ceramic teeth sends tingles of excitement rushing up through your belly and into your throat. You wonder if this is what it's like to kiss someone real until your questing tongue tastes silicone, feels the cottony disappointment of the gauze, is stymied by the unresponsive ceramic.

The warm waves in your belly break into washes of shame and impotent fury. Already your brain subconsciously works over the best way to seal the silicone over the gauze and allow the teeth to open for you. Some small black worm drowning in the deepening well of your self-disgust, of your *alone*, tells you that this won't rid the prototype of the smell of warm plastic.

With mental palms, you search out that reasoning worm and mash it, slamming it into the well's bottom, but you only manage to splash up more of that sickening hatred. You hate that it won't die. You hate that you can't use this well to drown it.

Your breath comes in quick, hard bursts, as though you've been chasing something real. Your legs tingle with sleep and you wonder how long you've been sitting here, prototype staring at you through its blank, unpainted eyes. You decide it doesn't matter. You decide that giving it eyes might make it feel like you're being seen and loved.

A few faux wood tables away from you, your crush pulls out a tube of ChapStick. The scent of fake cherries wafts to you even from that distance. You asked once, in that classroom that smelled of crayons and citrus cleaner, if you could borrow some.

She said no, of course.

Your crush looks up at you when you pass by with your lunch tray. It's that same look of horror, but at least now you remember her eyes are brown.

You can't find the exact shade of her eyes when you shop for paint on the way home, but you figure it's close enough.

Your fourth prototype is soft silicone anchored to a hard plastic skull that sports ceramic teeth. You painted the eyes yourself: small black circle, larger brown ring, the rest filled in with white. The colors don't help you imagine being seen like you thought they would. The eyes still look flat, dimensionless, frozen and staring at something you can't see. You think maybe it sees your soul. At least you won't have to see yourself in their reflection.

This time, you sealed up the lips around the gauze rolls and smeared some cherry-flavored ChapStick on them. It's the same brand your crush uses, though of course you only found this out by accident. You even put this prototype on its own stand with a lever at its base that will open the mouth for you. You can work the lever with your feet and pretend it's just your toes curling in ecstasy.

Your lips glide over the ChapStick on prototype four. Its mouth gives softly under yours. You curl your toes and poke your tongue through the parting teeth, hoping for reality again, but there is nothing in the mouth to meet you but a hollow plastic cavern.

As you pull away, the ChapStick has worn off under your lips, and the taste of silicone is back. No flavor, no spray of perfume, will make silicone smell or taste of anything but silicone.

You expect to be upset by this, but the deep well within you stays calm. You understand how you might make it better.

You stay up all night looking up cross sections of human faces, skin, and lips to the background music of your mother doing anything but baking or thinking of you. Your mother's cigarette smoke creeps into your room through the vents. You still hate her because today is not one of your good days.

Your fourth prototype watches with passionless, frozen eyes as you wonder how you will replicate human skin.

You spend the weekend on your computer, touching your own skin and wondering whether your lack of beauty has changed its texture. It probably has. You remember the warm, smooth feel of your mother's arm when you laid your cheek against it.

You feel the rough, flaky texture of your own face, and the well deepens. Your mental hands chase the worm of reason at its bottom, pretending to need its help even as they seek to drown it.

Your fifth prototype required a sacrifice because, as your research has found, there is no material that smells and tastes like human skin besides human skin.

You decided in your desperation that any skin would do, and it was easy enough to blackmail the boy who threw you down the stairs last week into meeting you in the woods. From there, you only had to hit him with a carefully chosen rock until he stopped moving, and that was easy, too. It wasn't as easy to remove the skin from his face with the paring knife you stole from your mother's drawer. Blood is more slippery than you thought it was, and you had to remove his eyelids when you tore them.

You attached the skin to your fourth prototype's skull after it was clean and then smeared the ChapStick on its lips.

Without the silicone skin, there are no painted eyes to stare into what you think is your soul. Only huge dark hollows where the skin's eyelids were. You thought the lack of eyes would comfort you, but it seems the eyes were only stopping the prototype from really seeing you. You close your eyes as you lean in so you can't see the glaring darkness pouring from its eye sockets.

Prototype five's lips are slightly chapped, but they still taste of sweet fake cherries. You see now that the gauze rolls did not have quite the right give. You're not surprised. What you are surprised by is the taste of dried blood when your toes pull the lever and you poke your tongue through the gap in the teeth.

You gasp and let go of the lever. The teeth clamp down on your tongue and the stand falls over, pulling you with it. The gamy taste of the inside of the skin floods your tongue as you feel desperately for the lever. You can hear your mother climbing the stairs to investigate the noise, as if she really cares.

Your fingers find the lever, slip off.

The landing at the top of the stairs creaks under your mother's feet.

You slam your palm down on the lever and yank your head back. Your tongue is aching, but free, when your mother opens your bedroom door. You hate the look of not-quite-guilt on her traitorous face. When she asks, you tell her that you fell, and she doesn't hesitate long before leaving.

That black worm of reason swims up from the bottom of the well of sloshing disgust and alone, where you hoped you'd drowned it. You sit and stare at the ceiling without really seeing it as you listen. It tells you that you could have been caught. It tells you that silicone was enough, that with enough time and use it wouldn't have smelled like rubber anymore, but now you have killed someone. Now you can't go back.

Did you hide the body? You can't remember anything but the haze of the boy's sobbing screams and your own panting, humid breaths.

But if you can't go back, you tell the worm, there's nothing left but to go forward. And there could be a prototype better than this one, with one more sacrifice.

Your mother seems frightened of you as you prepare for what you hope is your final sacrifice. Did she see your fifth prototype? Can she smell it now that it's been in your room for a few days? You don't think she could in her cloud of cigarette smoke, but it's hard to tell.

Your research on your crush finally bears fruit and you swirl cherry ChapStick around your lips. You send an email from a throwaway account. You don't wait for a reply.

Your sixth prototype, which is not really a prototype, lays heavy and not yet stinking in your palms. This one had cherry-flavored ChapStick on its lips before you even acquired it. This one has long, silky brown hair that spills through the cracks between your fingers just the way you always hoped it would when you saw it in the hallways of your high school.

Your crush was almost as easy to blackmail as the boy who pushed you down the stairs. This makes you wonder if she is really your crush anymore. But it had to be someone. You needed it to be someone, and why not her? She would never have had you anyway. She only ever poured more disgust into your well.

It was harder to kill her than the boy. But you figured it out. This time you took your mother's largest knife from the kitchen. You knew you would need it to remove the head when she died. It took you half an hour to do it, but you got it done.

You whistle your way past missing posters for the boy on your way home.

You don't like the way your mother looks at you when you walk in the door. It's almost that same mixture of pity and disgust you're used to seeing at school every day. She doesn't say anything, though, so you bring the head up to your room to finally get your perfect practice.

When you sit on the carpet, you realize you carried the head home in your hands. They're slippery with her blood now.

With your backpack still on, you kiss her unmoving lips. They taste like sweet wax cherries, and they give, give, give beneath your mouth until they press—just right—against the barrier of her teeth. You move her jaw with your thumbs, and her mouth has all the parts you want it to have: slick teeth; smooth, cool tongue; and none of the coppery plastic death taste of your previous prototypes. It all moves the way you want it to with a little encouragement. You wish, fleetingly, that you didn't *have* to encourage, but someone has to lead a kiss, and it might as well be you, and you close your eyes to let this perfect moment drown you.

But she's cold. Not warm like your skin, or warm like she was when she struggled under your knife. Cold. Close, but not real. Close, but not quite her. You know, somewhere deep and reasoning, that you led this kiss because no one will kiss *you*. No one will lean into *you*, you will lean into *them*, always, because no one wants *you*. Not the way you want them.

Screaming, you throw the head across the room, and it almost hits the police officers bursting through your bedroom door.

You resist at first. You do an awkward crab-shuffle, still screaming, until your back hits the wall. You kick at the officers advancing on you, their hands spread in placating shapes—

And then you see, really see, their hands. Reaching for you. As if they want you. And in a way, you suppose they do. In a way, they are leaning into you.

You realize, smiling, that they want to touch you.

So you stop. You go still. You offer up your wrists, grinning, and sink into the gentlest touch you've felt since you last smelled baking from your bedroom.

Wetwork

By Elton Skelter

FADE IN
INT. THE MIDNIGHT DINER–NIGHT

He sits alone in the vinyl booth, elbows resting at the edge of the sticky tabletop, fingers laced together beneath his chin. The peak of his baseball cap casts a shadow that obscures his eyes, which are trained on the muted TV set on the far wall. Images of newsreels pass silently, muted, set to an innocuous soundtrack of some instrumental cover of an early '90s pop song he can't recall.

A waitress in a standard-issue dress approaches, her entry punctuated by the stick and squelch of an unwashed floor underfoot. She is unremarkable, mousy hair streaked with gray tied up above her face, which folds into a practiced and insincere smile.

From beneath the cap, he lets his eyes scan her face, sees the affectation, and mimics it, his lips curling up into a smile to match. He flashes teeth, then—*no, too much*—and replaces this with the coy smile he's been practicing since he was a kid, the one that uses only half his lips, adding undeserved innocence to a weathered face.

The waitress drops a plate in front of him—two eggs, two bacon, double serving of home fries, nothing touching—and steps back.

WAITRESS:

Can I get you anything else, hon?

He looks her over, the way an animal might regard prey: her thick frame; her forearms, strong, marked with burns and cuts, some long healed and silvered; her jaw set and strong, her sagging jowls doing nothing to hide a stony determination from years of simply surviving. He imagines she would be a fighter, that she could hold her own, that she wouldn't go down soft or stay down long. On her breast, a name tag embossed with a faded name, the paint flaking from within the shallow grooves: Shelley or Sheila, the name is indistinguishable and doesn't matter. After he finishes his meal, he will never see or think of Shelley or Sheila again.

He nods, and the waitress beats a retreat from the booth and back behind the counter, leaving her squish-and-squelch footprints in her wake.

In gloved hands he lifts a knife and a fork, tackling the food one at a time. First bacon, cut to squares, eaten individually and to completion. The same with the eggs. And the home fries he chews two at a time.

Shelley or Sheila returns with the coffee pot to top him off, and he nods his thanks, focusing on the expression of humanity.

She smiles and is again lost to him in a wet thud across a vinyl floor.

CUT TO
EXT. DOWNTOWN–MIDNIGHT

The pitch black of the night is at once both dead and alive. Something invisible yet palpable punctuates the air and crackles audibly.

He makes his way down Lakeview, takes an underpass beneath the turnpike, turns right onto a residential estate, which leads him down into the dockyard. He sticks to the shadows, skirting the motion sensors mounted high above the hoists and mounts of all the boats out on the water. Their absence has left the yard a cemetery of gargantuan bones.

Past the dock, he walks the rough-trodden path to the shore and takes the beach along the coast until a new-build high-rise looms in silhouette against the black-brown of the night sky.

His footsteps are silent pads on crackling asphalt, inaudible and practiced.

He inhales, warm air filling his lungs, as he approaches the high-rise. Avoiding the front entrance, he makes his way to the workers entrance out back. The door, he knows, is unlocked, and all security, save that which is intended, dies beyond this point.

Everything dies beyond this point.

BEGIN FLASHBACK
INT. HOME–DAY

He punches the time card at the rear entrance to the factory and leaves without saying a word. The shift has been long; his muscles ache in protest. It's early, so he walks the three miles back to the house, navigating through the various terrains he knows by heart. He undresses as soon as he is inside, showers the night away, and by the time he is ready to lie down to sleep, his cell phone begins to ring, a wail that echoes through the house.

The agency.

He recognizes the script from the last agency that called, and the one before that and the one before that and the one before.

AGENCY:

Sorry to call so early. So, we have some bad news.

The speech follows the same format as always: *not a team player; makes people feel uncomfortable; would be more suited to working alone; we'll call if we have something more suitable.*

He knows they won't call again, much like every agency he has worked with before.

His whole adolescence had been spent pretending, mimicking the expressions and emotions of the people around him, trying to conform and fit in to make life easier. It was exhausting. In one way or another, he had always revealed himself, reached so far into happiness or so deeply into rage that the mask had slipped every time.

As an adult, he has cast aside the need to pretend, dispelled the expectations and the accompanying exhaustion of trying to be something he knows he can never be.

He searches online for work—something, anything, to tide him over financially and keep the lights on, to keep him fed and housed. So little out there for someone who works best without the nuisance of company.

His last resort is the classifieds.

He scrolls absentmindedly, barely letting the impossibilities register.

—home massage (read: *pervert*),
—laundry services (read: *pervert*),
—straight-up fucking (read: *honest pervert*).

His eyes find it, an advert that speaks to him:

Needed: lone worker, no limits, not afraid to get your hands dirty. Negotiable rate. Instant start.

He hits reply, and the cycle starts.

Two days later a burner phone is delivered to his doorstep. It rings the second he opens the box. They are watching. They have him.

Intrigued, he answers the call.

END FLASHBACK

INT. HIGH-RISE–NIGHT

The service elevator takes him to the top rear of the building. He treads lightly past the reinforced iron door of apartment 22DD and approaches the neighboring apartment without detection.

With a flutter of anticipation, he slides open the metal barn-style door, enters the apartment, and closes it behind him with a hydraulic swoosh. Silence envelops him: the benefits of the soundproof cladding built into the walls of every apartment on the twenty-second floor.

The apartment is unfinished, every surface coated with a layer of plastic wrap. Long metal benches bring to mind an operating theatre.

Or an abattoir.

The air is frigid. He can see his breath in the makeshift clinical space, transparent clouds of frosted stale air that billow about him as he approaches the bank of high-tech, high-definition monitors that frame 22D from a range of angles, covering all the space within. There are twelve large screens, each date stamped and numbered, and as he removes his jacket, his pants, his undershirt, he lets his eyes scan across the enhanced digital translation of the happenings inside the neighboring abode.

There are more than two dozen cameras built into the soundproof walls of 22D, tucked into bookshelves, hidden in skirting boards, built into the upper corners of every room, and into hanging pictures, vases and lamps. He watches the carousel of images as they stagnate for fifteen seconds before reassigning to different locations.

On the screens, three young men, clad only in shorts, snort lines of white powder from a low coffee table. The floor around them is littered with discarded tins and bottles, and they take turns to snort their fill of what he assumes are supplied narcotics.

Two cameras on tripods watch them keenly from within the room, decoys that the young men look toward to flirt, to grab themselves and each other, to perform for what little money was offered them to appear in the lie of this movie.

They do not know why they are really here or that, with every drink and every line, they are in more and more danger.

If he could feel guilt, he might feel bad for them, for he knows what's coming.

To the left of the monitors, a rail holds his clothing, his costume for the performance, and one by one he dons the garments. To perform as he does, he must remain hairless, so he is shaved close to the skin on every part of his body save his eyebrows and a small thatch of public hair. He pulls on the undershirt, long-sleeved to cover his arms, and thermal leggings to cover his legs. Over this he draws on waterproof waders, a brushed flannel shirt, and a large butcher's apron fashioned from thick rubber and fastened in front with a dense industrial buckle. His boots are heavy, steel toed, and disposable. Black shiny rubber gloves run the length of his arms all the way to his shoulder.

The lower half of his face is covered by a surgical-style mask in thick leather, and his head is crowned by a long, straggly lace-front wig held in place with single-use wig tape and a bandanna.

To finish the look, he applies a tool belt to his thick waist, all loops and pockets securing various blades and weapons. This is the look they have chosen for him, a horror from a nightmare or a movie that he would never willingly watch. He is the star.

The young men continue their sexualized performance for the cameras that record nothing while the rest of the room observes with the endless memory of digital hard drives. He steps up to the monitors and, obscured from beneath the curtain of fake hair, appraises the men, each appearing shorter, each weighing less than himself. He had not anticipated three, but their size and frame, as well as the effects of the drugs on their bodies, does not faze him. They are settled into the couch, their tongues tasting each other mouths, necks, and skin convincingly. He supposes they might be hustlers or sex workers, the performance so enthused as to look real. It's all about selling the story.

He makes his way to the window, opens it, and climbs onto the fire escape, the low-hanging machete at his waist making a gentle *ding* against the window frame. Twenty-two floors below him, the city is dead—beautiful in its serenity, with only the sound of the wind and the distant call of surging traffic to break the imposed silence of this desolate location. He moves slowly along the metal catwalk to the outside of 22D and slides open the window, setting the performance, finally, into motion.

INT. HIGH-RISE–NIGHT

The reality of his performance doesn't register with him. He treats it like a game—hide and seek, where he is both hiding and seeking. The back window in the rear of the apartment pops open, freeing the sound from inside. He crawls gently through the window, a hand securing the machete, and into the dark and empty bedroom.

This room is familiar to him now. He knows the best ways to move to avoid detection. He knows how to angle his form for the best visuals based on where the cameras are hidden. He stalks the room, fully immersed in the game.

It's typical horror movie fare. He places himself behind the open door, gently pulling it closer to his body to cover his silhouette against the moon beyond the window.

Now he waits. Beyond the bedroom door, the music reaches a heavy crescendo and then fades to nothing. Laughter permeates the room, another thick inhale, the sounds of frottage and a gentle moan. He closes his eyes and trains his ear: the sound of bare feet padding on the floor, growing gradually louder.

VOICE:

I gotta piss and take a shower. I'll be right back.

The footsteps increase in volume, a strange haphazard staccato as they slalom throughout the hallway. The level of cocaine in this man's blood would be enough to raise his awareness, making the possibility of resistance all that more delicious.

The sound of the bathroom light being turned on rings in the next room, and the door creaks as it is partially closed. Then, the sound of running water as the shower turns on.

Let the games begin.

INT. BATHROOM–NIGHT

He eases the door closed behind him, waits for the sealing hiss to know the soundproofing has them encased. The shower is giving off plumes of thick steam that fill the room, fogging up the mirror above the basin. Through the shower curtain, he appraises the figure, his trim waist and wiry limbs, his high buttocks and thin muscular legs. He puts the guy at five-eight, maybe a hundred and thirty pounds.

He knows the way they like the first act. A silent strike; no screaming.

This limits his methods to a few quick and extreme options: beheading, slit throat, drowning, traumatic brain injury, choking, suffocation—all sudden, all requiring the element of surprise to reduce the risk of eliciting a scream from the victim. The first kill needs to fall into this set of rules but also needs to be visually arresting, to live up to the standards of what is expected from the performance.

He withdraws a length of leather cord from inside a pocket on the apron and, as the young man washes his hair and face beyond the frosted shower curtain, sets to wrapping it tightly around one fist, holding the other end taut in his free hand.

Then he strikes.

The young man's face is wet and lathered with soap, and his hands fly up instinctively to defend himself. The timing is perfect. He spins the young man, still blinded by soap and shampoo, to face the most encompassing camera and wraps the leather cord around his neck, pulling tightly to stifle any audible retort. He hoists the naked figure to him, holds him close as the man wrestles and wriggles in protest, clawing at the gloved hands that hold the binds and control his breathing. Wet gurgles are punctuated with small clouds of soapy bubbles as he fights the constraints, kicking and scissoring his legs, finding purchase against nothing but the wet plastic of the shower curtain.

The method is adequate, but hardly spectacular.

He hoists the man to the toilet bowl, half filled with piss, and thrusts the man's head beneath the surface and into the porcelain. A wet thud knocks him senseless and, for a second, the struggle subsides. The push was too hard, and the toilet water starts to turn a rusty orange with blood, suggesting a nose broken or lip split apart when the youthful face connected with the ceramic pan.

More blood clouds the water, and as the young man's wits return, he flounders, attempting to pull the flush, doing so blindly, unable to locate it.

A minute more, and they both know the game is over.

The minute passes, and the young man's struggle ends.

The first act is complete.

He lets the man's body rest against the floor and checks out his work. A thick bruised line forms a choker on the young man's neck. The odor of ammonia and copper fills the air, and the man's face is a bloody ruin. His front teeth have shattered and perforated his lips, his nose an explosion of cartilage and pulp. If he wanted spectacle, he had succeeded.

The shower curtain, half torn down, becomes a shroud for the body, and he lifts it easily in his arms, a prop to initiate the second act.

INT. BEDROOM–NIGHT

With the body posed beneath the bedsheets, its ruined face turned away from the doorway, he positions himself in the dead space beneath the bed and waits. The music down the hallway continues to rage its heavy beats, and the sounds of the young men laughing and fucking and indulging in each other's bodies provides a sick soundtrack to his proposed second act.

His arms are tired from the fight, and he lets the muscles rest as he waits a while, gathering his patience.

This section of the show can be pruned back in post, edited for time if needed, spliced with whatever pornographic footage is being committed to digital memory beyond the bedroom.

He controls his breathing, slow and steady, and prepares himself, huddled beneath the bed, until, finally, a voice from beyond the door echoes into the room.

YOUNG MAN #2:

Hey, Rudy, where'd you go?

The figure appears at the doorway, nude save for his underwear, his bare feet small and dainty, and this is all that falls into view from his vantage point beneath the bed.

YOUNG MAN #2:

Dude, come on. My ass is killing me, and *you* gotta spend time on screen to get the money.

No reply. Frustrated, the man walks into the room and to the side of the bed nearest the door, uses one foot to push the backside of the figure beneath the sheets.

YOUNG MAN #2:

(angry)

Get up, asshole. I seriously need a break. That creep has done more than half the blow and he literally won't quit.

He kicks the body again and, in his impatience, strips back the sheet. What follows resembles a mewl from an injured animal more than a scream, soft enough not to be heard by the last remaining young man in the distant room.

From below the bed, he tracks the man's motions as he turns, in horror he suspects, and stifles another sickening moan behind his hands.

Act two begins with a razor-sharp blade dragged across the back of the young man's ankles, the tendons making a snapping noise like the sound of torn elastic.

These screams are audible, and continuous, and the young man falls to the floor, desperately searching for the source of his pain. Their eyes meet, the man's go wide, and finally he slides from beneath the bed.

The second victim can be as loud as it wants after being incapacitated. The only purpose it serves now is to prepare the final victim for the chase. Apartment 22D is not expansive and does not allow for a chase as such, but this is the opportunity for the spectacle he is constantly pressed for.

He hoists himself to his feet as the young man tries to drag himself away using only his blood-soaked arms. The man is useless to him in that moment, and so he bypasses him, exits the bedroom as the music comes to a sudden stop.

YOUNG MAN #2:

(screaming)

RUUUUUUUUUUUNNNNNN!

The scream is piercing, dripping with fear and helplessness. Cinematically, it will make for an excellent soundtrack once the video is cut together for viewing.

As he exits the bedroom, he spies the last victim, unclothed, pupils the size of satellites, nervous energy visibly coursing through him. The man flings himself out of the lounge and toward the front door. He rips and pulls furiously at the lock.

The door, of course, will not open. It's auto-lock function is designed to stop anyone escaping without the aid of some unseen crew member to release the bolt remotely.

They truly have thought of everything.

He moves slowly toward the third man, shoulders hunched, making himself wider and meaner, glaring through the fronds of someone else's hair forming a curtain across his face. He quickens his step as his victim backs away and draws the machete from its holster.

It's typical of what you might expect: the young man runs, and he pursues. They circle the couch and the coffee table, clumsily kicking at and tripping over bottles and cans.

The young man tries the window that, again, won't open without someone on the outside flipping a switch.

Our killer postures for the cameras, maneuvering the scared young man to the places where his fear can be immortalized in the best light, with the closest shots of his anguish. The man moves quickly, the coke in his system like a fire inside. He is sweating gloriously, skin thick with a sheen of sweat that makes him sparkle under the dipped lights.

Eventually, the dance must end.

Eventually, the man's neck is in his hand.

Eventually, the screams of this stranger are stifled by the pressure at his throat.

Eventually, his back is prone to the wall, and he is immobilized.

The young man's breath is locked in his lungs, his gaze turns to panic, and he views his attacker's face from beneath that thatch of fake hair obscuring his eyes, his lip turned up in a sneer of cruelty, of anticipation.

Finally, he drags the machete through the tight skin of his victim's abdomen. His mouth forms an 'o' shape as his insides fold and roll beneath the blade. Blood erupts in a thick curtain down his front, coating his legs, staining his white boxer briefs a hideous dark red-brown.

Inside him, the feeling threatens.

With a grunt, he hoists the blade once more and slams it through the man's chest, pinning him to the wall.

The man's eyes start to go vacant, but he grabs his chin in his hand and draws his attention back to his gaze. He needs the contact for this to work; he needs to relate.

With his spare hand, he rakes the young man's insides from the gash and lets them paint the floor at his feet, blood and ichor sloshing on the disposable boots, drowning the front of the rubber apron in strands of viscera.

The man's eyes widen for a second, and then he is gone.

The feeling hits him: raw human emotion. It floods his system like a narcotic drip and tingles along the edge of every extremity, crackles over his skin like static.

He does not know what the feeling is, but the fact that he can feel it is enough. Is it horror? Guilt? Shame? Does it even *fucking* matter?

He rides the wave until it subsides, and, as quickly as it came, it's gone.

From the bedroom, the second young man screams once more.

The feeling was fleeting, but he knows he has one more chance to recreate it. Perhaps he will savor that last kill, soak up every feeling he can, rinse the experience for all it is worth. If he keeps his camera angles clean, he has carte blanche to do whatever he wants to the final victim, no holds barred.

He looks away from the entrails erupting from within a ruined body.

There are still weapons to discover in the holster at his waist, most of them painted in the gore of the last victim or sloshed with sour piss from the first.

He considers his options, considers a way to slowly drain the life from this man while he—a vampire, a horror movie come to life—feeds on every last drop of emotion.

He is in this for the feeling, and feeling is something he has never been able to do.

Once he is done with the scene, someone, some nameless and faceless being, will cut the footage into a movie, enhance the soundtrack, fix the image with filters, saturate or color the lighting.

From there, someone will sell it to the highest bidder, stream it for a fee, and whoever pays the most will consume it for their own amusement.

It doesn't matter to him that the feelings he gets from these encounters are so dark and horrific; it matters only that he feels anything at all.

And in those final seconds, when the life drains from the face of his victim, he finally feels like one of them...

A person.

A monster.

Just like everyone else.

FADE OUT

Hair

By Francesca McDonnell Capossela

"My hairline is receding."

Samantha's mother pointed with her arthritic finger to the place where her oily forehead met tufts of baby hair. "See?" she said. She ran the soft pad of her finger over the line, making the little hairs stand on end.

Samantha tilted her head to the side to feign concentration. She reached out and touched the limp blond strands. Augusta's hair was brittle from excessive highlighting, but it was also thick and long, and it seemed unlikely that it would abandon her at sixty.

"And there's this bald spot." Augusta pointed to a coin-sized patch near where her hair was parted. "Can you tell?" She leaned towards the mirror and squinted.

Samantha sighed. "Turn back towards me, Mom."

Augusta turned, smoothing her hair back behind her ears, a nervous tic.

Samantha examined her mother's face, unnaturally tanned and coated in several layers of moisturizer. Her thick eyebrows framed deep brown eyes. The area above them was red now, as Augusta was in the middle of tweezing, but Samantha knew that she could cover up the irritation easily. The skin around Augusta's mouth and eyes was wrinkled, a crumpled sheet of paper that someone had tried to smooth back out. But, somehow, this sign of aging lent her a kind of glow, like the result of a soft focus camera lens.

Samantha turned away from her mother and instinctively checked her own reflection in the mirror, paying special attention to her hair. Did too much of her own scalp show?

She often wondered that. The part that the hairdresser had given her, along the right side of her head, was a thick line of pale white skin. At several places, small dots were visible like goosebumps—her skin was so unreliable—and, in the shower, she often pulled clumps of hair off her hairbrush. Maybe her mother's predicament was contagious.

Though she was younger, firmer, and smoother than her mother, Samantha's nose, inherited from her father, was too large for her face and was dotted with blackheads that makeup failed to fully disguise. If it hadn't been for this nose, she would have been, without question, more beautiful than Augusta. But the protrusion distorted her, and the question remained.

Besides her nose, Samantha had also inherited from her father the apartment in which she and her mother now lived. This apartment, with a view of Central Park, had once been vibrant with guests, buzzing with music and bubbling with champagne, back when her father was alive and their lives were prescribed and predictable. Now, they had long days of nothing to do, allowances paid to them monthly from a trust. The house was empty, and every floor-creak was a scream in the silence.

"Samantha?" Augusta motioned impatiently at the bald spot.

"We'll just cover it a bit," Samantha said glibly. "Can you put your hair half up?"

Together they worked at the hairdo, using a lock of hair to cover the spot of skin, and securing the tresses with a barrette at the back of Augusta's head. When Samantha snapped the barrette into place, she saw Augusta wince as the hair clip pulled at a sensitive strand of hair. Samantha felt a pinprick of pleasure. The bald spot, she noticed, was still visible if you looked closely. She was glad; it would highlight her own youth in comparison.

"How do I look?" Augusta asked.

"You look great." Samantha smiled, enjoying those three words that can, when said between women, mean anything. She'd have said the same three words if Augusta looked horrific, or if she looked her most beautiful, and her mother knew it.

Samantha could tell that Augusta felt the itchy anxiety of the phrase. Samantha picked up her martini from the dresser and took a sip, and Augusta returned to her previously abandoned task, plucking her eyebrows with some venom.

Eyebrows clean, thin, and arched, Augusta turned next to the matter of foundation, and began the seven step ritual that had been perfected over the last forty-five years. Samantha watched her mother, sensing that Augusta's frustration was bordering on violence. For a moment, she was afraid that Augusta would dig her painted nails into Samantha's skin, but her mother merely reached for her lipsticks.

Samantha and Augusta were in the master bathroom—which had two marble countertops and two sinks—and they worked with their backs to one another. *Sexy Sienna*, *Walk of Shame*, *Bond Girl*. Colors chosen carefully, as if by a painter, spread over moisturized lips, assets dignified and cared for. A hint of blush, mascara top and bottom, eyebrow pencil for extra arch, a nude on the eyelids.

Samantha's father had died from a heart attack in a hotel hot tub during a business trip to Beijing. In the year since his death, Samantha and Augusta had gone from getting seven hours of sleep a night to getting sixteen. They slept during beauty treatments, facials, massages, tanning sessions. They fell asleep with their heads in the big fishbowl sinks at the hair salon, faces raised to the ceiling, the bobbles around their heads resembling astronaut helmets. They slept during blow outs and manicures, pedicures and exfoliating scrubs, Swedish and Thai and East-West and acupressure massages. They slept in experimental sensation deprivation tanks, in meditation classes. They slept with needles poking out of their ankles and the base of their skulls during acupuncture. They slept to cut down on calorie consumption. They slept to escape boredom. They did *not* sleep during their Brazilian waxes. But sometimes, when they were home in their beds, they dreamed about the sensation of hair being yanked off their assholes, that final tug. The dull, bearable pain.

When they were not sleeping, Samantha and Augusta endured pain like only women can. They tried laser hair removal and asshole bleaching; they plucked eyebrows and froze fat. Did burpees in the gym until their vision blacked out. They starved themselves on juice cleanses and emerged battered from occasional plastic surgery sessions. But—during their limited stretches of consciousness—the exhaustion was far worse than the pain. There was always something to retouch, to remodel. They had to run miles just to stay still.

"They're downstairs," Samantha singsonged, and the thrum went through them both. The moment for which they had been waiting, planning, sharpening themselves all day. This dinner with men, this feast. It was not the most titillating of company—Samantha's father's cousin and his son—but company at all was a special treat. Especially the company of rich, unmarried men.

"I look like a whore," Augusta said, morosely as they walked to the elevator.

"I look like a fat little piggy," Samantha said.

The restaurant was old-fashioned, complete with a jazz band in the corner, and swanky velvet curtains separating its patrons from the outside world. They had the sense of being underground.

Samantha ordered a kale salad, without dressing, and a martini, and spent much of dinner watching Augusta shovel forkfuls of penne with vodka sauce and bacon into her mouth, barely pausing to chew. While the men talked, Samantha smiled and nodded and did some calculations in her head. One slice of dry whole wheat bread: 69 calories. Kale Caesar salad with no dressing: 250 calories. Caramel macchiato: 250 calories. Two double chocolate chunk Quest bars: 360 calories. Vodka martini: 124 calories. Mixed green salad without dressing: 40 calories. Total: 1,093 calories. She would have to do better tomorrow.

Chad and his father, Craig, could only have two motivations for being at the Waldorf Astoria with Samantha and Augusta that night. The first was a sense of duty towards Samantha's deceased father. The second was a hope that the women might invest in their new venture capital fund; their last business endeavor had been recently shut down under suspicious circumstances.

"We've been raising capital for our new project," Craig was saying. "It's a very safe investment with a guaranteed high return. Something your husband would have certainly participated in."

Augusta picked the olive out of her martini. "It's so sexy when men talk business," she said. "Do you have a girlfriend, Chad?"

"We'd love to show you the deck," Chad said. "It's a great opportunity."

"I bet you can't be tied down," she continued, rolling the olive around in her mouth. "Unless you're into that." She gave a horsey laugh and winked.

Chad was the type of thirty-something man who seemed attractive until you looked at his face. Then you saw that his milky eyes were too small and that he resembled one of those online face mashups that predict what a celebrity couple's child might look like; two faces that were attractive on their own but looked wrong when collaged together. Craig, meanwhile, had a long handsome face and gray hair. He looked like the type of creep who would get away with pleading that the preteen had seduced *him*. He kept telling the women that he was working on becoming a "better man," whatever that was.

All in all, the men were dreadfully boring. They talked in soundbites about stocks and politics, about Samantha's grandmother, her great-uncle, and some child to whom she was not sure she was even related. They said the necessary diplomatic things about the new president—a gleeful *he's nuts* and the classic *I hated both candidates*—which made it clear that they had voted for him. Samantha slid her bare leg towards Chad and allowed her toe to sneak up the leg of his trousers until it was prodding his mid-calf. She tried to go up farther, but the angle was awkward, and his pants were tight. He squirmed but did not push her away. He was not technically even her second cousin, as she was pretty sure Craig was not his biological father. But it was hard to be certain with these things.

Augusta was becoming increasingly drunk on her third martini of the night, and fifth that day. "You must be so relieved to be separated from your ex-wife," she said to Craig sympathetically, "She was such a demanding woman."

"She *died,*" Craig said, rather ineloquently. "She had cancer."

Augusta shrugged. "Now that you're both bachelors again, I wanted to ask you something." She smiled naughtily. "What do you boys think about feminine rejuvenation? Have you ever been with a woman who had it?"

The men were silent. They probably had no idea what Augusta was talking about, Samantha thought. They probably lived in a porn world of perpetually tight pussies, where skinny hairless bodies were the product of nature, not hard work. They had no idea how much sweat and blood went into the upkeep of their fantasies. Men were so naïve; you had to pity them.

"I know for myself and Samantha," Augusta went on, unaware of the blank stares she was receiving, "we do our Kegels every day, and we've had rave reviews. I mean, one man said I felt like a thirteen-year-old girl. Do you remember that, Sam?" Augusta giggled wildly, and for a moment, Samantha wasn't sure her mother would be able to stop laughing. Then she reigned herself in. "But of course, we're always in the market to improve, so if it really does work..."

Samantha knew this was too much. Her mother miscalculated more and more these days, and Samantha had trouble stopping her. It was embarrassing, and she wondered, not for the first time, whether she would have to stop going out with her. After all, Augusta would have to understand. It was she who had taught Samantha to be attractive in the first place; ugliness, they both knew, must be obliterated.

Samantha was beginning to panic. She could feel the men's eyes retreating from her and her mother. They were looking at their plates, at each other. Samantha looked at Augusta and saw that her hair had come out of its updo. The bald spot was now blatantly visible, as if a spotlight were aimed on it. She felt a surge of hatred for her mother's ugliness, a hatred that was not her own. She felt her underarms prick with sweat.

Had she put on deodorant? She couldn't remember. Couldn't remember getting ready at all, couldn't even remember who these men sitting across from her were. Connor? Christian? She felt faint with hunger, imagined that her skin looked gray. She couldn't hear out of her left ear, and she was seeing spots on the periphery. She excused herself to the bathroom.

In the dimly lit single stall, she slapped herself across the face several times until the spots in her vision vanished and her cheeks looked rosy again. She could barely see herself in the dark room. She had to turn the light up, she thought. There had to be a way to make it brighter. She found the light switch, looked for one of those dials that control brightness, but it was a simple switch: On and Off. She began to cry, pulling the switch up and down furiously, the movement jerky like that of an awkward hand job. The light went from dim to dark from dim to dark. She turned back toward the mirror and gripped the sink with white knuckles. She couldn't see herself clearly. She felt a scream at the back of her throat and swallowed. She leaned as close to her reflection as possible, straining her eyes until they ached. She couldn't see herself.

When she returned to the table, the conversation had resettled itself. The men had drunk a bottle of wine between them and were less intimidated by these women than one might expect. The conversation turned again to market conditions, and Samantha contemplated slitting her wrists in the bathroom; businessmen were so unbearably boring. Looking over at her mother, she saw that Augusta had mascara smudged under her left eye. She looked like a sad clown. Samantha didn't tell her. The two of them sat there, their perfect faces marred by exposure to the real world, like two ugly witches in a fairy tale.

They ate dessert: chocolate mousse for her mother, crème brulé for Chad, an espresso for Craig, an Americano for Samantha. She could smell the rotten hunger on her own breath. Her mouth polluting itself, sabotaging her. Making her disgusting. Why did your breath smell when you were hungry? Shouldn't it smell as you ate, consuming disgusting conglomerations of fat and carbs and sugars and artificial flavors? As you consumed the things that destroyed you, that made you flabby and heart-attack-prone, that gave you type 1 diabetes and blood clots and possibly early-onset Alzheimer's? She tried to swallow the smell of decay.

Despite renewed efforts, she was getting nowhere with her toe inside Chad's trousers. And anyway, even if she got him in a prone position, ready to be conquered, he would probably faint at the smell of her, her rancid breath, the odor of a body breaking down. She got up again, motioning to the bathroom as explanation. She didn't want to open her mouth and risk letting any of the trapped air out. She hoped they didn't think she had diarrhea; she hadn't shit in ages.

At the sink, she rinsed out her mouth with water. It made little difference. Desperate, she pumped a bit of soap into her hand, mixing it in her palm with the running warm water, and then rinsed her mouth again. It tasted sour, the pearly pink soap, but there was the stench of perfume too that masked the smell of hunger. Less like roses, and more like detergent, but still.

When she returned, the check was on the table in its black leather envelope. Her mother reached dramatically for her wallet, moving slowly to maximize Craig's time to stop her. He let her fumble in her purse for a moment before he produced a Platinum American Express that Samantha knew weighed as much as her left hand.

"Would you boys like to join us at the house for an after-dinner drink?" Augusta tittered at her own proposition, as if she were a schoolchild enjoying the innuendo. "It's such a large house, and we'd hate you to have to go back to Brooklyn tonight." She said *Brooklyn* like she said *pubic hair*.

Craig and Chad were not looking at each other, or at Augusta and Samantha. Allied again, mother and daughter grinned at each other, batting their eyelashes in unison. Both faces flushed with the possibility of sex, of more alcohol, of company and entertainment, of conquest.

"I'm afraid we've got an early meeting tomorrow," Craig said, "with the Board of that company I was telling you about." Samantha had to suppress a yawn. One good thing about her dad dying had been no more talk of Board meetings.

"That's unfortunate," said Augusta, but there was the slightest undertone of relief in her voice. Samantha understood. Their sex routine was exhausting: silky nightdress put on in the bathroom, stray hairs plucked while sitting on the toilet, the teeth brushing, the squatting over the bath faucet to clean the asshole completely. The perfect moans, never guttural but high-pitched and delicate, the squeezing of the vaginal walls, the constant prayer to some nameless god *not to sweat, not to queef, not to leak anything*. And then the peeing, the shower, the perfuming, the antiperspirant, the makeup redone, the kiss goodnight or the walk to the door, the early morning wakeup to brush teeth and reapply foundation. It was easier, much easier, to look beautiful when you were alone.

Samantha had known what to expect after dinner, and had only made a show of covering her ears when her mom opened the cab door at a red light, stuck a finger into her mouth, and excavated herself of the pasta, cream sauce, and bacon, which came up in the pinks and oranges of a sunset.

Augusta slammed the door and wiped a bit of spittle from the corner of her glossed lips with her stiff finger. "What a delicious dinner," she said. "I wish you'd eaten, Samantha. You're always such a killjoy."

Samantha was overcome by a sudden wave of anger. Hot salty liquid rose in her throat. Again, she saw black spots at the corners of her eyes. She lunged for her mother and grabbed the lump on the back of her head that was the barrette. She yanked hard and Augusta cried out, a strangled, ugly noise.

"Ma'am? Everything okay?" the taxi driver asked. The women locked eyes, and Augusta reached a shaking hand forward to pull closed the partition.

Samantha let go and turned away from her mother. There were loose hairs on her black sweater like an animal had shed on her. She thought of the splatter of vodka sauce on the side-walk and felt achingly hungry. If only she could stand the finger down her throat, she could be more like her mother.

The whole way home, Samantha fingered the fat that rose over the waistband of her jeans, the little bit of flesh that she hated more than anything in the world. She imagined having a serrated knife with which to saw at it.

She felt lightheaded by the time they got up to their apartment, and she poured herself a glass of vodka, chewed two Tums (20 calories), and sat down on the couch.

She looked for her phone for a minute before realizing that she was holding it. She had opened a photograph of her and her mother from two years ago. They looked happier, but their tans were patchy.

When she felt steadied by the antacid and the alcohol, she went to the master bathroom where she pulled out the sleek metal scale that had been a birthday present when she was in middle school. Standing on it, ready for the worst, she was surprised to see she had lost a pound since that morning. It was probably just water weight, but still. She reapplied her makeup in the mirror, holding onto the bathroom counter with one hand. This room, like every other room in the house, was spare and impersonal, like a hotel.

Makeup done, she turned to her hair. Letting it down, she found that it was matted and oily. It reminded her of the texture of doll's hair, felt repulsive in her fingers. For a moment, she was overcome by another wave of nausea, disgusted by her own body, by the so-called appendage of the skin that was her hair. The anatomical term was accurate in its nastiness; *appendage* sounded like a sack of flabby flesh, a protrusion.

She tried to brush out her hair, but the knots were so dense that the brush caught again and again. She yanked the brush furiously until her eyes watered, but when she'd finished the first clump of hair, she saw that she had only made it bushier, wilder than before. She picked up a bottle of dry shampoo, sucked in the chemical smell of it, but it only made her hair greasier.

She was filled with a rage she knew well. It was the feeling she got when the sensitive skin of her vulva was ripped at with hot wax. Something so sharp and hot, she felt she could kill.

It was the fury of being subjected to pain, again and again, of being both the victim and the sadist. She remembered her mother's favorite lesson: *a woman's hair is everything.*

Samantha woke with drool coating her left cheek. She checked the time on her phone. She had seven likes on her Instagram photo. She stood up and swayed. She checked the time. An Apple News alert. 4 a.m.

She walked slowly to the bathroom. In the dark, she could see the counter, scattered with lipsticks and eyebrow pencils. The cleaning lady had been there yesterday and already it was a mess. Then Samantha noticed something odd, a bundle, perhaps a pile of clothes, near the sink. She moved towards it and touched it with her pinky finger. It was coarse and strangely oily. She recoiled, looked around, and then picked it up.

It was a wig.

She looked again at the counter and noticed that there was something in the sink. Her eyes were adjusting to the dark. Something was dripping slowly into the basin from the wig. Something runny. She saw little hairs scattered around.

She reached in and touched the liquid. It was warm. She brought it to her nose. She couldn't smell anything. She checked that nobody was watching her and licked her finger. It was blood.

She looked down at the wig. What she had taken for the wig lining was not lining at all. It was patches of something bumpy and oily and warm. Patches of scalp.

Samantha screamed.

Though Augusta was not the ideal mother of mommy blogs, she was a mother nonetheless, and hearing her daughter scream reached the most primal part of her. She jumped out of bed and ran to Samantha's bathroom. She still had on her moisturizing gloves and socks, and she slipped a little on the tile floor. "What happened?" she demanded, her voice screechy with nerves. She turned on the light, and then she also screamed.

Samantha was standing in the dim light of the bathroom, holding her own hair, bald and bleeding from the places on her head where her scalp was missing.

"What have you done?!" Augusta shrieked.

Upon seeing her mother, Samantha remembered the sweet violence of the night before; the freedom of mutilation. She remembered the bald coin on the crown of her mother's skull. She looked down at the thing in her hand, and a faint grin tweaked the corners of her lips. She was more terrifying than ever.

"How do I look?" she asked. She was still clutching her hair in her left hand; an ancient warrior brandishing the head of an enemy. "Mom, how do I look?"

Paypig

By Jeremy Megargee

If anyone tells you that sex work is easy, they're lying through their teeth. It took forever to build up my social media platform, endless hours of content creation on TikTok, Twitter, and OnlyFans. It was about establishing the brand that is Goddess Penelope, a findom dominatrix, and if you haven't heard of findom before, I'll give you the short and sweet version. It means financial domination. It's about coercing desperate and pathetic men into signing their lives over to me and financing my life in exchange for attention and degradation. These men are subs (aka submissives) and they identify as paypigs. You'll find them in the dark corners of the internet kink community, and you really have to break them early and appeal to their fantasies of absolute servitude to a superior creature.

I've gotten really good at it. Verbal humiliation. Telling them how small and inadequate their cocks are. Forcing them to drink hand soap and scrub their genitals raw with a Brillo pad. Sometimes I'll fuck my boyfriend while on FaceTime with them and make them watch, and after they beat off to it, I'll force them to eat their own semen. I guess some people would find it disgusting, but I've always had a sadistic streak in me, so if anything, I'm amused by it. When I'm not wearing the neon green wig that is the staple of Goddess Penelope, I'm just Tabby, mother of three kids, homeowner, and generally a normal looking twenty-three-year-old. My subs have gotten me to the point where I just bought my own house, a brand new Lexus, and I'm pampered to the point of never going without anything that I want. But a recent issue has affected my finances. One of my most loyal and subservient paypigs ended up committing suicide, and that fucked up my whole revenue stream, because this guy was literally giving me thousands and thousands of dollars for my mortgage, utilities, clothing, spa visits, nail salons, etc. It's a huge inconvenience to lose his money, but I'm all about getting my bag, so I'm on the hunt for a new paypig to replace him ASAP.

I got a tip on a private forum, and a new potential has already reached out via DM. His username is Vermilion, stable blue collar worker, unmarried, has more money than he needs, and meek as a kitten. Exactly the kind of prey that is perfect for being robbed blind. And the best part? It's all legal. He literally wants to be stripped of his finances because he has no self-worth. There's probably an ocean of childhood trauma behind that, but it's not my business, and I don't care. I'm a goddess, not a therapist, and my only goal is to separate that cash from his bank account and get it transferred into mine.

So, things were a little rocky there for a week, but it looks like a new resource has entered the playing field. Time to sink the claws in and get him locked down quickly. Findom is a competitive world, and only an ambitious goddess can survive...

Vermilion drags the straight razor across its cheek, splitting the flesh into ribbons, a wound that gapes and taunts. It squirts claret, and a thumb is pressed into it, wiping new hot blood against scar tissue that decorates hatchet-like features. The hoodie is pulled down low, eyes just jackal shine in the dim lighting of the bathroom, and the razor flicks back and forth, seeking unmarked flesh, tearing into that which lies beneath.

Superficial wounds, shallow cuts that bleed and hurt, but nothing fatal. It is merely leeching out the lament. Occasionally, it howls and trembles, hating that reflection in the mirror, loathing the scars and the maker of the scars. It thinks of another, the lost one, and it boils to the brim with hate.

It hates from a house of straw, this piggie, this pain piggie, this broken-brained lurker of 24/7 diners where cockroaches live on caffeine. And when it hates, it trolls the forums. It's looking for her. She's gotta be the right one. There are thousands of them, the goddesses, the ones offering feet worship on Twitter, chastity cage torture on OnlyFans, verbal teardowns on pornographic subreddits.

A thriving market that caters to the lost, the lonely, the fetid, and the damned. So much ugliness in that world, a callous disregard for humanity, and Vermilion knows ugliness. It has spent many days recently picking at scabs and carving into itself. Self-mutilation to suppress emotional anguish. And perhaps the cycle would have continued until it was nothing but strips of flayed meat on dirty tiles, but lady luck came, and she kissed...

Vermilion found Goddess Penelope with her bright green hair, her dark fuck-me eyes, and lips with the perfect curvature to be cruel. It found her in the nothing hours between 4 a.m. and 5 a.m., and it reached out.

Care for a new sub?

A little pain piggie in a house of straw.

And don't all paypigs go to heaven?

She's winding down after a cam session with a sub, and it's so damn relaxing to release the leather clasps from around the thighs and waist, the strap-on coming off slowly, big floppy obsidian-colored dildo shining with lube, and she tosses it into the upstairs bathtub to be disinfected later. Strap-ons are so much heavier than most vanilla people would realize, and they put a strain on the hips trying to support the weight of a huge, artificial, rubber cock. For a goddess, it's the equivalent of a career woman taking off her bra after a long day the office.

The wig comes off and gets placed on a mannequin head, the makeup is scrubbed from the pores, all those greens, blues, and reds swirling down the drain, and the necklace with the universal key to hundreds of locked penises in chastity cages is removed and placed into a little jewelry box for safekeeping.

It's like shedding the skin of Goddess Penelope, much like a reptile removing dead scales that no longer suit its purposes for the moment. Tabby emerges bare-faced and looking especially casual in an oversized lavender sweater and black leggings, her hair up in a messy bun. Tabby is the real person, and she's who the goddess is, with all masks cast aside. She's a mother above all else, and it's time to feed, bathe, and put the kiddos to bed.

She has two toddlers and a newborn, and they are an absolute handful on any given day. She makes enough money to have in-home daycare, and luckily, her "office" for making content and communicating with submissives is separated from the main house via a spiral staircase and a big red door that stays permanently locked when she's not working. She has to do that, because the lives of Goddess Penelope and Tabby can never intersect. They're as different as night and day, and she doesn't want her kids knowing about what she does for a living. They all assume that she's an accountant that works from home due to the pandemic situation currently happening in the world.

She wastes no time paying the sitter and sending her on her way, and then she focuses on getting in some leisure hours with the kids before it's time to start getting them ready to turn in for the night.

The work phone vibrates a bit as Tabby flicks through Netflix to find the little ones a cartoon to watch. It's Vermilion. She has to at least entertain a response if she wants to keep this one hooked, so she leans back and takes a quick selfie with a Snapchat filter, eyes squinted and lips pouting just enough to torture him.

A finger with an acrylic nail stabs down, and with deep satisfaction, Tabby sees that the picture has sent.

Vermilion sits on the edge of a pitted rooftop, brick digging into its frail hips, eyes flickering over glimmering city lights. An insect hive down there, full of drone cars and drone people. The nightscape is less loud, and so it has the capacity to soothe neurotic thoughts. It plays with a claw hammer, the rubber handle wrapped up tight in electrical tape for a better grip. It smashes the hammer down across the brick at random intervals, watching red chips fly, little bits of shrapnel to feed the starving dark.

It thinks bad thoughts of winged things. Birds, bats, planes, and fat dumb moths that stalk streetlamps. It thinks of flight. In another life, before its mind turned to chaotic soup, Vermilion was an active and fairly normal human being, and it remembers the time that it went sky diving with a group of smiling friends. The adrenaline rush as the door to the plane slid open, wind tearing into its hair, and nothing below but a gaping stretch of emptiness, and patchwork fields thousands of feet down. There was a lump of fear in its throat, and then the instructor pushed them out, and all that remained was weightlessness and carelessness. The world and its little problems ceased to exist, and there was serenity in the drop. Vermilion was almost sorry when the parachute unfurled and put a stop to that feeling of free fall…

Is that what he felt in the end? That same serenity before the inevitable splat?

It shakes its head violently from side to side, trying to dislodge that question and the ruminations that come with it. It barks at the moon, a dog rabid by the circumstances of tragedy, and it lifts the hammer and swings it wildly, letting the sharpened claw slice through the air.

A buzz from the smartphone in its pocket, and the hammer and the dark memories are momentarily forgotten. It brings the phone up, squinting against the surrounding black, and it sees the self-proclaimed Goddess. She is filtered, a little homely beneath the false face. She lacks divinity in this picture, but she is most certainly the one…

It smiles, because the search was long, and many hours were lost in the hunting. It does not notice that its gums are bleeding, and it swallows the plasma without caring, a vague taste of copper in the throat.

It starts doxxing, and when it finds her home, the worship can truly begin.

• • •

Tabby dances through the kitchen with a glass of red wine, Ariana Grande's "Positions" playing from the AirPods nestled into her ears. She's just vibing and unwinding after putting the kiddos to bed, doing a little light cleaning here and there. She tiptoes up the staircase, dusting as she goes and allowing her hips to sway as she feels the music, booty shorts clinging to her toned cheeks. A draft catches her, whipping at the back of her hair, and she notices the upstairs hallway window closest to the exterior storm gutter is open, curtains billowing inward. She shakes her head while smirking, chastising herself for being so scatterbrained and leaving the window gaping like that.

She closes it, and then dances her way quietly to the baby's nursery to make sure he's still in the crib and peaceful. She stops in her tracks in the doorway, not understanding. The lights are all on, and all three of her children are present in the room. The toddlers are kneeling in the center of the room, eyes big saucers of fear, and the infant is wiggling on the carpet next to them.

"Guys...why are we outta bed?"

They yell and beg mommy to turn around. Before she can, she feels a solid impact to the back of her skull, and then she swims in a sea of black.

She awakens in the same room, groggy, and with a massive throb emanating from the back of her head. Her wrists flex, and she sees that they're zip tied tight to the rocking chair that she keeps in the corner, along with her ankles.

Her kids are still in the center of the room, looking like their blood has run cold, and for the first time, she registers the other figure. It lingers in a corner where the starlight projector of the baby's room barely illuminates it, a dark, dead star in an otherwise soothing galaxy. It moves forward, showing more of itself. Scabrous features, the face a latticework of scars and fresh cuts, skin like melted pink wax. It wears a dark hoodie with the hood pulled low, and it has breasts beneath, giving the vague idea that it is female. A claw hammer dangles loosely from the right hand, fingers barely touching the length of it...

The eyes are hard to discern, like an animal glow on the side of a backroad at night, but there's something in them Tabby doesn't like. It's difficult to define, but it looks like derangement to her, a person who has long since given up on being a person. It speaks, the voice confirming its femininity. It sounds like daises wilting softly in a meadow that has been abandoned by the sun.

"You know me as Vermilion. I'd like to show you something."

It reaches out a hand, fingers scabby and picked at, the nails torn down to the quick. A glossy photograph is placed in Tabby's lap. It's an extremely average looking middle-aged man with drooping features, glasses, and balding gray hair. The sort of man you wouldn't give a second glance to in a public place. It takes her a minute, but then it registers where she's seen the face before...

It's one of her paypigs. This is the one that she considered her main cash cow, the poor schmuck who had been dropping thousands on her per month. The same one that ended up committing suicide, though she had only received the most rudimentary details about his death from other sex workers in the findom community.

"My father. Dear old dad, and he was a good dad. I didn't find out about his fetishes until after he had jumped from the rooftop of a high-rise. Imagine that. Finding out your dad had a humiliation kink after he's just gristle being cleaned up off a sidewalk."

A little titter, and Tabby is once more disturbed by the amount of detached derangement there is in that laugh. Vermilion seems...untethered to reality in some essential way.

"He was deeply depressed. He was lonely. He had no sense of self-worth, and he was in debt up to his ears. Debt he had accumulated each day from you. Paying you every dime he had for you to remind him of what a worthless piece of shit he was. Paying you to dehumanize. Paying you to tear him down, over and over again..."

"Listen, just untie me, let me go console my kids, and we'll talk about this, alright? It's a kink. It was totally consensual.

He sought ME out! I was just doing my job, for fuck's sake. You can't blame a sex worker for something your father chose to do. He should have sought therapy instead of putting his money into my pockets…"

Vermilion greets this with a long period of silence. The claw hammer lifts in the air, and it runs an index finger along the head of the hammer, testing the steel.

"I don't know how much responsibility you have in this on an ethical level. I cannot bring myself to hate you. You are a vulture, yes. You pick at the scraps and the bones of the lonely, the mentally sick, and the broken. An accomplished carrion eater, a happy buzzard stripping the meat from something that is already too weak and sad to stop you. But he did come to you. Perhaps he wanted that pain to push him to the place he always wanted to go…"

Vermilion shrugs, looking downward at the carpet. Tabby still can't see what color its eyes are. Everything about the stance and personality of this person makes her think of a hyena draped in human skin…

"I inherited his pain in the end. I've tried to bleed it out. I've tried to crush it into submission. I've tried everything, Goddess. Nothing works. That kind of pain is special. Something you love with everything that you are, reduced to blood and gristle. A smear where there was once a smile. Pain like that just…eats you up. And there is nothing inside me left to eat."

A few soft footsteps across the carpet, Vermilion's shoulders hunched, hammer swinging at its hip.

"I take no joy in this. But I have to share this pain, and you're the best person to share with."

Tabby expects it to drive the head of that hammer into her face at any moment now, and she's attempting to mentally prepare herself for the blow. She vows that she will not scream in front of children, even as her blood sprays and her bones are turned to powder. She won't scar their ears with the screams of the mother that birthed them. But that first blow does not come. Something far worse happens. Vermilion pivots, facing away from her, and it lightly touches the head of the hammer to the temple of Tabby's young son, the boy sitting there, staring at her, his small body racked with tremors. Tabby immediately realizes that the suffering intended for her will be to witness the purest souls in her life turned to gristle. The same gristle that Vermilion found splattered so artistically on the asphalt after her father's last great leap...

Tabby tries to breathe, to struggle, to do anything at all, but her consciousness is fading in and out, each rabbit-like inhalation causing her head to droop into a sea of black. There are sounds. Meat being hammered. The flash of red, a faucet opening and pooling somewhere behind a crib. Whimpers from innocents, and purity bludgeoned down into smears of scarlet paste. Tabby lifts her head, eyes barely open, so sore and raw and aching.

Vermilion's hands are grimed in the remnants of what it has done, and it rises to a vertical base before her, fetching a deep sigh from within its chest.

Tabby is vaguely aware that she is roaring profanities at this monster, telling it how she will kill it, how she needs to be untied to go to her children, just an incoherent mess of raw grief and barely realized anguish. Huge gushes of snot drip down from her nostrils, and they're like strings caught in her nose as she whips her head from side to side, a mental breakdown tearing her slowly apart.

Vermilion approaches while swiping the sweat and blood spatter from its brow. Tabby cranes her neck as far forward as it'll go, desperately snapping at it with her teeth, trying to will herself to get close enough to bite.

It looks at her face, seeming to study her expression.

"It's in you now. That pain I mentioned. I can see it as clearly as a reflection. I'm glad you can finally understand."

It lifts the hammer, and it positions the claws up against the side of its throat. When it looks at her, there isn't even a hint of humanity remaining.

"Thank you for letting me share."

The hammer is yanked aggressively to the left, and Vermilion uses the claws to snag and rip through flesh, opening up its own jugular, a big chunk of blue vein splitting to the side and allowing the blood to splash out in a torrent, splattering Tabby's screaming face, some of it landing like warm bathwater on her tongue.

The murderer collapses in on itself, just frailty in a hoodie, and it curls its knees into the hollowness of its chest as it dies.

Tabby sweeps her gaze around the abattoir of the room, her children's bodies littering the floor in various states of gore-streaked perversion.

It feels like a dream. A horrible dream…

Her traumatized mind travels back to one of her sessions as Goddess Penelope, remembering the words that dripped like honey-dipped venom from her tongue.

"You're disgusting. You're a worm. You're vile, pathetic, and no one will ever love you. And honestly? Now that I think about it…"

"You should just kill yourself."

Barry & Lich

By Stephen S. Schreffler

You know the van. It's one of those vans from like the '80s, three wolves howling at the moon painted in photographic detail along the side. Bumper sticker mosaic plastered over the rear doors, Jesus Christ bobblehead on the dash, rattles like a grocery cart, and the whole rig drifts to the right. I bet you could guess just who might be driving it, too. Big fella for a high schooler, mop head for hair, sleeveless acid-washed jean jacket. It's decorated like a five-star general's uniform, but instead of purple hearts and stars of valor, it's all pins and buttons that say things like *Punk You, No Smoking,* and *Hurts Donut*. Safety-pinned between the shoulders, a Misfits patch. Neurosis T-shirt under that. An open can of Olympia between his wide thighs, and yeah, those are leather pants.

That's Barry. He works at Guitar Center.

Can you imagine the type of accomplice Barry might patter around with? There in the sheepskin passenger seat is a guy as skinny as Barry is rotund. Tall as Barry is squat. He's got the build of a telephone pole, wires for arms floating outside a Punisher T-shirt that could fit a sumo wrestler. Their Dungeons and Dragons group one time called him a "Lich" and so that's who he is. *There,* rolling down the window, ripping a joint like he was born for it.

So, Lich, he manages the drum section at Guitar Center.

They don't know it yet, no one does, but tonight they'll commit multiple homicides. Five high school girls and three high school boys. Schoolmates.

These boys. Always ready to bring a good time. Good enough to wash out all the bad ones.

I mean, how do you think a van like that, Barry at the helm, Lich-is-my-copilot, how do you think a van like that is handling the winding roads up Pine Mountain to a lonely cabin in the middle of nowhere on a late summer night? Yeah. Not pretty, is it? "Tom Sawyer" is blasting through the premium sound system; the one thing Barry was always dropping his paychecks on aside from dank weed and piss beer. Hell, though, they're having fun. They're all jacked on THC and alcohol and good vibes, baby.

They're actually not bad kids. Lich rolls a hell of a spliff, and he'll walk you through Rush's "2112" with a scholar's intellect if you have a free Friday night. Barry can play "Stairway to Heaven" on his dad's Gibson SG perfectly. Close your eyes and it's Jimmy Page in the flesh. They have a good, honest time. They don't know they're about to commit multiple homicides; you could argue it's not their fault anyway. Like I said, it's not like they planned on this. They're just committed, believe in the sacrosanctity of something like playing a role.

Look, I know that sounds weird, but hear me out. Barry and Lich? They're three years deep into a Dungeons and Dragons campaign, should be at home with their fellow social outcasts slinging D20s, talking in character. One time, Barry, or should I say Bludzorg the Dismemberer, got so into the session, he shouted in his best orcish and pulled out a real sword no one knew he even had, and I kid you not: cleaved the entire fucking table in half. Dice went flying, papers fluttering like scattered pigeons, beer and mountain dew dousing everything. Everyone went nuts. Lich, or should I say Priestess of Carnage, held a staff high and declared this sacred ground. So point is, they come there ready to take on a role. Bludzorg the Dismemberer. Barry knew the role well. Priestess of Carnage. Lich embodied the role.

Plus, they work retail. Got to be at the ready, know their stuff, help their customer do stupid shit like play "Smoke on the Water" through a solid state redline Peavy amp. Or hit every crash in the soundproof cymbal room. If you walked into that Guitar Center, man I'm telling you, they would hook you up. So even there, they can play the role of Guitar Center Corporate Payroll'd Certified Em-Ploy-Ee.

Obviously, there's high school, where they play another role. The sufferers of nasty looks, the butts-of-the-jokes, two punchlines walking. Getting the shit kicked out them when the teachers aren't around, or sometimes worse than that. Smoking joints by the dumpsters, skipping school, pretending like they're so despised because they're above all this high school bullshit. Not outside it, above it. The Weirdos. They got that role down to a tee.

Can't forget about their respective roles at home. Lich chopping hot dogs in a slurry of ketchup for his younger brother and sister, sure to save a squeeze of ketchup for himself even though he knows there won't be a hot dog to go with it. Their dad's long gone, but their mom's only gone for a few nights or weeks here and there. Lich's brother and sister start kindergarten next year, which means they'll learn for the first time what it's like to have lunch every day, and not just the lunch that Lich stashed from school, pulled from a sweaty JanSport to their applause and laughter, like it really might be the big surprise Lich assures them it will be. He announces in a British accent that "dinner is served." Here's the finest steak money could buy, he tells them, as he unwraps a tray full of three kinds of slop. Good big brother. He plays the role as best he can.

Barry is "another kid with daddy issues"—those are his words, often followed by a hardy-har. He jokes with Lich about how maybe their dads ran off to the same place; Beer Heaven, or something. Burning in Hell, maybe. Barry Sr. burning in Booze Hell for all eternity. In the meantime, there's this man-shaped void in Barry's house, and his mom spends just about every other week trying out a new jigsaw for the empty slot. Some men are too nice for Mom. They never last long. Some are the right kind of mean. They laugh at Barry, toss him a five-dollar bill when they need the house to just them and Barry's mom. Then there were the Real Bad Men. Those guys? They would say things about Barry's mom he'd rather not know. What she likes, what she looks and feels like down there, and what they do about it. Real Bad Men. Usually, Barry ends up knocked out and bloodied by them, having charged with white-knuckled fists and a lungful of hate. His naked mom screaming in the background. Barry wasn't the jigsaw on nights like that, but maybe one day he would be. Until then, he'll play out the role.

The role they imagine.

Or, the role assigned.

Or, the coveted role.

But we're here to see them play out a brand-new role they never planned on.

I mean, here's what happened, why they're on Pine Mountain Road. The girls, they thought it would be just the funniest thing ever to invite our boys to this little cabin weekend.

Ha ha. Good jokes and big laughs. Imagine girls like that inviting Barry and Lich to something like a cabin getaway where there'd be no adults. How excited these boys were about joining them. They nearly convinced Lich that they were ready for that master class on Rush, bring his vinyl along. Like that's what this was about. But no, they gave Barry and Lich the wrong address. Which had our boys standing at the wrong house, six pack in each hand, a sandwich baggie of weed in their pockets. The address was Mr. Comely's, school principal, so that was an awkward interaction. Ha ha. Good one. It's Friday night, and Mr. Comely already had plans for Monday morning. "See me in my office", he'd said as he tightened his bathrobe.

So, there's a little bit of a fuck-the-man vibe in the van tonight as they pull into the gravel driveway up to the actual cabin these girls and boys are at. The end of the world is due Monday morning, better make the most of the weekend. Locating the cabin had been easy, they both knew that photos would show up on social media soon enough, and they also knew that at least Amber had geolocation tagging turned on by default. This wasn't the first time Barry and Lich had been just oh-so-curious about where Amber might be on a given Friday.

They're pulling on a couple of rubber masks they grabbed at Spirit Halloween. It was the first stop after Mr. Comely's, *after* hatching a plan about how they could get back at the girls with a prank of their own. Really vile masks, too. Like, have you been in a Spirit Halloween lately? Shit would make Michael Myers blush. Barry had grabbed his Bludzorg sword on the way out. Lich? Oh god, Lich. Man, I love that guy. He'll tell you about how Rush just commits to every song, how that's what makes the absurdity of it actually work. So, Lich is committed to this prank. He's got an actual chainsaw he found in the garage. How funny is that? Get it running, get it screaming with gas-powered rage when he rips that pull chord.

The plan is this: peek in some windows, tap on the glass with the sword, get that chainsaw roaring. Work up a good scare. Who's laughing now? Renegotiate the van down Pine Mountain Road.

Innocent enough. No harm, no foul. No one gets hurt over a joke, do they? Barry and Lich know that better than anyone.

Barry shuts off the headlights as the van crunches to a slow stop in the gravel driveway. There's like ten cars out front, and Barry recognizes Chet's Pontiac Trans Am. He knows that car because he covets the thing. Chet. God. Chet is the quarterback for the Owls, the school's football team. Of course he and his cronies got the *real* invite. If Barry had to guess, linebacker Patrick was there. Probably Chet's wide receiver George, too.

Good, Barry thinks, the more the merrier. He and Lich exchange a glance like they know without a word spoken that this has also become about humiliating Chet, Patrick, and George in front of the ladies. Just as Chet, Patrick, and George have often done to Barry and Lich. Turn the tables.

So, there's five ladies, like I said. Amber, Jenny, Kat, Steph, and Denise. A mix of the cheerleading squad and Denise, captain of the high school girls' volleyball team. All legs as far as Barry and Lich are concerned, sorry. They're in high school and can't avoid how thoughts about the opposite sex pass through a cheesecloth filter of hormones. They're about to find out the thrill, the power, that comes with making said opposite sex scream for their lives and they might have some more thoughts bouncing around by the time this is over. So, sorry again. Just hang in there because it's about to get out of hand.

Here's how it starts. They do the peeking, the tapping of sword on glass, but see that the cabin is empty. Regarding each other through the gruesome rubber visage and pencil-troll-hair, they think to each other: now what? And then the lodgepole pines towering over them echo back the laughter of five high school girls and three high school boys. A glance towards the pine tops reveals the orange flicker of firelight. Sounds like the party's out back. They make their way around the cabin to where everyone is. They're improvising now, and Lich will tell you actually *that's* what made Rush great. Improvise, feel the crowd, jam it out. Commit. Play the role. On the count of one-two-three-four, Lich revs the chainsaw.

Amber, Jenny, Kat, Steph, and Denise scream immediately. I mean, right away.

Ha ha. What a joke.

Now Chet, QB and captain of the Owls, is shouting in the darkness where Lich is hiding.

"Hey! Who the fuck is there?" He shouts over the rumbling chainsaw.

Chet's a Mormon. He says *fuck* like he might get in trouble for it.

"Oooh, I'm so scared," Barry whispers to Lich through his rubber mask, and they laugh together. God, it's just too good. Being on this side of it.

Patrick and George stand at attention on either side of Chet like they can take on anything.

That's about how it goes for the next whatever minutes. Barry and Lich rev the chainsaw or hack at a tree somewhere in the woods, run around to some other area, do the same thing. Chet and the football goons puff their chests and shout about all the things they'll do if they catch them. The girls scream. Oh, look, Chet has taken off his shirt. How precious.

So, there we go; mission accomplished for Barry and Lich, right? Came out, scared everyone, good times had. The plan, then, was to leave. Maybe. Or hell, maybe it's just a good time that can get better? You know Barry and Lich; they're down for that. So maybe they can come out of the darkness, unmask themselves, everyone shares a laugh.

Barry says as much all in one look through his cheap Halloween mask. Lich maybe agrees. Hard to tell because seriously these masks are nasty as all hell. It's ludicrous, but the boys, they feel like this is what Chet, Patrick, and George must feel like. Powerful. Well-equipped.

Barry makes his way towards a shed at the edge of the firelight like that good time can indeed get better, like a shared laugh is sure to follow. Why shouldn't it? It's high school. It sucks, it's awesome; it's whatever you make of it, as far as Barry and Lich are concerned. Maybe this can be an inside joke they share, and maybe it'll be enough to forget all the other stuff, like sending Barry and Lich to Mr. Comely's. Or the worse stuff. Chase the moment here, boys. Commit to it. Play the role.

But then, about the time they're feeling all silly about it, Amber says something. Says something that turns the whole night the wrong way. "I bet its Barry and his stupid friend. Did you guys see the look on their faces when we invited them?"

Everyone laughs.

Ha ha. Good joke.

"Oh my God, I know," says Kat.

"Ugh," Steph shudders. "Those guys give me the creeps. They're so gross."

They all start talking shit. Saying some hurtful things.

Things like:

—I hate them so much

—Ew, they smell like BO all the time

—I bet they get all their clothes from the thrift store

—So pathetic

Barry's kind of leaning around the back of the shed and he remembers hearing his mom's last boyfriend once say something like that. Soaked in cigarettes and Olympia beer, calling Barry pathetic. *Pathetic.* Some words just hit harder to some people. That's Barry's word. *Pathetic.* It's a part of who he is, echoing around between his ears even on the best of Friday nights.

Barry is gripping Bludzorg's sword ever more tightly.

Pathetic is a word that smells like alcohol, like rotten teeth and stale Camel Reds. Feels like a busted nose, spitting teeth, blurry in one eye for a week. Weighs a ton.

He's breathing heavily, seeing motes wink in and out of his periphery.

Pathetic is his missing dad's reason for going AWOL. Pathetic is what all the men in line outside his mom's bedroom have to say about it. Pathetic is Barry's own mom giving her firsthand account of why there's a line, and why Barry can't ever do anything about it.

His jaw tightens. Back stiffens. Breath hot and loud in his mask.

Lich feels that sting too. He glances down at his oversized Punisher T-shirt that he indeed got from the thrift store. It was the only one long enough to cover his wiry torso. His mom takes him and the twins there once every few months, uses some of the money they got from returning cans to get them "new" clothes. How pathetic he needs to make himself to get his brother and sister to eat, dancing like a butler. How pathetic he felt looking up Amber's geotag again.

Pathetic is thinking even for a moment they could pull a prank and maybe go out and have a laugh with some new friends about it. The more pathetic they feel, the heavier the sword gets. Pathetic is all that gasoline sloshing around in the chainsaw.

Then Kat kicks off a whole new conversation about all the things they would prefer over fucking Barry and Lich. Stuff like: pass up a briefcase full of a million dollars; shoot their own PTA moms; eat dog poop for the rest of their lives.

Barry and Lich feel the fun of a Friday night leeching from them. They feel like they're losing again. Not the plan. And when Jenny says she'd rather have all her arms and legs and her very head cut off, and the girls each agree, Barry looks at Lich. He can only see wet eyes through the cheap Halloween mask. He thinks, well let's just see about that.

"Fuckin' losers." Chet's trying on the F-word again, and it doesn't land any better than the last time. He's on his way to the shed to "take a piss" which he announces like its foreplay or something. Of course, his cronies Patrick and George need to piss at that moment too. Like they're thinking "Dicks out over here!" they shout while pissing, as if that might be tantalizing to the girls. They end up farting-distance from Barry and Lich. Amazing they don't see the boys, but they've stopped caring because they've got the world on a string. They're close enough that both Barry and Lich can feel the delicate pinprick of piss droplets on their skin, hear it on their weapons.

Patrick recalls "this one time" about Lich. And then Lich is back in a memory he tries as best he can to forget. Goes like this:

—Surrounded by muscular naked high school boys in the locker room: Chet, Patrick, and George.

—Lich gets hard, tries to hide it

—They see it

—They laugh

—Want to suck my dick, don't you?

—Now he's getting pushed down

—Now they've got him in some kind of wrestling pin and they're trying to pry open his mouth

The three friends all laugh at the memory, laugh like it happened just yesterday. Ha ha.

Lich remembers, too. He can still hear his own screams from that day in his head, and he needs something to drown them out, something louder. He rips the pull cord, and the chainsaw roars. That should do it.

It's like a war trumpet to Lich, fills his veins with gasoline. He brings the chainsaw down on Patrick's swiveling head with all the strength he couldn't muster that one morning on the wet tile floor of the locker room. And when it connects, Lich keeps going, dragging it through that entire memory until the chain is all gristle and bone and hair, and two halves of what used to be Chet fall on either side of Lich. There's no stopping now. For the rest of the night, he's got Neil Peart's Birmingham '88 "XYZ" drum solo playing in his brain, start-to-finish, on repeat. Lich steps through both sides of Patrick like the curtains have opened, covered in the refreshing spray of viscera from his chainsaw. He's breathing manically when he spots Chet. The QB is trembling, pale, shocked, just like you would be had you just watched that drum solo. Lich wonders what happens when you *stab* with a chainsaw. Intends to find out.

Then there's Barry watching this. First, he's shocked as anyone. Then, the warm splatter of Patrick's insides fleck across his mask. His wide-open mouth curls into a slow, wide-open smile, helped along by the gentle nudge of a gradually nodding head. When both parts of Patrick land, Barry gets it. He's heard Lich's master class on Rush. Commit. Play the role. What else can a good friend like Barry do but help? Barry leaps into the air, higher than he's ever leapt before, eyes red with blood rage, Bludzorg's sword gripped in both hands overhead. He howls like a wolf, like the three wolves on the van, and pulls the sword down upon George. He chops and chops and chops. All in perfect rhythm, a 4/4 beat to match the song in his mind. "Good Vibrations," a la Beach Boys.

They're both covered in gore when Denise shows up to see what's the matter. Denise, why did you do that? What do you *think* is the matter? That's a chorus of power tools and death throes by the shed. Don't go there. What can someone like Denise do about it? But she doesn't think, just goes, which means she's next. Has to be. A masked Barry and Lich and their tools of reckoning is what's the matter, Denise. All the parts around them that used to belong to three high school boys. And then, she tries way too late to say something nice. But all Barry can hear is the conversation by the fire, agreeing that she'd rather have her head chopped off than even kiss him. So, he grabs a fistful of hair, aims her gaze at the night sky, and obliges.

They didn't plan on this, back in the van, outside Mr. Comely's. It's just sort of happening. Like it needs to. Nothing pathetic about this.

I mean, need we go into detail from here on out? Lots of screaming, lots of blood. Denise's head tossed at the flames until the rest of the girls realize what it is, which is right when Barry and Lich come out of the darkness with a heavy sword and a screaming chainsaw, masks glistening and dripping. And then they're the only two left, our boys, surrounded by what would take you a good while to realize are the remains of five high school girls. Arms here, legs there, heads rolling.

It's like the fire had been built for them, the way they stand alongside it. The role was offered to them. And didn't they just kill it? Barry and Lich can't help but laugh. Out of breath. Filthy. They have their masks on still, playing out the role. They're not pathetic. They're not pinned down. They're Barry and motherfucking Lich.

You see the van again, don't you? Tearing down Pine Mountain Road. They're passing around a joint and smoking it through the mouth hole in the Halloween masks. Stereo blasting. Wow, that was crazy, man. I know.

Ha ha. Good joke.

What's funny is that homecoming is next weekend and there's no QB1 for the game. Not as many cheerleaders as last week. But there's still going to be a dance, and after-parties that Barry and Lich won't be invited to. But maybe they'll show up anyway. Step through the gym's steel doors into an atrium of dangling ribbons, drifting balloons, couples slow-dancing and oblivious to how good these two got it. This week's top-40 hits playing over the rented PA as Barry and Lich enter like they're the main act of the evening, masks with a week's worth of filth clinging. Masks that haven't been removed even once since having been donned. A van still running in the parking lot as the door closes behind them. Barry and Lich. Always ready to bring a good time.

Me & My Shadow

By Linda D. Addison

The first time It saved my life,
I looked young, full of softness,
the street razor sharp with others waiting
for something fresh & new,
but I knew Its teeth were sharper,
my hunger deeper.

I went with one of them to the woods,
they tore my clothes, as if I was a toy.
This was a game, my shadow's game,
surprise—surprise, when my knife opened
their neck, their hot blood—sweet,
my hunger fulfilled.

Moving on, new towns to find,
new necks to open, fresh meat to taste,
my shadow never tired of promising
something innocent, something unique,
their animal minds easily dazzled by my smile,
each time It consumed a different piece.

On a planet crowded with too many people,
who could blame Us for helping rid
the streets of those who are not good people.
Does that make me & my shadow bad?
It tells me I'm just different, special
& that makes me happy.

Acknowledgments

Human Monsters, A Horror Anthology, would not have been possible without Rob Carroll, Editor-in-Chief of *Dark Matter Magazine*, and his belief that we had it in us to curate a whole-ass anthology. Thank you for bringing this opportunity to us and walking through this process with us every step of the way.

Our families have been huge supporters of this project, giving us the time and quiet we needed to read hundreds of stories.

We want to thank the Dark Matter staff, Anna Madden, Marie Croke, Phil McLaughlin, and Marissa van Uden, for reading submissions alongside us and for your valuable insight.

Thank you, Alex Woodroe, for sharing your expertise and knowledge. We're so honored and thankful that *Human Monsters* is the first of three 'Monster' anthologies to be released by *Dark Matter Magazine's* trade imprint, Dark Matter INK. We can't wait to support the next two in the Monster trilogy.

Thank you to all the writers who submitted stories of human monsters during the open call. We were blown away by the constant buzz and enthusiasm surrounding this project. The horror community at large rallied around our very first editing journey, and we feel very thankful for the support. We were overwhelmed with emotion by the volume and quality of stories we received.

Lastly, thank you to our Night Worms customers. For three years now, we have curated horror for you and have developed a real sense of what the genre has to offer and how we can best represent it to passionate readers like you. Thank you for trusting us. It has made projects like this possible by giving us the confidence to listen to our guts and our hearts when it comes to good storytelling. We truly believe we know what readers love when it comes to horror...our happy place.

—Sadie & Ashley

About the Authors

Linda D. Addison is the author of five award-winning collections, including *How To Recognize A Demon Has Become Your Friend*, and is the recipient of the HWA Lifetime Achievement Award, and SFPA Grand Master of Fantastic Poetry.

Gemma Amor is a Bram Stoker Award-nominated author, voice actor, and illustrator based in Bristol, in the UK. Her debut short story collection *Cruel Works of Nature* came out in 2018. Since then, she has released *Dear Laura*, *White Pines*, *Six Rooms*, *Girl on Fire,* and *These Wounds We Make*. Her novel, *Full Immersion,* is published by Angry Robot books.

Jena Brown grew up playing make-believe in the Nevada desert, where her love for skeletons and harsh landscapes solidified. A freelance writer, she currently contributes to various outlets. You can find her short story, *They Don't Eat Teeth*, in the anthology, *What One Wouldn't Do*.

Nat Cassidy writes horror for the page, stage, and screen. His critically-acclaimed, award-winning horror plays have been produced across the United States, and his horror novel debut, titled *Mary: An Awakening of Terror*, is published by Tor Nightfire. He lives in New York City with his wife.

Venezia Castro is a Mexican writer of literary and speculative fiction in English and Spanish. Her work has appeared in magazines in Mexico, Canada, and the United States. She is currently living in Scotland and working on her first novel.

Andrew Cull is the author of *Bones*, *Remains*, and *The Cockroach King*. His writing has been described as a masterclass in emotional cinematic horror fiction. He lives in Melbourne, Australia.

Andy Davidson is the Bram Stoker Award-nominated author of *The Hollow Kind*, *The Boatman's Daughter*, and *In the Valley of the Sun*. His work has been listed among NPR's Best Books of the Year, the New York Public Library's Best Adult Books of the Year, and *Library Journal's* Best Horror. Born and raised in Arkansas, Andy makes his home in Georgia with his wife and a bunch of cats.

L. P. Hernandez is an author of horror and speculative fiction. His stories have been featured in anthologies from Cemetery Gates Media, Sinister Smile Press, and Soteira Press, among others. He has two short story collections including the fully illustrated *The Rat King*. He is a husband, father, and a dedicated metalhead.

Laurel Hightower is the author of *Whispers in the Dark*, *Crossroads*, and *Below*. She co-edited the following anthologies: *We Are Wolves*, *The Dead Inside*, and *Shattered & Splintered*. She lives in Kentucky with her husband and son.

C. S. Humble is an award-winning American novelist, living in East Texas. His latest novel, *All These Subtle Deceits*, is the first book in his Black Wells series, published by Dark Hart Books. His horror western trilogy is forthcoming from Cemetery Dance Publications.

Emma Alice Johnson grows wildflowers and writes. She lives on a farm dedicated to conservation of endangered pollinators. She is a two-time Wonderland Book Award-winner. Her short fiction has appeared in *The Dark*, *Dark Discoveries*, and many other publications. Her latest book, *Unicorn Wasteland*, was published by Everybody Press.

Jeremy Robert Johnson is the author of *The Loop*, *Entropy in Bloom*, *In the River*, *Skullcrack City*, and *All the Wrong Ideas*. He lives and writes in Portland, Oregon.

Stephen Graham Jones is the Bram Stoker Award-winning author of more than a dozen novels, including *The Only Good Indians*, *My Heart is a Chainsaw*, and *Don't Fear the Reaper*.

Rebecca Jones-Howe writes neo-noir and gothic horror from her home in British Columbia, Canada. Her work has appeared in *PANK*, *Pulp Modern*, and *Dark Moon Digest*. Her collection of short fiction, *Vile Men*, is published by Dark House Press.

Caroline Kepnes is the New York Times bestselling author of *You*, *Hidden Bodies*, *Providence*, and *You Love Me*. Her work has been translated into thirty-two languages and inspired a television series adaptation of *You*, currently on Netflix. She grew up in Cape Cod, and now lives in Los Angeles.

Samantha Kolesnik is an award-winning author of *True Crime* and *Waif*. She is a two-time Splatterpunk Award winner, and was nominated for the Bram Stoker Award for her work editing the anthology, *Worst Laid Plans: an Anthology of Vacation Horror.*

Chad Lutzke Chad has written for *Famous Monsters of Filmland*, *Rue Morgue*, Cemetery Dance, and *Scream* magazine. His books include *Of Foster Homes & Flies*, *Stirring the Sheets*, *Cannibal Creator*, *Skullface Boy*, *The Same Deep Water as You*, and *The Neon Owl* series.

Josh Malerman is the New York Times best selling author of *Bird Box* and *Daphne*. He's also one of two singer/songwriters for the Detroit rock band, The High Strung. He lives in Michigan with the artist/musician Allison Laakko.

Catherine McCarthy Text Catherine McCarthy is a spinner of silky stories with macabre melodies. She is the author of the collections *Door and other twisted tales*, *Mists and Megaliths*, and the novella *Immortelle*, published by Off Limits Press..

Francesca McDonnell Capossela grew up in New York City and holds an M. Phil from Trinity College Dublin. Her publication credits include *The Los Angeles Review of Books*, *Columbia Journal*, and *The Point Magazine*. Her debut novel, *A Terrible Beauty*, is forthcoming from Lake Union press.

Jeremy Megargee weaves tales of personal horror from Martinsburg, West Virginia, with his cat Lazarus acting as his muse/familiar. He is an active member of the West Virginia chapter of the Horror Writer's Association.

Tim Meyer dwells in a dark cave near the Jersey Shore. He's written and published over fifteen novels and novellas, including *Malignant Summer*, *The Switch House*, *Dead Daughters*, and *Limbs*.

S. P. Miskowski has received two National Endowment for the Arts Fellowships. Her second novel, *I Wish I Was Like You*, was named This Is Horror 2017 Novel of the Year. Her books have been finalists for a Bram Stoker Award twice, and for a Shirley Jackson Award four times.

Archita Mittra is a writer, editor, and artist, with a fondness for dark and fantastical things. Her work has appeared in *Tor*, *Strange Horizons*, *Zooscape*, *Anathema Magazine*, *Hexagon*, and elsewhere. She has been nominated for the Pushcart, best of the net, and other prizes.

Stephanie Nelson is a writer living in Boise, Idaho, with her husband and kids. This is her first horror publication, and she has another forthcoming in *Mother: Tales of Love and Terror*, published by Weird Little Worlds.

Leah Ning lives in northern Virginia with her husband and their four pets. Her short fiction appears or is forthcoming in *Writers of the Future Volume 36*, *PodCastle*, *Beneath Ceaseless Skies*, and *Apex Magazine*, among others.

Cynthia Pelayo is the author of *Loteria*, *Santa Muerte*, *The Missing*, *Poems of My Night*, and *Into he Forest and All The Way Through*. Her horror novel, *Children of Chicago*, won an International Latino Book Award for Best Mystery (2021).

Sam Rebelein has work in *Bourbon Penn, Coffin Bell Journal, Press Pause Press*, Ellen Datlow's *Best Horror of the Year*, and elsewhere. HarperCollins' crime and horror imprint, William Morrow, is publishing his debut horror novel, *Edenville*, in fall 2023.

Belicia Rhea was born under a waning crescent moon in the Sonoran Desert. She writes horror, weird fiction, and poetry. You can find her work in *Nightmare Magazine, Ligeia Magazine*, and *Miracle Monocle*, among other places.

Stephen S. Schreffler is an author of science fiction and horror. He lives in Bend, Oregon, with his Boston-Frenchie, Huxley, and spends his non-writing time exploring the Pacific Northwest, or playing guitar for rock bands, The Chaw, and Bad Bad Blood.

Greg Sisco is a novelist, screenwriter, and film director. His short fiction has appeared in the anthologies *Worst Laid Plans, Halldark Holidays*, and *Nox Pareidolia*. His most recent novel is *In Nightmares We're Alone* from Off Limits Press.

Elton Skelter is new on the fiction scene. He has a number of short works forthcoming, and his debut novel, *Life Support*, will be released in 2023 through D&T Publishing.

John F. D. Taff is a multiple Bram Stoker Award-nominated author with five novels and more than 150 stories in print. He lives in the wilds of Illinois with two pugs, one cat, and a long-suffering wife.

Dana Vickerson is an architect and writer living in Dallas. Her short fiction has appeared in *Trembling with Fear* and *Tales to Terrify*. She has drabbles in *Drabbledark II* and *Wyrms*.

Kelsea Yu lives with her husband and children in the Pacific Northwest. Her stories appear in *Classic Monsters Unleashed, Death in the Mouth*, and elsewhere. Her novella, *Bound Feet*, is published by Cemetery Gates Media.

About the Editors

Sadie Hartmann (aka Mother Horror) is the co-owner of the horror fiction subscription company, Night Worms, and the Editor-in-Chief for horror fiction imprint, Dark Hart Books. She's currently writing a non-fiction book about horror for Page Street Books, coming in 2023. She lives in the Pacific Northwest with her husband of twenty-plus years, where they stare at Mount Rainier, eat street tacos, and hang out with their three kids. They have a Frenchie named Owen.

Ashley Saywers is a wife, mom, and lover of all things spooky. She is the co-owner of horror fiction subscription company, Night Worms. When she isn't reading, you'll probably find her listening to a true crime podcast, shopping for Halloween, or drinking a Pumpkin Spice Latte. Yes, she really is that basic.

About the Cover Artist

Oliver Jeavons (Olly) is a UK based artist also known as *artofolly*. He works with many different medias and styles, and he is always pushing his creativity further. Comic book art, book cover art, and commissions of all types are included in his portfolio.

Permissions

Also Available from Dark Matter INK

Linghun by Ai Jiang
ISBN 978-1-958598-02-3

Monstrous Futures: A Sci-Fi Horror Anthology
edited by Alex Woodroe
ISBN 978-1-958598-07-8

Frost Bite by Angela Sylvaine
ISBN 978-1-958598-03-0

Monster Lairs: A Dark Fantasy Horror Anthology
edited by Anna Madden
ISBN 978-1-958598-08-5

The Bleed by Stephen S. Schreffler
ISBN 978-1-958598-11-5

Available from Dark Hart Books

All These Subtle Deceits by C. S. Humble
ISBN 978-1-958598-04-7

Rootwork by Tracy Cross
ISBN 978-1-958598-01-6

All the Prospect Around Us by C. S. Humble
ISBN 978-1-958598-05-4

Mosaic by Catherine McCarthy
ISBN 978-1-958598-06-1

CPSIA information can be obtained
at www.ICGtesting.com
Printed in the USA
BVHW080518051022
648678BV00005B/21